ALL EYES ON US

ALSO BY KIT FRICK

SEE ALL THE STARS

ALL EYES ON US

KIT FRICK

MARGARET K. McELDERRY BOOKS
New York London Toronto Sydney New Delhi

Author's Note on Content: intense flashback scenes depicting abusive conversion "therapy" tactics; characters exhibiting homphobia

MARGARET K. McELDERRY BOOKS
An imprint of Simon & Schuster Children's Publishing Division
1230 Avenue of the Americas, New York, New York 10020
MARGARET K. McELDERRY BOOKS is a trademark of Simon & Schuster, Inc.
For information about special discounts for bulk purchases, please contact Simon & Schuster Special Sales at 1-866-506-1949 or business@simonandschuster.com.
The Simon & Schuster Speakers Bureau can bring authors to your live event. For more information or to book an event, contact the Simon & Schuster Speakers Bureau at 1-866-248-3049 or visit our website at www.simonspeakers.com.
Book design by Michael McCartney
The text for this book was set in ITC Legacy Serif STD.
Manufactured in the United States of America
First Edition
10 9 8 7 6 5 4 3 2 1
Library of Congress Cataloging-in-Publication Data
Names: Frick, Kit, author.
Title: All eyes on us / Kit Frick.
Description: First edition. | New York : Margaret K. McElderry Books, [2019] | Summary: In alternate chapters, Amanda faces family pressure to marry Carter, knowing he cheats, and Rosalie pretends to date Carter to alleviate family and church pressure about being a lesbian.
Identifiers: LCCN 2018024746 (print) | ISBN 9781534404403 (hardcover) | ISBN 9781534404427 (eBook)
Subjects: | CYAC: Family problems—Fiction. | Dating (Social customs)—Fiction. | Betrayal—Fiction. | Lesbians—Fiction. | Sexual orientation—Fiction.
Classification: LCC PZ7.1.F75478 All 2019 (print) | DDC [Fic]—dc23
LC record available at https://lccn.loc.gov/2018024746

This goes out to all my girls.

IF YOU LOVE ENOUGH YOU'LL LIE A LOT /

GUESS THEY DID IN CAMELOT

—TORI AMOS

AND IT'S HARD TO DANCE WITH A DEVIL

ON YOUR BACK / SO SHAKE HIM OFF

—FLORENCE AND THE MACHINE

1

Three hours into the party, I'm tipsy on more than champagne. My mother would say that's the feeling of power, but I think it's the feeling of being adored. Maybe they're one in the same. I'm standing at the top of the Shaws' balcony staircase with Carter, allowing a roomful of eyes to wash over us from below. They're looking because we light up the room. They're looking because someday, we'll run this town.

"Don't you want to go downstairs?" Carter asks. "Graham and Adele are all alone."

I follow my boyfriend's eyes to our friends in the great hall below us. The Shaws live in the most venerable of Logansville's many Victorian estates. From our vantage point on the balcony, we have an eagle-eye view of the entire party. As always, the great hall is host to Mr. Shaw's world-class antique art collection, and tonight, it's teeming with Logansville's oldest money and most auspicious up-and-comers. Graham and Adele are decked out in their New Year's Eve finest in the baroque-era corner. He looks suave in a crisp suit and forest green tie, his tight brown curls cropped close to his head. His hand rests lightly on Adele's back, and her bright gold tube dress really pops against the dark brown of Graham's skin. As usual, she's mid-brushing him off.

"Soon," I promise Carter. "Let's just take one more minute up here together." I give his hand a tight squeeze. One more minute with my boyfriend. One more minute before I have to share Logansville's golden boy with the rest of the madding crowd.

He extracts his hand from mine and trails it slowly across my back before letting it fall to the balcony rail. He's right next to me, but his mind is somewhere distant. Somewhere I can't go. The moment of tipsiness is gone, and suddenly I feel more exposed up here than adored. I let my eyes dance across my boyfriend's broad shoulders, his shock of blond hair, the faraway look in his eyes that makes my skin go cold.

Carter knocks back the last of his champagne, and a college girl in a cater-waiter tux appears to replace his empty flute with a full one. He downs half the glass in one gulp. She offers me a flute as well, but I decline. I need to stay sharp. I glance around the hall, searching for our parents, not that they'd care about Carter drinking. Ever since we became a couple freshman year, they've basically treated us like adults. After all, we're Amanda Kelly and Carter Shaw. We're their legacy. The thought makes my heart skip a beat, excitement or fear rattling inside my chest.

At seventeen, Carter's already a rising star in the community. Varsity athlete, senior class president, sharp mind for business like his father. His future is a dazzling display of success and certainty and respect. With him, so is mine.

I keep my eyes trained on the crowd until they land on Krystal, Carter's mother, who's talking to my mother beneath the Shaws' masterfully restored seventeenth-century Flemish tapestry. Linda is gesturing rapidly, a stack of platinum bangles sliding up and down her too-thin arms. She pauses to take a sip of something clear from an almost-empty rocks glass. She's probably working Krystal to secure the Shaws' large annual contribution for the upcoming benefit. The Logansville Museum of Fine Arts is one of the organizations for which my mother sits on the board. A bangle catches on the tip of one long powder-pink nail, and it takes her way too long to unsnare it. She's getting sloppy. Someone should probably cut her off.

I glance around, but I can't find my father in the crowd. If he were paying attention, he'd know the exact words to say to make her reel it in. But he's not looking. If it was me guzzling too much champagne and embarrassing myself in front of Logansville's elite, I'd be grounded until graduation. In moments like this, I can feel the scales tip another notch, the imbalance settling like so many lead bricks across my back. Watching her like this, it feels like my mother has removed herself from the equation entirely when it comes to our family's future. It's like she gets a free pass because I'm going to take care of everything.

I draw in a long breath and toss back my hair. My mother should be hosting, not boozing, but I can't tell her how to act. She leans forward and grips Krystal's shoulder, too hard. I can feel her grimace reflected on my own face. With my mother rapidly heading out of commission, I'll have to do double the hosting for us.

I turn to Carter. "Okay, let's go." His champagne glass is almost empty again, and he's running a finger absently along the edge of my dress, right where the delicate red satin meets the outline of my shoulder blades. His touch makes my skin tingle. From the great hall below us, we must look picture perfect. I glance over the rail, down to where one of my mother's museum friends is waving up at us, the gesture full of fondness for the town darlings. I wave back, then raise my eyes to meet Carter's. He's looking right at me now, but the distance is still there, thrumming right beneath the surface. I try to blink it away.

It's amazing how a change in perspective can transform the whole view.

Downstairs, I stop to exchange pleasantries with the Beaufords and the Steinways while Carter is absorbed into the crowd. Every so often, I catch a note of his rich, rough laugh or see a flash of those deep dimples, white teeth. Everyone wants a minute of his time—it'll take him all night to reach Graham and Adele. I tell myself it's fine. I have my own mingling to do. I'm in the middle of laughing at one of Mr. Steinway's terrible jokes when the cater-waiter from the balcony touches my arm.

"Sorry to interrupt, Miss Kelly, but I couldn't find your mother."

I glance around. She's right. The space below the Flemish tapestry is empty, and Linda Kelly is nowhere to be found.

"We're running low on the Kobe and Stilton toasts and crab

rémoulade, and Carla wants to know if we should run across the street to restock now or after the ball drops."

I've lived directly across the street from Carter since we moved here in second grade. The move had something to do with the fallout from the financial crisis; Dad changed jobs and my mother thought a small town would be a nice change of pace for our family. Carter and I were in school together, and our parents became fast friends. They've been cohosting the annual New Year's Eve party for as long as I can remember.

The cater-waiter clears her throat, waiting for my response. It's tradition for the Kellys to arrange the catering and host the staging area in our highly functional kitchen across the street; I don't think anyone has actually prepared a meal at the Shaws' since the Victorian era. Her question is minor, a detail. But I can't screw this up. I squint up at the giant grandfather clock at the base of the stairs. The face is so intricately designed, it's almost impossible to read.

"It's eleven twenty," she says, waiting patiently for my verdict. Her bow tie is slightly askew. It's all I can do to resist straightening it out, keep my hands busy.

I take a deep breath. My mother should really be handling this. If I get it right, she'll never notice. But if I get it wrong, I'll never hear the end of it. "Send two staff over to the kitchen and make sure they're back with the Kobe and crab by a quarter of. Tell Carla to keep the rest here circulating, okay?" I force my voice to stay steady. If she notices my nerves, she doesn't let on.

She leaves to find her boss, and I excuse myself from the Steinways to look for Carter. I just need a second of his time, a quick kiss, a reminder that he cares. That he's in this with me. Because in a few years, Carter and I will be throwing parties like this one. In a few years, no more training wheels. The torch will be passed, and it will be our arms thrusting the bright, hot flame into the Logansville night. Together.

I'm slipping through the crowd, making eye contact and smiling, when my phone chimes. Instead of the usual message preview, the words *Private Number* light up the screen. I glance around, then step out of the hall and into the entryway. Perched on the lip of the Shaws' stone fountain, my red Louboutins flashing against the blue marble floor that looks like the ocean, I open the text.

> New Year, New You. Wouldn't you look
> better without a cheater on your arm?

I look around, fast, but aside from the coat check girl in the corner, I'm alone out here with the fountain and marble floors. The very small circle of people who know the truth about Carter's one bad habit are twenty steps away, right inside the party. And none of them would send a message like this. My fingers hover over the reply box, but there's nothing to say. Someone who thinks they know something is trying to ruin my night. And I'm not about to give in to a coward hiding behind a blocked caller ID. I toss my phone back into my bag and run my fingers through my hair, smoothing the glossy strands that frame my face. When I breathe in, I'm the only one who can hear the air catch against the back of my throat. Then I walk back into the party.

"Mandy, Mandy!" Adele is grinning and waving wildly at me from the great hall's baroque corner. Only Adele is allowed to call me Mandy. Our mothers were Kappas together, and we've known each other practically since the womb. Adele's mom was a major reason my parents chose Logansville when we relocated from Pittsburgh ten years back. So Adele gets a pass. To everyone else, it's Amanda Kelly.

I make my way through the sea of satin, lace, and Jo Malone to my friends. Adele wraps her arms around me in a sloppy hug, practically lifting me off my feet with the force. The gold sequins on her tube dress bite into my skin, but she's too drunk and amped up on the gleaming, beguiling promise of New Year's Eve to notice me squirm.

"Sorry we were late getting here," she says, releasing me from the hug and locking me into some intense, boozy eye contact. Her lashes are thick with mascara, and the long, blond streaks in her hair have been freshly touched up at the roots. Adele is always immaculately put together, and people who don't really know her would never believe that just beneath her feminine exterior is a total firecracker with a passion for improv and a silly, brash sense of humor. "Ben's shitty car got a flat on the way over, and we had to wait for Triple A."

I groan and roll my eyes at Ben, who's engaged in some full-on geekery with Graham. The words *Gotham*, *DC*, and *Bronze Age* rise above the peels of laughter and clink of glasses that fill the hall in surround-sound. Ben's mouth is stretched wide into his usual dweeby grin, and he's definitely recycling the same too-short pants and too-big jacket he wore to last month's winter formal. It's something I can't quite put to words, an itch beneath my skin, but Ben brings out the worst in me. We all tolerate him because he's on varsity lacrosse with the rest of the guys, and he's actually a really good midfielder, but Ben still conducts himself like we're in middle school, like he's not part of Logansville South's most enviable group of seniors. If you hang with us, you represent us. And all Ben represents is a complete lack of savior faire. I suppose I should feel bad because his mom left them when we were in fourth grade and maybe he's been lacking in fashion and life advice, but seriously.

"Why did you let yourself be shuttled here in Ben's rattle-trap?" I hiss at Adele beneath my breath. "What's wrong with Graham's Escalade?"

I sound like my mother, but I can't help it. Just watching him hook his arm around Graham's shoulder makes the back of my neck turn hot.

Adele glances at Graham, then leans in too close to my face. "I didn't want to give Graham the wrong impression about tonight, okay? Like he's my date or something? So I said Ben could drive us, like a group thing."

"Why couldn't Graham have driven you, like a group thing?"

Adele stares at me blankly for a second. I draw in a deep breath and try to push the nastiness out. I hate when I get like this. But before I can apologize for snapping at her, Adele breaks into a slightly wobbly tap routine in her pointy heels, immediately capturing the attention of everyone around us. It's totally inappropriate, yet absolutely charming. The guys pump fists in the air and cheer her on. This is classic Adele. Diffusing the moment, choosing comedy over confrontation. Redirecting the course of the night.

I love Adele because she's been there for me forever. Because she's funny as hell. Because when my mother turns the screws too tight, Adele can just sense it, and she's at my door with mocha caramels and the latest *Vanity Fair* and *Vogue*. I should cut her more slack when it comes to Graham, and guy stuff in general.

When she's accepting a round of applause and tugging her dress back in place, I flash her a warm smile. "Sorry. I'm glad you're here."

"I love your dress," she says, tacitly accepting my apology. "Where did you find it?"

"I picked it out on a trip to the city. There are actually a few cute boutiques on Wood Street now."

The city is Pittsburgh, the closest place to West Virginia's Northern Panhandle to resemble an actual metropolis. We lived there for the first seven years of my life, but I don't really remember much before Logansville. The panhandle—that skinny strip of land nestled between Pennsylvania and Ohio—is part southern charm, part Hicksville. Logansville, naturally, brings the charm. Pittsburgh is about a forty-five-minute drive from here; my dad makes the commute every day to the investment firm where he's newly a partner. He was already a partner at his old firm, but his job kind of fell apart along with the economy. It's been a long climb back to where he is now, and we're far from the top of the mountain.

I'm totally lost in thought when Trina arrives with a heaping plate of hors d'oeuvres. I raise my eyebrows.

"What, they're for sharing." She holds the plate out to me.

Trina is tall and model-thin, and she can eat like a horse. It's going to catch up to her someday, but at the moment she looks amazing in a sapphire mermaid dress that only she could pull off and a new cascade of ombré hair. She had the wave put in so her bone-straight Japanese locks would "flow like the ocean." Her words. Trina's beloved Canon EOS 5D is slung around her neck. The clunky camera kind of ruins her elegant silhouette, but Trina would never attend a society function without it. She would also be the first to take down any joker who makes a crack about camera-obsessed Japanese tourists. Trina may love her selfies, but she's no hobby photographer. Or tourist. Trina's going to be a professional.

I pluck a Kobe and Stilton toast off her plate and pop it in my mouth. The staff must have returned with the fresh round, which means it's getting close to midnight. It also means everything's running smoothly, not that I'll get an ounce of credit. I close my eyes for a second, and the anonymous text message flashes across the back of my lids. *Wouldn't you look better without a cheater on your arm?* I shiver. Someone is trying to shake me up, and it's not going to work.

"Where's Carter?" Trina asks. My thoughts exactly. I haven't heard his laugh rising above the din since before I stepped out of the hall. I glance around at our friends. Bronson has joined Graham and Ben in the corner, although his eyes are fixed on his phone. Any money says he's texting Alexander, his boyfriend, who goes to school across town at Logansville North. Alexander was invited tonight, of course, but he's still in Tulum with his family. Graham makes a show of trying to read Bronson's texts over his shoulder, and Bronson shoves his phone in his pocket and joins the conversation, which has turned from comics to skydiving, their new obsession. Only Bronson has actually jumped before; his dad's in the military and Bronson is kind of an adrenaline junkie. The guys all want to immortalize their friendship by jumping out of a plane together before we graduate in five months. It's ridiculous, but not as ridiculous as Batman versus Wolverine. Anyway, Carter's not with them.

Adele and Trina are standing on either side of me, scarfing canapés. Except for Carter, that's all of us. I scan the rest of the room. Winston and Krystal Shaw are strategically positioned with my dad, Jack, near the entryway, should they need to greet any extra-fashionably-late guests. They're glowing, the royalty of Logansville. My mother should be with them, but it's probably best if I don't spend too much time thinking about where she's gone off to. Two years ago, I found her passed out in the gun room, her face pressed against a glass case housing one of Mr. Shaw's many antique revolvers. Since then, the Shaws have kept their little vintage armory locked up tight during parties. I'm sure she's found a regular bed to pass out on this time. At least she had the good sense to make an exit before she went from sloppy to fully lit.

My eyes rove through the rest of the crowd, searching for Carter. The great hall is filled with my dad's investment colleagues and their families, many of whom drove from Pittsburgh to be here tonight; the board members from my mother's organizations, the Museum of Fine Arts and the Northern Panhandle Land Trust; and the bigwigs from Shaw Realty, the largest, most successful corporate firm in the area. Carter's already slated to head up sales in one of their regional markets as soon as he graduates from college.

My eyes dart back to my friends and then around the hall one more time. I squint again at the grandfather clock. It's 11:55. I can feel my pulse spike.

"There he is." Adele's pointing up to the balcony. Carter's leaning into the wall, back pressed against the ornate cream and gold wallpaper, texting furiously. His fingers pause, and he stares at the screen for a beat. Then, his face transforms into a wide grin.

My heart sinks, blood rushing to my face. I know I don't look pretty wearing this mix of hurt and fury, but I can't help it. It's five minutes until midnight, and Carter's texting with *her*. Again. Adele takes one look at my face and turns to Graham.

"Get Carter down here. Now."

Graham glances at me, then follows Adele's gaze up to the balcony. A shadow passes over his face when his eyes find Carter. He squeezes my shoulder and presses past me. "On it."

Trina flags down more glasses of champagne, and soon everyone's crowded around me in a tight circle, guzzling bubbly and laughing hard at something Ben says that's not even funny, but it keeps me almost entertained until Graham reappears with Carter. I take a deep breath to clear my head. Whoever sent that anonymous text struck a nerve. But they're wrong: Carter belongs on my arm. I belong with him.

She is just a temporary distraction. I'm forever, and deep down, Carter knows it. He squeezes through to the center of the circle and takes his place next to me at exactly thirty seconds to go until midnight, just as the whole room starts counting down.

"Sorry, babe," he whispers in my ear. "Family stuff with my cousin. Lost track of time."

Carter thinks I don't know about her. I smile thinly and let the lie fade into the chant: *eighteen, seventeen, sixteen* . . . My fingertips glide across the gold chain around my neck until they find the small onyx heart at the end. Carter gave it to me because black is eternally classy, and it goes with everything. Because Carter knows what I care about, knows me inside and out, knows we belong together. I repeat it over and over inside my head until I believe it. Then I draw his eyes to the heart with my fingertips, remind him that he's here with me. He smiles, his eyes locked into mine.

Twelve, eleven, ten... All around us, our friends lift their champagne flutes toward the ceiling. Bronson scoops Adele up in both his arms, and she tilts back her head, letting her hair plunge down toward the floor in a sea of gold. Trina raises first her Canon, then her phone, and snaps a series of pictures. I smile wide. *Six, five, four*... Carter touches my chin and draws my face toward his. *Three, two, one*... His lips find my lips, and this is how tonight is meant to end. Carter and me, together, surrounded by cheering and glasses clinking, surrounded by our friends who are toasting the new year and toasting the two of us, together. We're at the center of everything. All eyes on us.

ROSALIE

SUNDAY, DECEMBER 31

Three hours into the party, I could claw out my own eyes. Literally. Figuratively. *Allegorically.* Inside the neon cage of this church basement, the night is frozen in time, and I'm frozen along with it. Unable to move forward. Trapped in the sticky web of lies that both fill me with doubt and keep me alive. I burrow deeper behind the overstuffed coat rack as if the wall of polyester and wool might protect me. It's only ten thirty. There's still an eternity between this moment and the countdown to the ball drop, that saving grace that means we'll all get to go home. Praise Jesus.

I breathe in the mix of damp wool fibers, sparkling cider, and dust, then I dig out my phone and shoot my girlfriend Paulina one last text.

Have fun tonight!
See you next year!

I try to be happy. Pretend I'm not jealous of her night out dancing with her brother and his friends while I'm confined to the bowels of God's Grace Fellowship of Christ to ring in the new year with the members of Jesus' army.

It doesn't work.

Paulina doesn't text back. They must already be at the club, where it's too loud to hear, and there's probably no reception anyway. I slip my phone into the back pocket of my stiff dress slacks where I can feel it vibrate, just in case, then push myself up off the coat room floor. I've been hiding in here too long; people will notice. My parents will notice. I reach my arms toward the ceiling, stretch out the kinks. Then, hair check: still styled. Shirt check: slightly wrinkled, but passable. I slip off my glasses and rub the lenses against someone's coat sleeve until they shine. Then I slip the boxy blue frames back across the bridge of my nose. Deep breath. I can do this.

Back in the event hall, I look around for my little sister, Lily. The finished basement beneath the titanic evangelical chapel isn't fancy, but it's proportionately big. And crowded. Pretty much every member of the Fellowship is here tonight, hundreds of believers mingling over cookies or stationed around card tables, chatting earnestly for hours on end. Which is to say, no one would have missed me tonight, but other plans were not an option. The church gathering is the only acceptable New Year's celebration for the Bell daughters, and my parents' word is law.

Finally, the rose-pink flash of Lily's dress catches my eye. Two boys in miniature dress pants and miniature ties are chasing my sister and another girl. One catches the tail end of Lily's sash in his hand, and she squeals before disappearing with her friends through the door to the kitchen.

For the second time tonight, I try not to be jealous. Of Lily's youth. Her innocence. Her unfettered ability to just enjoy the party. Maybe she'll be lucky. Maybe for her, the Fellowship's path will be easy. Maybe she'll never have to learn how rigid and airless these walls can be for anyone who doesn't fit the scripture's mold.

I believe in God. And I like girls. They're not switches you can flip on or off, pieces of me you can take or leave. But the Fellowship of Christ isn't just any Christian church. Some evangelical congregations are moderate or even progressive, but the FOC is one of the most reverent, most dogmatic. And the Fellowship teaches that love can only exist between a man and a woman, that it's God's plan. We believe scriptures are inspired by God, and to stray is to fall short of His glory. *We. They.* It's not that simple.

With Lily out of sight, I'm forced to look around for someone else to talk to. Or somewhere else to hide. The event hall is absolutely packed with bodies, but I don't have any friends here. Friends treat you like an equal, like a *person*. This congregation has only ever treated me with concern at best and fear at worst. For four years now, they've tried to *cleanse me*. To guide me on *the path to eternal life*. I used to believe—really believe—they had my best interests at heart. That their love was God's love, and if I opened myself up to enough of it, it might save me.

On the worst days, I still can't shake the voice that says, *What if they're right? What if you're going to hell?*

I walk over to the cookie and juice table to give myself something to do. All the women in the congregation baked for tonight. There must be ten different varieties of bars—lemon, pecan pie, coconut—and every possible chocolate chip option known to man: nuts, no nuts, gluten free, sugar free, vegan. I don't have much of an appetite, so I grab a bottle of orange juice instead. The cap unscrews with a satisfying twist.

"Rosalie." I feel my mom's firm, steady presence even before she speaks. We look as unrelated as I feel. My petite frame, dark hair, and bad eyesight all come from my dad's side, but then again, I don't feel much of a hereditary bond there either. "There you are. Emily Masters is right over there. Why don't you go say hello?"

I take a gulp of juice so I don't have to answer.

Mom frowns, her mouth tugged down into those classic Julia Bell lines of disapproval that I know so well. "You need to make more of an effort, Rosalie."

This is not a new conversation. Mom's target is the daughter of one of the most esteemed ecclesiastical ministers across the entire Fellowship of Christ evangelical denomination. Brother Masters is revered nationally for his fervent and compassionate outreach to souls lost in sin. The reputation he developed through his landmark To Seek and Save program is the number one reason my family relocated to Culver Ridge almost four years ago. My mom has been dying to see Emily and me become friends since the instant the moving van pulled up.

The problem is, I have tried to be friendly, and despite what

Mom thinks, Emily has zero interest in buddying up to the weird, "confused" girl whose affections might turn ungodly at the bat of an eye. I am the furthest thing from attracted to her, but I know exactly how she sees me. *Ill. A pariah. Possibly contagious.*

"I don't think Emily and I have a lot in common," I say quietly. As soon as the words are out of my mouth, I regret them. I'm causing trouble. I should just say *okay* and drop it.

Mom places her hands squarely on my shoulders and turns me to face her. Her touch makes me flinch. There's a grit about her, a fierce righteousness that demands my focus. Emily is the church, and therefore Emily is good. The right kind of influence. Mom locks her eyes into mine. "I'd like to see you try to have more in common. Understood?"

I turn my gaze toward Emily. She's sitting across the room on a plastic folding chair, talking to Beth Clark, a junior who follows her around like a puppy. I've always gotten the sense that Emily likes the attention more than she likes Beth, but who am I to judge. I don't really know these girls. Emily lifts her hands to gather back her hair, then lets it fall down her shoulders. She has the kind of luscious blond tresses that I used to covet when I was too little to know anything about being my own person. Tonight her head sparkles almost unnaturally in the neon basement lights. I reach up automatically and touch my sharply frayed bangs. Now, I wouldn't trade my short, jagged cut for anything. My parents don't love it, but they haven't made me grow it out yet either.

I could try my heart out, but Emily Masters and I will never be friends. I imagine looking into her pale blue eyes and perfect pink lips and telling her all my secrets. What happened in middle school. Why my parents pulled me out. How I was homeschooled for a year, why we moved across the state to Culver Ridge the summer before ninth grade.

I shudder thinking about the secrets she already knows—or thinks she knows. Emily made it perfectly clear as soon as we arrived in Culver Ridge that, as Brother Masters's daughter, she knew all about my history. My "struggle." Her tone, the way she reached for my shoulder as she spoke and almost—but didn't quite—touch it, spoke volumes. I'm almost positive she's the reason the whole congregation seemed to think they could see down to my very soul from the moment my parents guided me through the God's Grace doors.

Emily might know some facts about me—the stints in counseling, the summer at Camp Eternal Light—but she doesn't know the first thing about being Rosalie Bell. Emily's never been made to feel subhuman by people who think they speak a higher truth, who fervently believe their principles come straight from God's mouth. She's only been on the other end of that spite.

Some days, I feel dead inside. And others—days like today—the anger courses like a current through my veins. I used to blame my parents for everything they put me through, everything they believe. Now I take the anger, curl it up into a ball inside my stomach, save it all for the Fellowship. It keeps me focused on living one more day, and another, and another, until eventually I can leave this place behind.

I turn back to my mom. "Understood." I've put this off as long as possible. That I would go talk to Emily was never really up for debate.

Mom smiles. Julia Bell's evangelical conviction that I've been cured, that I've received Christ's gift of salvation, keeps her hopeful that her daughter might legitimately befriend a pastor's daughter. Part of me feels guilty for deceiving her. The other part of me knows that deception is the only thing keeping me together with my family, with Lily, keeping me with Paulina, keeping a roof over my head, keeping me alive.

Mom gives me a gentle shove on my behind like I'm a toddler, and I walk toward Emily and Beth, the orange juice bottle clutched so tight in my fists that the plastic bites my skin.

"Happy New Year," I mumble, grateful for the stock conversation starter.

Beth keeps talking like she didn't hear me, but Emily glances up and gives me a tight smile. She is nothing if not polite, at least on the surface.

"Have you made your resolutions, Rosalie?" Emily manages to make even the most standard question feel loaded. "I'm sure my father would be willing to meet, if you're . . . struggling. His door is open to every member of God's Grace."

"I'm good, thanks." It takes all my willpower not to tell her to shove her condescension where the sun doesn't shine. But blowing up at Emily Masters would hurt me way more than it would hurt her. Within Fellowship walls, I can't afford to make any mistakes. My everything depends on my ability to keep it together.

"How about you, Beth?" I turn to the younger girl, bringing her into the conversation as if we're just three FOC kids having a regular chat.

"Yeah, sure." She leans physically away from me, dismissing me with the whole of her being.

I can't do this. I take a step back. "Well, have a nice evening," I say. "I hope the new year brings you all of His blessings."

As I turn, I'm pretty sure I hear them both laugh. I know Mom's watching from across the room, silently admonishing me for not trying hard enough, for coming up short. Again. I need to get away from them, their laughter, the sear of Mom's eyes on the back of my head. I'm letting my feet carry me fast toward the coat room, the bathroom, anywhere, when I feel my phone buzzing in my back pocket. I push through the door to the women's room. It's mercifully empty. I lock myself in a stall and check my texts.

> Do you have any idea how much I miss you right now? 😟

Sweet. But definitely not Paulina. I hesitate before typing back.

> There's a church basement full of people out on Rural Route 12 just dying to meet you.

Which I can say only because he would never actually show up.

> I wish I could whisk you away.

I laugh, picturing Carter Shaw rolling up here in his Mercedes to rescue me from the saved souls of Culver Ridge. In reality, Carter's place is with his girlfriend, Amanda, at that superposh party their parents throw, and he knows it. Besides, Carter doesn't actually want to be here. With me, sure. But not here. Twenty minutes outside Logansville, Culver Ridge calls itself a suburb, but it's barely even that. More rural than suburban, the landscape is home to cows, chickens, and the mostly white, mostly working poor. There are three shops within walking distance from my house: a CVS; a liquor store that also sells ice cream out of a Plexiglas window in the summer; and Margarita's, a take-out pizza joint home to West Virginia's soggiest crust. O'Malley's, the catch-all discount store, is a ten-minute drive, and there's no grocery store, so whatever you can't get at CVS or from a roadside stand means a trip into Logansville.

Carter does not belong here. Not in Culver Ridge, and certainly not in the basement of the most reverent fundamentalist Fellowship in northern Appalachia. What he wants is fun Rosalie. Date night Rosalie. Rock-show-going, junk-food-eating, devil-may-care Rosalie. His slice of adolescent deviance, his escape from all the responsibilities that come with being Carter Shaw: a college-to-career pipeline, money and property and prestige, Amanda Kelly.

It's been almost exactly four months since we met, since Carter became the smoke screen keeping me out of the phony, destructive kind of "therapy" my parents think delivered me back to God's path. In March, I'll turn eighteen, and in May, I graduate. Staying far away from church counseling for a few more months is my number one priority. It has to be. Even though I'm deceiving Carter, who thinks we're for real—and inclination for cheating aside, he is a pretty nice guy. Kind. Caring. Someone I might actually be friends with, if things were different. And there's no denying how much pain I'd cause his girlfriend if she ever found out. Or how I'm putting Paulina in an impossible position, asking her to let things between Carter and me be okay for now, just for now. When I think about it too much, the guilt starts to slosh around in my gut, nestles up against the ball of anger I'm keeping there.

I draw in a deep breath that does nothing to quiet my jangling nerves. My phone is buzzing again.

> I bet you smell amazing. I can't wait to
> see you again.

> Yup, see you Thursday

Then I wonder if my text sounded a little harsh, so I add a green heart emoji.

> I'll text you again before midnight,
> okay?

Before midnight. Of course. Not *at* midnight, because then he'll be with Amanda. Pressing his lips against her lips and guzzling Dom Pérignon from crystal champagne flutes with Logansville's old-money Republicans in their lavish dresses and suits. I tell myself they're so steeped with privilege, so untouchable, I could never possibly hurt them. That whatever arrangement they have, Amanda's okay with it. But I know a lie when I hear one. The guilt gives another slosh, just for good measure.

> Don't get in trouble.

The clock on my phone reads 11:29. I should probably actually pee and then get back out to the party. One more half hour, and then we can finally go home.

But when I open the door, I know I can't face the event hall again. I can see my dad across the room, twirling Lily in circles. She spins around, and around, and around, her giggles pitched high with delight. I want to run over to them. I want to laugh like that, dizzy and delirious. But I can't fake happy anymore tonight. I can feel my mask slipping and my resolve slipping with it. If I were a better person, maybe I could figure out how to just be content and grateful to be here tonight with my family.

The thought stops me in my tracks. Those aren't my words. A cold chill runs down my spine, the familiar premonition of an old memory that wants to be shaken loose. A memory belonging to a cold church office or sweltering camp rec room, both options equally petrifying. Both threatening to drag my mind somewhere I can't let it take me. Not now. Not with all these people around. I jam my fingertips into my temples, will the memories to stay lodged deep in the recesses of my mind where they belong.

Before I can lose this fight, I turn around and take the hall all the way to the end. I don't even stop to grab my coat before running up the stairs. At the top, I turn away from the megachapel and head instead for the doors at the back. Outside, the cold air is a shock to my bare arms. It's always too hot in the basement, but out here it's appropriately freezing for the last day of December. I don't mind. I lean back against the concrete wall of the church and watch my breath stream out in front of me in white wisps, then disappear. My glasses fill with fog, and I take them off, close my eyes. I draw the air in, then out, try to get my breathing under control. My mind back in the present. In, then out. The cold air makes me feel clean. Like I'm freshly scrubbed, and each breath is polishing my insides until they shine. I picture my body stretching out across the blue glass surface of a winter lake. It's just me, and no one's poking or prodding or judging. It's all going to be okay. It's silent. It's perfect.

The door bangs behind me, snapping me back to reality. I nod to Mr. Hagan, stepping outside for a smoke.

"Rosalie," he says.

"Happy New Year, Mr. Hagan. Did you and Mrs. Hagan have a good trip to Baltimore?"

"We did." He keeps a good five feet between us. "She's still there with the kids. Marcy and Brian gave us a new grandbaby for the holidays. Born right on Jesus' birthday. A real miracle."

"You must feel very blessed."

"We are," he replies, staring straight at me. "Family is a blessing. New life is a blessing." He stops there, but his unspoken words hang in the air between us: *A union between a man and a woman is a blessing.*

"Well, happy New Year," I say again. Mercifully, he nods and continues on away from the church, into the parking lot, to light up his cigarette.

Alone again, I lean my head back against the wall and close my eyes until my phone buzzes, a text from Carter, as promised, wishing me a happy New Year. I tap out a quick reply. Maybe someday, when all of this is behind us and I'm living in Pittsburgh with Paulina, maybe Carter and I could really be friends. But probably not.

It's 11:55. All up and down the East Coast, people are cozying up to their loved ones at house parties or bars, fingers laced with fingers, bare skin brushing against bare skin, setting off sparks. Champagne breath mingling with champagne breath.

Carter doesn't write back, but it doesn't matter. It's not Carter I want here with me tonight. Downstairs, the giant flat screen is switched on. Cheers and the bright chime of bells filter out into the night air. My family is gathering together to watch the ball descend on Times Square. I should go in. I should join them. But it's easier out here, alone. It's midnight, and for a moment, I don't have to pretend. Out here, the world is perfectly still.

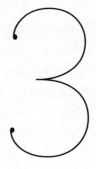

AMANDA
TUESDAY, JANUARY 2

At seven fifteen on the first morning back after break, Dad is shut in his office with a thermos of coffee, doing prework before driving to the firm. And my mother is still in bed. Family meals are a rarity in the Kelly household, breakfast in particular. I have a vague recollection of bright, early-morning chatter over juice and toast in our old house, but like most things that used to make my parents happy, that habit died in Pittsburgh.

I open the fridge, already knowing I'll find an assortment of boxed hors d'oeuvres from Sunday night and not much else. My mother was too hung over yesterday to do much beyond watch an endless stream of *House of Cards* reruns in her bathrobe, and I can't remember the last time Dad did the shopping. I pour some cereal into a bowl and drain the last of the almond milk.

At seven thirty, when there's still no sound of my mother stirring, I pluck the list from the wicker basket on the counter and head upstairs.

"Mom?" I stand outside my parents' bedroom door and hold my breath. A minute later, I knock again. "Can I come in?"

A muffled groan that might be *yes* or *go away* filters through the door. I grasp the handle and push it open partway. Inside, I'm greeted by pitch dark. The heavy drapes are drawn all the way across the windows, and it may as well be midnight in here.

"What is it, Amanda?" My mother's voice is sharp and edged with last night's drinks. My eyes adjust to find her propped up on one elbow in bed. Her sleeping mask is shoved halfway up her forehead, her hair bunched in the elastic. She looks less than happy to see me.

"I saw the list on the counter." I choose my words carefully. "Should I go to the store after school?" A younger version of me would have whined about there being nothing to eat. Now I know to skip straight to the part where I offer to go shopping myself.

She collapses back on her pillow. "I think you should. I have the Land Trust luncheon at one, and I don't know when I'll find the time."

Because she won't be out of bed until noon. Because she'll tell Mrs. Steinway that the car's not running right, so she can get a ride, so she can make it a three-martini lunch.

I've pulled the door almost closed when she adds, "Amanda? Don't use the family card. There was a fraud alert last week, and they said something about deactivating. Take the Amex from my purse."

I pause, fingers on the door handle, mouth half open. There are so many things I want to say right now, but all of them would make this worse. Did she forget I used the family Visa at the florist on Sunday, and it was fine? My mother lies like she knocks back top-shelf vodka—liberally. She must think I'm entirely oblivious. There's nothing wrong with the card except the balance, which is probably near the limit again.

The Amex is my mother's private card; I don't think Dad knows she has it. She uses it to pay for spa days and liquor store runs and pays it off from her personal savings, which have been floating all the things we can't really afford anymore but apparently can't live without. Based on my mother's recent spike in stress and alcohol consumption, I'd wager her savings are nearly tapped. My parents have never talked to me about it, not directly. But I've seen the statements. I know we've been making the minimum monthly payments since middle school and racking up debt of the many-zeros variety. Now that Dad's a partner again, things will get easier. But getting out of debt this deep won't happen overnight, especially at the rate my mother keeps spending.

"Okay," I say softly. I close my mouth, then the door, and fly back down the sleek wooden staircase into the dark gleam of the kitchen—all marble and stainless steel—where my mother's purse slouches on the unused breakfast table. My fingers close around her wallet, and along with it, a sheet of white printer paper, pristinely folded. Feeling only slightly guilty for snooping—she did send me into her purse, after all—I open it up, expecting a spa pass or agenda for her all-important luncheon, but it's an email from Carter's dad.

> I can't stop thinking about Sunday's
> tête-à-tête. In truth, my skin tingles
> nonstop. I fear it's become a bit of a
> rueful habit, and yet, I've no resolve
> to effect its end. Have you?
>
> But to the point: You need an answer,
> N or V. Always V, my dear. In the end,
> always V.

My eyes skate to the top of the paper. It's from last night, sent from Winston's personal account to my mother's. I tell myself it's just a few short lines of obscure parental prose, but I drop it back down into the cave of her purse like it has teeth. I need to get the credit card, get to school. Inside her wallet, in slots below the American Express and family Visa, are three new cards I don't recognize. I slip the Amex into my pocket, shove her wallet back into her purse, and head down to the garage.

Most people listen to music on the way to school, but I like the silence on the drive to Logansville South. Sometimes it's the only quiet in my entire day. Once I hit the parking lot, Adele and Trina will be waiting to meet up with me for the walk to the main entrance, and then everyone wants my attention the second we hit the doors. That's the price of being Amanda Kelly—and 98 percent of the time, I love it.

But the coupé is my sanctuary. For seven minutes every day, I'm not private Amanda: walking on the eggshells that line the floors at home, or proving myself to Carter, again and again.

And I'm not public Amanda, either: beautiful, sharp-tongued, admired, feared. Queen of the senior class. For these seven minutes, I don't have to be any of those girls. I can just be me.

And today, the real me is a ball of nerves. As I drive, I try to shut the anxiety-spiral down, but the thoughts keep coming: How my dad practically lives at the office and we still can't pay the bills. How deeply my mother has sunk into her well of 80 proof and delusion. And how they've pinned all their hopes on my relationship with Carter. What marrying into the Shaws would mean for our family. It's the last thought that makes my stomach churn and my knuckles whiten against the wheel.

This summer, I'll turn eighteen. In the fall, Carter and I will join WVU's incoming class. He's a legacy there, and of course I'll join him. I can only imagine what kind of strain a private university would put on our family, and following Carter to WVU is the kind of smart financial choice my mother can get behind.

But first, I have to endure a few more months of *her*. Hopefully, she won't last that long. As I wait for the light on Foster to turn green I take in a long, slow breath. Carter may have one glaring flaw, but otherwise, he's perfect for me. And even more importantly, he's perfect for my family. A life with Carter means making my parents' lives good again. I can make that happen.

As soon as Rosalie gets out of my way.

Whenever I want to drive out to Culver Ridge and strangle that home-wrecker-in-training, I repeat my mother's words like a mantra: *Don't treat other girls like the competition, and they won't be.* My mother may be a lush, but she is the authority on maintaining a powerful relationship.

Once we get to college, Rosalie will be out of the picture, and maybe then, everything will go back to normal for Carter and me. Back to the way it used to be. For a quick moment, my fingers find the onyx heart around my neck. WVU's French department may not be as highly ranked as the language programs at the other schools where my guidance counselor insisted I apply, but my eye is on the goal. I don't need the best French degree in the country. Being Mrs. Shaw will open doors and maybe even give my parents back a bit of the happiness that seems to have drained away with their savings.

The light changes, and traffic on Foster starts to move again. I flick on my left turn signal and wait for a break in the line of cars. Recently, my seven-minute drive has been extended to nine because of the addition they're putting on the school. We're getting a new science wing and a second gymnasium (because Logansville taxpayers were not about to fund any large-scale expenditure not somehow tied to the varsity athletics program) and so the front entrance to the parking lot is closed off during the construction.

As I wait for the traffic in the opposite lane to clear, I scan the work boots and hard hats for David Gallagher, who's been working here since November. Ben's older brother is a freshman at NPCC-L, the Logansville branch of the Northern Panhandle Community College, but he was still a senior here last year. He's trim and athletic to his little brother's awkward lank, at once laid back and outgoing. I honestly don't know how he and Ben are related.

I spot David hauling a wheelbarrow full of something covered in a gray tarp just as the lane finally clears and I'm able to make my left past the site and the little lot where the construction vehicles are parked, and on into the main parking lot. I can see the outlines of his arm and chest muscles through his jacket. I honk my horn as I pass by, and he looks up and waves. Early freshman year, before Carter and I got together, David took me out to the movies a couple times. We were never a couple, but we had fun. Carter doesn't know—will never know—that David was my first kiss.

There's some beef with his dad and Carter's, though, so we pretty much stopped hanging out when Carter and I started dating. Never stopped Ben from hanging around, of course. I always kind of wanted David to hook up with Trina, but his family's a mess, so it's probably for the best that it never happened.

As I leave the construction site behind and circle around to the parking lot's back entrance, I try to dial the anxiety down to a dull roar. It's time to be public Amanda: game face on. I pull into the lot and whisper under my breath, "You've got this."

I shift into park and close my eyes, allowing myself one more moment of silence. The air inside the car is still vibrating with the echo of my whisper. I feel centered, energized. I'm Amanda Fucking Kelly. My phone buzzes, but I ignore it. I just need one more minute.

"Bitch, it's freezing out here." Adele's voice snaps me out of my daydream. Her face is pressed against the window, and she's fogging it up on purpose. She presses her lips together and leaves a smeary kiss right in the center of the glass. "Our asses are turning into icicles." She reaches over to smack the back of Trina's puffy coat, somewhere in the neighborhood of where her ass would be if she actually had one. Trina lets out a yelp.

Time to turn it on. Sharp wit. On top. In charge. I throw open the door and a second later I'm standing next to them in the parking lot, shivering and jumping up and down like it's a lot colder than it actually is.

"If you want to survive the Logansville winter, you've gotta shake it, ladies." I shimmy from my shoulders all the way down to my boots, and we all burst out laughing. Adele lets out a giant snort, and then we're doubled over, laughing twice as hard, and Trina's yelling, "I'm peeing! I'm peeing!" even though she's totally not.

All around us, car doors are slamming and everyone's staring because we're the loudest people in the student lot. We play like we don't give a shit what anyone thinks, and it's not like they're judging us, anyway. They want to know what we're cracking up about. They want in on the joke. It's the first day back to school after break, and it's clear that we had the best time. We have the best stories. And this morning, we're having the most fun.

Game on.

We start walking, arms linked together, puffy sleeve into puffy sleeve. Marshmallow arms. My phone buzzes again as we're about halfway across the lot, a reminder of the text I ignored. "Please hold," I say, making all three of us wait so I can dig it out of my bag.

I click on the screen and a selfie of Carter and me raising champagne flutes lights up in the background. My sleek brown hair and pearl-pale skin look stunning against the bright red of my dress. Cutting across the background photo, the new message indicator reads *Private Number*. I suck in my breath and click on the icon.

You're so beautiful it hurts.

"Who is it?" Trina asks.

I stare at the five words on the screen. My heart flutters, just a little. "I don't know. There's no caller ID."

"Let me see." Adele grabs my phone, not waiting for a response. "Ooh, flirty. Did Carter get a new phone?"

"I think I would know." I grab my phone back and start typing.

Who is this?

No answer.

Hello? Who's phone is this?

"Can we do this inside?" Trina is hopping from one foot to the other, her white wool scarf and the pompoms on the ends of her spotless white boots bouncing up and down against her long black coat. "I promise we can still play detective where there's actual heat on."

"You look like a penguin," Adele giggles. She turns out her feet and hands like flippers and proceeds to waddle in a circle around Trina. "I'm Chilly Willy the peeeeenguin!" she trills while Trina swats at her with her scarf.

"Fine." Something about that text makes me feel jittery. I can't tell if it's good-jittery or bad-jittery, but suddenly my heart's racing. I fix my gaze on the massive brick and sandstone structure that is Logansville South. Time to get my head back in the back-to-school game. I speed-walk across the rest of the parking lot, Trina matching my pace and Adele struggling to keep up in the doubtlessly too-tight dress beneath her metallic silver coat.

Inside, we push through the crush of kids loitering outside the auditorium and head straight to my locker, which sits in a quiet alcove off the main first floor artery. My boots make a steady *click-click-click* like a heartbeat against the white-and-gold-flecked floors. It smells like it always smells in winter: stale air mixed with melting crayons, the scent our old boilers pump out through the vents when the heat's up full-blast. I check my phone twice on the way, but there's still no response.

"It's probably a wrong number," Adele suggests. "I bet there's a great story behind it." She crosses two spread-open palms through the air in front of her, setting the scene. "Get this: Some girl typed a random number into some dude's phone at a party over break, and he thinks he's texting *her*, but really she's in Morgantown somewhere. . . ."

I try to tune her animated chatter out. She's probably right, but I don't want to believe her. Adele finishes her story, and I dial my combination while she squats down over her bag, rummaging around for something that must be buried deep at the bottom, and Trina leans back against the wall. I didn't tell either of them about the text on New Year's. They would have spent the rest of the party trying to crack the case of the mystery texter, and I was not about to give this Private Number person that kind of satisfaction.

But maybe this isn't the same person. *You're so beautiful it hurts.* What if this morning's text really *is* from Carter, some mystery he's cooked up involving burners and a scavenger hunt? It's definitely not like him. Carter is two dozen roses on Valentine's Day and tiny onyx hearts on gold chains and the tasting menu at Taviani's downtown. He's traditional. He's not the games and intrigue type, and I've never wanted him to be until this moment.

I can't explain it, but I'm suddenly hooked on the idea of this new Carter. My heart is still jumping just a little as I hang up my coat and grab my books. Adele is still buried deep in her bag, tongue sticking out through her teeth. Whatever she's doing, she looks possessed. Finally, she gives up and turns to Trina. "Lip gloss?"

Trina hands over a tiny blue canister just as my phone finally buzzes again.

> Consider me your secret admirer.
> You're way too good for that Carter
> guy.

My heart sinks. It was silly to think it might be Carter. I want to tell this so-called "secret admirer" to shove it because what is this, fourth grade? But a part of me, just a tiny part, is curious. Someone wants to play my White Knight.

"What'd it say?" Adele asks, standing and trying to read over my shoulder. I click off the screen and toss my phone back in my bag before she or Trina can get a look.

"You were right. Wrong number."

"Sucks." Adele makes an exaggerated pouty face, then unzips her coat revealing a burnt orange sweater dress. "God, it's a million degrees in this place. Can't it just be a normal temperature?"

"You know they always crank the heat way up after break." Trina takes Adele by the elbow and starts guiding her toward the stairwell. Their lockers are one floor up.

"See you in Aiden's," Adele calls over her shoulder, making a show of fanning herself and faux-stumbling as they walk.

"Bye," I call back, my words dissolving into a laugh.

In the fall, we discovered our studio art teacher, Mr. Parker, is Mr. *Aiden* Parker, so now we secretly call him Aiden because it's the sexiest name ever. We all take art as an elective, even though Trina's the only one of us who's any good. Her obsession with that high-end Canon is a bit extreme, but she does have a kind of amazing talent for photography.

I wave and wait for them to disappear into the stairwell. As soon as they're gone, I shut my locker and turn my phone back on, heart beating fast.

> Who IS this?

> Are you messing with me?

This time, there's no delay. I get three texts back, one after the other.

> Of course not.

> I know you love a good game.

> And don't you dare tell Carter Shaw about me.

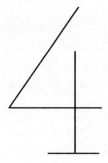

ROSALIE
THURSDAY, JANUARY 4

My life is negotiation. With my parents, with Carter, with Paulina, with myself. Carter's scheduled to arrive at five, so that means by four thirty it's time to get stoned. The charade of our relationship is keeping me safe—but it's not something I can face sober.

I shove my desk chair up against the door (no locks allowed at the Bells) and pull the cardboard box that holds the shoes from my Holy Immersive Baptism out of the back of my cramped bedroom closet. I push aside the tissue paper to reveal my vape pen and the jar that holds my stash. Then, I plug the vaporizer into its charger.

Drugs of all kinds are strictly prohibited by the Fellowship of Christ. Christian teens are high on life! But vaping is hardly the most serious of my FOC infractions. If the church's principles are right—which they aren't because I can't let myself think that way—the afterworld already holds a punishing lake of fire with my name on it. In this life, I'm getting stoned.

There's something calming about the ritual of charging and packing the pen, knowing my own little nirvana awaits. I hover over the wooden desk that doubles as a dresser and press the weed into the chamber, not too loose, not too tight. Then I sit back on my twin bed, spread up with the same worn yellow quilt I've had since grade school, and wait for the pen to charge.

Paulina and I tried pot for the first time freshman year, after her cousins swept through town, gifting her three pristinely rolled joints from their plants in Washington State. Pau never really got into it, preferring the cigarettes that are surely killing her faster, so when they mail her "care packages" of vacuum-sealed baggies packed in rolls of toilet paper, she passes them on to me. She hooked me up with the bright purple vaporizer too, which my parents would never recognize as an instrument for smoking pot. But they'd definitely recognize the smell, so I'm meticulous about hanging out the window and exhaling into a towel. If my parents found out, there would be something way worse than a punishing lake of fire waiting right here on Earth. But it's worth the risk. Getting high is like stuffing my ears full of cotton; the noise doesn't stop, but it muffles the daily reality of existing in my own house.

I check the time on my phone. 4:40. The light on my pen blinks from red to green, and I raise the window next to my bed and draw in a deep hit. Pau's cousins call the stuff they grow Smucker's since the plants are in an area that used to be berry patches. They swear it has "notes" of raspberry jam, but as I draw the vapor into my lungs, all I can taste is the sweet burn of oblivion.

Before I head downstairs, I return the shoe box to its place in my closet and grab the bottle of lavender body spray from my dresser slash desk—deodorant and face lotion on one side, books and school supplies on the other. I angle a spritz onto each wrist and two into my hair. Then, a final spritz near the window just to be safe.

When I'm returning the bottle to its place, something catches my eye: On the other side of the dresser top, my small collection of novels is out of order, a blue spine next to a pink one, disrupting my neat organization by color. My parents have been snooping again. *Monitoring.* I resist the urge to return Gayle Forman to her rightful place and shove my hands into my cardigan pockets. Deep inside my stomach, the ball of anger glows orange.

Downstairs, Lily's doing her reading comprehension homework on the den couch. I can hear the clatter of Mom and Dad in the kitchen, starting dinner and waiting for Carter to arrive, Faith NOW blaring. The nasal pitch of twenty-three-year-old talk radio wunderkind Billy Love Williams whirrs high and sharp like a swarm of angry bees. My throat tightens, and I half close the den door behind me.

"Hey, Lils." I plop down next to her on the couch, bumping my hip against her hip and making her giggle. "Whatcha working on?"

"A Job for Rob." I glance at the work sheet balanced on her lap desk. It's full of words ending in *-ob*: *cob, mob, sob.* At the bottom of the page is a cartoon of a man holding a big barrel of corn.

"That's corn on the *cob,*" Lily says, pointing to the cartoon triumphantly.

"So it is." I give her a big kiss on the top of her head. I don't remember having so much homework in first grade, but by midway through the year, these work sheets are already much too easy for Lily, so I guess it's paid off. "Are we still on to read *Anna, Banana* together after dinner tomorrow?" Lily likes to pretend Anna's adorable wiener dog, Banana, is ours.

"Obviously," she says to me, her eyes big and serious.

"Carter should be here soon," Mom calls from the kitchen, voice rising above the radio.

"Any minute," I call back. Which means I have to finish getting ready. I push up from the couch.

Back upstairs, I slip past the open door to Lily's room and into the bathroom. When Lily turned six this year, Mom gave up the hall storage and Dad broke down a wall to give Lily her own room, but it's still basically a closet. She'll move into my room the second I'm out of the house.

I stare at myself in the mirror. It's easy to recognize the girl I see, but she's not really *me*. Skinny jeans. Navy blue top that Mom picked out and a long beige cardigan. My clothes say nobody girl. Plain Jane. Basic. Inside my head, I'm wearing a fitted leather jacket over a soft gray T-shirt; a short black skirt; and tall, chunky red boots that could kick some serious ass. I close my eyes and the girl inside beats her fists against my rib cage, desperate to get out. *Just a few more months*, I promise her. *Just until we're safe.*

I adjust my glasses across the bridge of my nose, then smear some Bed Head on my fingers and run them through my hair. The dark brown strands stick out in all directions in a rocker girl, messy-on-purpose way that makes me feel alive.

A minute later, Carter pulls up front and my heart sinks deep into my stomach. I can't see the car from up here, but I can hear the crunch of tires against the gravel drive and the smooth *whoosh* of the car door closing.

When he knocks, I let my parents get the door. Dad's a teacher, so he's always home early, but Mom traded shifts at the grocery store today just to be here for these ten minutes. I can hear their three voices turn to laughter almost immediately, but I don't rush downstairs. Carter's good with my parents. He always makes the right jokes, puts them at ease. And most importantly, he's a Christian. Entering into a relationship with a nonbeliever is a practice expressly prohibited by the gospel according to everyone from Deuteronomy to Nehemiah to the Corinthians. In Richard and Julia Bell's perfect world, Carter would be FOC, but my parents will take a good Presbyterian boy as long as he lives a godly life. Since he knows it's important to me, he always turns it up for my parents.

"Rosalie? Carter's here!" Mom's voice floats up the short set of stairs to my room.

"Be right down!" I rinse off my hands, then grab my bag from my bed. I'm still rubbing my palms against my jeans when I arrive at the bottom of the stairs. Mom glares disapprovingly. When she looks at Carter Shaw, she sees a lucrative church endowment and her daughter's salvation, all rolled into one. Eyes fixed on the wet streaks on my jeans, she says, "There are two perfectly clean hand towels in the bathroom."

"I know," I mumble. "Sorry."

I glance around our living room, seeing it through Carter's eyes as I can't stop myself from doing every time he's here. Mom keeps our house meticulously clean; there's not a speck of dust or cobweb to be found. But no amount of vacuuming or dusting can disguise the worn beige carpet in need of replacing. The secondhand furniture. The thrifted art on the walls. It's not that I'm embarrassed by it; our house is what it is, and I actually like our thrift-store decor. I picked some of it out myself. But Carter *notices*. Even though he's far too polite to say it, I know he's making mental comparisons to his family's estate.

Dad doesn't seem to notice my discomfort. He's all smiles and deep chuckles this evening; Carter always puts him in a good mood. "What's tonight's plan?" His tone is amiable enough, but the truth is he'd never let me out of the house without knowing my whereabouts, even with a good Christian boy he trusts.

"Dinner in the city," Carter replies. "If that's okay, sir?"

My parents smile and nod, entirely charmed. "Of course," Mom says. Her voice is filled with hope.

The guilt draws back its lips, baring razor-sharp teeth. I take a deep breath and let everything smooth out around the edges, leaning into my buzz. With each stray thought about the precarious web I've spun, another thread snaps. Too much thinking, and it'll all rip apart.

I smile at Carter and walk over to him, sliding my hand into his. "Ready to hit the road?" I ask. The skin on my palm itches.

"Absolutely." He beams down at me, then turns to my parents. "Bye Mr. Bell, Mrs. Bell." He steadfastly refuses their offer to "call us Richard and Julia," and my parents find his insistence on formality endearing.

"Back by nine thirty," Mom says as I dart into the mudroom for my coat. "On the dot."

"Yes, ma'am," Carter replies, and we head out the door. Carter is always angling for a weekend date, when my curfew gets extended by an hour, but it's never been too hard to push back. He may want to take me out on a Friday or Saturday, but really, he can't. His weekends belong to Amanda.

We slide into the front seat of Carter's much-too-fancy-for-Culver-Ridge car, and he backs out of the drive, gravel pinging the tires. He fiddles with the stereo controls on the dash until the newest album by a pop-punk band we saw together blares out of the speakers. I try to relax and start bouncing along to the music, willing it to boost my mood.

"Where are we going?" I shout.

He turns the music down a little. "I could definitely go for some salt and grease tonight. Want to hit the 'O'?"

"Sure, I've never been."

Carter reaches over and squeezes my hand, a big grin bringing out a dimple on each cheek. "You're going to love it, Rosalie. Zero ambiance, but the cheese fries are out of this world."

I nod. "Let's do it."

The first couple times we went out, Carter made a big production of explaining that he wanted to expand his horizons, explore new things, see the world outside Logansville. But deception was clearly not his strong suit; beneath those dimples and bright blue eyes, he was hiding something.

On the night we met last August, I was playing wing woman for Elissa at a club in downtown Logansville. Sneaking out that night had meant risking my parents' wrath, but Elissa had just broken up with her boyfriend and needed me, so I'd slipped out through the mudroom after my parents went to bed. It was 21 plus, but Elissa got us in because she knew the sound tech. Inside, we spotted a group of high school guys at a table behind a velvet rope. Elissa said she recognized one of them from a youth leadership conference, Ben Gallup or Gallagher, so we went over.

The guys must have paid their way in. They had bottle service, and two gin and gingers later, Ben's friend Carter was telling me how beautiful I was, how *unique*, how bad he wanted to take me out. He was handsome if you're into that preppie, blond heartthrob thing—or guys in general—but when he asked for my number, I said no.

Later, when we were waiting for the bus back to Culver Ridge, Elissa asked me did I know who I'd turned down back there. I'd shrugged and said some rich kid from Logansville, I guessed. I'm not out to Elissa. I'm not out to anyone except Pau.

"That's Carter *Shaw*," she'd said. "As in Shaw Realty? His parents own like half of West Virginia."

I looked him up on my phone at four in the morning when I was home, under the covers, my parents none the wiser. Facebook didn't tell me much, his profile was set to private, but Google did. The first hit was a photo-rich feature from the previous December's *Logansville Gazette*, touting his parents' real estate agency as the *model West Virginia family business*. The article included profiles on his dad, founder and CEO; his mom, the CFO; and Carter, who was clearly being groomed to take over one day. It listed his many accolades: Logansville South lacrosse team captain, homecoming court three years running, leadership roles on a long list of school clubs and organizations. Under normal circumstances, I wouldn't have given him any more of my time, but summer before senior year had been pretty low, my parents' suspicions simmering and popping, threatening to boil over. I spent my days slinking around the house, fear buzzing beneath my skin.

So when Carter tracked me down via Ben, via Elissa, I'd said yes to a date. And when he'd made a big deal about avoiding Logansville, I'd called him out on it.

Carter had blushed deep red and sputtered something about being on a break with his long-time girlfriend, Amanda.

Girlfriend. We were in the middle of date number two. I'd almost called it off right then.

"You're really on a break?" I'd pressed.

"We've been together a long time. We have a kind of arrangement." He said it was fine, really, but hanging out in Logansville would be kind of like rubbing it in her face.

I'd let his words settle. My parents had been positively glowing since the day I'd introduced them to Carter—they had to vet anyone I was hanging out with, of course, male or female. I'd printed out the article from the *Logansville Gazette* at school, had brought it home to show them. The paper hadn't mentioned a girlfriend.

I'd wanted to believe him, didn't ask any more questions. But eventually my conscience got the better of me, and I looked Amanda up online. She had a lot of photos set to public, the albums absolutely bursting with pictures of Carter. Recent pictures. Pictures I pretended I hadn't seen.

Sometimes, we drive out to a diner in Wheeling or this movie theater that's kind of in the middle of nowhere, but most of the time we drive the half hour into Pittsburgh where there's plenty to do and three hundred thousand people to lose ourselves in. It's amazing how fast cows and cars propped up on cinder blocks turn into bridges and office buildings, a bright glimpse into my future.

As we drive on Forbes Avenue past Primanti's, another Pittsburgh culinary institution, and the building that looks like it used to be a small castle that now houses a noodle shop and T-Mobile store, my skin starts to tingle. Atwood Street, Oakland Avenue, South Bouquet. We're almost here—at the "O," but more importantly, at the University of Pittsburgh, its campus right in the center of the city. Paulina and I will both be freshmen there next year, assuming we get in. Which we will.

Carter finds a spot down the block from the restaurant, and we get out of the car. In front of us, a group of students cross above Forbes in the enclosed pedestrian walkway that connects one side of campus to the other. Next year, that will be Pau and me. I'm so wrapped up in my fantasy that I don't notice Carter next to me on the sidewalk. He fake-tackles me from behind, picking me up and spinning me around and around. "I love the 'Burgh!" he shouts. "And I love being here with you!"

I yelp, caught off-guard. A chill races down my spine, and this time, I can't stop the memory from coming. *It's sophomore year, Halloween, and I'm in downtown Logansville with Donovan Miller at a theater showing* Donnie Darko *after school. My hands are folded in my lap, my eyes trained on the screen. He leans across the armrest and presses his lips into my long, limp hair. "I love being here with you, Rosalie," he whispers.*

My stomach curdles, rejecting the sugary combination of Dr. Pepper and Swedish Fish sloshing around inside. I mash my fist into my mouth and struggle to keep it down. I want to like him the way I like Paulina. I want those feelings that Brother Masters calls "a homo-SEX-ual sickness" or sometimes just "the sickness" to go away. I want, so badly, to be normal.

At our new home in Culver Ridge, my parents are celebrating or praying, probably both. The FOC counselor in our old town told them our sessions together had worked. He called me a "success story" with a kind of pride that made my insides heave because I knew it was a lie. I'd just gotten really good at pretending, anything to make the sessions stop. They believed it because they wanted to believe it, but they haven't loosened up. They're afraid I'll slip back into sin, that the cure won't stick. If they knew what Paulina and I do sometimes—kiss and trade secrets in the clearing behind the school, bodies pressed against each other, then snapped back like rubber bands, breath hot and sweet in the air between us—they'd put me back in FOC counseling faster than anything. And I'd never see Pau again.

We are friends who sometimes kiss, have not yet found a language to describe what we are to each other. Or I haven't. Paulina wants to be my girlfriend, but putting a name to what we are, what I am, means admitting something I'm not ready to admit.

I stare straight ahead, but I'm not really seeing the movie. My stomach churns and churns. I've been back in regular school since we moved here, but I'm still under glorified house arrest. Having a boyfriend could change all that. I picture my parents relaxing just a bit. I picture myself at the library, working part-time. I picture myself in the fall play. I picture myself never seeing another FOC counselor, ever again.

I picture myself with Paulina, when my parents think I'm out with Donovan.

"Me too," *I whisper back.*

Carter puts me down, then spins me around to face him. "I just can't get enough of you, Rosalie Bell." He places his hands on either side of my face and tilts it up. "You are so freaking special."

I plaster on a smile. My stomach churns, Dr. Pepper and Swedish Fish all over again. I squeeze my eyes shut until it passes. When I open them, Carter's standing in front of me, all dimples and white teeth. "Come on." I shove aside the voice that says no matter what I do, I can't win this. "Cheese fries await."

Inside, we place our order at the counter and slide into a booth in the back. The Original Hot Dog Shop is a Pitt favorite, and even though it's January, it's packed with students. They bring us our fries and chicken strips and Carter completely lights up as we scarf them down. It doesn't take a genius to figure out that he doesn't eat too many cheese fries with Amanda. Or that meals with his family are more likely to be chef-designed than deep-fried. I'm the girl who will order chicken strips and a Coke and call it dinner. The girl who doesn't care about labels or the future. I'm the girl he can be real with. Even if I'm not real with him, not even a little bit.

"There's supposed to be this amazing fry shop out by WVU," Carter says when we've cleared our plates. "They deep fry candy bars, marshmallows, you name it."

I frown and change the subject to live music. There's a band playing at Milk & Honey in a little bit, and when it comes to Carter, I only want to think about the present.

After the "O," we climb back into his car. I key in the address for Milk & Honey and pull my vape pen out of my bag while Carter drives. He seems to think my penchant for dry herb makes me edgy, along with my haircut and big, boxy glasses. In Carter's world, I'm some kind of religious rebel, a thought that would almost be funny if it wasn't so freaking sad.

We park a few blocks down from the coffee shop, and I pass Carter my pen. He draws in a deep lungful of vapor and closes his eyes. His head falls back against the headrest.

"This is the most fun I've had all week," he says, his eyes still shut.

If I'm really being honest, I'm having fun too. I wish I hated Carter, that he wasn't so nice. If I loathed every minute with him, this would almost be easier. I look out the window when I respond. "Me too."

"Seriously, I mean it." His eyes are open now, and he's looking right at me. "I know this seems like no big deal to you, but I can't be like this at home." He draws in another deep hit.

It strikes me then that Carter and I might have more in common than I've been admitting.

"Like what?" I ask, genuinely curious.

"Just . . . relaxed. When I'm with you, it's like, no one's watching me. Is that a weird thing to say?"

"Totally weird," I reply. His face falls until I laugh, and he gets that I'm joking. He passes the pen back and I take another hit, but it's basically kicked. "Let's go in."

As it turns out, the band is pretty terrible, but it's still early, so we stay at the coffee shop for the full set. I let Carter hold my hand. With my eyes closed, I can almost pretend he's Pau.

At the end of our second or third date, Carter suggested we drive up to Culver Ridge's eponymous bluffs. The ridge is the local make-out spot, and I shut that down hard and fast. I think he finds it a little confusing—how I'm obviously not as devout as my parents, but when it comes to sex, I'm basically the Virgin Mary. I told him I'm religious, take it or leave it. FOC kids save themselves for marriage. He's never suggested the ridge again.

After the set ends, we get back in Carter's car. When we're parked in my driveway, and I know my parents are peeking through the living room window, I let him kiss me good night.

5

AMANDA

THURSDAY, JANUARY 4

Two days later, I haven't heard another word from my "secret admirer," but I can't get the texts off my mind. The words keep popping up at the most inconvenient times, throwing me off my game. *You're so beautiful it hurts.* Instead of worrying about my family on the drive to school, my brain is a skittery mess. *You're way too good for that Carter guy.* Is this person into me? What does he know about my boyfriend? *Don't you dare tell Carter Shaw about me.* Who is sending those texts?

The whole week is just kind of off. By Thursday night, which feels like Wednesday night because we started back to school on a Tuesday, I'm going stir crazy in my bedroom, texting with Adele and Trina and not doing my homework. I sprawl out on my bed, which my parents upgraded to a king for my sixteenth birthday last year, even though they probably shouldn't have, and tuck my feet into the folds of the silky duvet. I can't focus. Carter's working for his dad tonight, which really means he's out with Rosalie. Which means my thoughts are running wild.

I click over to Facebook to stalk her one more time, but the girl either maintains zero internet presence, or she really knows her security settings. She's only posted one new picture since the holidays, a stiff, posed shot of her standing with a girl who looks about six, probably her kid sister, in front of a sad-looking artificial Christmas tree. She's pretty enough, I guess, if you're into short girls with hipster frames and ugly, angular hair styles. I bet she thinks she's "indie," but she's obviously a poser. I do not get what he sees in her.

I shove off my bed and walk over to my desk, which is piled with the homework assignments I should be doing. I ignore my books and pick up a framed photo instead, the one that's been keeping me company since freshman year. It's a picture of Carter and me at our ninth-grade spring formal, almost exactly three years ago. He's standing behind me, arms wrapped around me tight, leaning down to kiss the top of my head. His eyes are closed, and my face is split wide in a giant grin. Fourteen-year-old Amanda is all teeth and giggles. I'm wearing a silky purple gown with little spaghetti straps that are embarrassingly freshman year. Carter's hair is a bit longer and even wavier than he wears it now, and the deep dimples in his cheeks are still baby-smooth. We look more sophisticated now, like we've grown into ourselves. Into the people we're meant to be. But still, this is my favorite picture of us. It's the one that reminds me I'm living in a fairy tale. For a moment, I close my eyes, and I remember how lucky I've been, how lucky I still am.

For the first couple years we were together, I was deliriously happy. When it became obvious my parents saw Carter as more than just my boyfriend, it didn't feel like pressure because we were in love. Carter's successful family was just icing on an already perfect cake.

The summer after sophomore year was the first time he cheated on me. I think. Three kids came down with mono at camp, and they sent us all home a few days early. When I got back to Logansville, Winston said Carter was at the pool; I walked in on him making out with Brie McLain in the shady area behind the locker rooms. While Brie ran away shrieking, literally, her blue bikini straps sliding down her shoulders, Carter told me it was a huge mistake. He'd missed me so much. He swore it would never, ever happen again.

I'm not naive. I was raised by Linda Kelly; I know how to sniff out a lie. But I wanted to believe him. I didn't want to break up. When I finally told my mother, she took both my hands in hers. *You're a compassionate person, Amanda,* she said. *Carter's very lucky to have you.* Her words sounded like the truth.

I look at the picture again, at fairy-tale us, and my stomach doesn't fill with the usual butterflies. Changing course now isn't really an option; there are too many wheels already in motion. Winston and Krystal practically treat me like their daughter-in-law already. Last year, Carter and I were photographed as the state's most promising young couple for a "Twenty Under Twenty" feature documenting rising influencers. And the truth is, I still love Carter. I just don't know if he's still in love with me.

I turn the picture face-down on my desk and wander out into the hallway. It's dark and quiet, so I switch on the hall light. I can hear Dad shuffling around in his office, performing his evening ritual of letting college basketball play on mute while he reads financial blogs and unloads his work stress into his assistant's inbox. I didn't hear him come in. I don't think I've actually seen my father since dinner Tuesday night, the last time he was home early enough for us all to sit down together. But his presence in the house is unmistakable, a tense knot of anxiety and determination.

From the top of the stairs, I can see my mother in the kitchen, pouring a vodka soda. My mother is best avoided after drink number three, but it's only a quarter after nine. I do some quick calculations. She had drink number one with dinner and number two right after. So this could be either her third or fourth. I decide to risk it and start down toward the kitchen.

"Hi, honey," she purrs, patting the stool across from her at the marble-topped island. She looks surprised but pleased to find me in her nocturnal domain. Tonight, the sleek surfaces and rich, dark paneling in here suit my somber mood just fine. "Come join me." Her voice is toasty and smooth, but she's not slurring yet.

This is about as motherly as Linda Kelly gets. It would never have occurred to her to come upstairs to check on me, but now that I'm in her sight, she's remembered that face time is key to a healthy mother-daughter relationship.

I grab a Vitamin Water from the fridge and sit down across from where she's standing at the island, her hands resting against the cool marble. She reaches over and runs four gel-tipped fingernails through my hair.

"Such a beautiful girl," she murmurs.

I scowl and untwist the cap on my drink.

"Amanda Kelly, what is that face?"

I take a long gulp and wipe my mouth with the back of my hand. Now it's my mother's turn to scowl.

"Use a napkin." She motions with her eyes toward the cloth squares neatly folded in a basket on the neglected breakfast table. I push myself up and walk over to grab one.

"What is with you tonight?" she asks when I'm perched back on the stool, napkin in hand.

I'm being a pain, and I remind myself that Linda is the reason I found my way into the kitchen in the first place. As hard as my mother's advice is to take, it usually calms me down. Those texts have gotten to my head. I need her reassurance.

"Carter's out with that skank from Culver Thrift again."

"Amanda, language."

"Sorry, I meant Carter's out with that boyfriend-thief from a socioeconomically depressed suburb." The thing is, I don't *know* Rosalie. Maybe she doesn't know that Carter is off the market. Maybe she's actually nice. But until either of those things are confirmed, it's easy to hate her.

"And you're feeling self-conscious." My mother's voice is flat. She sighs and sits down across from me. Before she speaks again, she takes a long drink. The ice cubes clink merrily against the glass.

"Amanda, you know your father and I support you and Carter completely." This is an understatement. Linda and Jack don't just support Carter—they're *invested* in him. Sometimes, I think they're too focused on the power and stature behind the Shaw name. But I get it. Logansville runs on old money, old customs, old ideals. For ten years, we've been faking it. With my future linked up with Carter's, we'll have finally made it.

"So do Krystal and Winston," my mother is saying. "We're all behind you one hundred percent."

I nod. She's right—Carter's parents do genuinely love me. If they suspect the Kellys are living minimum payment to minimum payment, they've never let on. They either don't care or, more likely, my parents have done an impeccable job of convincing them we're worth every penny our house and cars suggest.

"But, Amanda," she continues, "boys will be boys. And people—men, especially—make mistakes. Relationships are a long game. There are going to be other women—"

"Mom—"

"Listen, Amanda. I know you don't like me saying this, that you think it's not *feminist*, but, honey, you have to make some allowances. Do you think I haven't done the same with your father? That Krystal hasn't with Winston? You can't hold on too tight, Amanda. A tight leash snaps. You have to play strategically, let Carter get those other girls out of his system. They can't compete with you, honey. Not in the end."

I let my mother's words sink in, but the usual rhetoric isn't having its desired effect. I don't know what I want her to say. Something better. Something more satisfying. "It's not other girl*s plural*, Mom. It's just Rosalie."

"And you need to understand that she may not be the last girl Carter experiments with. But she won't last long, honey. You and Carter have such a bright future ahead, and he will *always* come back to you. This girl is nothing you need to worry about."

She drains the last of her drink and lifts the bottle of Ketel One. Drink number whatever is my cue to go.

"You're right," I say, even though the tightness in my chest says otherwise. I need to forget about those texts, get my head back in the game. "I have AP Euro to finish. I'd better get back upstairs."

"Of course," my mother nods, glancing at the clock. It's 9:40. I wonder if it occurs to her that *she* should be the one asking *me* if I've finished my homework. She squints at the numbers, then brings her glass back to her lips.

I turn toward the stairs.

"Everyone has your back, Amanda. You and Carter are meant to be together. The Kellys and Shaws are not going to let you fail."

I don't feel very comforted as I walk back toward my room. My mother's pep talks are never really pep talks. They're reminders that failure isn't an option. That my future lies with Carter, and I'd better figure out how to make it work.

I walk back into my bedroom and let the niceness of it all sink in. The polished wood floors and soft area rug. The photo collage of me and the girls above my bed. The gorgeous oak bureau and rose glass lamp. I want my parents to be able to relax, to stop worrying that we're on the verge of losing all this. And I want Carter, and everything a life with him promises to be. But I want more than that. I want love and trust and forever and ever.

I know my mother has my best interests at heart, that I should trust her, but lately, I've felt less and less sure her way of handling things is going to lead to my happily ever after. Her voice is still ringing in my ears as I close the door behind me. *Do you think I haven't done the same with your father? That Krystal hasn't with Winston?* I grab my phone from the top of my duvet and sit down at my desk. I want more than compromises and willful ignorance. I want everything our parents have—but better. And I want it to work with Carter. So everyone gets to be happy. My fingers gravitate toward the onyx heart, and I slide it back and forth along the chain.

My AP European history book sits in front of me unopened. I thumb through to somewhere near the middle and stare at the chapter I'm supposed to be reading. The words swim across the page, so I close it again and pick up my phone, flipping it over to stare at the screen. There are a few new texts from Trina and Adele, and two unread messages from Private, from 9:23 and 9:36. My breath catches in my throat.

> Have you been thinking about me?
> I've been thinking about you.

> Your boyfriend's not thinking about
> you at all tonight, but I'm not like him.

> WHO IS THIS?

I'm furious, but I can't stop my heart from leaping into my throat. I wait three long minutes. No reply.

> Why are you blocking your number?

> Don't you want me to know who I'm
> talking to?

This Private person is definitely messing with me, but maybe it's because he really cares. . . . Part of me wants to nip this little distraction in the bud, but another part of me is dying for a glimpse behind the mask, to figure out who's been spending so much time with me on their mind.

And then it hits me. This person isn't showering me with attention because they care. If Private were really a "secret admirer," he'd be sending me a lot more compliments and a lot fewer digs about Carter. I've been looking at this all wrong. These texts aren't from someone who *likes* me. They're from someone who wants to play on my insecurities, rub Carter's cheating in my face, and break us up. Something inky dark swirls at the edges of my vision, causing me to pitch forward and clutch at the edge of my desk. The pads of my fingers go white against the wood.

Because she *must* know about me.

Rosalie.

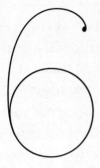

ROSALIE
FRIDAY, JANUARY 5

I sing Grace VanderWaal with Lily on the way to the bus stop. We hold hands and belt as loud as we dare, eyes flashing to the neighbors' windows as we pass by. No one complains. They never do. Houses in Culver Ridge are spaced far apart and set back from the road in an uneven jigsaw of crumbling wood and siding, fenced-off dog runs, and the odd piece of farm equipment left out to rust. We keep to the sidewalk, then hug the outskirts of trampled lawns when the sidewalk runs out.

"She's coming to Pittsburgh in May," Lily says when we finish our off-key rendition. "On tour."

My heart sinks. "You know we can't go, right, Lils?" Unless it's a Christian rock band touring the Fellowship circuit, transforming the God's Grace mega-chapel into an arena for Jesus, concerts are strictly off-limits.

"I know." Her voice is soft.

"Maybe they'll make a TV special," I suggest, halting our walk to squat down at eye level. Her mittened hands are warm in mine. Not that it'd be likely to air on local access. But I could probably get us permission to watch at a friend's. "If they do, I'll bake Rice Krispie treats. We'll make it a party."

She grins. "Deal." We keep walking.

Culver Ridge isn't populous enough to get its own school district, so we're bussed even farther into the sticks with kids from four nearby townships to Greater Logansville elementary, middle, and high. The three schools share one plot of land—"the pasture"—in the township of Logan Mills. Not that it's pastoral. Think lowest percentile rankings in most measures of academic success in the Northern Panhandle. Think shared lockers. Think five sports teams, one coach. The pasture is just a training ground for the next generation of West Virginia poor kids.

The little kids' bus does its pickup twenty minutes before the bus to the high school. When we arrive at the stop, which services both the school and public routes, I'm surprised to see Miss Larkin waiting. The teachers mostly carpool, but she must not have a ride today. She beckons us over with a friendly wave.

Miss Larkin teaches fourth-grade science, which I only know because she's former FOC. In Fellowship circles, that makes her infamous. Parishioners who publicly reject the Fellowship's teachings are essentially exiled in a practice called Ecclesiastical Extradition. If the unbeliever is thought to be a poisonous influence, the church compels the family to sever ties.

Our first year in Culver Ridge, she reached out to me. I guess I'm a little infamous in FOC circles too. I stopped by her class-room, once. She told me she was Extradited from a congregation in Missouri. When I asked why she chose to make Culver Ridge her new home, she said it was for the job, and we left it at that. I've seen her with a guy, a boyfriend or fiancé, and I wonder if he's Christian. If he's the reason she left the church, denounced it, if it was worth it to never speak to her family again. She let me know she was there, if I ever wanted to talk. Mostly, I've been too nervous to be seen anywhere near her.

When I look at Miss Larkin, I see my future. Someday, I'll slip up. Someday, I'll no longer be able to keep my identity under wraps. I'm going to keep trying, for as long as I can, but someday, that shunned unbeliever could be me. I grasp Lily's hand tight, hold on.

We chat for a couple minutes, and I'm overwhelmed by the same feeling that always hits when I see her: I want to ask her everything, and just as hard, I want to run far away. When their bus comes, she looks over her shoulder, her eyes repeating her offer: *If you ever want to talk . . .*

I get Lily on board with a kiss and a wave, then wait. Shiv-ering in the cold bite of early January and burrowing deep into my coat, I stamp my feet back and forth, watch the storefronts across the street. It's still early; neither CVS nor the liquor store is open, but there are already cars in the lot they share. Waiting. People need to fill prescriptions before work. People need bread and peanut butter. People need wine, vodka, rum.

Normally, I like this pause before the rest of the high schoolers arrive. It's quiet, just me and the cars in the lot. There's nothing to negotiate, no compromises. But today, skin still crackling and pricking with Carter's touch, another unwanted memory starts to unspool.

I only went out with Donovan a few times, but I pretended we were still together for weeks after I'd admitted I didn't like him the same way he liked me. I'd tell my parents I was seeing him, then hang out with Paulina instead. I got careless, forgot how small Culver Ridge is. When my mom ran into his mom in the CVS cosmetics aisle, my lie was exposed. *Rosalie? We sure do miss her; it's too bad things between her and Donovan didn't work out.*

That summer, my parents doubled down on their bid to save me. The familiar chill tingles along my spine, a cold far deeper than January and sharper than a blade of ice, until suddenly, I'm sweating in my winter coat.

I'm sitting in the rec room at Camp Eternal Light, a prayer circle of twenty-six of us sinners. The hot metal folding chair presses against the backs of my legs, making my skin sweat and itch. The single ceiling fan's thin blades do almost nothing to cut through the deep swelter of the Tennessee summer. My dark green camp shirt clings to my stomach and armpits, the cloth damp where the slogan reads: DELIVERANCE THROUGH GOD'S DESIGN. *My parents took out a loan they can't afford to send me here, a last-ditch investment in my salvation. It's been three years since my first FOC counseling session, and this time, I know I'm not broken.*

Pastor Ray is leading us sinners in prayer. I bow my head and pray for God to reset my moral compass (2 Corinthians 5:17–21). I pray that I might recognize my homosexual behavior as outside God's plan (Romans 1:25–27, Leviticus 18:22, Genesis 2:24). I pray for the strength to live my life in conformity to scripture (1 Corinthians 6:9–10, 1 Timothy 1:9–10). I pray and pray, and beneath the words I say out loud, I pray for the strength to stay alive. The strength to lie.

I look up, and Pastor Ray's eyes find mine. They're filled with fire.

"Rosalie, hey!" Elissa's voice snaps me back to the bus stop. She wraps her arm tight around my shoulders in a surprise side-hug, and my entire body goes stiff.

"You okay?" she asks, pulling away. Her tight blond curls bounce against her chin, but her face is etched with concern.

"Sorry, fine." I force a half smile. "You just startled me."

"Okay good, because I need your advice." Elissa launches into her history group project woes, and I nod sympathetically until I can shake the memory off, be a good friend.

On the bus, Elissa checks her apps while I stare out the window and picture Carter and Amanda and their fancy friends driving their fancy cars to Logansville South this morning. I asked Carter once, early on, why he didn't go to prep school. He said his family felt strongly about maintaining a presence in town, that sending their son off to boarding school delivered the wrong kind of message. I guess real estate is all about *networking* and *messaging*. I didn't ask about Amanda because we don't talk about Amanda. Not after that first time. But I assume she's at Logansville South for the same reason. She's part of the "family brand." Or maybe it's simpler than that. Maybe it's just because wherever Carter is, that's where Amanda is too. *Don't think too much.*

Eight hours later, the dismissal bell is ringing and I'm scrambling to get to my locker like everyone else. I have a few friends here— mostly just Paulina and Elissa—but I keep a pretty low profile at school. The less people know about me, the more I blend into the background. It's safe in the background.

I head out the main entrance and into the pasture. Kids are

spilling into waiting busses out front, or walking toward the converted barn between the high school and middle school that houses the mat room and gym. No one's just milling around outside today; it's too cold for that. As I cross through the brown, patchy field, grass brittle and crunching beneath my feet, the school buildings grow smaller and smaller at my back. I guess this area could be farmland, but there's nothing being farmed. It's just beaten-up weeds, trampled by hundreds of feet, a parking lot, and then a ways out, past the school boundaries, the woods.

That's where I'm headed today. I cut through the lot, which is practically empty because no one has a car here except some teachers and administrators. Then I'm officially off school grounds. When I'm sure no one's looking, I slip into the woods. The last bus back to Culver Ridge—the one meant for athletes and other kids staying late for extracurriculars—leaves at six, which means I have almost three hours when I don't have to be the person I am at school or at home or at church or with Carter. I can be the person I am with Pau. The real me.

There's a little clearing about ten minutes into the woods. I know the route like it's a map of my own face. Right before you arrive, there's an old tree that got hit in a lightning storm years ago. Paulina and I have stashed all sorts of things in its hollowed-out trunk: two mats from the gym, a sleeping bag, pillows wrapped in plastic bags, flashlights. One mat and a pillow are already gone, so I know Pau's beat me here. I grab a second pillow and head toward the clearing.

"*Chyoo-chyoo-chyoo-tseee!*" I whistle right before I push through the trees.

"*Kicky-chew, kicky-chew, kicky-chew!*" Pau whistles back.

Paulina and I both took acting as our elective in ninth grade. Mom thought acting class would be a good way for me to meet people at my new school, and turns out she was right. On the first day, the teacher made us sit in a circle and share one thing that made us special, some talent or skill. Pau and I both said we could do birdcalls. My dad taught me when I was little, and until Pau, I'd never met anyone else my age who knew how to call. Now, we always greet each other with the most ridiculous new calls we can learn. It's our special thing, just like this clearing is our special place.

Pau's sitting on the mat, back pressed up against a tree and a cigarette pressed between her lips. Her long, dark hair spills out around her scarf and coat in loose ringlets. Her jeans are cuffed at the ankles, revealing a row of lace eyelets at the top of her socks. Pau calls her style femme-boy, as in half femme, half tomboy. It's supercute. She takes a drag and blows the smoke out the side of her mouth. I hate that Pau smokes cigarettes, but I don't really have a bargaining chip.

She plucks the cigarette away from her lips with two bare fingers and waves it abstractly toward the sky. "It's fucking freezing out here."

I don't say the obvious, that she'd be better off stubbing out that cigarette and putting on some gloves. Instead, I plop down next to her and unzip my backpack.

"I brought Smart Pop."

"Great, I'm starving."

The two of us can go through a large bag in one sitting. I don't know how she can eat and smoke at the same time, but I let that slide too.

For a moment, we just sit together on the mat, crunching on

popcorn and not talking. I breathe in and out, and it feels like the first real breath I've taken all day. When Paulina finishes her cigarette, she leans her head against my shoulder. Her body melts into mine, butter into warm bread.

"Long week?" I ask.

"Technically, I guess it was a short week," she says. "Only four days. But it felt like an eternity."

I turn my head and Pau lifts hers from my shoulder, then her lips find mine. Kissing Paulina is like a warm bath on a winter night. A welcoming. A relief. Her lips taste like they always taste— salt and smoke.

"I missed you, Lee-Lee."

"I know." I kiss her again, deeper this time. I haven't seen Pau since Tuesday. Not really, not like this. Wednesday I watched Lily after school and Thursday we both know I was with Carter.

"What did you two do last night?" she asks between flickers of lips and teeth and tongue.

I stop.

"Let's not do this. Just this once."

Paulina pulls away and leans back on the mat.

"I hate that you have to have a *beard* like it's the freaking nineteen twenties. But I hate not knowing even more."

"I just don't see why you need the play-by-play." My mouth is dry, coated in a thin film of popcorn dust that tastes suddenly stale. I spit into the dry mud and pine needles. One more negotiation.

Paulina reaches into her coat pocket and pulls out her pack. She taps it briskly against the palm of her hand, then slides a fresh cigarette between her fingers and lights it.

"Because," she says, exhaling a slow stream of smoke, "at least if I know everything, I don't have to imagine it."

I sigh deeply and run my gloved fingers through my hair until the strands stick out to the sides. I hate that she's right. If I had my way, I'd keep Carter Shaw and Paulina Flores completely separate. Carter flung across my body like a human shield, and Pau sealed up tight in the chambers of my heart. I owe Paulina better than Carter and secret clearings in the woods and stories about dates we didn't go on together. But for now, this is how it has to be. So that in five short months, it can be much, much better.

"We ate cheese fries," I start. "At the 'O.' Then we drove to the South Side to hear this really bad electro-pop band. The show was crap, but you would have liked the scene. A bunch of indie kids, and not all white either. A couple of black guys and even one Latina chick."

"Cool." Paulina's voice is noncommittal, but she really would have liked Milk & Honey. She puts up a tough front, but I know she's constantly reminded of how white it is in Culver Ridge. She's practically the only Latinx kid at school now that her older brothers have both graduated. Most of West Virginia is really white. Paulina's parents are both Mexican-American; her mom's family has been in the area for decades and her dad moved here for school. They met in college and settled in Culver Ridge for some incomprehensible reason.

"And then what?"

"Huh?" I fiddle with the zipper on my backpack. Paulina knows I'm stalling.

"After the bad electro-pop show with the marginally diverse audience. Then what?"

I stare at the cracked gym mat beneath us, the brown grass poking up through dirt and pine needles. "Then he drove me home. End of story."

"And?" Paulina presses.

I snap my head up and force myself to look at her. "He kissed me good night. One short kiss. Is that what you want to hear?"

"Yes. It is." Paulina smashes her cigarette into the dirt even though it's only half gone and stares back at me. "Anything else?"

"No!" I practically shout. "That other stuff, it's just for us, okay? You know that."

Pau slips her hand into mine. Her bare fingers slide easily between my gloved ones. We fit—sand and salt air, moon and stars. Her voice is soft when she speaks again. "I know you wouldn't. But trusting you doesn't mean trusting him. And I don't trust him around you for one second."

I squeeze her hand. "Carter Shaw is a cheater and a liar and he's probably really *confused* and *tortured* about how hard it is to be the blond-haired, blue-eyed, cis-het heir to the family fortune." I grin, and then Paulina giggles, loosening up a bit. "But I know how to handle him, okay?"

Paulina squeezes my hand back. "I know you're tough, Rosalie. I know you're a survivor, and you can take care of yourself. But this isn't about me being jealous, I promise."

I crunch down on a bite of popcorn and raise my eyebrows.

"Okay, it's not *just* me being jealous. You being with Carter—it's not healthy. It's, it's . . ." Her voice trails off and her face twists up. "It's *sick* that you have to do something so harmful to keep yourself safe."

"You're right," I say quietly. Because it is harmful. Even though

I only see him a few times a month. Even though I keep our dates strictly PG. There's no way I'm coming out of this unscathed. But whatever harm I'm inflicting pales in comparison to the alternative. My lies are my shield, protecting me from the kind of "therapy" I can never go through again.

"I can't watch you do this to yourself for five more months," Pau says. "That's practically forever."

"It's not," I insist. "You and me, we're forever. Carter's just until graduation."

"What would really happen if you ditched him?" Paulina asks. "There's a million freaking miles between staying in the closet to protect yourself at home and having a *real, live boyfriend.*" Her voice is strained, and her lips start to tremble. "I'm just so scared for you."

I lean in and wrap my arms around her tight. Then I whisper, "I know. But just saying I'm straight now isn't enough. Carter makes them believe it."

She pulls away and wipes at her eyes. "This sucks."

"Trust me, if I broke up with him, the fallout would suck much worse." My words are bitter, acid and blood. We're both silent for a moment, thinking about the summer after Donovan, how my missteps triggered all my parents' fears.

"They can't send you away again," Pau says. "Not once you're eighteen; it's not legal."

"There's ex-gay ministry right here at God's Grace. And I can't—" My voice breaks.

"Of course not." Pau grabs my hands, holds them tight. "I will never let that happen to you again, ever." Her voice is fierce; it zips straight down my spine. I squeeze her hands back.

I'm alone in the almost-dark. One dim bulb flickers in a plastic fixture overhead. Today, there's a new wasp trapped inside. It flies into the hot glass, then falls back stunned. I watch it stumble around in a daze for a minute, two, until it falls still next to the bodies of its sisters. My eyes smart from staring into the light. There are four tiny bodies outlined now against the plastic shell. I guess alone is relative.

I stare at the notebook in my hand. Through the light spots dancing across the page, I can barely read the verse I've copied out, again and again. The wrath of God is being revealed from heaven against all the godlessness and wickedness of people, who suppress the truth by their wickedness. . . . *I flip through the pages. I've copied this verse from Romans 1 twenty-eight times now. It's not nearly enough to earn my passage out of this locked, airless room. My hand throbs, and my legs and butt ache from sitting on the concrete floor. I don't know how long I've been in here. Someone brought me breakfast, but they forgot about me at lunch. Forgot or chose to forget. I scoot up against the door and press my ear to the metal. Outside, I can hear voices coming from the chapel. I can't tell what they're singing, they're too far away. My stomach cramps up, and I wrap my arms around my waist. Singing means it's almost dinnertime. They have to take me to the bathroom, let me eat.*

Above me, the new wasp stirs, buzzes, thrashes angrily against her plastic cage. She's still alive. But the truth convulses in my throat: She's going to die in there.

I pick up my pen, balance the notebook on top of my knees, and start to write. The wrath of God . . .

Paulina and I hold hands and stare into the trees, remembering. Those dead months—me in Tennessee, her here and no way to reach me—hang in the air around us. Paulina shivers, and I fold her into my chest. Through the padded fabric of my coat, her cheek is a perfect fit against my collarbone.

"You know you can come live with us," she says finally. It's not the first time she's offered her brother Ramon's old room as a refuge. "In March, the second you're eighteen."

"I wish I could." Pau's family has always been more than welcoming; I know they'd help me however they can. But leaving home would break my family forever. The Fellowship would turn them against me.

I would lose Lily.

In five months, I'll be independent. I have enough saved. I'll move out and start college, keep my family and my personal life far, far apart. It's going to work because it has to.

Paulina sighs and rests her head back against the tree. "I can't tell you what to do, and I'm there for you no matter what. But the offer stands."

"I love you, you know? Only you."

"I love you too," Paulina says back, and I know she means it. My parents' love is laced with fear, but Pau's love is unconditional. "How much more time do we have?"

I click my phone on to check. "Almost two hours."

"Wait here." Paulina disappears for a minute, then returns carrying our sleeping bag from the hollowed-out tree. "That's plenty of time."

It's freezing when I slide off my coat, even under the sleeping bag. In a few minutes, I don't feel the cold anymore. What I feel is warm and shuddering and loved. Paulina's lips move across my skin and her hair tickles my legs. I feel free. Finally, for the first time in days, I feel like myself.

7

It's Friday night, Carter's arm is wrapped tight around my shoulders, I am surrounded by friends, and I will not let her words burrow like thorns beneath my skin. *Think big picture*, I tell myself. *Think happily ever after.* I let those texts throw me. No one has been trying to bring the charm—Carter, or otherwise. Whoever sent the nice ones sent the nasty ones too. Now that I'm sure that someone is Rosalie, I can focus on what to do next.

We're in our usual booth at the Sunny Side Diner—the big round one in the corner, the only booth large enough to seat all of us. Carter and I are right in the middle, Adele and Graham are next to us, and Bronson, his boyfriend Alexander, and Trina are on Carter's right. Bronson leans over and whispers something in

Alexander's ear that makes his face light up in a lopsided grin. We're just missing Ben, by which I mean he's bound to show up eventually and squeeze into our booth.

There are at least ten better places to eat in downtown Logansville, but the Sunny Side is the only full-service restaurant that will let us hang out for hours. I prefer the vibe at Vanilla Bean, the coffee shop on Springvale, but the guys just could not survive a Friday night without a burger and basket of fries.

I order my usual Greek salad (hold the onion, dressing on the side) and Diet Coke and assume my recurring role as mediator between Graham and Adele. Graham has been basically in love with Adele since kindergarten. They dated for about two seconds in seventh grade, but then he screwed up epically by kissing Karen Kowalski during a game of spin the bottle while he and Adele were going out, and she's never forgiven him. At least that's what she claims. Really, she just loves making Graham squirm.

"Sunday," he's saying. "Brunch at Verde. You and me and the most important meal of the day. Don't make me cancel the reservation."

Adele's lips twist to the side. Verde is the newest restaurant in town, and it's also the most high-end. They just started serving brunch last week, and Carter's parents came back raving about the shrimp and grits and Bellinis with house-made pear nectar. Now everyone wants a table. Adele is such an open book; I can see her thoughts plastered across her face. She wants in on that reservation, but she can't let Graham win. I wish she would give it up and go out with him already, but Adele enjoys the game more than she actually wants a boyfriend.

Out of the corner of my eye, I can see Carter texting

one-handed under the table. All up my arms and down my legs, the thorns prick and bleed. I make myself ignore him and turn to Adele. "Any socializing that happens on a Sunday morning can barely be called a date. I'm sure Graham would agree." I raise my eyebrows at him.

"Yeah, sure, not a date. Just you, me, and some short-rib hash."

Adele scowls. "You make it sound so sexy when you say it like that."

"You want sexy? I can give you sexy." Graham lifts Adele's Sprite from the table and slides the straw between his teeth.

"Ew, Graham, give it!" Adele snatches for the glass, nearly spilling pop across all three of us.

I roll my eyes. "You two are hopeless." They're also both stubborn as mules. I run my hand lightly across the top of Carter's thigh, reminding him that I'm here, I'm the girl at his side. His phone is back on the table now, but he, Bronson, and Alexander are lost in conversation about top-of-the-line skydiving gear. I mean, shouldn't all equipment designed for jumping out of planes be top-of-the-line? I catch Alexander's eyes and raise my brows—he's the only one of them who's not obsessed, *normally*, but tonight he flashes me his off-center grin and continues debating the merits of investing in new versus used reserve canopies. I squeeze Carter's leg through his jeans, and he breaks away from the guys just long enough to give me a rough peck on the top of my head. Then he's gone again. I can feel the spot where his lips met my hair tingle, then fade.

I glance around the three of them to Trina, who slips me a poised smile before snapping a selfie. Her lipstick perfectly matches the cranberry of the booth back, and I wonder if she did that on purpose. She gestures for me to scoot around and join her, but I shake my head. I keep my hand on Carter's thigh until our food arrives. He presses his lips against my ear as the waitress is setting down our plates. "You're so sexy, babe," he whispers. He places his hand on top of my hand and squeezes. The thorns retract to a dull throb beneath my skin.

I pick at my salad. Out of the corner of my eye, I watch Adele watching Carter and me. He's still got one arm wrapped around my shoulders while he shuttles sweet potato fries to his mouth and jokes with the sophomores who have stopped by our booth to pay homage to Carter and the other guys. But mostly Carter. I half listen to their conversation, my eyes still on Adele. These must be the current JV-hopefuls, angling to get in with the seniors. Carter grins and passes out words of encouragement. It never ceases to amaze me, how he can be that nice to every single person, day in and day out. A minute later, he's squeezing out of the booth to give an acne-spackled sophomore tips on proper cradling technique, an abandoned umbrella serving as the make-shift lacrosse stick. Adele takes a sip of pop, her eyes transfixed on his lips. Does she have to be so *obvious*?

The other reason that Adele shoots Graham down, the one I try not to think about, is that Adele has been mildly infatuated with my boyfriend for as long as we've been together. Not that she'd ever act on her feelings. My best friend would never betray me like that.

Okay once, when Carter and I were broken up for a month last year, he and Adele hooked up. The breakup wasn't even a real breakup. Carter had been flirting with this apple-cheeked freshman, and I froze him out to send a message. My mother practically disowned me, but I knew what I was doing. Carter came crawling back, no more apple cheeks, end of story.

But for a heartbeat in time, Adele got it in her head that Carter and I were finished. That he needed comforting and she should be the provider of said comfort. When we got back together, Adele came to me sobbing. She was *so sorry*. She had *no idea* I was going to take him back. There were so many things wrong with that picture: How she should have been comforting me, not Carter, how it's never okay to move in on your best friend's ex. How bad she hurt me. It's basically the shittiest thing she's ever done, but our friendship has been otherwise rock solid for seventeen years. Adele is the most constant, most familiar thing in my entire life. Carter swore it was a one-time mistake. Adele swore it was a one-time mistake.

I let it go.

"What did that salad ever do to you, Kelly?" Bronson's voice snaps me out of my not-so-pleasant stroll down memory lane.

I'm gripping my fork so tight my knuckles are white. I drop it, and the metal clatters against the plate. Bronson and Alexander shoot matching worried stares in my direction.

"Excuse me." Suddenly, I'm feeling really hot. I stand up and make Adele and Graham move so I can get out of the booth. "Makeup refresh."

For a second, Adele looks like she's going to try to come with me, but I shoot her down with a hard stare. I need some air. Alone.

I lock the door to the one-person bathroom and lean against the wall beside the hand dryer. I am usually so much better about ignoring Adele's ridiculous crush on my boyfriend. She swore nothing like junior year would ever happen again, and I believe her. The truth is, I'm not actually mad at her—not when I have much bigger things to worry about.

Adele is just distracting me from the real threat. The girl whose affections Carter actually returns. If I hated her before, now that I know she's the one taunting me, I full-on *loathe* her. I reach into my bag and grab my phone. No new messages. Okay. Deep breath. I need to take a minute and get my head together before going back out there.

I open Insta and scroll through my feed. Trina has already uploaded three photos from tonight. Her and Alexander sticking out their tongues. A selfie with her ombré hair half covering her face and some filter that makes it look like she's at a disco. And then one candid shot from early in the night: Graham looking at Adele with puppy eyes, Adele taking a sip of her drink and gazing up at Carter, me adjusting my hair, my face tilted up toward the ceiling, and Carter staring straight at the camera, grinning. Trina has an uncanny talent for capturing the truth.

Just as I'm about to drop my phone into my bag, a new text pops up. Private.

He's not thinking about you, but I am.

Game over. I know who you are.

Doubt that.

But I'll give you three guesses.

I don't need three, bitch.

I'll count that as one. Wrong.

Whatever. Stop harassing me.

You're NOT going to win.

If you don't start listening to me,
you're going to be the ultimate loser.

What's that supposed to mean?

I'm seething. Who the hell does Rosalie think she is?

You think he'll give you your dream
future, but he'll only give you a future
of misery. Better get out now, Princess.

I half scream, half growl, then throw my phone into my bag. I've been doing my best to follow Linda's advice and just ignore her. But this string of provocations is testing my resolve. I walk up to the mirror and add a fresh coat of Peaches & Cream gloss to my lips. I run my fingers through my hair, smoothing the strands. I check the corners of my eyes for any smudges. I breathe in really deep. Then I'm ready to go back out there.

When I step through the door, Ben's here, sitting next to Trina. I can feel heat prick the back of my neck; I am so not in the mood to deal with him right now. My eyes travel across the rest of the booth. Carter's sitting again, and the sopho-mores are gone. Bronson and Alexander are lost in their own private conversation. Adele's staring at her phone. It must be something really interesting, because Graham's arm is wrapped around her shoulder and she hasn't shoved it off yet. I start to walk toward them, but then I see David standing at the counter.

"Hey, handsome." Before I can think better of it, I slide up next to him and lean my arms across the polished metal surface, covering up the menu he's been reading. "On chauffeur duty tonight?"

"Amanda Kelly." David gives me a big grin. "Ben's car's in the shop. Again." He shrugs and shoves his hands deep into his pockets. "Had to drive him out here in the truck."

"Oh, sorry about that." My eyes flick across the room to Carter. He's watching us.

"Why don't you join us? There's room in the booth."

"Can't. Paper due tomorrow." He looks disappointed.

"Tomorrow's Saturday."

David shrugs, his jacket stretching against the muscles in his back. When did he start looking way more than one year older than the rest of us? He's more chiseled, probably from the construction gig, but also more serious. More adult. "Welcome to community college." He slides the menu gently out from under me and turns to the woman behind the counter. "Can I get a burger, well-done, no tomato, to go?"

"You want fries?"

"Just the burger. And a Coke."

I stand up straight and adjust the strap of my bag against my shoulder. "Nice seeing you, David."

"Hey, can one of you give Ben a ride home?"

"Of course," I say in my most gracious voice. "It would be our pleasure." As I turn to walk away, I bump my hip, almost imperceptibly, into his.

David smiles, and I watch Carter flinch out of the corner of my eye. "Nice seeing you too, Amanda."

Back at the booth, I go around to the other side and slide in next to Ben. He flashes me a smile and runs his fingers through his hair, which needs a trim. The ends stick out where his fingers left messy trails.

"I forgot to tell you," he says as if he's picking up on a conversation we never started, "I ran into your mom outside Mason and Vine after school on Wednesday." I can feel the muscles clench along my jawline. Mason and Vine is my mother's favorite wine shop. When she's easing off vodka sodas, she's doing it with Chardonnay. As if a bottle of white were somehow less serious than the clear stuff. "I helped her carry the cases out to her car," he continues, too loud, oblivious to my discomfort. "She had five or six. Are you throwing another party?"

"How noble of you," I bristle. Show me a perfect family, okay? It's not mine, and it's sure as hell not Ben's. I narrow my eyes against his wide, puppy dog stare. He's either entirely clueless or going for the jugular. "Squad goals, Ben," I mutter beneath my breath. I'm not about to sit here in the Sunny Side and invite a diner full of rubberneckers to a front-row performance of *Our Dysfunctional Families*. It's like I actually need to explain the concept of social finesse.

"What?"

I grit my teeth and let it go, move on to the reason I came over here. "You have to get a new car. We can't be shuttling your ass all over Logansville."

"Yeah, I know," he mumbles, chastened. "I'm picking it up in the morning. So you'll drive me home tonight?"

"Maybe."

I get up, leaving Ben to stew, and move around to the other side of the booth. Graham and Adele let me back into my regular spot next to Carter, and I grab two of his sweet potato fries. Suddenly, I'm starving.

"What was that all about?" I watch his eyes flicker to David, still waiting at the counter.

"Someone needs to give Ben a ride home 'cause his shitty car is in the shop again. That's all."

Carter narrows his eyes at me, and the hot flush of irritation on the back of my neck turns to shame. Flirting with David in front of Carter was probably a brainless move. But allowing Ben to burrow under my skin, once again, was even worse. He doesn't know my mother, only sees her at social events, where she's usually the host. Of course he'd think she was buying wine for a party. And of course I'd bite back like he'd made an intentional play to wave the Kellys' dirty laundry in my face.

Carter doesn't say anything further, but his eyes tell me I'm not trying hard enough. He's always treated Ben like a little brother in need of protection. Partly, from me. I look away, but I can't un-see the subtext: If I could just be *better*, maybe Carter wouldn't seek out other girls. Once again, I've come up short. I wrap my arms tight around my waist.

Carter turns to Graham. "Think you can give Ben a ride, man?"

"Course," Graham says. They bump fists and lock eyes. Then Graham leans across the table toward Ben. "I've got you, man."

I try to catch Adele's eyes—*she'll* sympathize with me about Ben's utter lack of tact—but she's busy making a huge show of disentangling herself from Graham. I raise my eyebrows deliberately at her, but it's as if she's intentionally avoiding my gaze.

Carter watches David's retreating back as he disappears into the parking lot with his food. Then, he turns to me, and this time the disappointment in his eyes has been replaced by lust. Maybe flirting with David wasn't such a bad idea after all. "You ready to jet?" He tosses two twenties down onto the table, which is way more than enough to cover our food, but we're probably springing for whatever Ben orders too. I press my lips together and force a rising jab back down my throat.

Then I lock eyes with Carter. All night, he's been focused in turn on each of our friends. It's one of Carter's best—and most impossible—qualities. He has a way of making everyone feel special, included. I'm the only one who's been feeling left out. And now his light is turned entirely on me. "More than ready," I say.

Five minutes later, we're in Carter's Mercedes, driving too fast down the Logansville streets toward our houses. But really, toward his house because we both know that's where we're going. There's a side entrance that leads past the closed-off antiques wing and straight up to the third floor, to his bedroom. It's not like our parents won't notice his car pull into the drive, but no one's going to bother us. Our parents actually seem to get that sex is part of a healthy relationship.

I can't wait to get inside. My whole body is thrumming. Rosalie, Ben, David, Adele. My mother. Those awful texts. I want to shut it all out. I just want to be with Carter, alone, my body pressed up against his body in his bed where everything is normal and good.

We slip through the side door, and Carter flicks on the entrance light. I start toward the stairs, but halfway down the hall, we both stop. The door to the antiques wing is open, and all the lights are on. Inside, someone's humming.

"Linda?" The humming stops. "In here."

"It's us, Dad," Carter says, peering inside.

Winston Shaw emerges from behind a large, cloth-draped triangular structure, possibly a harp. "Kids," he says, looking startled. He steps into the hall and shuts the door behind him, as if our very presence might devalue his loot. He's holding his phone, a clunky old BlackBerry, which he flicks on and off before shoving it deep into his pocket.

The wing that serves exclusively as storage for the majority of Winston's vast collection is off-limits to prevent damage. I haven't been inside in years, but when we were kids, Carter and I used to sneak in all the time. It was the best spot in the estate for hide-and-seek: three temperature-controlled rooms chock full of tarp-draped statues, Queen Anne chairs, mirrors, and framed canvases. I never quite understood the point of owning so many antiques that will never see the light of day. Sure, a bunch are on display throughout the estate, but Winston should probably open his own gallery or donate a few relics to the Museum of Fine Arts. I'm sure Linda and her board would be thrilled.

"Is my mother . . ." I start to say, not really sure what I'm asking.

"She was supposed to stop over an hour ago," Winston says. "The caterers left a serving platter and a couple boxes of flutes."

"Oh." A relief I can't quite place floods my chest. "I'll bring them home tonight. Not a problem."

"Thank you, Amanda." He smiles at me kindly. "Since you're here, can I interest you two in a quick listen? The remastered 1930 *Boléro* just arrived, and it is spectacular in the listening room."

Winston also has a deep fervor for classical music, a hobby that Carter can't stand but I find rather fascinating. I've learned a lot from him, especially about the French composers. *Boléro* is Ravel's most famous work, and I *do* want to hear it in Winston's "listening room," a small space on the second floor furnished with powerful surround-sound. Regardless, a polite evening with Carter's father is not exactly what either Carter or I had in mind.

"How about tomorrow?" I ask. "If you have some time in the afternoon, I could come over for *Boléro* and cookies. I just baked a batch of white chocolate cranberry, and I'm the only one eating them at home."

Winston lights up. Carter will never take an interest in his father's hobbies, but in me, Winston's found an avid pupil. And he has a rabid sweet tooth. "Come over after lunch," he says. "You're in for a treat."

When we're finally alone in Carter's room, he mumbles, "That's real nice of you. Spending time with my dad."

I shrug. "I actually want to hear the recording. It's nothing. Now can we stop talking about your dad?"

Carter grins, all dimples and bright white teeth. Soon, we're tearing off our clothes with some terrible pop-punk music on in the background, probably the furthest thing in Carter's collection from Ravel. I would normally hate this band, whoever they are, but tonight I want the loud, harsh sound. It drowns everything out. When I'm on top of Carter, my legs on either side of his hips and his breath fast and raspy below me, I can finally forget about Private and Rosalie and Ben and Adele. For a moment, everything feels normal between us.

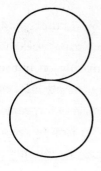

ROSALIE
SUNDAY, JANUARY 7

From my spot behind the Info Desk, I can see the late afternoon sun swell into a fat golden orb, then begin its slow drift through the spindly January trees. We're the ones in motion, but it doesn't seem that way. I stare through the library window at the wind and sun and cars on the road and feel the world moving fast while I'm motionless, caught. Between my parents' fear and my future. Between my future and Lily. Between church doctrine as familiar as the air I breathe and the truth buried deep in my heart. Between the past damage still coursing through my veins and the harm I'm inflicting, even now, a fracture to stave off a catastrophic break.

I answer questions, make recommendations, guide patrons

toward the right aisles, and watch the clock tick toward four. It's my usual weekend routine: library, church, library, homework. I love my job, but today by closing time, I'm itching to get outside, get on my bike, throw my body into motion. I'm so eager to go, go, go, I forget to check in with Dad before I start home.

I jam my feet down on the pedals, ride fast and hard for the first few minutes until my calves start to burn and the wind stings tears from my eyes. Then I slow down and take my time biking along the two-lane road, stretching the fifteen-minute ride into thirty. The small branch where I work is technically in Bracken Hollow, the next township over, but there's not much to distinguish the rural communities surrounding Logansville. On my right, a barbed-wire fence keeps grazing cattle in and curious humans out. The air smells of manure mixed with a sharp winter tang. I try to relax into the motion of the bike, start planning out the English paper I have to write when I get home, but as I ride, my mind does what it likes to do when I'm alone: spiral. I picture Lily, her small face jumbled together with flashes of Carter and Pau and Carter again. The good feelings and the ugly feelings whirring and spinning inside me until they're all the same messy fear.

When I get home, I lock my bike in the shed out back and let myself in through the mudroom. The car's gone, which means Mom's still at God's Grace. She spends every Sunday afternoon volunteering, something she'd like me to do more of. Fortunately, my need for a job is paramount seeing as my parents can't really give me an allowance. Working at the library pays for my phone, which is my lifeline since we don't have internet or cable in the house, and everything else goes straight into the account I set up for college.

I kick off my shoes and hang my coat on the empty peg by the back door. Then, I head to the den to check in with Dad. He's in his usual spot at the big table in the corner, camped out in front of two stacks of math papers. When he looks up from his grading, his face tells me I've screwed up big time. I glance at the clock, and it hits me all at once. Fifteen minutes later than I should be, *and* I forgot to call before I left.

"I'm sorry," I say automatically before he can lay into me. I think about making up some excuse, but that would only make things worse.

"Where have you been?" His voice is clipped, edged with fear. That I've done something much worse than coming home late. That I've *strayed*.

"I'm sorry," I say again. "Just biking home. I lost track of time."

He stands up, and I take a step back.

"I don't know what to do with you, Rosalie. There are rules in this house."

"I know," I mumble.

"Do you?" His voice pitches up.

I swallow. I don't know what else to say. It was thoughtless to forget to call, even more so to dawdle on my way home. I did this to myself. "I'm really sorry," I say again.

"Lily!" Dad calls, his body leaning in the direction of the stairs. She must be up playing in her room. I know what's coming. He's calling her down so we can pray together. About me.

In a minute, she appears in the doorway to the den, Lily-Barbie, her favorite and therefore eponymous knockoff, clutched in her fist.

"Come here." Dad holds his hands out to both of us. We take

them without question and kneel in a small circle on the den floor. Lily-Barbie drops to the carpet. Dad recites from heart: "Then some Pharisees and teachers of the law came to Jesus from Jerusalem and asked, 'Why do your disciples break the tradition of the elders?'" It's Matthew 15, from the New International Version, the preferred Bible of the FOC. I, too, know this verse by heart and join in, the words ticking like times tables off my tongue.

"Jesus replied, 'And why do you break the command of God for the sake of your tradition? For God said, "Honor your father and mother" and "Anyone who curses their father or mother is to be put to death. . . ."'"

I close my eyes, and the coarse grain of the den carpet against my knees and the dry scratch of my father's palm against mine take me back to another house, on the other side of the state, where my parents and I kneeled to pray for my soul almost nightly the year I turned thirteen.

My heart pounds furiously in my chest, a sharp staccato beat I can't slow or steady. I clutch Mom's hand to my left and Dad's to my right. Lily, barely more than an infant, whimpers in her bassinet by the window. Together, we recite from Timothy 1, the verses that teach that homosexuality is immoral, a sin on par with those of killers and slave traders. I press each word through rattling lips, pretend I'm tattooing them to my skin. If the words become part of me, I'll remember them. If the words become part of me, I can change.

Last week, I went to my parents because I was afraid. I wanted them to say Jesus would accept me anyway. I wanted them to say they'd love me unconditionally. I wanted it to be okay.

Dad's face turned to stone. Mom asked me question after question.

Had I kissed a girl? Was a specific girl leading me into sin? *It's not like that, not for me. It's not one person; it's a million feelings that add up to one thing I know for sure about myself. It's the lilac shampoo smell that floats from Cat Heaton's hair when she passes by the orchestra room every day before lunch. It's the brush of Mila Astin's knee against my knee in the girl's locker room last Thursday, changing for field hockey practice. The way she doesn't shave her legs, and the powder-fine hairs tickled my skin. It's Emmy Rossum in* Beautiful Creatures, *the way her eyes glowed with a darkness and light that sent a shiver straight through me. The way I snuck back into the theater to see her a second time.*

Dad says it's not too late. Temptation itself is not a sin. If I can overcome these thoughts before they become sinful behaviors, I can still find salvation.

If not, Mom, Dad, and Lily will go to heaven, and I'll burn in hell. Alone.

My heart is still pounding, rapid fire. My palms are slick, and I grab my parents' hands tighter. I need them. I can't go to hell.

Later, after dinner, I'm supposed to be doing my homework at the table in the den. My parents are in their bedroom with the door closed. I wriggle under the table and press my ear to the heating vent.

"I don't know what I did wrong, Richard." Mom's voice is tinny, bounced against the vent's metal edges. I squirm closer, press my ear hard against the slats.

"It was a mistake to let her join field hockey." Dad's voice is deeper, clearer. "You heard her; those locker rooms are the devil's playground."

Mom whimpers. "We didn't know." A pause, then: "I'm still waiting for Stan to approve my request to go part-time." I draw in a deep breath. Part-time?

"He'll approve it. It'll work out."

"You're the teacher. I don't know what I'm doing."

"I'll help, you know I will. She'll do math and earth science with me in the evenings." A pause, then: "The sooner we get her out of that school, the better. It's too dangerous for her to be around so many girls." My mind whirs. No more school?

"Her sessions with Michael start on Wednesday, praise Jesus. Rosalie says she's ready to work hard."

I am. Next week, I'll start meeting with a counselor at church. Michael. I'm to do everything he tells me. I'm to work harder than I've ever worked before. I'm ready. I'll do anything to save myself.

Dad drops my hand. The room is thick with silence. My parents believe I have sought redemption for my "choice" to like girls through confession, repentance, and faith. They believe I've made another "choice"—to change. I look up at Dad, force myself to meet his eyes. When he speaks again, his words are soft, filled with love.

"We worry for you, Rosalie. We only want you to live according to His path." He's talking about today's infractions, but really, he means so much more.

"I know." I push myself up from the carpet, legs trembling. Lily scrambles up beside me. "I'll do better. I promise." I reach down and give Dad a hand up. When he's standing again, he folds me into a huge hug.

"I love you," he whispers in my ear.

"I love you too."

For a moment, we're silent. Lily fidgets beside me, doll back in her clutch, unsure if she's been released to her room.

"I have that English paper due tomorrow."

He nods and returns to his desk, his stacks of papers. I take Lily's hand and start toward the stairs.

"Rosalie?" he calls after me. I freeze. "Your mom's going to be home late tonight. They're kicking off the Winter Campaign at God's Grace. So it's just the three of us for dinner." That's code for, *Can you figure out dinner, Rosalie?* Hopefully it also means he'll let my transgression slide without alerting Mom.

"Of course," I call. "I'm on it."

Upstairs, Lily drags me into her room. We don't talk about what happened downstairs. Prayer sessions like that—usually a Bible verse followed by specific prayers from Mom or Dad—are a regular occurrence. Usually when Lily or I have messed up. Usually me. I used to find comfort in family prayer. The verses were like a script: Do this, and you'll be okay. You'll be saved. Simple. Now, that comfort has been replaced by a cold dread that settles in my stomach and refuses to leave for hours after we pray.

Lily plops down on the little strip of floor next to her kid's bed. She's surrounded by every doll she owns. From where she's sitting, you could easily touch the bed with one hand and the wall with the other, elbows bent, but Lily doesn't seem to notice. At six, my sister slips with ease between the worlds of dolls and pop stars, Disney princesses and the Blessed Virgin. The world isn't yet carved up for her, godly and secular, childhood and adulthood, fantasy and reality. Despite the rules that govern Lily's life, anything still seems possible.

I'm caught between a rush of envy for her innocence, and pity—because anything *isn't* possible. Not if Lily wants to keep her place in this family. And even then, eventually, she'll have to choose: our parents, or me. God, or me.

I swallow, thinking about Miss Larkin, how she hasn't seen her family in years. How their love for her has been replaced by fear at best, bitter contempt at worst. How someday, that could be me.

"What's up with Lily-Barbie?" I ask, shoving the thoughts deep inside and crouching down to my sister's level.

"She's sad because Rachel-Barbie moved away. Lily-Barbie's mom is getting her a dachshund puppy, but Lily-Barbie doesn't know it yet." She pronounces it *dash-hound*.

"Sounds like she's going to love that surprise."

"Yeah." Lily picks up her dolls and begins playing like the earlier interruption never happened.

She was only three when we moved to Culver Ridge, but she still talks about Rachel, her best friend from our old town. Mom helped Lily send Rachel a few letters when we first moved, but now we only hear from Rachel's family at Christmas. It's hard to keep in touch when you're a little kid. I feel a stab of guilt. If it wasn't for me, we'd still live in our old town. Lily would probably be playing Barbies with Rachel right now.

"Mac and cheese for dinner." I give Lily a kiss on the top of her head. "You'll help me make a salad?"

"Now?" Lily asks, eyes wide.

"Later. I'll come get you."

For a minute, I stand frozen in the doorway, watching my sister play with her dolls. I want to watch her grow up. I want to know the person she'll become. As badly as I want a life outside a faith that condemns me for being myself, I want a life with Lily in it. Inside my chest, my heart shudders and throbs.

I turn away, crossing the hall to my room, and close the door behind me. It's after five and completely dark outside. Instead of switching on a light, I walk over to the window. The gray swell of a gibbous moon illuminates the sky. In the space of an hour, the world has transformed, light to dark, golden to gray. I grip the sill with my fingers and wonder how much longer I can hold on.

AMANDA

SUNDAY, JANUARY 7

On Sunday afternoon, I call the girls over for some emergency detective work. It's not like I couldn't do a Google search on my own, but honestly, I could use the moral support. Carter messing around is one thing. I hate it, but it's not exactly new. Normally, I can tap into Linda's advice and keep my emotions in check. But I got three more texts yesterday, and at this point I'm seriously pissed.

"I thought you said it was a wrong number." Adele is sprawled out next to me on my bed in head-to-toe magenta velour, hugging Huggie, the stuffed elephant I've had since I was three, to her chest. She's gotten her highlights touched up to an even whiter blond, and her lips are frosted pink beneath a layer of clear gloss. Her aesthetic says Real Housewife of tomorrow.

"I knew it wasn't really a wrong number," I admit. "I just thought she'd drop it. But she's definitely not dropping anything." No one is allowed to talk about Carter's cheating unless I bring it up. I would rather die than let my friends pity me. But today, there's no way around it. We have to talk about Rosalie.

"So you're sure it's that weird Culver Ridge girl?" Trina is already sitting at my desk, penguin coat and scarf combo slung across the back of my chair and emerald green nails flashing against my laptop keys. I peer over her shoulder; she's typing *how to look up a private phone number* into Google. "I can't believe Carter's still sneaking around with her."

Adele was the first to find out about Rosalie. She heard it from Graham, who was at this club in town with Carter the night they met last August, right before the start of senior year. Graham told Adele that Rosalie was there with a friend, and that she blew Carter off. We Facebook-stalked her anyway, and she was obviously not a threat, so I was not prepared when Trina came back from a gallery opening in the city three months later with pictures of Carter and Rosalie on her camera.

"I walked in, took some quick shots, and walked right back out before Carter saw me. It sucked too, because there were some amazing photographs in that show, and I had to make a whole other trip into the city to see them."

I had bristled when she'd first told me. Was she actually weighing something as trivial as a missed gallery opening against my happiness? But really, we both knew she'd done me a giant favor. If Carter is messing around, I need to know about it.

In November, I was prepared to wait it out. It had been less than a year since I'd broken up with him over the apple-cheeked freshman. You have to be strategic, which means never making the same play twice. I didn't think Rosalie would last. She's from the sticks, for Christ sakes. She has the world's ugliest haircut. But now, everything's different. She's forcing my hand.

"It has to be her," I tell Trina. "She thinks she's making some big move. Like if she scares me, I'll roll over and deliver Carter on a silver platter. We need to prove it's Rosalie sending those messages."

My friends nod, their faces appropriately serious.

"But it seems like she's mostly just telling you how beautiful you are," Adele says. "That seems like a weird way of saying, 'back off, bitch.'"

I shrug. "It's a strategy. She's obviously not naive. She knows telling me to step off would get her nowhere. But she's graduated beyond compliments. Here, look." I open the stream of messages from Private and scroll back to the ones from the diner Friday night. I hold my phone out to Adele, who snatches it eagerly and reads aloud.

He's not thinking about you, but I am.

"Well, that's creepy as shit," Trina says.

"Wait, it gets creepier. Mandy says she knows the stalker is Rosalie, and the stalker denies it. Then she says Mandy's going to be 'the ultimate loser' if she doesn't listen to her, and Carter's only going to give Mandy 'a future of misery.' That's pretty low."

"Hold up," I say. "You think this qualifies as *stalking*?"

Trina shrugs, ombré hair fluttering around her shoulders.

"She's sending you creepy texts, and she's obviously obsessed with you and Carter. I'd call that stalking."

I grab a pillow and hug it to my chest, suddenly feeling cold. The texts are annoying and a little vile, but they're just a power play. It's hard to imagine Rosalie could actually be dangerous. . . .

"Keep reading," I instruct Adele.

"Okay, these three are from yesterday." She scrolls.

> You know you need to end things.
> You've known it for a long time.

> You may be the prettiest girl at school,
> but things are going to get real ugly if
> you don't start listening to me.

> Don't be scared, Amanda.

"What the hell does that last one mean?" Trina asks. "Don't be scared to break up with your boyfriend so I can lap up your sloppy seconds? Or don't be scared *of me*?"

"Right?" Adele agrees. "That's messed up. And pathetic."

Something inside my stomach twists, but I bite my tongue. I think Adele would like to pretend we've both forgotten how she tried to lap up my sloppy seconds with Carter last year. I forgave her a long time ago, but no one's doing any forgetting. Subconsciously, my fingers brush the onyx heart at my neck.

"It really is textbook," Trina sighs, returning to my computer. "Veiled threats. Taking out her aggression behind a screen. I should probably refer her to my mom." Trina's mom is a psychiatrist or psychologist, I always forget which. I smile thinking about Rosalie pouring her heart out on Trina's mom's couch.

"Have you showed the texts to Carter?" Adele asks. She has a few strands of blond highlight clenched between her teeth, and she's chewing furiously.

"Obviously not. And not because she forbid it. The last thing I need is a fight with Carter right now. No one breathes a word to him, got it?"

I lock eyes with each of them, and they both nod. I am dead serious.

"Going to Carter like a wounded puppy is not the right play." I exhale long and slow, then toss the pillow aside and smooth down my hair. "We need to handle this without Carter. Prove she's sending the texts. Expose her."

"On it." Trina starts typing again, and the screen fills up with search results for blocking your caller ID.

"So what exactly is your plan?" Adele asks while Trina scrolls through the links. "For exposing her, I mean?" Her tone lacks its usual levity. Maybe this whole taking-Rosalie-down thing will have the added benefit of disabusing Adele of any lingering notion that Carter might be hers one day. She really needs to get over herself and get together with Graham already so we can put this awkwardness squarely behind us.

"I don't know yet. But I'll figure something out."

"Amanda?" My mother's voice accompanies a swift rap on my door.

I turn to my friends. "One sec." Then I slip into the hall and close the door behind me. I haven't seen Linda yet today, and past experience has taught me not to invite her into my room when

I have people over unless I've had a chance to assess her alcohol content.

When I get into the hall, though, she looks surprisingly bright eyed and bushy tailed.

"I'm not allowed to come in?" she asks.

"Adele was trying on an outfit," I lie. "Just giving her some privacy."

She accepts my excuse and leans against the wall. "I thought I heard voices. Are both Adele and Trina over?"

I nod.

"Well, they're welcome to stay for dinner. Your father has business in the city, so it's just us girls." She says this as if it's not "just us girls" 90 percent of the time. I guess the only difference is that it's Sunday, not that the days of the week seem to mean much in the finance world.

"Okay," I say hesitantly. If she's still this with-it in a couple hours, it might actually be nice to have Trina and Adele stay. . . .

"Why don't you ask them, because if I don't call Lynn by two, there's no way we'll be able to get her for tonight."

Oh. Lynn is the private chef we hire when my mother feels the need to impress. The chance of her having a last-minute opening seems slim, but more importantly, we can't afford Lynn right now. My mother is doing this because Jack has deserted us tonight. Which I'm sure is only because his meeting is important for business, which means he's doing it for us. I know my mother misses the days when Dad was the head of his division, when weekend obligations could be shuffled off to a junior partner. I barely remember that life, but it's like a ghost in the house, dogging my father at every turn. And raising my mother's hackles. I don't want any part of the barbs and daggers, the financial tug-of-war that has come to define their marriage.

"It's just Trina and Adele," I say. "Takeout's fine."

My mother stiffens.

"Trina was just telling us about this new Peruvian place off Springvale," I press on. "I'll check with the girls and see if they deliver, okay?" I lean over to give her a peck on the cheek.

"Peruvian sounds interesting." She eyes me suspiciously.

"Seriously, I've been craving it all day," I insist. She relaxes just a little before releasing me back to my room.

I close the door, and Trina looks up from my computer. "Everything okay?"

"That Peruvian place deliver?" I ask. Trina nods.

"You should both stay for dinner, then. My thank-you for playing detective."

"Speaking of which," Trina says, "if we're going to trace these texts back to Rosalie, first thing we need to do is figure out how she made her number private."

"Is private the same as unlisted?" Adele asks.

"Not exactly," Trina says. "Unlisted means your number isn't in the phone book or the White Pages online. My mom keeps our landline unlisted. She likes to keep family and business separate." I'd keep my home number unlisted too if I had tons of psych patients with twenty-four-hour access to my cell phone.

"Private's like anonymous or blocked, right?" I ask.

"Right." Trina turns back to my laptop. "This site says if you dial star-sixty-seven before typing in a number, it will block your outbound caller ID. But I think that only works for calling, not texting." She clicks back to the search results and opens a new link. "Okay, here we go. Apparently there are web-sites you can use to send anonymous texts, but most of them don't let the person on the other end text back. You've been writing back to her?"

"Yeah, and she's been responding."

"Okay, so scratch that." Trina scrolls some more. "Here it says you can send anonymous texts via email, but I think then they would show up from an email account, and she'd also have to know your phone carrier."

I shake my head. "Keep going."

"So there are also a bunch of apps. I think most of them give you a fake number to use, but maybe some show up as 'Private'? The bad news is it's pretty impossible to figure out who's tex-ting you because you don't have to use your real name or number when you make an account. So, unless she's totally clueless, she used fake info."

"Can you schedule a text to send later?"

"Why does that matter?" Adele asks.

I shoot her a look. "Just considering all the angles. The texts from Thursday night, I know she was out with Carter. The more we can figure out about how she's pulling this off, the better."

Trina frowns and stares at the screen. "This article doesn't say. Sorry. Maybe on some of the apps?"

Adele switches out the piece of hair she's destroying for a new one. "That must be it, right? The app thing?"

"I guess so." I groan and collapse back into the wall of pillows on my bed. If Rosalie is using an app, there'll be no way to trace the texts back to her. This is impossible.

"Okay, wait." Adele grabs my hand. "If she's using an app, she had to download it, right? Like through the Apple Store or whatever? That's totally traceable."

"Sure," Trina says. "If we had her phone. Or if we were the FBI."

"Wait a second." I sit up straight. "That's it."

"We're going to take this to the FBI?" Trina raises her eyebrows at me.

"No. The FBI wouldn't give ten shits. But the Logansville police might, if she screws up."

"What do you mean?" Adele asks.

"Right now, she hasn't done anything illegal, right? I mean the texts are a little stalker-ish, but she's probably not breaking any laws. But what if she directly threatens me? That's illegal harassment."

"And then you could get the police involved." Adele sticks another strand of hair in her mouth, and I glare at her. "I get hungry when I'm thinking. Sorry." Trina digs out a Kind bar from the box on my desk and tosses it over.

"Jack and Linda Kelly's daughter being harassed by an anonymous stalker? That's news. We can't trace the texts back to Rosalie, but the police could. If she's charged with harassment, they'll confiscate her phone. They'd be able to figure it out."

"Right," Trina says slowly. "But how do we know she's going to do something illegal? Like you said, the texts aren't exactly law-breaking."

"Not yet," I agree. "But I'm pretty sure she's capable of taking things to the next level. 'Things are going to get real ugly?' 'Don't be scared?'"

Adele nods furiously, eyes wide. "That was totally creepy."

"If I don't give in, she'll have to up the ante. She just needs a little push." I smile, sinking back into the pillow wall again. Now, I have an idea.

"What are you going to do?" Adele asks through a mouthful of Kind bar.

"Right now, she has the upper hand. She's behind this shield of anonymity. But what if I remove the shield? What if I email her?"

"You have her address?" Trina asks.

"School account. I'll plug her name or initials or whatever into the Greater Logansville formula. Once I call her out, she'll have to back off or step up her game. Either way, I win."

Secretly, I hope she doesn't back off. Now I'm mad. Now I want her to threaten me so I can turn her in to the cops. That boyfriend-thief might think she's being all clever, but she doesn't know who she's messing with. I feel ten times better now that I have a plan.

Rosalie Bell is going to crash and burn.

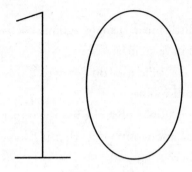

ROSALIE

MONDAY, JANUARY 8

By the time I get to the school library during fourth, I'm practically shaking from overcaffeination and lack of sleep. The computer screen is crystal-bright. My right eyelid is twitching. I slide my flash drive into the port and wait for my English paper to load. I stayed up far too late banging it out on the family computer in the den. I need to start scheduling my time better, but I just can't dredge up the motivation unless there's a deadline breathing down my neck.

While my paper prints, I open up my email. The school-issued accounts are really closely monitored, so it's mostly notes from teachers and administrators, redundant stuff from class and morning announcements. But there might be news from my theater teacher about auditions for the spring monologue contest.

When her name pops up in my inbox, the first thing I think is that I'm even more tired than I realized. I'm having waking hallucinations. The subject line reads *BACK OFF, SKANK* in shouty caps. The second thing is: Fuck me. She knows.

The cold dread from last night's family prayer session turns to sharp blades of ice in my stomach. I hunch over the desk, wrap my arms tight around my waist.

When Carter told me he and Amanda had an arrangement, I wanted it to be true. Even after I looked her up on Facebook, saw all those pictures of them together, I wanted to believe that I wasn't doing anything wrong, that even better, Carter was never going to get too attached to me, because in the end, he was meant to be with Amanda. When I told the story that way, it was perfect. But that's all it was: a story.

The last sheet of my English paper falls into the printer tray, and I take my time making sure all the pages are there and in order before stapling them together. Then I let the cursor hover over the unopened email, bracing myself for what's to come.

Subject: BACK OFF, SKANK
From: Amanda Kelly
To: me

Seriously, back the hell off. I don't
even know what you think you're trying
to pull, but spoiler alert: It's not
working. And if you keep this up, you're

going to have a whole lot more than an
angry email to contend with. In case it
never occurred to you, there are people
in Logansville who care about my health
and well-being. Who would do pretty much
anything to make sure no one screws with
my future. You think you're messing with
just me, but you're not. You're messing
with the Kellys.

Also, hi. We haven't formally met,
so let me take a moment to introduce
myself. I'm Amanda, Carter's girlfriend
of over three years. But that wasn't
really necessary, was it? You know
exactly who I am.

And don't think I don't know exactly who
you are. I probably should have reached
out a long time ago, but you know why
I didn't? Because you're so not worth
it. But this anonymous texting thing is
getting old. It's boring. I'm bored. So
now you have to stop. Let it be shown
for the record, I'm asking nicely.
Rosalie Bell: Please stop this immature,
harassing, borderline criminal behavior.

If you have something else to say, now
you know how to reach me. The normal

```
way. Not hiding behind some pathetic
private number like the coward you are.

If the texts don't stop, you'll be
hearing from my lawyer next.

Happy Monday, beyotch.

-AK
```

I'm shaking when I forward the email from my school account to my Gmail. Of course Amanda's furious. I've been fooling myself thinking that what I've been doing with Carter—even though it's not what it looks like, even though I have every intention of slipping out of his life by graduation and leaving them to live happily ever after—wasn't going to hurt her.

I delete any trace of her email from the school's system before logging out. Then, I text Pau.

Clearing after school. Need to talk.

Four hours later, I'm leaving the pasture behind and crossing the woods toward our clearing. Today, I walk right past the tree with the hollowed-out trunk without stopping to grab a pillow. Pau and I never meet up on Mondays because of Youth Ministry, but this can't wait. I have to catch the 3:45 bus back to Culver Ridge, but I have to see her first.

"*Vrdi vrreed vreed,*" I call.

"*Peet-suh peet-suh peet,*" she calls back.

She's standing with her back pressed against a giant oak, lighting a cigarette. She's still not wearing gloves, but she has a kelly green hat pulled down over her dark brown curls. Kelly green. Perfect.

"Fancy meeting you here on a Monday," she says, grinning.

"I need you to read this." I cut straight to the point, holding out my phone, and her face folds into lines of concern. "Here."

Pau takes it. After a minute, her back slides down the trunk until she's squatting against the ground. She looks up at me. "Shit."

"I know." I sit down next to her and press my fists into my lips until I can feel the skin bruise.

"You've been sending Princess Amanda anonymous texts? That's pretty baller, Lee-Lee."

"What, no! I don't know what that's about. The point is, she knows who I am."

"Yeah." Paulina takes a deep drag, then tilts her head back, blowing the smoke straight up into the sky. "You had to kind of figure she was going to find out eventually, right? No offense, but Carter's not exactly covert ops material. And you have to think he's probably done this before."

I raise my eyebrows.

"Cheat, you know? You're probably not the first. I'm sure Amanda has eyes all over the Northern Panhandle."

"Shit." I take back my phone and shove it into my coat pocket. "It's just I haven't heard a word from her all this time. I thought, I don't know. I didn't think she knew."

Paulina fiddles with the laces on her clunky brown boots, but doesn't say anything.

"If she knows about me, she could find out about us. What if she keeps digging? This could be really bad."

Paulina's silent for a minute. "So what are you going to do?" she finally asks.

"Write back to her, I guess. Tell her it's not me with the texts. Start being more careful with Carter."

Paulina shakes her head. "You can't keep seeing him; don't you get it? She's not going to let this go."

"You know that's not an option. We can't have this same conversation—"

"I know," Pau cuts me off. Frustration crackling across her skin, her hand flies up in the air between us. A piece of ash soars off the tip of her cigarette, and I flinch.

"Sorry." Her voice is quieter now, but there's something hard and biting lodged beneath her words. "But this isn't okay. We need a new plan."

My spine starts to tingle, and I wrap my hands tight around my body. I think the words I can't bring myself to say out loud: *There is no other plan.*

It's my third session with Michael, a twitchy, clammy-skinned FOC counselor dedicated to making gay kids straight again. Michael used to be SSA, the church shorthand for same sex attracted; now he's married to Evie, a nice woman in our congregation. They have a three-year-old daughter. Ex-gay ministry worked for him. He's going to make it work for me.

We sit across from each other in a small office in the basement of our old church, in our old town. It's already April, but it's still freezing down here. I tug at my shirtsleeves, wrap my hands in the soft pink cotton. Our first two sessions were what he called "talk therapy," but he's not a licensed therapist. My parents say a regular therapist can't help me. Not with this. In order to redirect my attraction from girls to boys, I have to trust the church and our methods.

I suck in a sharp breath. Michael's holding a picture in front of me, something torn from a magazine. It's a grown-up woman, naked, one long, stilettoed leg wrapped around a tall metal poll. You can see her boobs and everything. She's staring straight at me with eyes that look half asleep.

"What does she make you feel?" Michael asks. Flecks of spittle collect in the corners of his mouth.

"Um, nothing." I look down at my lap, embarrassed. She's old enough to be in college, probably older.

"Does your stomach tingle?" he asks.

"No." I lift my arms and wrap them tight around my chest. I don't have boobs yet, not like that. Hers are huge, way bigger than my mom's. "I just feel weird."

Suddenly, Michael's grabbing my hand and plunging it in a bowl of ice water on the desk to my left. I gasp. It's so cold, my hand feels like it's on fire. I try to jerk away, but he holds my arm in a vice grip.

"Look at the picture," he commands. He's holding it too close, right in front of my nose. I peek over the top of the page and up to his face. It's red and splotchy. There's sweat collecting where his forehead ends and hairline begins. I whimper.

"Look at it, Rosalie."

I stare at the too-close photo until my eyes cross and my hand feels like it's going to crack off my wrist. Tears leak down my face and drip onto my jeans. Finally, he releases my arm and drops the picture to the floor. I clutch my hand to my chest.

"Here," he says gently, handing me a soft yellow towel. I wrap it around my hand as Michael holds up a new photo. It's a black-and-white *ad for Wrangler jeans. In it, a man is running across a dirt road at the edge of a wheat field. His shirt is torn open and flaps back in the wind, revealing a muscly chest. His hair is long for a guy and the wind kicks it out in all directions as he runs. I fix my eyes on his hair and wrap the towel tighter around my stinging hand.*

"No," I say to Paulina, my voice firm. "I'm going to handle this. I'll write to Amanda, explain I'm not sending the texts. I'll tell her I'm ending things with Carter. And then I'll talk to him. We'll find different places to go. We'll be more careful."

Paulina's mouth twists into a deep scowl. She stabs her cigarette butt into the ground like it's the enemy.

"This girl means business, and she's got lawyers and shit. If whoever's bothering her keeps it up, she's coming after you. What are you going to do if those texts keep coming?"

"I'll cross that—" I start to say, but Pau holds up her hand again, cutting me off. We never fight like this. The flash in her eyes makes me shiver.

"Cut Carter loose," she says. "Please. We'll figure something out with your parents."

"There's nothing to figure out with them," I practically spit. I jump up and grab my backpack, slinging it roughly across my shoulders. "This isn't about logic or being reasonable. FOC doctrine is nonnegotiable. I'm sorry I can't be a better girlfriend, but you've known the deal since we met. If you can't handle a few more months like this, then you need to tell me. Do you want to break up?"

"No." Pau stands and grabs at my arm, pulling me to her. Every nerve in my body lights up. I can feel her breath hot on my face. "You know I don't want that."

"Then you need to trust me."

For a moment, Paulina doesn't say anything. In the silence, I can hear our hearts beating together: *ker-thunk, ker-thunk.* I think of Lily, and a little piece of me dies. Soon, there are tears stinging my eyes, and I break her hold to wipe roughly at them with my coat sleeve. "I have to go. I'll miss my bus."

"Rosalie, I'm sorry." Before I can turn back toward the woods, Paulina is pulling me into her again. "I do trust you. We're going to get through this. We're pros at that."

I let her hold me for a minute, breathing in and out into her thick tangle of curls. Paulina's parents may not be Dan Savage-level supportive, but she's out at home, and it's fine. Her older brother Ramon is gay, so he kind of paved the way. She's lucky in a way I can't even imagine—and she knows it. For years, she's been my rock. Without Pau, I'm not sure I'd be even close to okay. I'm not sure I'd still be here at all.

"I really have to go." I tilt my chin up, and the press of her lips is a reminder that after everything, I'm still me. I'm alive. For a moment, I let myself sink into the kiss. And then I turn into the woods and start jogging toward the parking lot. I have eleven minutes to get to my bus.

I'm winded in no time. I'm good on a bike, but running is not my friend. I stop to catch my breath. Behind me, twigs crunch. I spin around, and a two-tone blur like piano keys or lane markers on a highway disappears behind a tree halfway back to the clearing. The crunching stops. Images of Pau and me kissing flash across the back of my eyelids.

"*Vrdi vrreed vreed.*" Even before I finish the call, I know there won't be a reply. Paulina's coat is brown.

Part of me wants to go back, and part of me wants to pretend I didn't just hear footsteps or see a white-and-black streak disappear into the trees. I glance at my phone. My bus leaves in nine minutes. It doesn't matter what I want. After yesterday's transgression with Dad, being late to Youth Ministry isn't an option. I'll have to sprint.

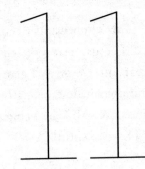

AMANDA

TUESDAY, JANUARY 9

When I pull into the student lot, Adele and Trina are standing in the spot next to Adele's bimmer, saving it for me. I tap the horn twice as I pull up, and they scurry out of the way like I might actually hit them. I'm out of the car with my phone out and email open before they can even say "good morning."

"Read this."

"She wrote back?" Trina asks.

"Last night. Here." I hand the phone over, and we start walking.

"Read it out loud," Adele insists, struggling to get a view of the screen.

> Subject: Re: Fwd: BACK OFF, SKANK
> From: Rosalie Bell

```
To: me

I'm sending this from my regular email
because in case you write back, you
can't use my school account, okay? They
monitor that shit.

I'm really sorry about Carter, and you
have every right to be angry. The truth
is complicated. I've given it a lot of
thought, and I'm going to end things
with him. I was never trying to mess
with your future. Promise.

About the texting. That's not me. I'm
sorry someone's bothering you, but
I wouldn't even know how to send an
anonymous message.

Take care,
Rosalie
```

When Trina finishes reading, we're all silent for a moment. She hands my phone over, and I slip it into my bag.

"Too easy," Adele says. "One email from you, and she's just going to roll over?"

"She's a coward," Trina says. "Maybe you should have done this two months ago."

"No, Adele's right," I say. "Something's off. 'I was never trying to mess with your future'? What else would you call what she's doing? And anyone can figure out how to send an anonymous text; it's not rocket science. We Googled four ways in ten minutes on Sunday."

We push through the main doors to Logansville South, and it's like walking into a wall of sweaty boy sound. Half the wrestling team seems to be staging an impromptu match outside the auditorium doors, and a group of freshmen clog the hallway mouth, eyes fixed on their phones, too obsessed with completing this week's Battle Pass challenge to notice we're coming through.

"Watch it." I shoulder one of the freshmen out of the way, in no mood for graciousness.

"Anyway," Adele says when we've made it through the press of the main entrance, "I don't buy it. She's feigning ignorance on purpose."

"Don't buy what? Who's feigning ignorance?"

Suddenly Ben is walking with us like he'd been there all along. My already thin patience bottoms out.

"None of your business," I snap at the same time Adele says, "Just some bitch who's bothering Mandy."

"Someone's bothering you?" Ben's face is filled with concern. He looks like he wants to hug me, but thankfully he thinks better of it and shoves his hands into his pockets. "Why would anyone bother you, Amanda?"

"Don't worry about it. The situation is under control."

We turn from the main hallway down the corridor that leads to my locker. I wish he would just leave. I wasn't done debriefing with Trina and Adele, but I'm definitely not continuing this conversation with Ben Gallagher hovering.

"Isn't the rest of the debate team waiting for you?" I put on my nicest voice, hoping Ben will get the hint.

He doesn't. "Huh? We don't have practice until Saturday."

"Holy shit." Trina stops in her tracks and flings out her long, skinny arms, pinning the three of us behind her.

"What the—?"

"Amanda," she cuts me off, "is that your locker?"

I stare down the corridor toward a group of kids gathered in front of what might be my locker. Then again, it might be any locker in my alcove; it's impossible to tell from here, especially with so many people milling around. Everyone is whispering and snapping pictures. All I can see for sure is that there's something bright red on the floor, and everyone seems to be freaking out in a hushed, slow-mo kind of way.

"Wait here," Ben says. "I'll go make sure it's safe."

I roll my eyes as he runs ahead of us down the hall like he's acting out some video game. We ignore him and start walking. Whatever it is, it's probably not a bomb. What does Ben think, he's going to diffuse it before we arrive?

It's obvious it's my locker from the way people stare when I get close. A few people step aside, letting me in.

"What the hell?" My locker door is covered in blood. It's streaked all down the gray paint and pooled on the floor in front. Resting in the middle are a dozen formerly white roses, now stained a sticky red, and a small teddy bear. Trina digs in her bag for her Canon and starts snapping photos.

"Evidence," she whispers, forehead scrunched in concentration.

Ben touches my elbow, and I flinch. "I don't think it's real blood," he suggests. "It's too bright. It looks like corn syrup mixed with red food coloring, like they did in old movies."

"Thanks, Sherlock," I spit. Then, I spin around and glare at all the shocked, vacant faces. "Who did this?" I shout. "Who saw something?"

No one says anything. They just stand there like a herd of big-eyed cows.

"Seriously? There are, like, eight hundred people in this school. *No one* saw who did this?" My locker alcove may be in a low-traffic zone, but this scene is unmissable.

My skin is hot; I can feel bright red blotches breaking out across my face and neck. This is not okay. This is taking things way, way too far. I reach down and snatch up the teddy bear. I need to throw something. I need everyone to get out of my face.

Adele lets out a shriek. The bow tied around the bear's neck falls to the side, and its head plops down into the pool of fake blood, splashing sticky red syrup on our boots. Yellow stuffing pokes out where its head should be. I'm so startled, I drop the body, and it sprays us with even more syrup.

"Shit." My hands are shaking.

"Who the hell did this?" Ben shouts into the crowd. No one answers.

"This is sick." Trina takes me by the shoulders and steers me away from the mess at my locker and toward the main hallway. "Let's get Ms. Walker, okay? She'll handle this."

A trip to the vice principal's office turns out to be unnecessary, because by the time we're halfway there, one of the Spanish teachers has noticed the crowd and suddenly all the teachers on the first floor seem to respond to some secret teacher radar, emerging from their classrooms to take charge. Everyone is ushered away from my locker and into homeroom. Ms. Walker is headed down the hall toward us. Someone must have called her.

"Amanda, please wait in my office, honey," she says. "You can help yourself to some coffee."

"I just need to wash my hands," I mumble.

She smiles at me kindly. "Of course. I'll be right back."

In the bathroom, I turn the water on as hot as it goes. My hands are still shaking as I run them under the stream. The water turns pink and then clear. Trina stays with me, dabbing at my boots with a wet paper towel. At least they're black; it's not going to stain.

A minute later, Adele bursts through the bathroom door.

"There you are. I couldn't find you."

I ignore her and stare at my face in the mirror above the sink. It's gone from blotchy red to pure white. I look like I'm in shock, which I guess I am. What *was* that? Fake blood. Teddy bears with severed heads. It's like I'm living in some Christopher Pike novel. What's next, a cow heart pinned to my desk with a butcher knife? Creepy chain letters and graveyard scavenger hunts?

"I thought you should see this." Adele is holding a little white envelope with my name scrawled across the front. "It was with the flowers. I grabbed it before the janitors came."

I take the envelope gingerly and flip it over. Inside is a white card, the kind florists use for writing greetings, but this one doesn't have a store logo. The note is in classic typewriter font, but the card looks laser-printed.

```
I asked you nicely. I told you he was no
good. Now you know I'm serious. Before
```

```
January 24, you will break Carter Shaw's
heart. Make it public, make it hurt. I
know I can count on you to make a scene.
End it—or I'll end things my way.
```

"What does it say?" Trina asks. I pass the card over. The look on Adele's face says she read it before she got here.

"'I asked you nicely'? What does that even mean?" Trina hands the card back to me.

"She wants Mandy to break up with Carter. Obviously."

"Isn't January twenty-fourth—?" Trina starts to ask.

"Carter's birthday," I finish for her. "That's two weeks away."

"Wow," Trina says. "That's just plain cruel."

"This bitch is out for blood." But even as I'm saying it, I have a tiny, nagging doubt that this was Rosalie. I want to rip up the note and flush it down the toilet, but I shove it in my bag instead. This is evidence.

"That email was such bullshit," Trina says. "She's all apologies one second and fake blood the next?"

"Maybe she has multiple personality disorder," Adele suggests. "Doesn't your mom have a patient like that?"

"It's called dissociative identity disorder now," Trina says. "Besides, you shouldn't casually diagnose."

I stare at myself in the mirror again. A little bit of color is starting to come back to my cheeks, and I pinch them to speed up the process. Unless Rosalie is truly brainless, which I'm pretty sure she's not, why would she do something that makes her look like a jealous freak in front of all of South? She'd have to know Carter would suspect her of targeting me. It wouldn't be a smart play. I smooth down my hair and check for mascara smudges. Then, I'm ready to get out of here.

"I have to go." I shove away from the sink and start toward the door. "Ms. Walker wants to see me."

"Do you need me to come with you?" Trina asks.

I shake my head, no. "I'm fine. Really. I'll handle this."

Adele and Trina stare at me, unblinking.

"Really." I raise my eyebrows at them. "I'm totally fine. You're both late to homeroom." Then I push open the door into the empty hall. Before I can get to Ms. Walker's office, my phone beeps. One new message from Private.

Your move, Princess.

I turn off my phone, the hard kind of shutdown that makes the screen go dead, and shove it to the bottom of my bag.

Three hours later, I'm sitting in the cafeteria with Carter, Graham, and Trina. The four of us have early lunch, which is the worst because I'm never hungry and then I'm always starving by sixth. Today, I can barely even sip my ginger ale. The smell of fryer grease and dish detergent makes my stomach heave.

By now, the entire school knows about the scene at my locker. The photos were all over Snapchat and Insta by homeroom. Carter was furious when he found out; Graham says he punched the whiteboard in Mr. Baum's class. Now his anger seems to have mellowed into a roving sort of concern. He alternates between petting my hair like I'm a puppy and shoving his hands in and out of his pockets.

"What did Ms. Walker have to say?" Graham asks through a mouthful of burger. Just watching everyone eat makes me want to puke.

"Mostly she asked a bunch of questions, like had anything unusual happened before, and did I have any idea who might have done something like this. She made me set up an appointment with the school counselor, and then she called my parents to appraise them of everything South is doing to ensure my safety. My mother was pissed, but she's pretty wrapped up in the museum benefit. Honestly she'll probably forget by tonight."

"So, do you?" Graham asks. "Have any idea who did it?"

I glance at Trina, a clear signal to keep her mouth shut. After three hours of not focusing in class, I'm more sure than ever that Rosalie didn't have anything to do with this. She doesn't go here; she wouldn't know my locker. And she wouldn't make herself look that bad in front of Carter. I need more time to think.

"No idea."

"I can't believe you're still here," Trina says. "You should take the rest of the day off, go home. Everyone would understand."

"Seriously, babe." Carter places his hand on top of my hand on the table. "I'll drive you. We can come back later for your car. You need to take it easy."

"I'm really fine," I insist. Going home is a sign of weakness. If whoever did this is here at South today, I need them to see me strong. Strong girls do not go home to cry to Mommy when someone pulls a *Carrie* at their locker.

For the rest of the day, everyone shows their support. Girls throw me sympathetic glances. Some supertall sophomore stops me in the hall to offer himself as my escort, which I politely decline. I smile at everyone and tell them how *grateful* I am to have *so many friends* at South and how I'm sure the school will get to the bottom of this childish prank in no time.

Inside, I'm a mess. I have to run to the bathroom between every class because my stomach is a swamp of anxiety. I'm filled with the ever-growing certainty that I'm dealing with something much bigger than Rosalie. And if it's not her, that means someone else is out to get me. Someone who wants to come between Carter and me, rip us apart. Someone who wants to scare me—or worse.

At the end of eighth, I pull out my phone and wait for it to reboot. But when the screen lights up, there are no new messages from Private. The last text is still from this morning. *Your move, Princess.* Somehow the silence is worse than anything that might have been there waiting.

12

ROSALIE

TUESDAY, JANUARY 9

Lily and I walk briskly home from the bus stop, although I'd rather take my time. The afternoon sun glints off stop signs and tractor sheds and the liquor store windows as we pass. It's a cold kind of sun, all flash and no fire. I squeeze Lily's hand and tuck my other glove up into the sleeve of my coat. At home, Dad will be waiting, watching the clock. In an hour, Carter will come to pick me up. I'd love to delay both interactions, but Sunday's screwup is still fresh.

"Can we read more *Anna, Banana* tonight?" Lily asks.

"Course," I agree. "I'm having dinner with Carter, but we'll read it before bed, okay?"

"Do you like him?" I swear my heart stops. She's looking up at me, her eyes big and lips parted just slightly.

I adjust my hand in hers, the fabric of our gloves scraping together. "Sure I do," I say after a minute. "Don't you think he's nice?"

"That's *not* what I mean." Lily twists away from me as if I'm making her say something embarrassing. "I mean, do you *like* him?"

I have no way of answering this. A thousand rusty nails collect in my throat. The thought of lying to her face makes me sick. But much as I love my little sister, I can't trust her with the truth. Not yet anyway.

"Sometimes you don't know right away," I say slowly, "if you like a person that way."

"Why does it take so long?" Lily asks, and the nails twist and scratch against my throat.

"You know how when you started kindergarten last year, you really wanted to be friends with Claire Beech? And you tried really hard, but she never wanted to play the same games as you?"

"Yeah." Lily pouts a bit at the memory. "What does that have to do with anything?"

"It can be hard to be friends, right? Even when you like a person and they're nice, sometimes you still don't have a lot in common. Well, dating is even more complicated. There's a lot to figure out."

"Oh." Lily twists her lips back and forth, trying to decide if she'll accept my shitty nonexplanation. I want more than anything to level with my sister. In my mind, I form all the sentences I can't say out loud. *No, I don't like Carter that way because he's a boy, and I like girls. The church believes same sex relationships are wrong, but the church isn't right about everything. And they're very, very wrong about this.* I don't want her to grow up with only the voices of the

Fellowship and our parents in her ears. I don't want her to grow up like I did, filled with prejudice and fear. Most of all, I don't want her to grow up to be afraid of me.

I keep my mouth shut. I vow to have a real conversation with Lily someday. As soon as it's safe. Whenever that will be.

When we get home, Lily scampers up to her room, and I wander toward the kitchen. I stop in the doorway; Dad's fixing a sandwich and blasting WRPK 96.5, his contemporary Christian music station, back turned toward me. The music's fine, at face value, but I can't stop my whole body from tensing up. As I hover in the doorway, I realize it's a Third Day song. I used to love them. I try to make my shoulders relax, afraid the Fellowship is crushing out of me everything I once enjoyed about being a Christian.

Mom's closing tonight, which means a slow ride home on the bus from downtown Logansville. She used to be an assistant case manager at the Office of Family Support. After we moved, she spent a year looking for a job in state government before becoming a Fresh Food Associate for a lot less cash.

Her job wasn't the only thing we sacrificed to move here. We gave up our house with only twelve years left on the mortgage, and I know my parents took a hit because we sold it in a rush. Our new house is smaller, darker; the listing said it "needed updating and plenty of TLC," but we haven't been able to give it much of either. I glance around our kitchen—peeling red-brown wallpaper trim, dinged-up and permanently stained linoleum floors, appliances that are relics from the eighties or nineties, whenever the house was built. It makes me sad and then furious when I think about it. How my family made so many sacrifices so they could save me. How we all believed I needed to be saved.

As I stand in the kitchen doorway watching Dad slather mustard on two slices of bread, I puzzle over the same question I've asked myself a thousand times in the last five years: What if I had just kept my mouth shut in seventh grade? It's a useless exercise that always leads backs to the same answer. When you're raised to believe that homosexuality is the fast track to hell, but that people can change, that we can be made new creations in Christ Jesus, silence isn't an option. Not when you're thirteen. Not when fear turns to broken glass on your tongue. Better spit it out.

Dad doesn't see me hovering. I stand still for a moment longer, trying to unclench my muscles, music still pulsing around me, and my thoughts wander back to yesterday in the woods. The flash in the trees. The footsteps. Someone was watching me. I watch my father spear two olives with a fork and put them on his plate. Ever since Carter came into my life, my parents have been more relaxed than they've been since seventh grade. But that kind of deep, faith-based suspicion and fear doesn't just go away. I know they're still terrified for my salvation.

I wrap my arms across my stomach and let my head fall against the door frame.

Dad spins around. "Rosalie. Didn't hear you come in."

"Hey, Dad." I give him a small smile. His eyes flick up to the clock above the stove, then back to the counter. He turns the radio down, and my shoulders drop.

"Want me to leave this out for you?" He gestures toward the sandwich fixings in front of him. I keep my eyes trained on his face.

"That's okay. Carter's picking me up soon."

"That's right!" His face opens up. "Date night."

He wants, so badly, to believe his little girl is straight, cured, saved. The assurances of Counselor Michael and Camp Eternal Light only went so far. In his eyes, Carter is living proof, the salve for my parents' fears. I scuff the toe of my shoe against my pant leg and try to smile.

"I'd like you to invite him to come to service with us on Sunday," he says. "Your mom and I are eager to introduce Carter to our family at God's Grace."

My chest gets tight. "I think he has church with his own family." It's probably true, but that's not the point. Carter can't come to God's Grace. Not ever, definitely not now that Amanda knows. There are too many people in the congregation. Too many eyes.

"They'd all be welcome," he says. "We would love to meet his family. You'll ask him tonight." It's not a question.

I nod, although there's just no way. My parents and Carter's parents will never meet. I can make up some excuse this time, but I have no idea how I'm going to put this off indefinitely. My heart hurts because I *want* to make my parents happy. And in the end, I can only let them down. They will never love me for me. The dark cloud always hovering at the back of my mind starts swirling and churning, making my vision go gray. It's not my fault, but then why do I still feel like a failure? In the eyes of the church, that's exactly what I am. My breath is getting shallow. The web is snapping, one thread, two.

"And, Rosalie?" He's holding something out to me, a small box. "Your mom and I have been waiting to give this to you, but now that things are starting to get serious between you and Carter, we agreed the time is right."

I reach out, take the box. It's feather-light and fits in the palm of my hand.

"Well, open it," Dad says, beaming.

I tear off the silver wrapping paper, then lift the cardboard lid. Inside, a ring. Its silver band is adorned with a cross etched into a small silver heart. Along the outside of the band, Psalm 51:10 is engraved: *Create in me a pure heart, O God.*

"Try it on," he says, and I slip the band onto my finger.

I force a smile. "It fits."

"This ring is a reminder of your self-worth, Rosalie. We want you to remember who you are, how important it is that you don't give away any pieces of yourself."

I swallow, hard. Dad reaches over and plucks a small piece of paper from the bottom of the box. It's a pledge card. "Let's read this together," he says.

Heart pounding, I find my voice: *"Today I make a commitment to purity—to God, myself, my family, and my future mate—until the day I enter into a biblical marriage relationship."*

My heart squeezes a little in my chest, and at the same time, a peel of laughter threatens to burst through my lips. I know how much this means to my parents, how much they care, no matter how misguided their thinking. But there's no place for the love I share with Paulina in that pledge. I'll never "enter into a biblical marriage relationship," not the way the Fellowship defines it. It's sad and infuriating and somehow wildly hilarious all at once. I choke the laugh into a cough that makes Dad's eyes crease.

"I'm sorry," I gasp. "I just need some water."

"We want you to take this seriously."

"I do." I drain a glass at the sink, get myself together. In the most literal sense, I've just pledged my abstinence until the grave. "Carter feels the same," I assure him. "We've already discussed it."

Dad nods, appeased by my lie. He puts everything back in the fridge, then picks up his plate. "Be sure to send Carter in when he gets here," he calls, pressing past me and into the den.

I stand frozen in the doorway for a minute, alone. The ring is snug on my finger.

Upstairs, I glance into Lily's room. She's curled up on her bed with a stack of library books. After I move out, I'll keep up both lives as long as I can, but I have this terrible fear that someday, no matter what I do, I'll lose her forever. I blow her noisy kisses from the doorway until she looks up and giggles, then I slip into my room and close the door, jamming the desk chair beneath the knob. I'd rather spend tonight goofing off with my sister, but Carter will be here in fifteen minutes. I open up my closet and take my shoe box down.

An hour later, Carter and I are seated in a booth in the far back corner of the Wheeling Eat'n Park. He keeps fiddling with his menu, even though he always orders the same thing: the Original Breakfast Smile with bacon, scrambled eggs, home fries, and white toast. I can barely think about food, but when the server comes, I ask for a turkey club and iced tea out of habit.

I can't stop glancing around the restaurant. Of all the places we go, the Wheeling Eat'n Park seems safest. Logansville has its own Eat'n Park, plus another diner and a bunch of classy restaurants. Why would anyone in Amanda's crew, or anyone from Logansville for that matter, drive almost an hour to get the same eggs and fried potatoes they could get right in town? Still, my entire body has been on high alert from the second I heard the crunch of Carter's tires in our drive.

When the server leaves to put in our order and we're alone again, I glance around the diner one more time, then look Carter in the eye.

"Something happened. We have to talk."

A muscle twitches in his cheek, and he jams his fingers into his hair. "How did you . . . ? I mean, what happened?"

"Don't freak out, but I got an email yesterday. From Amanda. I don't know how she found out, but she did. And she's not happy."

"Oh." Carter's face gets hard, those boyish lines settling into something distinctly grown up. He starts tearing at the corner of his paper napkin. "Shit."

"Yeah, shit." I stare down at the table. I want to accuse him of lying to me, misleading me about their supposed "arrangement." But I've been complicit in hearing only what I want to hear. And besides, now I need to ask him to lie. One more time. I take a deep breath, in and out, but the guilt clings tight to my insides. "Can you tell her we went out tonight, and I ended things?"

"Are you breaking up with me?" Carter asks. "Because if you met someone else, or changed your mind—"

"No!" My voice is too loud. I grip the tabletop until my knuckles turn white. "Nothing has to change, but she needs to think I broke it off, okay?" So she'll stop digging. So she'll never find out about Pau.

Carter looks up from the scraps of his napkin. He reaches across the table and takes my hands, prying my fingers from the table's edge. "You're a saint, Rosalie Bell, you know that? I wish

I could be more for you. I'm sorry it has to be like . . . how things are right now. I'll talk to her, promise."

He runs the pads of his thumbs across my hands, across the ring. "What's this?"

"Oh." I look down at the cross etched into the little silver heart. "It's a purity ring. Basically I'm engaged to God until marriage." I crack a half smile.

"A gift from your parents?"

"Yeah. They want to make sure we don't, you know . . ."

Carter smiles at me then, big and genuine. "You know I respect you a lot, right, Rosalie? Your parents don't have anything to worry about." I nod and pull my hands slowly away from his.

"What did you think I was going to say?" I ask, forcing a change in subject.

"Huh?"

"You started to say something, earlier. When I said that something had happened."

Before he can open his mouth, our server is back with our drinks. I mumble thank you and slip the wrapper off my straw.

When she's gone, Carter says, "Something happened at school today, and at first, I thought . . ." His voice trails off. I take a big gulp of my iced tea, no sugar, no lemon, lots of ice.

"Thought what?"

He shakes his head. "There was no way you could have known."

I look at him, puzzled, and our food comes. When we first got here, I didn't think I could eat, but now I'm starving. I sink my teeth into my turkey club, and it tastes amazing. Carter picks at his bacon.

"It's about Amanda. Is it okay if I talk about it?"

"Oh." Now I get why he's being weird. "Yeah, sure. Okay."

"Someone did something to her locker this morning. They poured fake blood on it; it was kind of scary."

"Oh wow." I didn't think popular girls got bullied at school.

"I've been furious all day. Who would do something like that?"

I give Carter a small, sympathetic smile, then return to my sandwich.

"But now that I'm here, I'm thinking about it all different."

"How's that?"

"No one messes with Amanda. She's not always the most"—he leans forward and lowers his voice—"generous person. But I literally can't think of a single person at school who would do this to her."

I can feel the color drain out of my face. I don't like where Carter's going with this. He can't seriously think *I* poured fake blood on Amanda's locker.

"Carter—" I start to say.

"But what if she did it?" he asks, cutting me off. "To her own locker?"

"What?" The blood rushes back all at once, whooshes through my ears.

"Hear me out. Amanda found out about us, right? You said you got that email yesterday. So she's pissed, and feeling kind of down? You don't know her. No attention is bad attention."

My mind reels back to the anonymous texts she claimed to be getting. "So," I say slowly, thinking it out, "what better way to get everyone's sympathy, and especially your boyfriend's, than to make the whole school think someone's out to get you?"

"Exactly." Carter piles a huge forkful of eggs onto a piece

of toast, but leaves it sitting on his plate. "You think you really know someone, but then something like this happens. I just feel really confused." A shadow passes over his face, something dark and fragile that I can't penetrate. I stare down into my iced tea, not sure where he's gone.

"I'm sorry," I say after a minute.

Carter lifts his head and gives me a weak smile. Whatever was there a moment ago is gone. "I'm the one who should apologize. Laying all this Amanda shit on you isn't fair." For the second time tonight, he reaches across the table to give my hand a gentle squeeze.

When the server comes back with our check, Carter pays.

"I'll talk to her," he promises on the drive back to my house. "We're having dinner tomorrow. I'll tell her then."

"Thanks." It's only seven o'clock, but outside, the world is a deep January dark. The moon plays hopscotch through the bare tree branches on the side of the road, casting a gray-yellow pallor across Carter's face, the dashboard, my own hands. I shove them between my knees.

This too shall pass. A Sufi poet wrote that all the way back in the middle ages. Carter will say I ended things. Soon, this will all blow over.

13

Carter insists on taking me to Verde for dinner, a four-course consolation prize for yesterday's mental and emotional anguish. Except for a few people still throwing me sympathetic glances in the hall, school was basically back to normal today. Ben following me around like a wannabe knight. Adele and Graham bickering like an old married couple. Bronson practicing parkour in the sixth-floor stairwell and Trina treating the occasion like a photo shoot. I let myself relax into the normalcy of it all. And most importantly, into the radio silence from Private. By the time I'm seated with Carter at a window table with the comforting view of twee Logansville in front of us, I can almost pretend that none of this creepy stuff ever happened. That there isn't a stalker, Rosalie or otherwise. Almost.

The only thing that isn't normal tonight is Carter. He's been all fidgety and extra attentive from the moment I climbed into his car. He even insisted on driving across the street to pick me up in my own driveway. After the waitress takes our order, he worries the corner of his napkin as if he could tear through the cloth.

"What's up with you tonight?" I finally ask.

"Huh?"

"You're all distracted and nervy. I thought I was supposed to be the head case."

"Sorry," Carter breathes into the tablecloth.

The waitress returns with our Perrier and two tiny rectangular plates.

"An amuse-bouche from the chef," she says. "Seared diver scallops on a bed of micro arugula and spring onions. Please enjoy."

Carter waits until I have a mouthful of scallop and micro greens to speak. "I've stopped seeing her. I wanted you to know."

I barely keep it together, washing the food down with a gulp of sparkling water. He's never mentioned Rosalie, not once, clearly thought I was in the dark. Her heart-to-heart must have come as a real shock.

I take a deep breath. "When?"

"Last night. She ended things."

"So that's what this dinner is really about?" Heat flashes across the back of my neck. "The tasting menu at Verde, Carter? Sorry I cheated, but it's over now?" I immediately regret my words. Yes, he should be sorry. I don't deserve any of this. But lashing out makes me sound like a baby. "I'm sorry," I say quickly, softly. "I'm glad you told me."

Somehow that concession makes me feel even worse. I'm

hysterical or weak. Pushy or a pushover. I look to him for reassurance I haven't ruined everything.

"Things are going to be different now, okay?" he says, and I can breathe again. "Trust me when I say I feel terrible. I want tonight to be special. This is a new us."

"A new beginning." This is all I've wanted since the day Trina showed me those pictures. Carter ending things with Rosalie. Carter making a real commitment to us again. But now that I'm getting exactly what I want, why do I still feel so shaken?

"A new beginning," Carter repeats. "It was just a slip. You know you're my everything. You and me, always and forever."

The waitress returns with our first course, four white tubes of bone holding richly roasted marrow served with toasted country bread, shallots, and a small dish of sea salt.

With a tiny fork, I remove the marrow from one of the bones and spread it across a slab of toast, and suddenly, I know why I'm still shaken. Carter didn't end things with Rosalie. *She* ended things with *him*. Because I told her to. All roads lead back to Carter and me, but what I wanted—all I've ever really wanted—was for Carter to decide on his own that he doesn't need other girls. That I'm enough, all he'll ever need. Is that too much to ask? My mother's voice rings loud in my ears. *You can't hold on too tight, Amanda. A tight leash snaps.*

"I'll be right back." I stand and lean across the table to give Carter a quick kiss. His wavy hair tickles my forehead. "I just need to run to the restroom. The marrow's really rich."

Carter smiles and raises a piece of toast. "Don't take too long, babe."

I have to wait for the restroom, so I lean against the

forest-green wallpaper and stare out the front window, try to take deep breaths. Across the street, a broad-shouldered man in a dusty black jacket, black snow cap, and tan work boots walks into Papa John's. A couple of years ago, there was a petition to remove chain restaurants from the small grid of tree-lined streets and Victorian buildings that make up Logansville's downtown. The community board lost the fight, but they did manage to pass a mandate requiring all business establishments within the downtown radius to put up facades in Logansville's mauve, gold, and navy. So now we have the classiest Starbucks, Papa John's, and Panera in West Virginia.

The restroom door finally opens, and I slip inside. I'm sure Rosalie didn't trash my locker, at least not personally. But she could have been working with someone at South. There's something way too easy about her apologetic email and lightning-fast move to dump Carter, exactly like I asked. I turn on my phone and pull up Private's last message. Then, I start typing.

> **You say you're not Rosalie. Prove it. Your move, Creep.**

When I get back to the table, Carter's watching the big man in the black jacket walk out of Papa John's with two pizza boxes and a two-liter bottle of Coke. The facade may be fancy now, but it's still the same subpar pizza. I just do not understand why anyone would go there when you could get a wood-fired pie from Taviani's right down the street. The man swings open the door to his truck, and I catch a glimpse of his face. It's Ben and David's dad.

"It's sad," I say, diverting the topic of discussion from Rosalie to something new. If this is really a new chapter for us, I'm ready to start writing it. "The way that family lives."

"Mmm." Carter acknowledges my observation without agreeing or disagreeing, and I immediately wish I could take the words back, swallow them deep inside my chest with all the other echoes of my mother's words I'd love to un-say. Maybe if the Kellys ordered a little more Papa John's and a little less Taviani's, we wouldn't be in such deep debt. The next course, steaming bowls of house-made bucatini all'Amatriciana, arrives, and I hope Carter will forget I said anything about the Gallaghers. He raises a forkful of pasta to his mouth and blows gently. "I feel bad for Ben," he says after a minute. "But not Mr. Gallagher. He only has himself to blame."

I pause, pasta halfway to my lips, and swallow. My mouth feels suddenly dry. It's a well-known fact that Ben's dad and Carter's dad don't get along, but I've never known the details. Some business stuff gone wrong. Mr. Gallagher used to work for Shaw Realty as a fancy kind of contractor, I think. Now he works hard-hat gigs, houses and condos, that sort of thing.

"What happened exactly?"

"With Crooked Carl Gallagher?" I've never seen so much animosity flash across Carter's typically altruistic face. "He screwed Shaw out of a bunch of projects back in the early two thousands. It was before we had the infrastructure we have now. My dad says Carl was siphoning clients to Firth and Sons, right before they signed an agreement with Shaw. Shaw would do all the legwork, and then Firth and Sons would get the gig. They were giving Carl some colossal 'referral fee' for stealing our clients for them. When my dad found out, he went ballistic, sued the shit out of Firth.

Crooked Carl destroyed his own business cred; the Gallagher name is dirt in realty now. He hasn't pulled a major client since."

"Oh." I force a tiny bite of pasta past my lips. "Remind me why we let Ben hang around?"

Carter frowns. "Ben's not his dad. You shouldn't blame him for how his parents screwed up."

I open my mouth to protest, to say I didn't even know Carl Gallagher's history until this second, how could I blame Ben for what his dad did, when it hits me that that's exactly what I'm doing. It's what I've always done with Ben. No, I didn't know the details. But strip away the gangly legs, the dweeby grin, the lacking social graces, and Ben is exactly who I'd be if my parents didn't keep up their iron-clad facade. I imagine our piles of debt laid bare like the Gallaghers' business scandal. Bankruptcy, social disgrace. It must have been easier for David somehow; he figured out how to keep his chin up, shake it off. But who's to say I'll be so resilient? If I lose Carter. If my family's shell cracks. I'm a complete bitch to Ben because I'm terrified that if we fall apart, I'll *be* him.

"You're right," I say, and Carter stares at me, surprised. "I never knew all that about his dad. That's terrible."

"Yeah, well." Carter mops at the side of his bowl with a piece of crust. "It all worked out in the end, I guess. Firth and Sons went out of business and Shaw Realty is the top firm in the state. You don't mess with the Shaws."

I smile. The fact that Carter can be friends with Ben despite their family's history says a lot. Carter's a good guy. Really good. It doesn't matter, in the end, who left whom. Rosalie's out of the picture, and Carter and I are finally back in a good place. I resolve to try to be nicer to Ben.

My good mood carries all the way through our final courses, rosemary-crusted lamb chops and chocolate soufflé. We chat about the photography exhibit Trina's planning for senior showcase—a series of old-fashioned portraits of our friends in twenty-first-century settings—and focus on the positive. Carter and Rosalie are over. We are back on track.

I kiss Carter good night in his driveway. It's only a little after nine; he looks disappointed when I say I have reading for French, but it's true. One night a week, I drive into the city to take college-level French literature at Chatham University, and the spring semester just started this week. I've been learning French since I was basically a baby; I skipped right to AP in ninth grade, so I've been taking college-level for years, and I'll major in French at WVU. I'm not sure yet what I'll do with the degree, but I'll have plenty of time to figure it out while Carter focuses on growing into his shoes at the firm. As I walk up the drive toward my house, my heart is still swollen with happiness over tonight's turn of events. For the first time in a long time, I don't have to worry about tomorrow.

When I let myself inside, I can hear the TV blaring from Dad's office. I slip off my shoes and hang my coat in the hall closet while some sports announcer lays the tragedy on thick in a story about a promising young athlete's career cut short in a drinking and driving accident.

"Amanda?" I've barely seen my dad in days. I pad quickly across the living room floor—my toes curling against the fibers of the ornate area rug that's more striking and somber than it is plush and warm—and stop in to give him a quick hug and tell him about my date. Dad's office is just a touch more lived-in than the rest of the house. I like it in here; it smells like his cologne and the old books that line the shelves. His desk is sturdy, formidable, but there are papers spread across the top, and the couch is cozy brown leather that's just starting to crack. Linda's been angling to replace it for months, but Dad's held firm. He listens to me chatter about Carter and Verde and nods happily. After a few minutes, though, I can tell he's anxious to get back to his email.

I say good night and slip quietly into the kitchen, expecting to find my mother, but the room is dark. She must have taken her third drink up to their bedroom. I hurry up the stairs and tiptoe over to their door. There's no crack of light spilling into the hall, only darkness. Maybe she had something for the museum tonight, something I've forgotten. When I press my ear to the door, I don't hear breathing.

When I'm in my room, I close the door and click on my phone. I've been in such a good mood since dinner, I almost forgot about the text I sent Private in the bathroom line. Now I have five new messages waiting.

> You want proof, Princess? Looks like
> your boyfriend isn't the only person
> Culver Ridge's biggest tease has
> been kissing. Would Rosalie send you
> these?

The next three messages are photos of two girls outside, in a wooded area. The shots are a little blurry, like they were taken from a distance on maximum zoom. I don't know the Latina girl, but I recognize Rosalie's angled haircut immediately. In the first two pictures, they're sitting on the ground, backs pressed against a tree, talking. The Latina girl has something in her hand, maybe a cigarette. I scroll down to the third photo and my jaw drops.

The last photo is the clearest. Rosalie and the other girl are kissing. Obviously, unmistakably kissing. I tap the photo to enlarge it. This is not some friendly peck. Mouths open, bodies pressed together tight.

Holy freaking shit.

While Carter's been cheating on me, Rosalie's been cheating on him—with a girl.

I tap the photo again, restoring it to normal size, and scroll down to the last text.

> Do you believe me now?

My fingers hover over the reply box. Private is definitely not Rosalie. So who the hell is harassing me? A cold shiver runs down my spine. This creep could actually be dangerous.

> I believe you.

The response comes right away.

> Good. Now send these along to peter.bell@SVHS.org

> Let Daddy put Rosalie out of action for good.

ROSALIE

WEDNESDAY, JANUARY 10

The Winter Campaign—the largest of the church's three annual fund drives—is an all-hands-on-deck situation, so by four o'clock I'm stationed at a card table in the God's Grace basement filing donor cards. *$25 gift, $50 gift, $15 gift. Paid, Outstanding, Paid.* The dollar signs shimmer and swirl on the baby blue cards, the cash adding up to a renewed investment in Brother Masters's To Seek and Save program. More outreach potential. More counselors trained statewide and expanding across the South. More people like clammy-skinned Michael to carry out "God's work." More damage that lingers for days that become years, baring its rotten teeth and then sinking them in deep. Promising to never really go away. I twitch involuntarily and squeeze my hands into the warm space between my knees.

"Are you all right, Rosalie?" Mrs. Hagan, the drive leader, is standing in front of me with a new stack of cards she's collected from callers around the room. Out of the corner of my eye, I catch Emily Masters's smirk. She's stationed at the next table over, explaining the filing system to two new volunteers who have just arrived.

"Of course." I pull my hands from under the table, hold them out to receive the cards with a smile. "How was your time in Baltimore?"

"Blessed." She places them in my hands. "Mr. Hagan shared the good news about our grandbaby?"

I nod. "Congratulations."

"It's such a blessing," she repeats. "Another child to be raised up in God's house."

A thin sheen of sweat breaks across the back of my neck. It's what my parents said about Lily when she was born. What they must have said about me. For my entire childhood, I wanted nothing more than to do right in God's eyes. To make Him proud. Even now, I still want a relationship with God, something not dictated by a fundamentalist interpretation of scripture. Something I haven't figured out yet. But in this particular house of God, I am an unwelcome guest.

Mrs. Hagan is flagged down by a volunteer with a question, and I glance across the room, searching for Mom. In her eyes, Brother Masters's good work saved her daughter from the devil's path. It's deeply personal in a way that makes the beads of sweat turn to ice on my skin.

But Julia Bell's calling station is empty. My eyes dart around the room until they find her in the doorway to the kitchen, deep in conversation with a tall woman with thick, salt-and-pepper hair that spills all the way down her back and shimmers in the neon basement lights. She's facing away from me, but even from behind, I'd be able to recognize a member of the God's Grace congregation. Before I can give too much thought to who she might be, Mom's eyes catch mine. I'm staring. She takes the woman by the elbow and pulls her gently into the kitchen. The door swings shut behind them.

I tear my eyes away, back to the stack of cards. The first one boasts a thousand-dollar gift.

After dinner, I help Lily get ready for bed while Dad outlines his lesson plan and Mom returns to God's Grace to help Mrs. Hagan clean up. When I close the door to my room, it's eight thirty. Carter and Amanda are probably at dinner right now. He's going to tell her we broke up, or maybe he already has. She'll believe him or she won't believe him. How good a liar is Carter Shaw?

I pick up my phone and text Pau.

Thinking of you.

Three little dots hover for a minute. Then, a rainbow of heart emojis fills up the screen.

I'm always thinking about you.

Going to a GSA meet-up with Ramon
after school tomorrow. Come with?

Like Gay Straight Alliance?

It's Gender & Sexualities Alliance now.

My fingers hover over the screen. Pau's always inviting me to come with her to meet-ups like this. Pride celebrations. Youth events. Things out teens do. My whole body aches for that kind of connection to the LGBTQ+ community. But sneaking around with Pau is barely safe. Doing something public is out of the question. You never know who might see you at a GSA meet-up. Who might tell your parents. I'm glad Ramon is home for winter break, that he can go with her.

Have to babysit Lily tomorrow. Clearing on Friday?

There's a pause before Pau responds.

Sure, I'll be there.

Hey Pau?

Yeah?v

You know I love you, right?

Of course I know. Wish we could skip ahead to Fri.

I'll set my time machine.

I tackle my homework and Paulina and I text back and forth until it's getting close to ten, then I head down to the kitchen to get a glass of water. When I pass by the den, my parents are sitting together on the couch, watching the news on one of the five local channels we get through the converter box. It's more coverage about that college basketball player who was killed in a drunk-driving accident early this morning. I guess he was supposed to take his team to the finals this year, get recruited into the NBA, go all the way.

It's really sad, but I don't know why my parents insist on watching this stuff. They're news junkies, addicted to the latest tragedy. Mom writes down names and includes them in her prayers. She prays they took Jesus into their hearts before they died, that he's watching over them now. And what if they didn't? I want to ask. How will your prayers help if they're burning in hell?

I duck into the kitchen and turn on the tap. I can still hear the news from the other room. The boy's mother is speaking now, her voice high and thin and on the verge of breaking. Outside, there's something else. The crunch of footsteps on gravel.

The kitchen window faces the wrong way, but the sound is unmistakable. There's someone walking down our driveway. Heart pounding, I slip out of the kitchen and back past the den into the living room. Then I stand on my tiptoes and peek through the little square of glass in the front door. It's completely dark out, but the porch lamp casts a glow on my parents' car in the drive and the little strip of grass that leads around the side of the house. For a minute, there's nothing, then a long shadow falls across the grass, caught in the lamp's yellow light. Someone is standing around back, on the grass that separates the shed from the mudroom. Someone very tall and willowy, or made so in their shadow's elongated cast. My breath catches, and the figure disappears.

Hands trembling, I check the door, make sure both the lock and dead bolt are secure. Then I walk quickly and silently back across the house.

"Rosalie?" Mom calls from the den.

I freeze.

"Just getting some water." I slip into the kitchen and grab the serrated bread knife from the butcher's block, then slip through the door that connects the kitchen to the mudroom. It's completely dark in here, but I'm afraid to switch on the light. I can feel the blood drumming against my ears. I inch closer to the door, stepping over boots and hats and Lily's T-ball mitt. I clench the knife handle tight.

When I get to the door, it's locked. I breathe in deep. There's no window, just a peephole. I press my eye to the tiny circle of glass.

Outside, all I can see is dark. It takes a moment for my eyes to adjust. Finally, I can make out the grass and the outline of the shed. I stand still for a minute that becomes two that becomes five, watching and listening. There's nothing. Whoever was here before is gone.

Eventually, my heartbeat slows to something resembling normal. I slip back into the kitchen and return the knife, then I check the window, making sure it's latched. I want to check the windows in the den too, but my parents are still in there. I slip upstairs instead. The door to Lily's room is half open, and I peek inside. She's in bed holding the pink stuffed cat she always sleeps with, breathing soundly. I tiptoe across her floor and make sure her window is latched, then check all the windows upstairs before going into my room and closing the door.

I can't prove the person I saw in the woods on Monday was the same person at our house tonight. But deep in my bones, I know it was. I would not put it past my parents to have me watched at school. But at our own house?

I switch off the overhead light but keep the lamp by my bed lit, then slip under the covers still wearing my clothes. I lie perfectly still. I leave my glasses on. I wish I'd kept the knife. For a long time, sleep doesn't come. Scraps of memory from afternoons in the cold church office in our old town blend together with Donovan and Carter and camp until it's all one thick swirl of fear. The person outside is watching me. The person outside is waiting to pounce. Finally around three, I slip into a shallow kind of sleep, that misty, tensile space between memory and dream.

I'm in Pastor Ray's office at Camp Eternal Light, crouched behind the desk and pressing the only phone on the grounds to my ear. I have exactly seven minutes until he's back from his morning stroll around the premises. I've been timing him for the three days since they released me from isolation, waiting for my chance. On the other end of the line, Dad's voice: "Hello?"

"It's Rosalie," I whisper. "I don't have a lot of time." In words that tremble and break, I tell him about the locked room and the dead wasps, the weight I've lost from meals they didn't bring, how I'm afraid they'll put me back there if they catch me on the phone.

At thirteen, I was too embarrassed to tell my parents what really went on during my sessions with Counselor Michael. I trusted, then, in his authority, let his version of the story—talk therapy, prayer—become the narrative my parents believed. But I can't protect them from this. I need to get out of here, need their help. If they know the truth, they'll come for me.

"Rosalie." Dad cuts me off, his voice an axe splitting wood. The words dissolve to sawdust in my throat.

"You've chosen a wicked path. This sickness has its claws in you, and you must suffer to be redeemed." Behind the desk, I cough and splutter. His accusations clash and spit. Is liking girls a choice or a sickness? It can't be both.

"If your faith in Christ Jesus were stronger, you would not find yourself in this position. Only your faith can save you."

The words spin around and around in my head, won't settle into something I can say to make him understand. Soon, it doesn't matter. There's only dead air on the other end of the line.

I wake with a start, clothes clinging to my skin and sheets soaked with sweat. I suck in one jagged breath, then another, then another until my heart settles in my chest. It's been months since I've woken like this, bathed in a slick film of fear and shaking from dreams that are reality made sharper in the dark. It used to happen almost nightly. In our old town, I'd startle awake from a dream about a girl, the toss of her hair in the breeze, the berry scent of her body lotion still lingering, even after I was sitting up in bed, heart pounding. I'd force myself to stay awake, determined not to dream my way into hell. It's not a habit I want to repeat.

I don't remember falling back asleep, and when my alarm goes off, it feels like I didn't sleep at all.

AMANDA
THURSDAY, JANUARY 11

On Thursday, I sit down at the dining room table with both my parents for the second time since Christmas. I used Linda's Amex to go shopping after school again today, and I'm feeling good about the reasonable yet impressive spread I assembled from the prepared foods counter. But as I dish chicken scaloppini and fingerling potatoes onto our plates, it's hard to ignore the fact that my parents are hardly talking.

Dad takes a bite and chews slowly. "Did you cook this?" His question is directed at my mother, who says nothing. "It's not that chef again, is it?"

She stiffens in her chair.

"I cooked," I jump in before she can respond. "Well, I prepared. It's from the store."

Jack frowns but keeps eating. He wishes Linda would cook more, or at all, and I hold my breath and will him not to pick that fight. Not right now. Not when we're all actually eating together and this meal was *almost* as inexpensive as homemade.

"Carter took me to Verde last night," I volunteer before he can decide to press. I've already told Dad about our date, but my mother, typically, wasn't up yet when I left for school this morning. "The lamb was really excellent."

"Any occasion?" she asks, raising her wineglass to her lips. She takes a small sip in a pointed exercise of restraint; I'd bet she has fund-raising calls to make after we're finished.

I want to tell her about Rosalie—that her exit from Carter's life was the occasion—but she'll find a way to twist around whatever I say. She'll make this about me gloating, not celebrating. She'll find a way to make it about herself.

"He was just taking care of me. After that stuff with my locker at school."

My mother takes a larger sip. "What stuff with your locker?" Dad asks. So I guess Linda didn't find the school's call important enough to share.

"Nothing," I say quickly, sensing the three of us edging dangerously near another fight. "Some prank. Carter was concerned about me, that's all."

"I hope you weren't too needy." My mother frowns into her fingerling potatoes. "It's nice that Carter took you out, but you have to grow a thicker skin. You're a beautiful young woman from a good family. Kids"—she gestures with her glass, a few drops of Chardonnay splashing onto the table—"are bound to act out of jealousy from time to time. You have to show Carter you're strong, that you're up for the job of being his partner.

Because it is a job, Amanda. Don't forget it."

I'm not sure whether her last statement is directed at me, my dad, or herself. Visions of steely, resplendent Robin Wright flash before my eyes. *House of Cards* is my mother's favorite show for a reason.

Dad stands abruptly and takes his plate into the kitchen, leaving me alone with Linda at the dining room table.

"I wasn't needy," I say, my voice small. "When Carter dropped me off, he wasn't ready for the night to end."

"Good," she replies, her words clipped. "Always leave him wanting more."

By the time I've finished clearing the plates, my father has retreated into his office and my mother has stationed herself in the dining room to make a round of calls to future Museum of Fine Arts donors. With the benefit less than two weeks away, her fund-raising efforts have been ramping up. She seems more stressed than usual about meeting her goal, which is entirely performative, because Linda Kelly *always* meets her goal. I slip upstairs before I get assigned a section of the call list. I've had enough of my mother's priorities tonight.

In my room, I perch in my desk chair and check my phone. No new messages from Private since the instruction to email that kiss shot to Rosalie's dad last night. First me, now Rosalie. Maybe I haven't been giving Private enough credit. Maybe this was never really about *me*. Maybe Private's end game is to take *Carter* down.

I try to think it all through. Rosalie only broke up with him two nights ago. When Private sent me the photos, she or he or whoever might not have known that Rosalie had already ended things. I have no love to spare for Rosalie Bell, but she broke it off. My business with her is done. Whoever else she kisses is beside the point, and anyway, I don't know this girl's family. If she's bi or whatever, outing her would be majorly vile.

I switch on my phone again and stare at the selfie of Carter and me on New Year's, the night all this began. We're stunning, but are we happy? I pick up the framed picture, the one of the two of us from our ninth-grade spring formal, and compare. My hair is done up in silly beauty pageant curls, and Carter's shoulders barely fill out his suit. One of the spaghetti straps on my dress is slipping down my arm. But both of our faces glow. I look back to my phone. On New Year's, we're dressed exactly right, posed exactly right. We look polished and elegant. Picture-perfect. But no, I decide, not happy. I switch the background shot on my phone to a selfie of Adele and me goofing around in oversized flannel pajama sets over winter break.

Then I take a deep breath. Carter and Rosalie are done. He took me to Verde to apologize and start over. Things are going to be better now, as soon as I can get this Private creep off our backs. We can be happy again. We're already halfway there.

I press my fingertips against my temples and try to think. Carter's birthday is in thirteen days. That's still a lot of time. I need to think two steps ahead, make a move before Private does.

I send the photos to myself, then open a new message and attach them.

Subject: Just thought you should know
From: me
To: Rosalie Bell

I'm not trying to scare you or anything,
but I wasn't kidding about those
anonymous texts. I know they're not
from you, but someone is out to get
me, and looks like they're out to get
you too. The texter sent me these with
instructions to send them to your dad.

Don't freak, okay? I didn't do it,
and I'm not going to. As long as you
stay out of Carter's life, we're good,
and honestly I don't want to waste
another second thinking about you, but
in case you don't want people knowing
you kiss other girls, consider this a
heads-up that someone wants to blow up
your spot.

You owe me.

—AK

I close out of my email and text Private.

Mission accomplished.

You emailed her dad?

I handled it my way.

Your way?

Straight to Rosalie herself.

Don't make me angry, Amanda.
I did not say you could do that.

You don't get to tell me what to do.

Silence. I've won. I turn off my screen and open up *Julie, ou la nouvelle Héloïse*, which I'm reading for class at Chatham. I curl into the pillow wall on my bed and let myself get lost in the story for over an hour until something that sounds like tiny pebbles pings against my window. A second later, it happens again. Carter hasn't thrown pebbles at my bedroom window since freshman year. My stomach fills with a rush of butterflies, and my fingers fly up to clasp the onyx heart at my neck.

I switch off the overhead light so I can see out, then pad over to the window. My bedroom looks out on the side of the house, a strip of landscaped flower beds that dissolve into a rock garden. I can't see much directly below me, but the garden lights are on. There's no one out there, but something that looks like little pieces of paper is scattered across the rocks. Love notes? The butterflies rise into my chest.

I slip on a warm sweater and shoes. Downstairs, Dad's still in his office, but the dining room is dark. It's a little after ten, too late to make donor calls. I grab a flashlight from the drawer and walk out the sliding glass doors onto the back deck.

Outside, I switch on the deck lights, but there's no one back here, either. I shine my flashlight on the lawn leading out to the gazebo and pool. Nothing.

Then I walk around the side of the house to the rock garden. Before I even get all the way down the path, I can see what the little pieces of paper really are. Not love notes—photographs. A million prints of the same picture: Rosalie and Carter, one arm wrapped tight around her waist, her face turned to the side, following the direction of his fingertips. His face is turned toward her, relaxed and smiling. He's pointing at something on the wall in front of them, a large photograph, the colors smeared out of focus in Trina's picture. Because that's what this is. One of the pictures Trina took in November at that gallery opening in Pittsburgh. The pictures that proved Carter was cheating. The pictures she swore no one would ever see but me.

I snatch one from the ground and hold it under the flashlight beam. I haven't looked at this photo since she showed me the shots. They looked different on her camera, smaller and less vivid somehow. Or maybe I wasn't looking as closely two months ago; maybe the past few days have worn me down. He's squeezing her close to his side, and even though I can only see part of his face, he's clearly happy. Not perfect and posed, the way he's been lately with me. Just totally happy.

"Fuck," I whisper beneath my breath. I drop the flashlight and drop to my knees. Trina swore she deleted those shots, but there must be hundreds of prints here in my yard. I scramble around on the ground, gathering them up, the rocks digging into my hands and knees and messing up my favorite pair of jeans. I don't care. Tears prick at the corners of my eyes.

I know they broke up, but it doesn't matter. Seeing this—how they were, just two months ago—still hurts just as hard. The tears spill over, and then I'm sobbing, mascara streaming down my face, lips twisted into an ugly, silent howl. There are too many photos. I can't hold them all. I run back around the house and grab a utility bucket, then I spend the next half hour finding every last photo in the rock garden until my nails are crusted with dirt and my face is streaked with snot and tears, and I know I'll never, ever be able to unsee the image of my boyfriend, happy and in love with Rosalie Bell.

When I'm upstairs again, I shove the bucket into the back of my closet and slam the door. Then I look at myself in the dresser mirror. I look like hell. I slip inside my bathroom, which connects directly to my bedroom, and turn on the shower, let it run hot. I strip off my clothes until they're in a dirty heap around me and pull back the shower curtain. But before I can step inside, my phone beeps. I think about leaving it, but I can't. I have to know.

I wrap my bathrobe around me and walk back into my room. The new message indicator is flashing, *Private Number*.

The first message is the same horrible photo of Rosalie and Carter, a digital copy, as if I didn't have enough. The caption reads, *Wake up and smell the truth, Princess*.

The second message is also from Private.

> You think it's over between Rosalie and Carter, but they're both lying to you. Send the photos to her father, and put Rosalie in her place.

My stomach clenches, acid pooling where there used to be

butterflies, and I know I'm going to be sick. I run back to the bathroom and crouch over the toilet, gagging and gasping until I'm trembling all over and there's nothing left inside. When I can move again, I stagger into the shower and stand under the hot stream until I finally stop shaking.

Trina took those photos, but she doesn't have any reason to hurt me. More likely, she lied about deleting the shots—sent them to someone or loaned out her camera. I should be furious with her, but right now, I'm too wrecked to be angry. Somehow, Private is everywhere. I start sobbing again, the water streaming down my face, mixing with the salt.

My heart is splintering into a thousand tiny pieces, but admitting how much this is getting to me means letting Private win. And that's not going to happen. Tonight, I'll curl into bed with Huggie and let the heartbreak wash over me. Tomorrow, when I have my shit back together, Trina and I need to talk.

ROSALIE

FRIDAY, JANUARY 12

I get through the day on a thermos of coffee and pure adrenaline. Amanda's email came in late last night, the pictures of Pau and me flashing across my screen like three little daggers poised to strike. For the second night in a row, I didn't sleep. I kept hearing noises outside, getting up to check the windows and locks. I know what I saw in the woods, and these photos are the proof. That I'm not imagining things, but also that I'm teetering on the verge of exposure. Three more threads, *snap, snap, snap*. The only tiny consolation is that whoever took those pictures can't be acting on behalf of my parents. There'd be no Amanda in the middle, and I'd be grounded by now, or much worse.

But I'm not out of the allegorical woods, not even close. Just because Amanda didn't send my dad the photos doesn't mean she won't change her mind. Or that the photographer, whoever it is, won't still take matters into their own hands.

After school, I take the bus home, then ride my bike to O'Malley's, the catch-all discount store about halfway between Culver Ridge and Logansville. I'm supposed to be at the movies with Elissa tonight, an excuse I can use about once a month. As I pedal, each house I pass holds watching eyes. Each car window conceals a camera lens. *Flash*.

The knowledge that I'm about to see Pau, that somehow she's going to help me get through this, is literally the only thing keeping me together. She knows the basics—that someone's been following me, that the clearing's not safe—but aside from texts and a few hushed conversations in the halls, I haven't gotten any alone time with her since Monday. I need her.

When I coast into the lot, it's packed with Friday shoppers, but no Paulina. I prop my bike against a post and wait. The sooner she gets to our designated meeting spot, the sooner we can get back on our bikes and get out of here. Meeting in Culver Ridge definitely isn't safe, and O'Malley's is borderline. If they ever spotted us together, my parents would look right past Pau's long, curly hair, mascara, and pink lips and zoom in on her cuffed jeans, collared shirts, and plaid blazers. They might not be able to pinpoint one particular thing that screams lesbian, but they'd just know.

I keep my helmet on and push my chin down into my scarf. A few minutes later, Paulina rides up. In place of her winter coat is an oversized blazer layered over a sweater vest and plaid button-down. The sneakers and cargo pants she was wearing at school have been swapped out for dark wash denim and tan loafers. She looks amazing, and suddenly I feel scrubby in the same jeans and sweater I wore to school. But at the same time, I'm a little pissed. Someone is threatening to destroy everything we have, and Pau took the time to change into a cute outfit?

"Hey." She's grinning big, and my anger dips. Paulina is the last person I want to be fighting with. I need her on my side. "I found a place. We're going into Logansville."

I raise my eyebrows. Logansville is Carter and Amanda territory.

"Don't worry," she says, reading my mind. "We're not going anywhere Carter Shaw would hang on a Friday night. It's open access at the museum. We'll debrief and see some art."

I frown. *Debrief and see some art?* Someone is following me. They took pictures. They showed up at my house. I haven't slept since Tuesday.

"This isn't *Harriet the Spy*, Pau. Why aren't you taking this seriously?"

She sighs. "I am, I promise. I'm freaked out too. But wallowing in the O'Malley's lot isn't helping anyone." She juts her chin toward the faded red awning that's probably needed replacing since before 9/11 and the sign announcing a sale on tractors, toothpaste, and fish tackle. "I promise we can still talk things through with Matisse in the background."

"Fine," I give in. We're halfway to Logansville anyway, and Pau's right—an art museum is probably the last place Carter will be tonight.

When we arrive, the museum is packed. Unsurprisingly, the elite of Logansville love getting something for free. We're not the only teenagers, but the crowd is mostly under ten or over thirty. I'm sure there's a preparty underway somewhere for whatever boozy event will be entertaining the Logansville South it-crowd tonight.

"Let's start in the Egypt room," Paulina suggests. "It was my favorite as a kid. I haven't been in there in ages."

I let her lead me through the French Impressionists and a special exhibition on Picasso's early drawings that look like they belong in New York, not Logansville, and into the room that houses the Ancient Egypt collection. We're greeted immediately by a display of alabaster vases and bowls, a tray carved with images of bread and vegetables, and several small human figurines that the sign says are called *shabtis*, representations of people who assist the deceased in the afterlife. The main event—a coffin holding the mummified body of a child—is surrounded by parents and toddlers.

Paulina motions me around the room, her face lighting up at each new artifact behind a glass case. I can see what she's doing. This is supposed to be a distraction, a little bit of fun. She wants to take my mind off the pictures, and my heart swells just a little because I appreciate it. It *is* nice to be here, surrounded by art and artifacts dating back hundreds and even thousands of years. It strikes me how good Logansville's collection is. The Museum of Fine Arts is like a mini Met. Really mini, but there's an impressive permanent collection and the exhibitions are always big-name artists. I'm no expert, but a museum of this caliber must be rare for a city of Logansville's size. Despite everything, it's fun to be here with Pau. Someday, I imagine we'll have nights like this all the time—only then, we'll be touching, holding hands, not holding anything back.

Pau wants to move on to the Impressionists, but I usher her upstairs to the cafe. We're here for a reason; it's time to talk. She gets a coffee and we find a little round table overlooking the museum lobby.

"You haven't even asked to see the pictures."

Pau shrugs, looking uncomfortable. "I guess I already imagined the worst."

"There's one of us kissing." I lean across the table, keeping my voice to a whisper. "You get what would happen if my parents saw it, right?"

She doesn't respond, just takes a long sip of coffee and stares at the table. I hand her my phone.

"I don't get it," she says after she's finished reading Amanda's email. "Why tell Amanda to send the photos to your dad? Why wouldn't they just do it themselves, cut out the middle-woman?"

"Whoever it is wanted Amanda to see. Maybe they thought she'd show Carter. I don't know. They're trying to ruin her life as much as mine."

Pau sits quietly for a moment, chewing on the cardboard lip of her cup. "Or maybe it's Carter they're really after. He must have enemies, right? Star athlete, superrich family. If I wanted to get at Carter Shaw, I'd go for his weak spots. It's messed up, but you and Amanda are probably just collateral damage."

I let her words sink in. If my dad saw these photos, it wouldn't just mean the end of Pau and me. My life would be over—including the part involving Carter.

"I need to do something. If Amanda finds out I didn't really break up with Carter, she has the photos, and she doesn't strike me as the forgiving type. We need to talk."

"Like face to face? You and Princess Amanda?" Paulina drains the rest of her coffee in one gulp and sends the cup flying into the nearest garbage can, basketball style. We get a few glares from surrounding patrons.

"Exactly. She could have sent the photos to my dad, but she didn't. She has a soul. And once she meets me, I become a real person. It's a lot easier to hate someone you don't even know."

"So what are you going to tell her?"

"Everything. The truth."

"That's a pretty big risk, Lee-Lee."

"It's a bigger risk not to." I stand and grab my coat from the back of my chair.

"You're right." Pau's words freeze me in my tracks. I look down at her, still seated at the cafe table.

"You're right," she says again. Her face is soft, and this time, there's a hitch in her voice. "It's a good idea, talking to Amanda. I just wish you didn't have to keep putting yourself through all this. I wish I could fix it."

I slouch back down, wanting more than anything to reach across the table and take her hands in mine. "Thanks for tonight," I say. "I needed a little distraction."

She smiles. *I love you.* Her lips form the words, soundless. "Now let's get out of here," she says out loud.

The whole ride home, I go over and over my options. Talking to Amanda is definitely risky, but what other choice do I have? This isn't the movies. No one's going to swoop in to bop the Bad Guy on the head. I could move into Paulina's brother's room and get myself Ecclesiastically Extradited. I could run away. I could sink my entire college fund into hiring a detective to find this creep, but then where would I be? No fairy godmother is sending me to college or reuniting me with Lily. They're not very good options.

Amanda's email is evidence she doesn't actively hate me, at least for the moment. And I know she's freaked out too. I can see the panic beneath every bitchy word. All I need is fifteen minutes of her time. If we're going to shut this creep up, we're going to have to work together.

When we get back to O'Malley's, Pau and I promise to text later tonight, then she stays in the parking lot to light a cigarette while I bike ahead into Culver Ridge. When I'm home and locking up my bike in the shed, my phone beeps. The caller ID reads *Private Number*.

I'm watching you, Sweetheart.

A lump forms in the back of my throat.

Who is this?

Think real hard. You know who this is.

You're the same person who's been
texting Amanda.

Bingo. I knew you had some brains in
that tousled head.

I grimace. The thought of this person knowing what I look like makes my stomach turn. But of course they do. They took those pictures, after all.

What do you want?

So thoughtful of you to ask. You
have until January 24 to tell Carter all
about your tryst with the brunette.
Don't even think about sparing any of
the details.

And under no circumstances can you
tell Carter about me. He needs to
think this is your idea, got it?

One more thing: record the
conversation and send it to me as
proof.

I almost drop my phone into the sink. I don't write back. Instead, I go calmly downstairs and eat dinner with my family. When I'm done putting the dishes away, I close myself in my room and email Amanda.

17

AMANDA

SATURDAY, JANUARY 13

The bed lurches below me. I smash my face into my pillow and breathe in, trying to grasp hold of last night. We were at Bronson's. Adele was pouring shots, some mixture of vodka and Frangelico that went down like chocolate cake. I must have had five. More. The bed lurches again, and I pull my knees into my chest.

When I drink at all, I am the two-drink queen. One to get the party started, a second halfway through the night, and done. When you live with my mother, you pay attention to your alcohol consumption. But last night, I was drinking to forget. The pinging against my windows. The avalanche of photos in the rock garden. The texts. *You think it's over between Rosalie and Carter, but they're both lying to you.*

I cornered Trina at the party, between shots two and three. She swore up and down she'd never sent the photos to anyone, that they'd all been deleted. "A few days after I showed them to you, promise."

I glared at her. *A few days?* That was a lot of time.

She also swore she never loaned out her camera, and I believe her on that. The thing cost as much as last season's Birkin bag, and it's pretty much never out of her sight. But someone could have taken the memory card.

"What about in Aiden's?" We usually left our bags piled in a corner in studio art. "Or at the diner that Friday?"

Trina considered. "I guess someone could have swiped the card, then replaced it later? It really could have happened anywhere."

I groaned and looked around for Adele. I needed another one of those shots.

Trina chewed on her lower lip. "Fuck, Amanda, I'm sorry. It was two months ago. I just don't remember."

Trina was officially on my shit list, but what else could I say? I couldn't expect her to remember something she'd never seen in the first place.

Unless she was straight up lying.

I swore Trina to secrecy about the rock garden incident, then found Adele. After chocolate cake shots three, four, and five, I wasn't sure what to believe anymore.

As the night wore on, I found myself wandering aimlessly through Bronson's parents' massive basement, avoiding Trina, avoiding Carter, weaving in and out of conversations at the pool table, the vintage jukebox, the restaurant-style bar. By two, I was ready to go home, but Trina was DD and I wasn't in the mood to ask her for a favor. Instead, I slipped through the sliding glass doors onto the pool deck and plopped down in one of the loungers. The plastic cushion was ice against my legs, and I curled them into my chest, tilting my head back to watch a massive American flag whip from the balcony. *Snap, snap*, chilly ribbons of red, white, and blue in the night. My thoughts flickered to Bronson's dad, an air force general with a lot of glistening stars on the shoulder strap of his uniform, away overseeing something classified in the Arizona desert. Nights there were probably freezing too.

"Hey."

I spun around to face the dim figure sprawled across a lounger by the deep end. The blocky pool house cast a dark slice of shadow from his face down to his chest.

"Alexander?"

"It's warmer over here. Trust me, you want to be by the heat."

I made my way over, scooting another lounger beside him. Up close, I could see that he had the door to the pool house propped open. Heat poured out against our backs.

"It's fine. Bronson does it all the time in the winter." He sounded entirely sober, and the lounger's built-in cup holder was empty.

"You're not drinking?" I asked.

"I never drink."

"Huh." My mind reeled back across all the Friday nights, the house parties and fetes, the endless social functions where Alexander had been present since he and Bronson got together in June. Half a year's worth of parties, and I'd never noticed.

"I don't either." I could taste the thickness of my words, how they wanted to stick to my tongue. "Not much, anyway. Not usually."

"What changed tonight?" he asked. Not pushing, just curious.

For a moment, I was silent. It hit me that I'd never had a real conversation with Alexander before, barely even knew Bronson in a below-the-surface way. Bronson was lacrosse and skydiving and daredevil stuff—stuff Carter liked. I'd only learned this year that he'd lived in nine different states and had two little half sisters—twin redheads—who lived with his mom. And I liked Alexander, a lot actually. But he'd always just been Bronson's boyfriend. That he went to a different school put him somewhat on the outside, maybe in a good way. He probably didn't even know about the vandalism at my locker.

"Do you ever wonder if you see yourself one way, but everyone else, they see something different?" I asked. "And you're the only one who can't see the real you?"

Alexander smiled, lopsided and toothy. "All the damn time."

"And maybe," I went on, "if people really cared, they'd tell you the truth. About yourself. About how they really feel. But no one likes to tell the truth."

Alexander tilted his head to one side and looked at me closely, as if for the first time. "Is someone lying to you, Amanda?"

"I don't know."

I force my eyes open, letting in the harsh morning light, and drag myself out of bed. My phone says 11:53. By the time I'm showered and dressed, I feel slightly more human. I take a long sip of coffee as my browser opens to its usual tabs: Gmail, Facebook, Atlantic-Pacific, and Weather.com, 'cause a girl's got to be prepared. I spend some time scrolling through Blair Eadie's latest posts, a winter-in-the-Cape-themed series complete with a gorgeous cashmere shawl and snow parasol, and then click over to my Gmail. Rosalie again. The email is from last night, probably thanking me for Thursday's act of goodwill. Not that she deserved it, apparently.

> Subject: Re: Just thought you should
> know
> From: Rosalie Bell
> To: me
>
>
> Hey. So, thanks for not sending my
> dad those photos. Will you delete them
> please? I think your anonymous texter
> was pissed because they got in touch. No
> caller ID, serious dirtbag?
>
> Something tells me I'm not the only
> one who got an ultimatum for Carter's
> birthday. I know I'm not your favorite
> person, but we need to meet up. Promise
> I'll explain everything.
>
> Here's my number: 723-958-6593.
>
> Rosalie

No way. When I stare at the email, the photos from Thursday night are all I can see. Her body pressed against Carter's. I jam my fists into my eyes, but the image is burned there. I take a deep breath, then hit reply.

Subject: Re: Re: Just thought you should
know
From: me
To: Rosalie Bell

I know you're lying. We are not about to
form some two-woman detective agency.
Figure it out on your own.

—AK

I add her number to my phone, just in case, then toss it in my bag.

I need to get out of the house. I need to drive. My stomach is still in knots, and my head is throbbing. I can't face an encounter with Linda or Jack right now, if he's even home. If she's even up.

When I slip into the hall and down the stairs, the house is mercifully quiet.

As soon as I hit the road, I feel a little better. My brain is still banging against my temples, but the knots in my stomach start to release. Despite the freezing weather, I crack the window to let in some fresh air. I don't really think about where I'm going, and when I find myself at the high school, I make my usual left at the construction site.

I drive past the crew, putting in a Saturday shift. In the time since we got back from winter break, the gymnasium has gone from a framework and scaffolding to something that almost resembles a real building. I pull into the parking lot and turn off the ignition, but leave the heat running. A minute passes, then ten. I don't know what to believe, who I can talk to. At Verde on Wednesday, I swear Carter was telling the truth. But on Thursday, someone wanted me to know he was lying. I picture Carter and Rosalie, still together, maybe together right now. Was his car in the driveway when I left the house? I can't remember. I didn't look. Maybe I didn't want to know.

I'm entirely absorbed in my dark fantasy of the two of them in Culver Ridge, doing whatever they do there together—drive around? hang out at CVS? make out in the backseat of the Mercedes?—when there's a tap on the passenger's side window. My eyes fly open. A tall, broad-shouldered man is standing next to my car, arms on the hood, face pressed close to the window. I shriek.

"Hey, it's just me!" He backs two steps away from the car, hands up in front of his chest.

"Jesus Christ on the cross, David Gallagher. Don't do that to me."

I wait for my breathing to even out, then press the unlock button. David grins and swings open the passenger's side door.

"Mind if I join you?"

"Get in, Gallagher. You didn't have to sneak up on me like that."

"Didn't mean to startle you, honest." David sits down and slides the seat all the way back, stretches out his legs.

"How'd you know I was up here?" I ask.

"Saw you pull in a while ago. Didn't see you leave, so I thought I'd come find you on my break."

I can't remember the last time David and I really talked. The other night at the diner barely counts. Ever since he graduated last year, I've barely seen him except around the construction site.

"Mind if I smoke?"

I'm about to tell him yes, I do mind, no cigarettes in the coupé, but then I notice that David's holding up a joint. I never smoke pot—Carter doesn't approve. I can feel him sitting between us, shaking his head in disappointment.

"Only if you plan to share that."

David grins and pulls out a lighter. Imaginary Carter narrows his eyes at me, sad frown lines tugging at his lips. David takes a long pull, then passes the joint my way. I hesitate, but just for a second. What Carter doesn't know won't hurt us. I suck the smoke deep into my lungs and immediately explode into a fit of hacking and choking.

"Easy there, cowgirl." David is laughing at me. "Hit it again, just take it slow."

I get the coughing under control, then do as instructed. This time, I manage to get the smoke in and out of my lungs without incident.

"First time?" David asks.

"Almost. Clearly I need more practice."

"Come round the school on Saturdays anytime. I'll smoke you up. You should bring Trina."

So David *is* into Trina. A smile flickers across my lips, then just as quickly dies when I remember Trina's on my shit list.

"Thanks, I might take you up on that." I glance down at the

construction site. "How's the project going, anyway?"

"Scheduled for completion in June. Too bad you'll graduate before you get to use it."

I shrug. "I guess."

"Seriously, Amanda? You should see the sad excuse for a track and field they've got out at NPCC-L." David used to play lacrosse for South, but he was never as good as his little brother.

"No team at community college?"

"Not exactly. But I'm getting out of there anyway."

I raise my eyebrows. He passes the joint back to me, and I take another hit.

"Oh yeah?"

"I'm applying to WVU, sophomore transfer. I'm pretty sure I'll get in. I just have to put together enough cash."

"You'll be there with Carter and me!" My voice is almost a squeal. For a moment, I forget that no part of my future with Carter is certain. And then I remember. If I lose Carter, I lose WVU too. Because how could I face four years on the same campus if we're not together? Which leaves me with the three other, significantly more expensive schools where I've applied, if I even get in. Which leaves my family where exactly?

"That's amazing." I try and fail to sound cheerful. "I really hope it works out, David."

"Yeah, well. It's not a done deal yet. WVU's state, but it's not exactly free."

Right. However bad we're struggling, David's family's struggling even more. I'm sure going to Carl for a loan isn't an option. I lean back into the headrest and close my eyes. After three hits, I'm definitely feeling something. Warm and almost weightless.

But something else too. I turn until I'm facing David head-on. We used to have fun freshman year. We never did anything fancy—the movies, the mall—but he always made me feel like the prettiest girl in the room. The only girl worth his time.

"Listen, I've gotta get back." David retrieves what's left of the joint and opens the car door. I wrap my arms tight around my waist, as if he might have seen inside me just now, as if I can stop him from looking.

"Just don't get on the road for a while, okay? Get some air, take a walk around the track."

"I'm not that stoned," I protest. But I know this was a mistake. David, the pot. The skin on the back of my neck prickles, Carter's disappointment mingling with my mother's, my father's. Somehow, I'm letting everybody down.

"Just looking out for you, kid," he says, a flicker of something I don't recognize flashing across his face, then gone.

"Don't worry about me." My voice is tight. David hesitates for a moment.

"Give Trina my regards?"

"Of course." But I know I won't say anything to Trina. It's selfish, but so what? Being with David isn't an option for me. I shouldn't even be thinking about it. I should be nice, set them up, but I feel bitter, mean.

He waves, then heads back down to the site. I sit in the car for a few more minutes, trying to enjoy the soft fabric and blasting heat. My headache's almost gone, but I'm not ready to go home.

I decide to take David's advice and step out of the car into the cold, crisp air. I head down toward the track. I've spent countless hours on the bleachers, watching Carter's games. Today, it's totally deserted. I leave the gate swinging behind me and start walking across the field. For a moment, I have this feeling like I've already graduated and I'm back in Logansville, walking out here like old times. The grass is cold and crunchy beneath my feet. That's the sound of high school, I think. The sounds of memories. I'm swaddled like a baby in my puffy coat; the cold can't catch me. I lie down in the middle of the field and close my eyes. Everything melts away—David, Carter, college, my parents. I'm floating.

Suddenly, there's the sharp bang of metal against metal. I sit up, heart pounding.

"Hello?" I must have fallen asleep; I'm groggy and freezing.

No one answers.

"David?"

I jump to my feet, then turn slowly in a circle. There's no one here. My heart is still pounding fast, too fast. The field, once familiar and welcoming, is menacing and cold. I have to get out of here. Now.

I start running, but when I get to the gate, it's closed, latch wrapped in a bike lock and fastened. I weave my fingers into the mesh of metal diamonds and shake, tears stinging my eyes. The field is surrounded by a tall chain-link fence on three sides. On the fourth are doors to the locker rooms, but they'll be locked up for the weekend. I make a half-hearted attempt to climb, but the mesh is far too fine. My boots scrape futilely against the metal. I'm trapped.

I sink to the grass, back sliding down the fence. This gate never gets locked. Someone saw me here. Someone did this to me on purpose.

I take out my phone, hands shaking, knowing full well there's going to be a message waiting for me. Sure enough, two brand-new texts from Private.

> You think you're smart, but you're just an animal in a cage. The sooner you learn that, the better this will end for you, Princess.

> You have 11 more days to pull off a public breakup. I know you can bring the hurt, Amanda—don't let me down.

I've been worrying about all the wrong things. While I was sweating over David and the pot, I should have been thinking about the person who *is* watching my every move. Not Carter, not my parents. Private. This is payback for Thursday night, for sending the photos to Rosalie instead of her dad.

I bang my head against the locked gate and scream, but there's no one around to hear.

I can't call Trina, or Adele for that matter. This is too embarrassing. I open up a new conversation and text Alexander.

> Hey, you around?

Yeah.

> I need you to come to South. Bring wire cutters, I'm locked in at the track.

What?

Just get here. Please?

On my way.

And Alexander? Don't tell anyone.

ROSALIE

SUNDAY, JANUARY 14

She knows I'm lying. When Carter and I didn't actually break up at Eat'n Park, someone was listening. Either Private tipped her off, or Carter Shaw is a very bad liar.

Amanda has the photos and Private has the photos. It's only a matter of time before everything rips to shreds. A thousand threads, *snaaaap*. In church, the shell of some other girl sings the hymns and recites the prayers while I sink into my chair and the long, cold fingers of my parents and the congregation and the Holy Spirit Himself squeeze tighter and tighter around my throat until there's no air left.

Richard and Julia are fully absorbed in the service, but Lily sees me shrinking in my chair, body caught somewhere between suffocating and disappearing altogether. She reaches over and slips her hand into my hand. Our fingers weave.

"Jesus loves you," she whispers. "His love is all around. Can't you feel it?"

I smile weakly at my sister, and tears well up in my eyes. All I can feel is the pulsing bass, which reverberates through the church's sound system. It pounds against my lungs, *thud, thud, thud*, until finally the tears spill over.

After service ends, I nibble cookies and try my best to make small talk with Ivan Brophy, one of the FOC kids I mind the least. From the seats behind us, I can feel Mom's eyes fixed on my back. She's deep in conversation with Mrs. Hagan, and their voices carry.

"You know he and Cecilia had a terrible go of it when he was growing up," Mrs. Hagan is saying. "She let him run wild, and now look what's happened." They're talking, it seems, about the Hagan's next-door neighbors, Philip Ireland and his mother, Cecilia. Before service, I'd overheard Beth Clark murmuring to Emily Masters that Philip had "run off to Dayton, with a man." He's a grown adult. I'm not sure leaving home to move in with your boyfriend qualifies as "running off," but this is the kind of occurrence that makes waves in Fellowship circles, even though the Irelands aren't FOC. It's gossip fueled by equal parts fear and disgust. The purity ring feels tight and hot around my finger.

"He was exposed to too many of the world's sins," Mom agrees. "And he doesn't have Jesus in his heart. It's people like that who ruin godly marriages."

The words crash down across my back. I'm not sure if they're for my benefit, or despite of me. I try to block them out, focus instead on Ivan Brophy's mouth. He's regaling me with an animated description of his volunteer plans for tomorrow's day off from school. When he asks if I want to join the outreach day trip for Mission Driven, I politely decline.

And then finally coffee hour is over, and the Bells are going our separate ways: Dad and Lily take the car home, Mom stays for her shift in the church office, and I take off on my bike. The road stretches out like a wide gray ribbon. I can't put enough distance between me and God's Grace, the world passing in a blur of barbed wire, frost-tipped grass, dairy cows. It isn't until I get to Bracken Hollow that I realize my jaw aches and my head is pounding from clenching my teeth all through service.

Inside, I hang my coat on an empty hook in the office and massage my temples. Our branch is small and the tech is about a decade short of modern, but I love it here. There's exposed brick on the walls and big open windows. It always smells like the plastic they use for library bindings and vanilla carpet freshener. I say hello to Marge, the librarian on duty, and settle in at the info desk. Within minutes I have a patron with a question, a blissful distraction from the din inside my head.

By the time my shift ends at four, my headache is gone and I've almost forgotten I told Carter to pick me up. We're supposed to be going to some coffee shop he found a few miles out, somewhere in a strip mall where he swears no one will spot us. The whole thing grates against my better judgment. I can't get high at the library, and there will be no Bell family face time tonight. But I need to see Carter. I don't know exactly what I'm going to say, but we have to talk about Amanda.

Through the row of front-facing windows, I can see him drumming against the steering wheel. Marge makes her final "library closing" announcement, and a minute later I'm in the parking lot, phone to my ear, reminding Dad about my date. Check-in complete, I strap my bike to the back of Carter's car and slide into the front seat.

He leans over to kiss my cheek, but freezes when I open my mouth. "Amanda knows we're lying."

"What?"

"I know you talked to her, but either she didn't buy it, or someone's been spying. And I think it might be the latter."

"Spying?"

Just talking about this makes me jumpy. Unless there's a bug in the Mercedes, no one could possibly be eavesdropping, but I lower my voice, just in case.

"Someone's been following me. At school, and the other night they showed up at my house."

"Oh my god." Carter grabs my hand and squeezes. "Did you get a look at the guy? Did he say anything?"

I shake my head. "I think it might have been a woman, but I'm not sure. I just saw her shadow. Someone tipped Amanda off that we're not really broken up. And someone's been following me around. So, two plus two . . ."

"Okay." Carter puts his other hand on top of mine and looks me straight in the eye. "We're going to figure this out."

"How? Amanda has . . . stuff on me. Stuff that can't get out."

"What kind of stuff?" Carter's grip on my hand loosens, and the corners of his mouth drop down. A somber gloom settles across his face, making him look much older than his usually boyish seventeen years.

I turn toward the passenger's side window and look out. Then

I turn back to Carter and lie to his face. "Stuff about my family; I don't want to talk about it. But Amanda could really do some damage, and she's definitely pissed." Because of course she is. Guilt balloons in my stomach, and I'm not sure what I want anymore. To keep myself safe, yes, but at what cost?

I look into Carter's eyes. The gloom has lifted; he looks like a confused little boy.

"Maybe we should take a break," I suggest. "A real one. Just for a week or two, until this blows over."

"No!" Carter smashes his fist against the steering wheel, and the horn lets out a sharp blast. I gasp. "I'm sorry, I'm sorry. I didn't mean to do that." He slumps back against the headrest. "I'll handle Amanda. Just don't do this."

I'd like to believe him, but Carter's not going to convince Amanda of anything. I'm sure he did his best last week, but Private's one step ahead of us.

"Just for a little while," I repeat. At least until January 24 is here and gone and this whole mess with Private blows over, Lord willing. I can hold my parents off for ten days. I'll tell them Carter's family took him on a trip for his birthday; that's something rich people do.

"I love you, Rosalie."

For a moment, there's a thin silence in the car. My stomach twists.

"I love you," he repeats. As if I didn't hear it the first time. As if destroying everything once wasn't enough.

I let the words hang. I'm the girl with zero expectations, his no-strings-attached commercial break from the regularly scheduled programming of being golden boy Carter Shaw. The guilt-balloon in my stomach expands and expands. He's not allowed to fall in love.

"I just need a little time," he says, pressing through my silence. "Leaving Amanda, it's not something I can just do. Amanda, me, our families, we're all tangled up in each other."

"I never asked you to leave her," I choke out.

"I know. I think that's why I fell so hard for you." The guilt-balloon bursts with a bang only I can hear.

I'm shoving open the car door and running around to unhook my bike from the back before I even have time to think. Something inside me is *just done*. I'm done lying to Carter about what we are, done hurting Amanda, done hurting Pau too. No matter what it means. Broken strands of my carefully woven web flutter around me, useless.

"What are you doing?"

Carter's out of the car, but I've already got my bike. I need to get out of here, now.

"Going home." I snap my helmet strap under my chin and secure my messenger bag across my shoulders.

"Wait. I don't get what just happened."

Of course you don't. I push off and bike out of the lot, onto the road.

"Rosalie! Shit."

The car door slams, and I pedal faster. The wind stings my face, and my eyes fill with tears. It's just the wind, I tell myself. I'm not really crying. I'll figure it out. I always do.

"Rosalie." Suddenly, Carter's next to me in the road, window down. He's driving halfway into the wrong lane, but there's no traffic. "Let's talk about this, please."

"Leave me alone!" I shout, mean on purpose. "You're crowding me."

He pulls all the way into the left lane, the wrong lane. "Please, babe, get back in the car."

Babe. He's never called me that before.

"I want us to be together," he shouts. "You and me."

"You belong with Amanda," I shout back. I pedal faster.

"What? I can barely hear you. Please get back in the car."

There's a red car coming toward Carter, driving too fast. He needs to slow down, drop behind me, get into the right lane. But he's not paying attention, eyes still fixed on me. Shit.

"Get over, Carter!" I shout.

The car starts honking. I pull to the side of the road, panting. Carter swerves into the right lane, then pulls up along the guardrail as the car passes in a red blare of honking and cursing.

He gets out and grabs my elbow. "Are you okay?"

"I'm fine. You're the one who almost got yourself killed."

He grimaces but doesn't argue.

"I don't understand what's happening, Rosalie. You have to talk to me."

"We have to break up. Not a break, break up."

"No. No way."

"This isn't a negotiation."

Carter is quiet. A muscle twitches along his jaw, holding back tears. Then he leans forward and buries his face in my coat. I lift my arms and let them rest lightly around his shoulders.

"I'm sorry," he says after I've been silent too long. "I don't know what I did, but I'm sorry. Please let me drive you home?"

I swing my leg off my bike. Wordlessly, we strap it to the trunk, then I climb back into the passenger's seat. For once, he doesn't turn on any music. We're silent for the rest of the drive to my house. When Carter pulls into the driveway, I know it's the last time I'll hear the crunch of his tires against gravel.

I slip out of the car before he can kiss me, then unhook my bike and wheel it up to the driver's side window. He doesn't get out of the car.

"Take care, Carter."

He doesn't say anything. I pretend I don't see tears spill down his cheeks. Then, I wheel my bike back around to the shed and listen to him drive away.

I make an excuse to Dad about the change of plans, some emergency at Shaw Realty. He seems to buy it. When I'm alone in my room, I take out my phone and open the conversation with Private.

I did it.

Send me the recording.

Not that. I broke up with Carter. So our business is done.

That is not what I asked you to do.

Who do you bitches think you are?

I suck in my breath. I'm seething. I know I made the right choice today, but at the same time, I just jeopardized *everything*. After all this, I can't risk Private leaking the photos too.

I thought this would make you happy.
Carter's crushed.

You need to stop thinking so much.

I wait, but they don't text again. I sink onto my bed and close my eyes. With Carter out of my life, Private better leave me the hell alone. It's not a lot of comfort. Now that I've broken up with Carter, it might not matter.

After a few minutes, Lily knocks on my door. "Rosalie?"

"Not now, Lily." My voice is a little too sharp. "I'm not feeling well."

I listen to her footsteps pad back to her room and hate myself just a little more. I should cherish every moment I have with my sister. I don't know how many more we have left. In my head, I try to map out what comes next. I can buy myself a little time with my parents, maybe two weeks. Then it all goes dark.

AMANDA

MONDAY, JANUARY 15

We're off school for Martin Luther King Jr. Day, which means a full day of preseason training camp for Carter and no French class for me. When my mother catches me moping, she puts me to work on the benefit. The board members are supercompetitive; it's about the arts, but mostly it's about Logansville prowess. Linda always comes out on top. Always.

And this afternoon, she is not happy. By the one-week mark pre-event, my mother should be fully in the black. The Logansville elite must be feeling stingy this year. She's been camped out in Dad's office since noon trying the big-ticket donors she hasn't yet reached while I'm on my phone at the kitchen table working my way down the new member list, thoughts running wild between calls.

It's been two days since someone locked me in at the track, and Private's been totally silent. Alexander thinks I was at school getting a book and the locker room door latched behind me. The lie doesn't even make sense, but fortunately he didn't ask questions.

When I'm not thinking about Private, I'm thinking about Carter, replaying his promises at Verde about new beginnings and always and forever. But photos tell their own kind of truth. In that Rosalie picture, Carter looked happy in a way I haven't seen in ages. That kind of happiness doesn't just vanish in a snap. He barely seemed to notice me avoiding him at Bronson's party. Then yesterday, he canceled our dinner plans, and his Mercedes was gone from the driveway by midafternoon. I'm not naive. I know he went back to Culver Ridge.

I pick at my nail polish and stare outside. The snow flurries that have been swirling all afternoon are starting to come down fat and thick. The absolute worst thing about Private—worse even than fake blood or headless teddy bears or horrible pictures or the stunt on the field—is that I think he or she might be right. I *do* deserve better than Carter Shaw.

The problem is, I don't know who I am without him.

For years, he's been my everything. Ever since we were kids, our parents and their friends loved to say how adorable we were together, how we were going to get married someday. When you hear it enough times, you start to believe it. I've known I'd be Mrs. Amanda Shaw for as long as I can remember. It's who I am.

Tears prick my eyes, and I punch another number from the donor list into my phone and reach yet another answering machine. When my mother emerges from the office at a few minutes after six, she's scowling.

"I can't reach the Beaufords."

"Maybe they're out?" I suggest.

"They're screening. Give me your phone."

"What?" I grab for it protectively.

"I'm going to try them from your number, Amanda."

There's no use arguing. I hand it over. "Fine. I'm starving."

My mother looks at the microwave clock as if she's just realized we didn't break for lunch, and it's already been pitch dark for an hour.

"Put in an order at Taro, please, darling? The spa bento; I need something light. Your father will want those tempura rolls he gets."

I don't bother to point out that they'll be cold and disgusting by the time he gets home. Instead, I say, "You have my phone." For a moment, it looks like she's going to give it back. She actually looks physically pained by the prospect of not outsmarting the Beaufords as soon as humanly possible. I sigh. "Never mind. I'll use my computer."

My mother smiles and disappears into the dining room to make her victory call.

Upstairs, I click through the menu options and punch in the numbers on the family Visa, which is now back in commission. My stomach is literally growling. Estimated delivery time forty to sixty minutes, with delays due to weather. I glance out my bedroom window into the swirl of white, then I wander back down into the kitchen to grab a fruit smoothie from the fridge. My blood sugar is crashing.

"Now, Jacques, that is not what I was expecting from you this year." My mother's voice carries from the dining room. She sounds determined in that dripping-with-honey way she has when she's trying to angle more money out of donors. "Well, based on prior giving history, of course." There's a pause. "No, Winston has nothing to do with this. Jacques, you know the donor lists are confidential."

Last year, Linda did a lot of her fund-raising across the street when our downstairs bathroom was being redone. She claimed it was too loud in our house to concentrate. Knowing my mother, she tried to reach Jacques Beauford from the Shaws' phone during last year's fund-raising blitz. By next year, they're going to be on to her little telephone game.

I drain my smoothie in a few large gulps and rinse out the bottle in the sink. There's another pause from the dining room. "I don't know what you're implying, but—hold on . . . No, there's a beep. No, it's Amanda's phone, I'm not sure . . . Jacques, I'm going to have to call you back."

I toss the bottle in the recycling and head toward the dining room. Whoever's calling, they're calling me. But when I get to the doorway, my mother's already picked up.

"No, this is Linda. I was— What? Winston, slow down."

I walk over and extend my hand for my phone, but she jerks her head away.

"The benefit has been tying up the landline . . . Yes, I'm glad you had Amanda's number too. Now, where are you?"

I drop my hand, but don't walk away. Linda's silky fund-raising voice has been replaced with parent voice. Something is wrong. Something with Carter. I can feel the smoothie I just inhaled sloshing around in my stomach.

"I'll go across the street. I'm sure Krystal just has her ringer off. . . . Winston, I'm happy to do it." Pause. "Yes, we'll be there shortly."

My mother places my phone down on the dining room table.

"What happened? Where's Carter?" I grasp for the chain around my throat, and my fingers find the little onyx heart.

My mother reaches for my other hand, but I yank it away. I don't want to be comforted right now. I want to know what the hell is going on.

"Just tell me."

"Sweetie, there's been an accident. The roads are very icy in the storm. Carter's in the hospital, but he's going to be fine."

Oh my god, oh my god. All my doubts, all my pent-up bad feelings about Carter . . . It's like I somehow *willed* this to happen. I spin around toward the kitchen. I need my bag, my car keys, I need to go.

"Sweetie, wait! He's going into surgery. You won't be able to see him yet."

"I don't care." I grab my coat from the closet and shove my arms into the sleeves. "Mercy or Presbyterian?"

"Mercy. Winston can't reach Krystal, but he thinks she's home. I'm going to call your father, and then I'm going across the street."

"Fine."

"If you wait, we can all go—"

"I'll see you there." I'm already halfway down the basement stairs. Going across the street to find Krystal sounds like a one-woman mission. I have to get in my car. I have to get to the hospital.

"Amanda, drive *slow*. It's very slick," my mother calls after me.

I wave at her from the bottom of the stairs, *okay okay*. Then, I slip into the garage.

The drive to Mercy takes forever. My mother is right, the roads *are* slick, and snow smacks the windshield in fat globs. Even at full speed, the wipers barely help. I switch on my brights, illuminating a blinding tapestry of white, then switch them back off. When I finally pull into the ER parking lot at a quarter to seven, I'm shaking.

"I'm looking for Carter Shaw," I tell the woman at the desk inside. "He was admitted here tonight."

She types, stares at her screen, then squints up at me.

"You family?"

"I'm his fiancée," I lie. I shove my hands into my coat pockets in case she thinks to check for a ring.

Her lips twist to the side. "He won't have a room until after surgery," she says after a minute. "He's in the OR." She glances across the room. "Your . . . father-in-law is here, if you want to wait with him."

I follow the woman's eyes to Winston, who's standing before the large bank of windows facing the parking lot, staring out into the storm. A minute later, I'm standing next to him.

"Winston." I place my hand gently on his elbow.

He turns to me, and for a second, it's like he doesn't remember where he is or who I am. His eyes are blank, wet discs. Then, he folds me into a tight hug. "Amanda. Thank god you're here." I feel stifled against the crush of his jacket, but I let myself be held. With Carter in surgery and Krystal not here yet, I'm the closest thing to family Winston has. I shove my complicated jumble of feelings toward Carter down deep and resolve to be strong. His family needs me.

Fifteen minutes later, my mother arrives with Krystal, looking frazzled. Carter's mom makes a beeline for the restroom, and my mother and Winston lock eyes. I dig in my bag and realize I must have left my phone on the dining room table. Adele's is the only number I know by heart, so I borrow my mother's phone and ask Adele to text everyone else.

By seven thirty, Krystal is settled at Winston's side and Adele, Graham, Bronson, and Alexander are clustered with us on the waiting room's dirty beige chairs. I burrow into my coat, even though it's hot in here. I feel better with it wrapped around me tight.

Graham says that Coach ended practice when the storm really kicked up around five. "Carter needed deodorant or something. He was walking down to CVS. Said he'd meet up with us at the diner." There's a CVS two blocks down on Foster. The parking lot is tiny and always full, so people usually walk from school.

Winston nods. "They told us Carter was walking back when a car drove up onto the sidewalk. It was dark . . . the storm . . . They think the driver lost control. But that fucker drove off, didn't even wait to see if our son was alive or dead." He slams the palm of his hand against the chair's metal arm. It makes a dull *thwack*.

"Winston," Krystal admonishes, grabbing his hand. Then, she bursts into tears, and my mother searches her purse for tissues.

Tiny, cold pricks rise along the back of my neck. "Did anyone see the car?" Something about this doesn't feel right. My hand moves to my throat. Sure, the driving conditions are terrible, but the stretch of road between Logansville South and CVS is all school zone. Twenty-five mph, streetlamps, wide sidewalks. You'd have to be driving like an asshole to lose control and swerve onto the sidewalk there.

"Not that we know of," Winston says. "A woman who lives across the street heard the crash and came outside. She found Carter and called 911, but the car was already gone. The police are reviewing footage, but the traffic camera outside the school faces up the hill, and if the driver's from around here, it's likely he turned around, went back the other way. It isn't promising."

"You didn't see anything?" I ask the guys.

"Graham and I left for the diner straight from practice," Bronson says. "Ben was running some errand for his dad, but he met up with us at like five thirty or maybe a little later. So yeah, we were all gone by then."

I glance over at Alexander.

"I was home, helping with dinner. Bronson picked me up when we got Adele's text."

"Where is Ben?" I ask. "And Trina?"

"Dunno about Trina. Ben left the diner before we did. He had to get home." Bronson turns to Adele. "You text them?"

"Yeah," Adele says. "Trina's skiing with her parents, remember? They were supposed to come back tonight, but they're taking an extra day because of the weather. She sends her love, or like, three heart emojis and that smiley face with a bandage." She pulls out her phone. "Still haven't heard back from Ben."

I press my lips between my teeth. I'm still pissed at Trina for being so careless with those photos, and while I've made a serious effort to be nicer to Ben since my lightbulb moment at Verde, it's for the best he's not here. I'd rather not have my resolve tested.

Finally, someone comes to tell us that Carter is out of surgery. He has three cracked ribs, a broken arm, and a concussion, but he's awake. He's going to be okay. She tells everyone except for immediate family to come back in the morning. I glance over at Winston and Krystal, and they nod. I go with them.

Carter attempts a watery grin when we walk in. His hair is a wispy, blond mess; one side of his face is bandaged; and he's clearly woozy from the anesthesia. I think I'm going to burst into tears, but then nothing comes.

The nurse tells us not to touch him, but Krystal ignores her and clasps his uninjured hand in hers.

"My baby."

"Hey, Mom."

Soon, a doctor stops by to update us on the surgery's success. Carter sustained a dislocated fracture to his left radius, which had to be operated on so the bone would heal correctly. He tells us that Carter will need rest and PT once his cast is off, but that he should be able to be released in a few days. The injuries, fortunately, are not severe.

After a few minutes with Carter, his parents slip out to review insurance information with a hospital employee, and Carter and I are alone. I pull up a chair.

"You're here." His tone is flat.

"Of course I'm here. Did you think I wouldn't come?"

Carter turns his head on the pillow and stares toward the window. Someone's drawn the curtain shut, so it's just a wall of fluttering beige and blue. He doesn't answer. After a moment, he turns back to look at me, as if he's surprised I haven't disappeared.

"Aren't you hot?" he finally asks.

I'm still stuffed into my puffy coat. I shake my head and wrap my arms around my stomach. Everything about tonight feels unsafe. Carter's arm is in a cast, and the concussion is serious. He's looking at me like he's not sure I'm real. Or like he's not sure he wants me to be.

"Thank god you're okay," I whisper. I try to look somewhere neutral, but my eyes keep landing on his injuries. This feels like a punishment—for doubting Carter, for believing Private, for flirting with David, even if it was all in my head. Only Carter's the one being punished.

"Out for the season, but I'll live." His voice is tight. It hits me that he's talking about lacrosse. *Did you get back together with Rosalie?* I want to ask. *Do you love her? Do you love me?*

"Do you remember the car?" I say out loud. "Anything about it?"

Carter shakes his head gingerly. "Not really. It came from behind, so I didn't get a look. I remember headlights, low to the ground. So it probably wasn't a truck or SUV. It knocked me into a snowbank. The doctors said I'm lucky 'cause it cushioned the impact when my head hit. But I don't remember that. I remember the lights, and then I was here."

I swallow and take a deep breath. Even if he has been lying to me, it's impossible to be mad at him right now. "I was so scared when your dad called."

"I'm gonna be fine." Carter grins, too wide. "Ouch."

I reach out and slip my hand into his. He squeezes it quickly, then lets his hand drop back limply on the bed. "Carter, something's not right. Who drives like that by school?"

"It was really snowing, though. Probably just bad luck."

I stare at my boyfriend in that hospital bed, and I just know. Nothing about this was luck. Someone knew Carter was out there walking. Someone hit him on purpose.

It's not because of my doubts or guilty conscience, but it's suddenly perfectly clear that this *is* happening because of me. Because I refused to do Private's bidding. Scraps of the texts flash across my vision. *Things are going to get real ugly if you don't start listening to me.* And that typewritten note that came with the flowers: *Before January 24, you will break Carter Shaw's heart. . . . End it—or I'll end things my way.*

Something cold and sharp twists deep in my gut. No matter how bad Carter messed up, he doesn't deserve this. No one does. This has to end. I open my mouth to say something, anything, but before I can figure out what, a technician comes into the room. I stand up to get out of her way.

"Just checking vitals," she says. "You're fine."

I lean back against the wall, and she turns to Carter. "How you feeling, honey?"

"Okay. Kind of like I got hit by a car."

She smiles. "A comedian."

"Do you know if they returned my stuff?" Carter asks.

The tech looks at him blankly.

"I had a backpack. Before I went into surgery, an officer said they'd give it back since there was nothing to enter into evidence."

I scan the room. There's a wheelie cart near the door; I can see Carter's backpack stuffed into the bottom shelf. "Found it."

While she finishes whatever she's doing and makes a note on

Carter's chart, I walk over and grab the backpack. It's unzipped all the way; the police obviously pawed through it thoroughly. Carter's books and a white CVS bag are inside. The technician says she'll be back in a couple hours, and I bring it over to the foot of Carter's bed.

"What did you get at CVS?"

Carter draws his lower lip between his teeth. "I don't remember. Gum? Everything right before the car hit me is a little foggy. Doctor said that's normal with head trauma."

I turn the bag upside down and the contents spill onto the bed. Two sticks of deodorant and a pack of cinnamon gum. I'm about to put it all back when something catches my eye. At the bottom of the backpack, half crushed beneath his history text, is a small teddy bear. I gasp.

"What?" Carter asks, straining to look.

"This bear. It's the same one from my locker. Did this come from CVS?"

Carter frowns. "I don't remember. Why would I buy that?"

"I don't know!" I fish around for the receipt, but there isn't one.

"Let me see your wallet."

"Huh?"

"The receipt. It's not here. Let me see your wallet."

Carter motions with his chin toward the little bedside table. On it are a pitcher of ice water, a cup, his phone, and his wallet. I snatch it and rifle through. Just his usual cards, ID, some cash. Carter's wallet is immaculate.

"Amanda, I don't think I bought that bear."

I turn it over, looking for a message from Private, something tucked into the ribbon around its neck. There's nothing. But on the merchandise tag, there's an orange price sticker from CVS. *Clearance $5.00.*

"I don't think you did either." I think about how some serial killers mark their victims or leave a token at the crime scene, and suddenly I'm freezing, despite my coat. Someone knew Carter was going to CVS. They put it in his bag, left it for me to find. Private wants me to know he was responsible for the hit-and-run.

I smile and take Carter's hand in mine. This time I hold it firm, don't let him pull away. A million dollars says there will be a message from Private waiting for me at home. I look up, and Carter's parents are back, waiting in the doorway for us to finish up. I shove the bear into my bag and lean over to kiss the top of his head.

"I should go."

"Can you hand me my phone?" he asks. "I'll be bored here without you."

I grab it from the side table and hand it over. "I'll see you soon," I promise.

At home, our delivery from Taro sits in a soggy bag on the porch. I pull into the garage, then walk outside to retrieve it. Inside, I shove it into the trash and grab my phone from the dining room table. It's almost completely dead, but I have a bunch of new messages. When I have it plugged into the charger in my room, I open them. Most of the texts are from Trina, but I have two new messages from Private. My hand trembles as I open the conversation.

It's a group text, to both me and Rosalie, from 8:31.

> You shouldn't have ignored me. Now
> look what you made me do.

The second message is from 9:42.

> You have 9 days until your boyfriend
> turns 18. You both have instructions,
> and they still stand. Ignore me again,
> and it will be much, much worse
> next time.

I close out of the conversation. In a few minutes, a new message comes through. This time, it's from Rosalie.

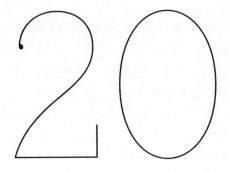

20

ROSALIE

MONDAY, JANUARY 15

At Youth Ministry, the memory of last night sticks in my throat like a stone I can't swallow down. When it's my turn to share my affirmation of the profound word, I tap into old reserves—the ones I learned from Michael. Flip the switch, get numb. Another girl's voice spills from my lips, professes how true healing can't begin until we know we're broken, how it's through darkness that His way is revealed as pure light. Brother Masters praises my bravery and leads us in a hymn about Jesus, our strong tower. I raise my arms and sway along with Ivan Brophy and Beth Clark and Emily Masters and everyone else, but my mind is a million miles from God's Grace.

I let this happen. When Carter came into my life, I thought I'd found my delivery from church offices and camp isolation rooms and my parents' watchful eye. I should have known better than to believe in miracles. I spin the purity ring around and around on my finger.

When we're all bundling up in our coats and scarves, Brother Masters pulls me aside. His hair, thick and blond like Emily's, is creased up at a funny angle from his snow cap.

"I liked what you had to say today, Rosalie. It is through recognizing the darkness within us that we come to see His light."

"Thanks," I mumble, jamming my hands into my gloves.

"But you seem distracted," he continues, and I know I'm not off the hook. As always, my performance was good, but not good enough. "When you focus on strengthening your relationship with Jesus, that's when true progress happens. This summer, I'm leading a mission trip to a rural community in Kentucky. It's a place a lot like Culver Ridge, and we have the special opportunity to bring our Fellowship ministry to the people there. I'll be announcing the details in a few weeks, but I wanted to tell you now." His look says this is a prize, a secret between us.

I nod, trying to keep my expression neutral.

"You'll be eighteen by July?"

"I will," I say hesitantly.

"I'd like you come, Rosalie. To assist me, as a Youth Ministry leader." He clasps my hand in his, and I can feel the force of his grip even through my glove.

His offer should be an honor, but it feels like a threat. I promise to think about it, then duck outside before Ivan can shower me with stories about his day with Mission Driven.

On the ride home with Dad, the snow is really coming down, a rush of thick, wet flakes that have already piled up three feet deep on the sidewalks. We drive slow, and I tell him about Brother Masters's mission trip. I talk as if I might actually go. As if I won't have already moved out, won't be living in Pittsburgh with Pau. More lies, but it's worth it for this brief moment. Dad looks delighted. This might be one of the last times he looks at me that way.

When I'm finally in my room with the chair jammed under the doorknob, I change out of my church clothes and start packing my pen. It's almost ten, and my nerves are shot. I just need to relax and crawl into bed. I crack the window and breathe the vapor in until my chest unlocks, a slow liquid warmth spreading from my lungs to the tips of my fingers and toes. Then, I lie on my bed, on top of the covers, and let myself float. Eventually, I turn my phone on and plug it into the charger. I haven't checked it for hours; no screens at Youth Ministry.

My notifications light up immediately. I have a series of texts, a missed call from a local number, and an unheard voice mail. I press play.

"This is Meghan calling from Mercy Hospital in Logansville. I'm calling at the request of a patient here, Carter Shaw. Rosalie, Mr. Shaw was in a car accident this afternoon. He's currently in surgery, but has asked that you get in touch with him as soon as possible."

My heart jumps to my throat. I need Carter to be out of my life, but also, I need him to be okay. To live out a long and happy future with Amanda, as if I'd never meddled. A small voice inside my head says this accident was somehow my fault. I pushed him away, didn't give him anything close to a real explanation. Maybe he did something dangerous, because of me.

I click over to my texts, and everything shifts into focus. Two new group messages from Private, claiming responsibility for something Amanda and I supposedly made him or her do. Carter in the hospital, Private's promise that *"it will be much, much worse next time."* This was no accident. I send a quick text to the other number on the chat.

> Is this Amanda? What's going on?

The reply comes right away.

> Stay out of this. I'll handle it.

> Fine, great.

She doesn't text back.

I don't feel fine or great. I feel dead sober. I feel scared. I also feel like the worst person in the world. I open up a new message to Carter.

> Are you okay? Someone from the hospital called.

> Rosalie.

> Hey.

> I through you wear ignoring the wounded.

What? Sorry. Youth Ministry tonight.

Ripe, forgot. Typing with once hand.
Can we FaceTime?

A fist of worry tightens inside my chest. This needs to be a clean break. I can't get sucked back in. But Carter's in the hospital, probably because of me—because I ignored Private's demands. My pesky, worthless conscience says I owe him a few minutes on FaceTime.

When he answers the call, he's a mess. Bandaged face, weird hospital lighting. He holds up his arm to show me the cast.

"You look like you got hit by a truck."

"I think it was a car. But yeah."

"What happened?"

"I'm not really sure? I was walking by school. You may have noticed there's a snowstorm." He cracks a smile. "Ouch."

"Out of control driver?"

"Yeah, drove up on the sidewalk. I don't really remember, but a snowbank caught me. Broke my arm and cracked a couple ribs, but I'll be fine."

"That's terrible. I'm so sorry, Carter." *Because I did this to you. Because this is my fault.* I force myself to smile.

"Rosalie, listen, I was thinking. About yesterday—"

"Carter, look—"

"No, let me finish. Remember that car? The one that almost hit me when you were on your bike, and I was in the other lane?"

"Yeah?"

"It's not a coincidence." His voice is dead serious. Determination radiates through the bandages.

"You think it was the same driver?" But that was *before* I texted Private.

Carter shakes his head gently. "No, listen. Yesterday, I almost got into an accident, but you were there. You saved me. Today, you weren't here."

I suck in a quick breath, and he continues. "Don't you see it, Rosalie? There's a connection. It's a sign we're not supposed to be apart." I start to shake my head back and forth, but he keeps talking. "It's like yesterday, there was a shield around me, and today, that shield was gone."

"Carter—" I start to say. He has it all wrong. He almost got into an accident yesterday because he was *driving in the wrong lane.*

"You believe in God, right, Rosalie?"

I stare at him on the screen, my mouth hanging open. He sounds like my parents, their believer's addiction to the twenty-four-hour news cycle. Is Carter Shaw about to ask me if I've taken Jesus into my heart?

"Rosalie?" he asks again.

"Of course I do," I say slowly. Despite everything the Fellowship has taken away from me, they can't take away God. Even if I can't picture what our relationship will look like once I leave the FOC behind.

Carter nods. "I've never been sure, until tonight. But this accident was a sign from God."

"I don't—"

"You don't have to say anything right now. Just think about it. We're supposed to be together, Rosalie. I love you so much. I really need you right now."

For the second time in as many days, I can feel the air being squeezed out of my lungs. I've told so many lies, and now, this is my punishment.

I force myself to take in a shaky breath. "I think you need some rest. This must be really stressful."

"Wish you were here," he says. "I miss you."

I give him a weak smile. "Take care, okay?"

Before he can say anything else, I end the video call. Carter could have been killed today. I slam my fist into my mattress with an unsatisfying thud. Here I am, still stuck in this mess. I have to unmask Private before we find out what's next, but the one person who could help me hates my guts. A heart-to-heart with my family is out of the question, and because of the holiday weekend, I haven't seen Pau since Friday. I am totally alone.

I get under the covers without brushing my teeth, then stare up at the ceiling and follow the lines where the paint has cracked. Just one of the many home repairs we never got around to making. If I look at it one way, it's a network, a road map. Endless paths. But when I look again, it's a just a broken web. My life on display, all the threads torn apart.

AMANDA

TUESDAY, JANUARY 16

In a rare display of parental empathy, my mother knocks on my door Tuesday morning to tell me she's notified the school I'll be staying home today. I can't even believe she's up. She says something about needing my rest after the stress of last night. I'll take it. I fall back to sleep and when I wake again, it's after eleven.

I check my phone. Adele wants to know where I am today. Graham says he's driving Ben and Bronson to the hospital at lunch, if I want to come. I can't deal with anyone right now, and most of all, I can't face Carter again so soon. I text back saying I'm sick.

The last text is from Alexander, a sweet note asking how

I'm feeling. I hesitate, my fingers hovering over the screen, then write:

Honestly? I'm scared.

And if I'm being really honest, fear is only the thick outer layer. Beneath that, I'm furious someone thinks this is part of a game I never asked to play. And sick to my stomach that Carter got hurt because I wouldn't surrender to Private. And even deeper? I feel like I'm breaking. Because we aren't happy, and we haven't been for a long time. This isn't really about Rosalie, much as I'd love to pin it all on her. This is about Carter and me, and I'm not sure there's any way to fix us.

I don't know what to say to Carter, where we go from here. But I'm not about to give some egomaniac with an anonymous number and an anger management problem the satisfaction of thinking he destroyed us. If we break up, it'll be on *my* terms. And I'm not about to dump my boyfriend of over three years while he's in the hospital. Which means I have a few days to think, figure out what I really want. And in the meantime, I've got to channel every ounce of anger and sadness and fear into exposing Private. It's the only way to end this.

My stomach clenches, and I realize the only thing I've eaten since breakfast yesterday was that smoothie before the hospital. I need food. I need to think. I need to go to CVS. That bear is going to lead me straight to Private. Game over.

Downstairs, Linda is in Dad's office with the door closed. More fund-raising calls. The TV in the kitchen is on mute, but the scroll bar at the bottom of the screen reads: *Police searching for unknown driver in Logansville South hit-and-run,* followed by a request for anyone with information to contact the station. I keep reading; they don't even have a make or model for the vehicle. Which means the traffic camera didn't catch anything. They have nothing. I leave a note on the island and head out.

An acai bowl and giant coffee later, I'm recharged. I leave a tip for the girl behind the counter at Vanilla Bean, then drive to CVS. There are no spots in the tiny lot out front, so I turn onto the side street next to the store and park illegally against the curb.

I pass the bin of stuffed animals on my way in. It's right up front, at the end of the service counter. I spy at least three identical teddy bears among the puppies and giraffes.

"I need to speak to the manager on duty," I tell the kid working the cash register. He's scrawny and pimpled and looks like he should be in school right now.

"Is there a problem?" he asks.

"No problem. I just need to speak to him or her, okay?"

He points toward a door at the end of the counter. "You can knock. Fred's in the office."

The door opens, and Fred motions me inside. He's a middle-aged guy with a too-tight cotton shirt tucked into his belt and a grease stain on his collar. A yellow wrapper with a half-eaten burger is spread out on his desk. He invites me to take a seat in the plastic chair across from him.

I put on my sweetest smile and tuck a strand of hair behind my ear. "So terribly sorry to interrupt your lunch. I promise I'll be very quick."

Fred smiles at me, charmed.

"I just need to ask about a purchase," I continue. "Were you the store manager on duty yesterday afternoon?"

"Sure was. You want to return something?"

"No, nothing like that. Someone bought a teddy bear from that bin of stuffed animals you have up front." I pull it out of my bag and show him the CVS price sticker on the tag. "Do you have sales receipts or security cameras or something? I need to know who it was."

"You need to know who bought that bear?" Fred raises his eyebrows, unamused.

I smile again, cranking up the charm. "Yes, yesterday. I just need to know who bought it for me."

Fred lifts the burger to his mouth and takes a big, greasy bite. "If you got it as a gift, we can take it back for store credit," he says around a mouthful of ketchup and bun. "Can't accept returns without a receipt."

This isn't working. I change tactics.

"You know the hit-and-run that happened up the road last night? I'm sure you saw it on the news." I stare meaningfully at Fred, letting the gravity of my words register. He blinks. "The bear is criminal evidence. I need to see security footage. Or I could just look through the stack of yesterday's receipts. You wouldn't even know I'm here."

Fred is glaring at me now. "Listen, ma'am. We can't show you security tape or customer records. If this teddy bear was driving the car, you'd better get the police involved. Now if you'll excuse me, I'm on lunch."

"No, wait—"

Fred stands and pushes past me, opening the office door.

"Out. If the police want to poke around, fine. You have to talk to them."

I stand and stumble back into the store, and Fred closes the door in my face. Jerk.

The kid working the cash register has been replaced by a forty-something woman with a bad dye job and a stone face. She gives me the side-eye as I snap a picture of the stuffed animal bin with my phone, but doesn't comment.

"Were you working yesterday?" I ask.

"Nope, off on Mondays," she says.

This is useless. I walk outside. The storm has been over for hours, but the snow is thick and crusted on the sidewalk as I tramp around the side of the store toward my car. When I'm about to cross the street, I notice the kid from the cash register smoking a cigarette next to the dumpsters around back. I spin on my heel and walk over to him.

"Can I have one of those?" I hate cigarettes, and the dumpsters reek, but I need an in.

He stares at me like he can't believe I'm actually talking to him. "Sure," he splutters, digging out his pack.

"I'm Amanda," I say, smiling. "You're Greg?"

"How'd you know that?"

I shrug. "I have an excellent memory. Read your name tag inside."

He hands me a cigarette and his lighter. I strike out three times in the wind before he takes the lighter back. "Let me do that for you."

"Thank you so much, Greg. I really appreciate it."

When I've successfully inhaled a foul lungful of smoke, I get serious.

"You work Mondays?"

"Yeah, afternoon shift pretty much every day. I study mornings. I'm going for my GED."

I nod like I care. "Awesome. Listen, someone bought me a teddy bear here yesterday. The kind from the bin up front. You know?"

He nods enthusiastically. "Sure, great deal. Clearing out all the little ones before we get in the big Valentine's Day order next week."

I smile and take another drag.

"Greg, I need your help. The bear was a gift." I lean in close and lower my voice. "Like from a secret admirer?"

He tosses his cigarette butt to the ground and grinds it into the slushy pavement with the heel of his boot. "Yeah?"

"And, it was really sweet and all, but I don't know who gave it to me. I'm just going wild trying to figure it out."

"Huh," he grunts.

"I need to know who bought it, Greg. Can you help me with that?"

He stares at me blankly. This kid needs a crash course in social graces. I touch his elbow and give him my most sincere gaze.

He shoves his hands into his coat pockets, and my hand drops. "I'd like to help you, Amanda. I really would. But we've sold lots of stuffed animals from that bin over the past couple weeks. Like I said, we're clearing them out. Sold five or six just yesterday." He pauses, deep in thought. "How do you know this secret admirer of yours bought it yesterday, anyway? We've had them in stock for ages, been on clearance for three weeks. Could have bought it anytime."

I'm about to tell him to shut up and think about yesterday's customers, but then it hits me that he's right. Private planted that bear on Carter yesterday, but he or she could have stocked up before staging the blood bath at my locker. This is totally pointless.

"Thanks for the smoke." I hold out the half-spent cigarette, and he takes it, surprised.

"Sure. Sorry I, uh, couldn't help more with the bear thing."

"Don't worry about it." I hurry across the street and get into my car, leaving Greg standing wide-mouthed next to the dumpsters.

On the drive home, I feel totally defeated. All that trip to CVS proved is that I'll never figure this out. But giving up means letting Private win. And I don't even want to think about what that might mean.

Think, Amanda. When did Private plant the bear in Carter's backpack? If they did it at the scene, wouldn't the police have found footprints? Or was it snowing so hard they were covered up by the time the cops got there? That's possible. Maybe Private was counting on that. Or maybe Private planted the bear *before* the accident, during practice. With school closed yesterday, the lacrosse team probably didn't even lock up their stuff. It could be one of them.

It could be one of our friends.

The thought is equal parts reassuring and terrifying. I can't imagine anyone we know doing something so cruel. But someone hit Carter with a car. Someone is out for blood.

I shiver. I thought I had this under control, but clearly I don't. Carter's in the hospital, CVS was a dead end. I need someone to talk to, someone who can really help. I think about Rosalie's offer to meet up. She might be useful, but I'm not exactly ready to team up with her either.

I need my mother.

At home, I knock on the office door.

"Yes?" She sounds annoyed. I should wait until this evening when she's done with her calls, but by then she'll be drinking. I need her sober for this.

"It's Amanda. Can we talk?"

I open the door without waiting for a response. She's sitting at Dad's desk, call list in front of her and a donor spreadsheet open on the computer. She rubs her temples.

"I suppose I could use a break."

I sit down on the couch and pull my knees up to my chin, like I used to when I was a little kid. I inhale the scent of old books and the faint spice of Dad's cologne. I thought I could be strong—for Carter, for his parents, for my parents. I thought I could be the person they all need me to be. The girl who won't disappoint them. But I can't do it anymore, not with Carter in the hospital, not totally alone.

My mother has her vices, but she's still my mother. She'll know what to do. I can't be Amanda Kelly right now—sharp wit, on top, in charge. In this moment, I just need to be a kid. I need my mom to fix this.

"It's about the accident," I begin, voice shaking. "The thing is, I don't think it was an accident. I think someone hit Carter on purpose."

As soon as I start talking, I feel a giant flood of relief. I tell her about the anonymous threats, the track, the teddy bear in

Carter's backpack. I remind her about the scene at my locker. The only thing I leave out is Rosalie. If I mention Rosalie, my mother will make this all about her. She'll jump to conclusions, insist that somehow this is me being petty. She'll turn my words back on me. So I leave Rosalie out and focus on Carter. How someone is trying to break us up. How this person is dangerous.

When I'm finished, Linda doesn't say anything right away. She's not a touchy-feely person, so I don't know why I expect her to leap from her chair and hug me, but I do. I expect her to pull me close and tell me she'll protect me. I expect her to be a real mother for once.

She doesn't move. "So you think the deviant who defaced your locker is the person who hit Carter?" Her voice is steady.

"I'm sure of it. I can prove that the person sending the texts was responsible. They contacted me after both incidents. After they locked me in at the track too. I don't know who it is, but I can prove it's the same person with the text history on my phone. It's why I have to go to the police."

I'm not sure I'm going to do it until the words are out of my mouth. But as soon as I say it, it's clear. I can't trace Private's messages, but maybe the police can. This is exactly what I was hoping for, back when I thought the texts were from Rosalie. That afternoon with Trina and Adele seems like a million years ago. Until yesterday, there was no real crime. Just creepy stuff and veiled threats. But now, there's already a police investigation into Carter's accident. A hit-and-run is a serious crime. The police are looking for leads, information that could help them find the driver. They'll take me seriously now.

"No. No police." My mother gets up from the desk and sits beside me on the couch without touching me.

"Why not? We need—"

"No police, Amanda. The benefit is less than a week away. This family needs to focus. An investigation is the last thing we need right now. It's good that you came to me about this. Your father and I will handle this privately."

"The benefit?" My voice is too loud. My mother flinches. "You want to withhold evidence that could lead to the driver's arrest because of *the benefit*?"

"Don't twist my words, Amanda. There are things happening on the board right now that you couldn't possibly understand. This is not a good time for an investigation. Besides, I just don't see how text messages from an anonymous number are going to help the police catch the person who hit Carter."

"I don't know, okay? I'm not the police. But isn't that their job?"

My mother gives me a sad smile. "I'm sorry that someone's been bothering you, darling. This must have all been terrible for you, and I wish you'd opened up to me sooner. But going to the police isn't going to help. The accident is hardly a secret; it was all over the evening news. Anybody could have turned on the TV and tried to take credit. It's sick behavior, but if someone wanted you to believe he was responsible, it wouldn't have been very hard. The police will see that immediately."

I sit in silence. That Private could have seen coverage of the accident on TV never even occurred to me. I think back to the texts. The earliest one was from around eight thirty, over three hours after the accident. By that time, they'd released Carter's identity. My heart sinks. Private could have just seen it on the news.

I start to cry. Big, hot tears spill down my cheeks onto my shirt. My mother dangles one stiff arm around my shoulders.

"Darling, it's going to be okay. You just needed to talk it out." She pauses while I grab a tissue from the box on the side table and dab at my face. "You know what we'll do? I have the best idea. We'll plan a family trip, after the benefit. You can bring Adele if you'd like. We'll get away for a few days, somewhere warm. Wouldn't that be nice?"

I try to smile. I picture Adele and me in our bikinis, stretched out in the sand. Somewhere tropical. Somewhere miles away from Logansville and Private and fake blood and Rosalie Bell. It's a nice fantasy.

"That sounds perfect," I say, playing along. "Maybe Turks and Caicos? Trina raved about this resort on Provo when she went with her dad last year."

"That's the spirit." My mother pats my shoulder, then removes her arm. "I'll talk to your father tonight. About the text messages and the trip. We'll handle this, Amanda, I promise. I don't want you to worry."

I stand and start toward the door. "I'll let you get back to your calls."

"Be strong, Amanda. When you have something that people want, they're going to try to take it from you. You have class, respect. You have Carter. I'm sorry to say this is only the beginning. People are going to be jealous of you all your life. You have to grow a thick skin," she admonishes me for the second time in a week. "An investigation invites scandal. The Kellys cannot afford to be the family who cried wolf. Understand?"

I nod. She's still looking at me. She's waiting for me to say it out loud.

"I understand."

"Good." My mother stands and walks briskly back to the desk. "Now go do some research. Turks and Caicos or wherever you want to go. It'll make you feel better."

My head is swimming when I close the office door. I'm more confused than I was before we talked. If Private isn't really connected to the hit-and-run, the police won't thank me for coming forward. It could look bad for our family. But what are my parents going to do? We're not the mob. No one's going to put a hit on Private.

Knowing my parents, their way of handling this will be to put in a call to our lawyer. Then, they'll forget all about it. And if Private really is dangerous, a phone call to our lawyer will do exactly nothing. If I don't do something, and fast, someone could wind up dead.

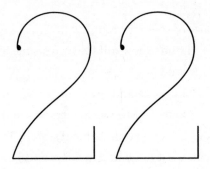

ROSALIE

TUESDAY, JANUARY 16

My parents think I'm at Mercy Hospital right now, visiting Carter. Instead, I'm in the O'Malley's lot, waiting for Pau. Since the museum on Friday, I've been sending her regular updates, and today we finally had school again, but it's not like we could talk about anything important in the Greater Logansville cafeteria. I've lived through worse days, but it's been a while. I'm not used to coping without Pau. By the time she pulls into the lot and I slide into the passenger's seat of her brother's car, I'm a giant ball of nerves and sparks. I sink into the seat cushion and blasting heat, and I can physically feel my muscles uncramp.

"You look like hell, Lee-Lee."

"I feel like hell."

"But you did the right thing, with Carter. I'm really proud of you." She's beaming.

We stare at each other for a minute. I want to lean across the seat and press my lips to hers, but we're in the middle of a parking lot.

"Let's drive."

Pau pulls onto the road, and for a few minutes we drive in silence. When we're halfway to the ridge, she says, "Talk to me about what happens now."

I'm grateful to Paulina for cutting right to the chase, but I don't have any answers. I'm no closer to uncovering Private's identity than I was before they put Carter in the hospital. Amanda still won't talk to me. And we're one email away from being outed to my dad.

"I wonder what it would feel like to be Ecclesiastically Extradited," I say finally.

Pau tightens her grip on the wheel. "I thought your church was supposed to evangelize the lost. Isn't banishing people kind of hypocritical?"

I shrug. "It's complicated. The FOC's mission is evangelical, and they don't Extradite everyone who leaves. It's all about fear. If the church thinks members of the congregation might be susceptible to your un-Christian influence, they'll make the family sever ties."

"And Lily . . ."

"They'd absolutely consider her susceptible."

Paulina whistles slowly through her teeth. "That's some messed-up shit."

"Welcome to the FOC, where the specialties of the house are God's love and messed-up shit."

We pull in at the ridge, and for a moment we sit in silence. I've never been up here before. I expected it to be crawling with cars, kids hooking up in the backseat, but tonight it's pretty empty. Probably the weather driving everyone inside. I've never even considered coming here with Pau—too public—but this might be one of our last nights together for a long time. The accident has been all over the news, and naturally my parents have been tuned in to every piece of coverage. Unless the story dries up fast, it's only a matter of time before Amanda gives an interview or Channel Eleven shows a picture of Carter with his "devoted girlfriend."

After my parents find out that I broke up with Carter, or about Amanda, or see the photos with Pau—whichever damning revelation gets out first—I'll be on lockdown at best. With everything falling apart around me, I need something good in my life. I need to be with the person I love.

I glance over at Pau. Now that we're here, we're both feeling the gravity of this week hard. To break the mood, I reach for her phone and settle on an oldies playlist she has saved. Some bouncy fifties tune fills the car with good vibrations, and my phone beeps. Carter.

I miss you.

I don't respond, and a minute later, he texts again.

I can't stand not seeing you. Come visit me?

You know I can't. Too public.

> Come after visiting hours. I'll sneak
> you in.

"Carter?" Pau asks.

"Yeah. He wants me to come to the hospital, but I'm not going."

I type a quick reply, the last.

> Can't talk right now. Sorry.

With a pang of guilt, I switch my phone to silent and toss it in my bag. "He's out of his mind. Over FaceTime last night, he was raving about the car accident being a sign from God that we shouldn't have broken up."

"No shit."

"It's like he suddenly found religion. He thinks we're fated to be together."

"You sure the car didn't hit his head?"

"He does have a concussion. . . ."

We both laugh. Then Paulina says, "The only one you're fated to be with is me."

I smile, in spite of myself. In spite of everything, I have Paulina. For now.

"Listen," she says. "I'm here for you, no matter what. I swear to Pussy Riot and David Bowie and all that is holy that I will do everything in my power to make sure the FOC doesn't get its hands on you. Even if it means kidnapping you until you turn eighteen."

I lean across the seat and press my lips softly against hers. "I love you."

She glances at the backseat and raises her eyebrows. "What do you say, lover? You, me, and this luxuriously cushioned Civic?" I follow her gaze into the back, which is clean and empty except for a couple blankets. "Let's make tonight about us. Tomorrow, we will face whatever comes."

I climb into the back and Pau follows. Under the tree where we're parked, it's pitch black and quiet except for the hum of the car heater. I kick off my boots, and Pau does the same. We twist around on the cushions until I'm on my back and Pau's half next to me, half on top of me, pretzeling our bodies into the small space. I'm used to the openness of the clearing, the chill of outside. In here, it's warm and close and strange. Paulina bumps my knee, then puts the palm of her hand down on my hair.

I giggle.

"What?"

"It's just so different. Than the clearing."

I scoot my shoulders so Pau has more room. Her lips brush mine in the dark.

"Good different," she says.

I nudge her lips apart with my tongue and kiss her deeper. I want to lose myself in her mouth, her body, her breath. I run my hands across her back and around to the front of her blazer. I slip them inside. My fingers find the softness of her breasts through her shirt. She shrugs her blazer off and tosses it to the floor of the car while I work down her shirt buttons, releasing them one by one until the only thing between us is the thin ribbed cotton of her undershirt. I trace one of her perfect, full nipples with my fingers, and Pau's breath catches.

She leans down and presses her mouth into mine, then unzips

my hoodie, and I scoot up in the seat so she can slip it off. Then, I pull her on top of me. I want the weight of her body against mine. I want the heat and the urgency. She slips her hand down into the waistband of my skirt, and I bury my face in her shoulder. In the darkness, stars explode against the perfect map of her skin.

When we're finished, first me and then her, we wrap ourselves in blankets and curl against each other. I rest my head on her shoulder and find her hand. Her fingers weave between mine, a perfect fit.

"I'm scared, Pau."

"Me too. But I am not going to lose you. I promise."

At home, I give my parents Carter's regards, then head upstairs. Lily's already asleep, clutching her stuffed cat to her chest. I give her a quick kiss on the cheek and get ready for bed. When I'm snuggling under the covers, a wave of exhaustion hits full-force. I think I might actually sleep tonight. Before turning out the light, I dig my phone out of my bag, where it's been on silent since we got to the ridge. Fourteen unread messages, all from Carter. I take a deep breath and open the conversation.

> Can you talk yet?

> What are you doing tonight?

> Why are you ignoring me, babe?

> Are you with someone else?

I'm sorry. They have me on some
serious painkillers.

The drugs are messing with my head.

You won't abandon me, right Rosalie?

Amanda doesn't know.

How the accident was a sign.
Everything changed.

I could have died, but I was saved.

We're supposed to be together.

I really need you.

Text me back.

Please.

I shudder and plug my phone into the charger. I'm sorry, Carter. But I'm not the girl for you.

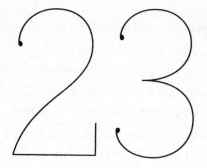

AMANDA

WEDNESDAY, JANUARY 17

When school lets out, I drive straight to the station. I should go to Mercy, but I'm still not ready to see Carter. I can't talk to him, not alone, not face to face, until I figure out exactly what to say. I send him a bunch of texts instead, and he doesn't seem too hurt that I haven't been there since Monday. He says he's mostly sleeping and watching old movies.

I park in the station lot and try not to lose my nerve. My mother is going to be furious, but if I'm right about this, I can bring the police right to Private. Which I'm sure I am. Almost.

Inside, there's a glass vase of half-wilted flowers on the Formica countertop that separates the entryway from the rest of the station, but no one's waiting to receive walk-ins. I've been standing aimlessly for a few seconds when a records clerk looks up from the file cabinets in back.

I explain that I have some evidence in the Carter Shaw hit-and-run and ask to see an officer working on the case. A few minutes later, I'm following Officer Cynthia Lu down a hallway into a small room with a desk and a wall of filing cabinets. It's just a regular office, not an interview room like on TV. She ducks outside to grab a metal folding chair from the hallway so I have somewhere to sit. The office is so cramped, there's barely room for me on the other side of her desk. I sit, knees pressed uncomfortably against the metal.

"Amanda Kelly," she says. "You're Carter Shaw's girlfriend?"

I nod. Officer Lu is a small woman with straight black hair pulled back into a clip. She's pretty, and she knows how to do her makeup to bring out her dark eyes and high cheekbones. She's definitely not the gruff, donut-eating, coffee-swilling cop I thought I'd be talking to. I try to relax. She seems nice, like she'll listen to me.

I draw in a deep breath. I'm really going to do this. My mother's face flashes before me, her eyes narrowing to slits. *The Kellys cannot afford to be the family who cried wolf.* But then I think of Carter, a sitting duck in his hospital bed. I can't afford to let this go any further.

"I'm here because I have some evidence in the hit-and-run. I mean, it could be evidence, and I wanted to turn it in." I open my bag and pull out everything I've collected: a handful of Trina's photo prints, the florist card, the teddy bear, and my phone.

Officer Lu stares at the objects on her desk for a minute without touching them. "Amanda, how old are you?"

"Seventeen."

"Do you have a parent with you today?"

"No."

"Okay. Or a lawyer?"

I shake my head. "I'm not in trouble, am I?"

"Of course not. But, Amanda, you're a minor. Are you sure you don't want one of your parents present when we talk?"

"I'm sure." I swallow. "I just want to tell you what I know."

She leans back in her chair. "Okay, go ahead."

I start at the beginning, with the texts. I pull them up on my phone, showing her the entire conversation with Private. I tell her about my locker, show her the photos still up on Instagram and the florist card with its cryptic message. I show her the photos of Rosalie kissing that other girl, and then the photo prints from the rock garden. I tell her about getting locked in at the track. Finally, I tell her about the teddy bear in Carter's backpack on the night of the accident, how Carter had no recollection of buying it or how it got there. I show her the CVS sticker on the tag and the photo I took of the clearance bin yesterday. I point to the headless bear in the locker photos, show her it's the same one.

Officer Lu listens quietly as I speak. She nods in the right places, but doesn't ask any questions. Finally, I show her the last messages from Private, the group conversation with Rosalie on Monday night.

"He sent this just hours after the accident. He's claiming responsibility for hitting Carter."

"And you don't have any idea who is sending these messages, Amanda?" Officer Lu asks. "Think carefully. It could really help us."

"At first, I thought it was Rosalie. But it's not; he went after her too."

"You keep saying 'he.' You're certain this is a man?"

"I think so? I don't know. It just seems like it is."

"I see." Officer Lu folds her hands together on top of her desk. Her nails are painted with a faint rose polish, and the tip of the nail on one index finger is chipped. "Any ideas, other than Rosalie? Maybe someone at school?"

"I don't know." My heart starts beating fast. It didn't occur to me that she'd ask so many questions. "Can't you trace the texts? Like with police software? That would be the fastest way, right? Then you'd know for sure who was doing this."

"We'll certainly look into identifying the number, Amanda, but text messages sent from numbers with blocked caller IDs are difficult to track down. The texter could be using a disposable prepaid phone."

"You mean a burner?"

"That's right. If the messages are being sent from a burner phone, we may be able to identify the number, but it's very difficult to connect disposable phones to their owners. Our best source of information here is you. Now can you think of anyone who might want to hurt Carter? Or damage his relationship with you, or this other girl, Rosalie?"

My heart is beating even faster now. I'm drawing a complete blank. I thought this would be simple. I'd tell them what I know and hand over my phone. They'd plug it into whatever police tracking software they use, and presto. Private would be revealed.

"Lots of girls would like to see Carter single," I manage. "But why would they hit him with a car?"

"Is there anyone at school who has a history with Carter? A fight, maybe. A disagreement. Something about Carter they didn't like."

"Everyone loves Carter. You have to understand, he's a really *nice* person. We have a close group of friends, but then he's friendly with everyone in our grade. The underclassmen look up to him. He's not just 'popular' in that fake way people mean. With Carter, it's *real*." It's true; no one would want to hurt Carter.

Officer Lu frowns. "Sometimes popularity breeds jealousy, Amanda." She sounds like my mother. "I want you to keep thinking, okay?"

I nod.

"And what about his family? They work in real estate, correct?"

"Shaw Realty."

"Do you know Carter's father well?"

"Winston? He's practically my father-in-law. We've lived across the street from the Shaws since second grade."

"That's very helpful, Amanda. So your parents are close with the Shaws, I gather?"

A growing clang of alarm bells starts to echo in my brain. This is exactly what my mother was afraid of: scandal.

"Amanda?" she asks again. I have to answer the question.

"We're neighbors."

She nods, pen flying across paper. "Does Mr. Shaw have any enemies that you're aware of?"

"Enemies?"

"Do you know of anyone who has a bad relationship with Shaw Realty? A competing firm, perhaps? Anyone who might be a business rival?"

"You think someone hit Carter to get back at his dad?"

"I'm just asking questions, Amanda."

"But that's what you're implying, right? That someone could be targeting Carter to get at the business?"

"It's possible. The hit-and-run may have been an accident. Driver lost control of the vehicle in the storm, got scared, drove off. Now that Carter's condition has been released to the media, and it's public knowledge that he will recover, we've been hoping someone will come forward to accept responsibility. But what you've shared with me today may change the nature of our investigation. We have to explore all the possibilities."

Cold, heavy dread pools in my gut. Carter's parents will be questioned. My parents will probably be questioned too. My mother was right; I shouldn't have come here. This doesn't have anything to do with our parents—I'm sure of it.

I smile politely at Officer Lu. "Of course you have to explore the possibilities. But none of Mr. Shaw's business colleagues care who Carter dates. I'm certain this has nothing to do with Shaw Realty. The person you really need to talk to is the manager at CVS. You need to figure out who purchased these teddy bears. I know it sounds silly, but that's your suspect pool."

"Mmm." Officer Lu clasps and unclasps her hands. "We'll take that under advisement. Thank you, Amanda."

She's not going to do it. I'm handing her the key to solving this thing, but she has it in her head that this is some sort of business revenge plot. That the adults are the ones she needs to interrogate. I try to push my chair back, but it's pressed tight against the file cabinet behind me. I stand up awkwardly and squeeze out.

"I think I need to get home."

"Amanda, if you think of anyone or anything else, please be in touch. Here's my direct number." She hands me a business card from a little black holder on her desk. "I'm afraid we'll need to keep your phone, at least until we've concluded our investigation. Would you please write down the password if you have one?"

She hands me another business card, this one flipped over so the blank side is facing up. I jot it down.

"So you'll still try to identify the number?"

"Of course. We're going to do everything we can to find the driver, Amanda. And that includes studying the digital evidence."

I feel a tiny bit reassured. I know it's a long shot, but maybe Private wasn't using a burner. Maybe they'll be able to track him down through the texts after all. Officer Lu studies me closely. Her eyebrows are drawn in, her lips pressed tight. I can tell she's unsure how seriously to take all this. How seriously to take me. Teddy bears, text messages, high school pranks. I know how it sounds. Like kid stuff.

"And CVS?" I ask again. "The manager's name is Fred."

"We'll be exploring all potential leads." Officer Lu extends her hand toward me. "Thank you for coming in today."

I take her hand and give it a quick shake. If the texts don't lead the police to Private, all I've accomplished today is causing a scandal. Just like my mother warned.

Instead of going straight home, I drive around Logansville for a while, trying to think. The only thing that really sparked Officer Lu's interest was the possible tie to Shaw Realty. My chest gets tighter and tighter, and finally I have to drive home. By the time

I'm pulling into the driveway and waiting for the garage door to open, I'm barely breathing.

My mother is on me before I reach the top of the basement stairs.

"Amanda Kelly. Get in here."

Officer Lu didn't waste any time. I want to bite back, tell her I know what I'm doing, but that's not even close to the truth. I *thought* I knew what I was doing, going to the police. Her face tells me I screwed up, big time.

I unzip my coat and take a seat at the breakfast table. My mother stands at the island, a tall glass in her hand. It's not even dinnertime, but something tells me the clear liquid she's tilting toward her lips isn't water. She doesn't join me at the table.

"I received a very unsettling call just now. Do you know who it might have been from?"

"Officer Lu?" My voice is barely a whisper.

"Speak up, Amanda."

"Officer Lu? From the station?"

My mother's lips are twisted into an ugly pink knot. She raises her glass and takes a long drink. I wince, hoping she doesn't notice. If she senses I'm judging her on top of everything else, it'll really send her over the edge.

Fortunately, she's too focused on her anger, and possibly a little too drunk, to notice or care. "That's right, Amanda. Officer Cynthia Lu. She told me that you came by the station, that you two had quite the tête-à-tête. I apologized profusely and told her your father and I were handling things."

A spike of anger flares in my chest. I feel bad about going to the police, about dragging my parents into this mess. But her words just confirm how seriously they are *not* taking me.

"How are you and Dad handling things?" I ask, my voice a bit too loud. I suck in a shaky breath, try to get myself under control. "I'm sorry about Officer Lu, I really am. I didn't know she'd get you and Dad involved. But can't you see that I'm scared?"

My voice breaks, the anger turning to hysteria. I'm actually shaking, tugged in a million directions. I'm angry at myself for thinking things would be easy once I went to the cops, for being naive. I'm angry at my mother for making my fear seem trivial, making it crystal clear my safety isn't her primary concern. And most of all, I'm scared. This has gone from creepy to violent, and Private is still out there.

My mother sets her glass down on the island with a sharp *clink*. "Is that what you think, Amanda? That your father and I are not concerned for the safety and security of this family, above all else?"

If she loved me, she would wrap her arms around me tight. If she really cared, she would see how bad I'm shaking, and she would want to stop it, make it all better. She doesn't move.

"Your father has been on the phone with Jackson several times since last night." For a moment I can't place the name, and then I remember he's the lawyer we have on retainer. "He's referred us to a very reputable PI, who we've hired, but with your phone locked up in evidence, I don't know what good that's going to do us now."

"A private investigator?"

"Someone to handle this quietly. Without the police rifling through our personal lives. You seem to have forgotten that's a priority. I told your Officer Lu that you were unstable, that this isn't the first time you've dreamed up a stalker. I assured her you were receiving the best treatment possible, and that we'd be involving your doctor immediately. I was very apologetic, and I think I've managed to undo most of the damage you've done."

"You told her *what*?" My mother's words strike like a punch to the gut. Tears spring to my eyes as if I've been physically hit. It *feels* that bad. I think about all the little lies and deceptions she lives by so she can keep being Linda Kelly. So we can keep being the Logansville Kellys. Fraud alerts and new credit lines and the incessant push and pull with my dad and fantasy trips to Turks and Caicos we could never really afford. The endless alcoholic haze. The fact that we're the only three people who know how deep our debt really runs.

It's because of her—not me—that we're on the verge of falling apart.

"Thank goodness I was able to think on my feet, and that she called me first, before involving the Shaws. I am acting in your best interests and the best interests of this entire family, and Carter's. This is an especially difficult time for them. The last thing Krystal and Winston need is the police on their doorstep, digging around in their business affairs."

I suck in a quick breath and wipe at my eyes. My hand comes away wet as my mind whirls back to dinner with Carter at Verde. I picture Mr. Gallagher carrying pizza out to his car. Carter said Carl and Winston hadn't spoken for years. I try to picture Ben's dad in his work boots and black jacket typing anonymous texts into his phone. No way.

"You're right," I say slowly. "I'm sorry. When I went to the station, I thought they'd have tracking software. Something they could use to identify the person who's been texting me. I didn't think they'd ask so many questions."

My mother grimaces and picks up her glass. She drains it in one long slug. "That's right, you didn't think. Thankfully, after my damage control, the police have agreed not to pursue this line of inquiry any further, for the sake of your mental health." She turns toward the sink, stumbling slightly against the counter. Once she's straightened up and placed her glass down, she turns around to face me.

"Amanda, we are concerned for your safety, but as we discussed yesterday, this texter of yours is an opportunist. Someone who saw Carter's name on the news and jumped to take responsibility for a car accident in the middle of a snowstorm, which thankfully wasn't any worse than it was."

I sink into my chair. I feel like a child. When she puts it that way, she sounds totally sane. And I sound like the delusional one.

"I assured Officer Lu that we're doing everything in our power to look after your health and well-being," she continues.

"Are they going to use the tracking software?"

"I don't know, Amanda." She sighs. "She didn't go into detail. I couldn't exactly tell her to pursue certain leads but not others."

"And we can't get the phone back? To have the PI do it?"

"I'm going to keep trying, but they're refusing to release it." She pauses for a moment. "I assume you did not have the foresight to erase your call record before turning it in."

"Call record?"

"My call to the Beaufords on Monday night. And then Winston's call while I was still on the line with Jacques. It doesn't look right."

I look at her blankly. "You were on the phone about the benefit. And then Winston called to tell us Carter was at Mercy. There's nothing suspicious about that."

My mother sighs. "Never mind. My work for the museum is private, that's all. If you'd have just listened to me yesterday, our family would not be in this predicament."

"I know." My voice is small. I should have trusted my mother to begin with. Instead, I went and did exactly what she told me not to do. Now the police won't bother us, but they won't try to identify Private either. The cold dread from earlier spreads from my gut through my entire body. How could I have known she really was handling things? Hiring a PI never occurred to me. I screwed up, but she could have told me. She's not entirely blameless here.

Suddenly, it hits me. There's still a way out.

"I'm going to fix this. I promise."

"No." My mother's voice is icy and thick with alcohol. "You've done enough. No more meddling. From this point forward, we work with Nathaniel. Everything goes through him. Clear?"

She doesn't explain who Nathaniel is, or wait for an answer. She disappears into my dad's office, then returns with a sticky note listing a phone number and email address for an N.Krausse@ Krausseservices.com. He must be the PI. Fine, that's exactly the kind of meddling I had in mind. If the police aren't going to track down Private, I'll get Rosalie's phone to PI Krausse so he can do it.

I fold the sticky and slip it into my pocket. "We're clear."

My mother softens, face smoothing out into her usual composed mask. She returns to the sink and rinses out her glass, then reaches into the freezer for the vodka. That's my cue to head upstairs.

When I get to my room, I reach for my phone, but then I remember. No phone. Instead, I open my laptop and compose a new email.

Subject: Need to meet
From: me
To: Rosalie Bell

Things have changed, we need to meet.
Come to my place on Friday at 6, and
bring your phone. Don't delete anything
from Private. Very important.

I assume you know where I live. House
directly across from the Shaws'. Phone's
out of commission, so email me to
confirm.

—AK

I hit send. There are seven days until Carter's birthday. I have seven days to figure this out, and Rosalie is my last resort.

ROSALIE

THURSDAY, JANUARY 18

Paulina says she found a new spot, somewhere safe we can go. Auditions for the musical are this week, so the theater's crawling with Greater Logansville's triple threats after school, but the scene shop is empty. Pau and I both do the fall plays, and I'll do the monologue contest in March, but musicals are definitely not my thing.

An empty scene shop, on the other hand, has promise. After school, I take the little staircase leading to the backstage area and walk toward the shop. The hallway is empty, but my stomach is still in knots. The clearing was far enough off school grounds to feel untouchable. Until it wasn't. Here, the voices of the cast warming up bounce off the walls around me. I take in a deep breath and press through the scene shop door.

Pau's perched on a stool, elbows resting on the worktable. The warm-up sounds are even louder, the cast's combined voice rising to a slightly off-key pitch.

"They're right there," I whisper. "Are you sure no one's going to come in?"

"No one's ever here until we're actually building sets. That'll be weeks." Pau smiles, and I relax a bit. I slip off my coat and drape it across the table. It *is* nice to be inside.

Pau reaches into her backpack. "I brought Smart Pop."

For a few minutes, it feels like old times. Like everything is going to be fine. We tear into the bag and shovel handfuls of popcorn into our mouths. I dig into my backpack and produce a bag of Twizzlers.

"Amanda emailed me," I say finally.

Pau's eyes get wide. "When?"

"Last night. She wants to meet, tomorrow, at her house."

"Can you get away?"

I nod. "I'll say I'm going to see Carter again. My parents won't question it."

Paulina peels a Twizzler from the package and starts to nibble. "What do you think Princess Amanda wants?"

"Not sure, but something changed. Maybe she finally realized she's not going to solve this on her own."

Paulina's face gets serious. "I have an idea."

"Okay."

"You should definitely talk to her, find out what she knows. But I think you should also do what Private's asking. Get them off your back."

"What?"

"Hear me out. You know the audio recording? What if you made a fake one? Ramon could pretend to be Carter. You'd 'confess' to him about us, and we'd tape it. We can do it on Tuesday; we're going to an all-ages Latin Night in Logansville. You'll come along, we'll record in the car." Her face is pleading, and it's not just about making the tape. *Come out with me, Rosalie.* I want to say *yes, screw it, I'm already on the verge of getting caught,* but something is nagging at me, something aside from the usual reasons. . . .

"Then we'll password-protect that shit," Paulina is saying, "and send it off to Private. Think about it: Private gets what they want, and Carter wouldn't tell anyone, because he'd never know."

It clicks, and suddenly there are two different trains of thought fighting for control in my brain. The first goes: *That would never work.* Even if Private bought the recording, they'd figure out the truth soon enough.

The second says: *I never told Pau about making a recording.*

"How do you know about that?" I ask. "The audio?"

Pau's face drops and my gut twists, hard.

"You told me?" she says, but it's more of a question.

"I don't think so." My mind races back to our conversation on Tuesday night. Pau wouldn't intentionally try to get me Extradited. Right? Her voice echoes in my ears. *I swear to Pussy Riot and David Bowie and all that is holy that I will do everything in my power to make sure the FOC doesn't get its hands on you. Even if it means kidnapping you until you turn eighteen.* Extradition would mean no more FOC, because I'd just be out. Disowned. It would also mean no more Lily, no more family at all. In the wrong hands, the audio file would ensure that happened, and fast. But Pau would never make that decision for me. . . .

I glare, forcing her to meet my eyes.

"I looked through your phone," she admits. "I'm sorry. You left your backpack on the table at lunch, and I looked. I'm worried about you. I had to see the messages for myself."

"You could have asked. You need to trust me."

"I'm sorry."

I let her words hang in the air between us. I believe her, almost.

"Since you've read all my texts—"

"I said I'm sorry. I really am."

"Fine. I'm not ready to forgive you."

"Fine."

"But since you've read them, there's something else I've been thinking about." I pull out my phone and open the conversation with Private. The latest string of texts came in last night. "Look at these."

Just a friendly check-in, Sweetheart.

You've avoided Mercy long enough.
Time to pay the patient a visit.

There's no better birthday gift than
the truth. Tick-Tock.

"Yeah?" Pau hands my phone back to me.

"How would Private know that Carter's been asking me to visit? And that I haven't gone."

Paulina is quiet for a minute. She chews the left corner of her bottom lip. "Good guess?" she says finally. "Private found the clearing, and they showed up at your house. Those probably aren't the only times they've been following you."

I shiver. She has a point, but it's not one I really want to think about.

"So if Private's been watching you, they know you haven't gone to the hospital. It wouldn't take a genius to figure out that Carter's asked you to visit. They made an educated guess."

My voice drops to a whisper. "Do you think they're watching us now?"

"No way." Paulina reaches out and takes my hands in hers. "We're safe here. But Lee-Lee, this person is not messing around. You know I don't give ten shits about Carter Shaw, but someone put him in the hospital over this. Let me help you make the recording. Let's end this."

I swallow. The recording. Even if I thought it would work, which I don't, I wouldn't let Pau anywhere near that audio file. For the first time in the almost four years she's been in my life, I'm not sure I can trust her.

She sees the panic on my face and squeezes my hands tighter. "Think about the future. In four and a half months, we're going to graduate and move into our apartment. And then school will start, and our whole lives are ahead of us." Her voice gets cold. "We'll finally be free of your parents and the church. Don't let some pervert jeopardize all that."

Her eyes flash with something that looks like rage. When she kisses me, I have to make myself kiss her back.

I leave the scene shop first and walk toward the bus. Five

minutes later, Pau climbs in and heads for the back row. All the way home, I think about how Private knew about Carter's pleas to go see him in the hospital. Pau could be right; it could have been a smart guess. But I told Paulina about Carter's texts on Tuesday. She's the only person who knows that Carter's been asking me to visit, and that I've been pushing him away. I follow her with my eyes as she gets off at her stop.

When she's on the sidewalk, she turns around and waves. I give her a small smile in return, then wrap my arms around my stomach. It aches. I probably ate too much junk food, but it's not just that. None of this feels right. When I get off the bus, I have to run to make it to the bushes in time. The panic pours out of me hot and sour along with the contents of my stomach and a flood of bitter bile.

25

AMANDA
FRIDAY, JANUARY 19

At school, Adele and Trina are all over me about a girls' night out at this lounge where Trina knows the DJ. I play the boyfriend-in-the-hospital card, tell them I need a long soak in the tub and a Netflix binge, and by eighth they let it drop. I would love to go out with my friends, forget about everything, or spend the night pruning away with bubbles and streaming, but Friday has other plans in store. Rosalie's coming over at six, and Trina and Adele can't be anywhere in the vicinity when she rolls up. In the last week, everything has spun out of control. The pictures, the track, the hit-and-run, CVS, the police, my parents. The more that's happened, the less I've wanted to share with my friends. It's not that I don't trust them; it's more like I don't trust anyone.

Or the fact that any opening up I have done—to my mother, to Officer Lu—has blown up in my face. I never in a million years thought I'd say this, but the only person I can really trust right now is Rosalie Bell.

On my drive home from school, all I can see is Carter's bandaged face in the hospital, how far away he felt when I finally broke down and drove to Mercy yesterday. The visit was strained, at best. First, he said he didn't want company, then he snapped at me for not visiting since Monday. Adele, apparently, has been visiting faithfully every day with care packages and flowers. She even snuck in Five Guys on Wednesday after school. It's all I can do to not roll my eyes at the mountain of magazines, snacks, and DVDs she's stockpiled in his room.

After half an hour of sparse conversation, Carter admitted how bummed he is about lacrosse, about spending senior year on the bench. When he apologized for taking things out on me, he sounded really sincere. He sounded like himself. For a moment, things felt almost normal between us. Before I left, I found a nurse who told me they're still monitoring Carter's concussion, taking extra precautions at the Shaws' request, and they expect he'll be released early next week.

And then what? I can't go back to the way things were. But when I think about life without Carter, there's a big blank space where the future used to be.

The thought makes me panicky, but not as panicky as the thought of Private forcing me into a messy, public breakup. I touch my necklace and swallow. There are five days until Carter's birthday, and Private does not get to dictate how this goes down. After what happened between my mother and Officer Lu, he is tripping if he thinks I'd do anything to embarrass myself, Carter, and both our families.

In a weird way, this isn't even about Carter anymore. This is about taking Private down.

When I pull into the garage and head upstairs, the house is empty. The benefit is on Monday, and the last-minute arrangements require my mother's full attention. She'll be at the museum until seven, and then Dad will join her and the other board members and their spouses at Taviani's. While they finalize plans for Monday, Rosalie and I will have the house to ourselves.

I grab some brie and grapes from the fridge while I wait. The new voice mail light is blinking yellow on the kitchen phone. I dial in and grab the notepad from its basket on the counter, prepared to take down yet another message from an arts patron needing to reach Linda Kelly stat.

But the message isn't for my mother.

"This message is for Amanda Kelly. Amanda, this is Officer Cynthia Lu from the Logansville Police. I need you to come back into the station as soon as possible. Please bring one of your parents with you. I'm sure your mother told you that we spoke on the phone on Wednesday after you left. I need you to give a written statement to clarify what you told me. This is extremely important, Amanda. False reporting is a serious offense, not to mention a waste of police time.

Your mother mentioned treatment, and I want to assure you that we have your best interests in mind. If you come back in, no one will pursue charges, okay? No one is trying to threaten you, but we need you to work with us to clarify the facts in Mr. Shaw's case. Please call me back as soon as possible, and we'll schedule a time for you and your parents to come in."

I listen to the message twice, then press delete. I can't deal with this right now. Everything I told Officer Lu on Wednesday was true. If I give a statement saying that I lied, *that* would be false reporting. I am not coming out of this with a police record. Rosalie will be here in less than an hour. I just need to get her phone, get it to the PI, and let him work his magic. I just need a little time.

The message reminds me, also, that I need a new phone. I run upstairs to grab my computer, then sink onto the living room couch and log into my family's wireless account. With a twinge of guilt about the additional expense, I click the option to add a new line to our family plan. I think about canceling my old number, but new texts from Private could still come in. Those texts might help the police, and if I ever get my old phone back, I might need it for the PI. I pick out the same model I had before, type in our area code, and presto, new phone, new number. I select the option for expedited shipping, and I'm done. By tomorrow, I'll have rejoined the modern era, and Private is not getting his hands on this number.

Mission accomplished, I switch on the TV and click through the guide until I find the local news. A segment on the benefit is just ending, and then the coverage switches to the day's top story: two toddlers hurt in a playground accident at a Logansville public park. My eyes stay glued to the screen until the doorbell rings at three minutes after six, but there's not a single mention of Carter or new leads in the police's ongoing search for the hit-and-run driver. Four days after the accident, the story has dropped off the news cycle entirely. Officer Lu's message and the complete lack of coverage confirms it: My mother's ploy worked. My parents think

I'm overreacting, the police think I'm lying, and I have five days to get to the bottom of this.

The doorbell rings a second time. I run my fingers through my hair, smoothing the strands, then check my mascara in the hall mirror before opening the door. Rosalie is standing on my doorstep looking flushed and out of breath. She's practically swimming in her winter coat, which is at least a size too big. Her glasses are fogged-up, and the tips of her hair stick out in all directions from beneath a fuzzy snow hat. She looks ridiculous and a little scared. Then, she sticks out a gloved hand and flashes her teeth.

"Rosalie Bell. This is weird, but I guess it's nice to meet you."

ROSALIE
FRIDAY, JANUARY 19

For a minute, Amanda stares at me unblinking. This—the two of us face to face, breathing the same Carter-less air—is definitely strange. I wasn't expecting a hug, but she could at least stop looking at me like I'm a space alien. She's taller than I realized from Facebook; she must have six inches on me. Otherwise, she looks exactly like I expected. Shiny manicure, fitted jeans and top, tiny gold earrings and necklace, fresh makeup. Curated. I realize I'm probably giving her the same judgmental look she's giving me.

She snaps out of it and takes my hand in hers, giving it a quick shake.

"Amanda. Obviously. Come in, you're letting out all the heat."

She backs out of the doorway and I step inside. After hanging my coat in the hall closet, she guides me through the living room, across the dining room, and into the kitchen. The niceness of her house is almost menacing. We pass three fireplaces and a dozen stone vases to match the intricate stonework that lines the walls. I'm surrounded by sleek, marble countertops, plush rugs, and lavish bouquets of flowers. Everything is dark and modern. Amanda catches me staring.

"My mother has a thing for stone accents." I wonder if she realizes she's touching the black stone heart that hangs from the delicate chain around her neck. "You want something to drink?"

"Water would be good."

She opens the fridge and gestures toward a SodaStream bottle. "Sparkling?"

"Just regular water."

"Suit yourself." She pours a glass of sparkling, then hands me a tall blue bottle that I guess contains spring water. "Come on, we'll talk in my room."

We take the stairs to the second floor, and I follow her down the hall toward the only open door.

"I'll be right back." Amanda leaves me alone to explore her bedroom, which is, to be expected, nice. The room is huge and was clearly designed to match the sleek, dark tones of the rest of the house. The colorful photo collage above her bed and messy pile of French novels on her desk are the only signs that a teenager lives here. Even her trinkets are displayed behind glass. I open the door next to her desk, expecting to find a closet, but it leads to a private bathroom with a whirlpool tub.

In a minute, Amanda's back with her laptop. She takes a seat in her desk chair, and I perch on the corner of her giant bed with my fancy bottle of water.

I've been in her house for eight whole minutes, and she hasn't asked about Carter yet. My eyes flit to the framed photo of the two of them that sits on her desk. I look quickly away. I need to clear the air, tell her the truth about Carter and me, but before I can figure out where to start, Amanda opens her mouth.

"Did you bring your phone?" Her voice is clipped, all business.

"Yes." I dig it out of my messenger bag and switch on the screen. "No new messages from Private since Wednesday. He also send you a friendly reminder?"

Amanda presses her lips together. "I turned my phone in to the cops on Wednesday. So if Private's been sending reminders, I didn't get them."

Right, her email had mentioned something about her phone. I'm hit by a sudden surge of hope. If Amanda went to the cops, maybe they have something on Private. Maybe this is almost over.

My optimism must be obvious, because Amanda says, "Don't get your hopes up. I had enough on my phone to connect Private to the hit-and-run, but my mother derailed the investigation. That's why you're here."

"What?"

She looks at me hard, clearly debating how much to say. "She thinks whoever hit Carter was an opportunist who saw the accident on the news. But she's wrong."

"Private texted us that same night."

"There was also this thing at my locker, with fake blood and a teddy bear." Amanda makes a face.

I nod. "Carter told me." And there it is: his name, hanging in the air between us.

Amanda sucks in a little breath. "Whoever hit Carter put one of those same bears in his backpack on the day of the accident."

"Like a message?" I ask.

"I think so. My parents hired a PI to investigate quietly, this Nathaniel Krausse guy. So that's why I need your phone."

"What?"

"Your phone. You kept all the messages from Private, right?"

I nod and grip my phone tight. I'm sure for Amanda getting a new phone is no sweat, but I worked hard for this. It's my only source of internet outside school, my only connection to Pau. I can't just run out and replace it.

"You'll get it back. God." She sticks out her hand and glares at me.

"When?"

"I don't know. A couple days. I need to get it to the PI so he can work his magic with Private's blocked number. We have five days, Rosalie. You get that, right? I thought you'd want to expose Private as much as I do."

I stare at her outstretched hand. Her eyes are flashing, but her fingers are trembling just slightly. She's as scared as I am.

"Fine." I hand over my phone and run my fingers through my hair. It's messier than usual, a casualty of static and the cold dampness that's been hanging in the air since Monday's storm.

"Thanks." She softens a little, my phone now in her possession. "I'll tell the PI he needs to return it as soon as possible. Here's his contact info." She copies something down on a sticky note and hands it over. "In case you need it."

"Thanks." I stare at the phone number and email address. "And what if he can't, you know, trace the number? What then?"

Amanda frowns, then slouches back in her desk chair. "I don't know."

"Me either."

For a moment, we're both quiet. If we're going to get anywhere, I need Amanda to trust me.

"You know the girl from the photos?" I ask. "The ones Private wanted you to send to my dad?"

Amanda nods, straightening in her chair.

"That's Paulina, my girlfriend. We're moving to the city after graduation, and we're going to Pitt together in the fall. Until Private found out, no one knew except her family. And now you know."

"So, you're bi?" Amanda asks.

"No, I'm not into guys. At all."

"I don't get it."

"Have you heard of the Fellowship of Christ?"

She makes a face. "Carter made me watch a PBS documentary about a woman who escaped. It was basically a cult except the people don't live on a commune, and the kids go to regular school. But they believe in the Rapture and eternal damnation and all that. They're fanatics."

"Oh." I never knew Carter watched that documentary. The woman was Extradited. It was a big scandal two years ago. But despite my feelings about the church, somehow hearing Amanda trash it stings. *Cult. Fanatics.* Her words hurt because they're true.

"Carter probably made you watch it because my family is FOC."

Amanda's eyes get big.

"When I was thirteen, I came out to my parents. I've spent the last four years in and out of what they call ex-gay ministry."

"Like, conversion 'therapy'?" Amanda forms air quotes around the word. "To try to make you straight?" She looks appropriately horrified.

"Yeah. Like that. They homeschooled me for a while, then we moved across the state for a fresh start in Culver Ridge. That's when I met Pau. I have zero feelings for Carter, I promise. He was just a good cover."

I flop back on Amanda's bed and stare up at the deep cream, crack-free ceiling and wait for her to lay into me.

Instead, she says, "So you never really loved Carter?"

"No, never."

"I'm not sure I did either."

I sit up and stare. Her eyes are shiny, but her face is composed.

"I thought I did." She's studying some spot above my shoulder. "I really thought this was love. It was always just a given that we were meant to be together. We were the perfect couple; everyone said it. But I was never enough for him. I thought he'd grow out of it, out of *you*." When she finally looks at me, it's all I can do to meet her gaze. "But you weren't the problem. I was the one who wasn't good enough. . . ."

The tears spill over, and I don't know what to do. I jump up and grab the box of tissues on Amanda's dresser and hold them out to her.

"Thanks." She snatches the box from my hand, and I wonder if she regrets opening up to me. If she said more than she meant to say.

"I'm really sorry," I say.

She shakes her head back and forth, fast, and blows her nose. It's a big, ugly sound, not the delicate sniffle I'd expected from Amanda Kelly.

"It's okay," she says. "If none of this had happened, who knows how much longer I would have stayed with him. We would have started college together in the fall. Do you know how many girls go to WVU? I would have pretended he wasn't sleeping with them. I would have married him."

"We never slept together. Not even close. Just in case you were worried."

She wrinkles up her nose. "I wasn't."

Then, she breaks into a grin, and suddenly we're both laughing. It feels great. I can't remember the last time I laughed like this.

"You know," I say when we've recovered, "you're wrong about one thing."

Amanda dabs at her eyes with a fresh tissue and takes a sip from her glass. "What's that?"

"The only one who isn't good enough is Carter. We both deserve better." When the words leave my lips, I know they're true. Carter may be supernice, but he's still a cheater.

In a few days, he'll be out of the hospital and my time will be up. I can't keep doing this—burying myself beneath a pretend girl, a girl I'm not. I'm going to have to decide what to tell my parents, what to do. I don't have any answers yet, but a hard, dark kernel of truth lodges itself in my chest: The lies were a shield and their own kind of bravery, but I can't carry that burden anymore. I'm not going back to that life. The kernel nestles into the hollow inside my rib cage, takes root.

"Thanks." Amanda's voice draws me back into her room. She runs her fingers through the strands of her perfectly straight hair, smoothing the tips. Her face is composed again. "I still kind of hate you. But only a little."

Before I can respond, she turns toward her computer and opens a fresh Google Doc. Then, she types: *Suspects*.

"If PI Krausse can't trace the number," she says, "we need a backup plan. Let's bring this fucker down."

I grin, feeling suddenly more alive than I have in weeks. Maybe longer. "Where do we start?"

We spend the next hour comparing notes. I tell Amanda about the person who's been following me, and we read through the texts on my phone. She tells me about all the creepy shit that's been happening to her and her conversation with Officer Lu. Finally, she shows me the screen shots she saved of the Private texts before turning in her phone and the bucket of photos in her closet, hundreds of prints, some candid of Carter and me at a gallery opening.

When we're done, we sit for a minute in silence. It's a lot of information, but it doesn't seem to lead anywhere. The only thing it adds up to is someone with a giant vendetta against Carter and, by association, us. My mind revolves back to Pau, like it's been doing constantly since yesterday afternoon.

"Whoever Private is," Amanda says finally, "this is personal. And I don't buy Officer Lu's theory that someone's trying to get at his dad through Carter. Why would anyone with a real estate bone to pick go after me? Or you?"

I shake my head. "It's definitely more personal than that." My eyes are fixed on Amanda's computer screen, the blank space below *Suspects*.

"Let's not think of this as a suspect list," I suggest. "Let's just start with a list of your friends. The people close to Carter."

"Okay." She stares at the screen, then starts to type.

```
Graham, Bronson, Alexander, Ben
Adele, Trina
Winston and Krystal Shaw
Linda and Jack Kelly
```

"Winston and Krystal are his parents, obviously. Linda and Jack are mine. The guys are his best friends; they're all on varsity lacrosse except Alexander. Graham's a sweetheart, Bronson's a daredevil, Alexander's his boyfriend, he goes to North. And Ben's the third wheel we let hang around." She makes a face. "Adele and Trina are my best friends. Trina could be a model, but she'd rather be behind a camera than in front of it. She took that picture of you and Carter at the gallery."

"She what?" My eyebrows shoot up.

"It's not her," Amanda says dismissively. "Someone got ahold of her camera, probably copied the memory card. Trina doesn't have anything against Carter. Or me."

"Okay . . . " Anyone remotely suspicious has my interest, if it means Pau might be innocent. "And Adele?"

"Adele's . . . just Adele." She looks like she wants to say something else, but then she gets quiet.

"What about Adele?" I press.

"Nothing. She's had this silly crush on Carter forever. But she's my best friend; she would never try to sabotage our relationship."

"Hmm." Both of Amanda's supposed best friends sound a little shady. "And what about Ben? You said he's one of Carter's friends, but you don't seem to like him very much."

She sighs. "Ben just tries too hard. He probably wouldn't be part of our group except for lacrosse, and he's smart enough to know it."

"Okay, so that could be something," I suggest. "Maybe he's jealous of Carter? Messing with his relationships would bring him down a notch. And Carter's probably not playing lacrosse anytime soon."

Amanda thinks for a minute, then shakes her head. "Ben Gallagher wouldn't have the guts to do something like this. No way."

I shrug. "It doesn't take a lot of guts to send anonymous threats. People will say anything behind the safety of a screen."

Amanda takes another sip of sparkling water. "If this is Ben, I am so going to kill him. But I really don't think so."

I perch on the edge of Amanda's desk to get a better view of the screen. I can't put it all together yet, but a neat little triangle is starting to form: Adele with the crush, Ben with the jealousy problem, and Trina with the camera. That gallery opening was in November. This means Trina, at least, has known about Carter and me for a very long time. Amanda and I should have put our heads together the second this all started; she's too close to see the forest for the trees.

I turn toward her, trying to sort out what to say, and Amanda's eyes light up. "Rosalie."

"Yes?"

"Does your girlfriend know about Carter?"

My stomach clenches. My Adele-Ben-Trina triangle theory is appealing, but what if I'm the one too close to see the truth? I try to imagine Pau behind the wheel, going after Carter in some sort of violent rage.

"She knows," I say slowly. "And she's not Carter's biggest fan, or the Fellowship's. But she wouldn't want you two to break up. Why would she mess with you?" My stomach is still in knots as I wait for her reaction.

"Right, I guess not." Amanda hesitates, then types *Paulina* at the bottom of the list. "I don't know, but I'm adding her anyway. We have to consider all the angles."

"Agreed."

We both stare at the list on the computer screen. Carter's parents, Amanda's parents. Six friends. Paulina. I can't shake the feeling that we're missing something. Something obvious, something we should be able to see. But I can't figure out what, and clearly, neither can Amanda. She closes her screen.

"Now what?" she asks.

"Now we hope your PI guy can deliver." I glance at the clock on her wall. It's after eight already. "I have to get home."

Amanda walks me to the front door and hands me my coat.

"How are you getting there?"

"Bus."

She frowns. "You walked from the stop? I'll drive you."

"That's not—" *a good idea*, I start to say. Who knows who might be watching, and what they'd think about Amanda and me together.

"I'm just taking you to the bus stop, not to Culver Ridge. Relax."

I relent and follow her into the garage. She drives a BMW. Of course she does. I pull my snow hat down low and sink into the passenger's seat as we drive.

"I'll email you," she says finally, when we're pulling up to the stop. "When I hear something from the PI."

I don't tell her I don't have internet at home. That my phone is my lifeline.

"Right. I'll watch my inbox."

"Want to wait in the car until the bus comes?" she asks. "It's pretty cold."

"I'll be fine. Thanks." But I don't get out of the car right away. We sit in her BMW and stare at each other for a minute that stretches into two. I don't feel much closer to solving this thing than I did yesterday, but I do feel better somehow. When this is all over, I'm going to move my life forward. We have a few possible leads. And Amanda's not heartless. She's just a girl whose entire future is on the verge of shattering into a million pieces. We're the same.

I get out of her car, and before she drives away, she waves.

Knowing the Kellys have a PI on the case gives me a tiny glimmer of hope. But as I wait for the bus, my thoughts turn again to Paulina. More than anything else, my mind keeps going back to one thing—those pictures in the clearing. Pau couldn't have taken them; she was *in* them. But she could have set it up so easily. The clearing was a perfect spot, untouchable. All this time, I've been thinking somebody followed us there. But what if my triangle is really a square, and Pau showed Trina exactly where to go.

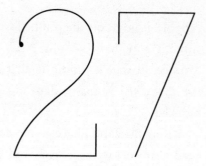

27

AMANDA

SATURDAY, JANUARY 20

First thing Saturday morning, Dad and I drive to a sad row of shops along the side of a two-lane highway about ten miles outside Logansville. After the police station fiasco, I resolved to keep my parents in the loop. I told them about Rosalie's phone as soon as they got home from Taviani's last night, and they agreed we should call Nathaniel Krausse right away. My mother's face went dark at the mention of Rosalie, but in the end she agreed. Her phone is our best bet.

The "agency" is an unmarked storefront with green, dust-caked Venetian blinds drawn tight across the window. I'm sure a low profile is part of the whole PI deal, but the sight of his office doesn't instill a whole lot of confidence. He sounded capable enough on the phone last night, though. Smart, measured. He made no promises, but said he could work with the texts on Rosalie's phone. That it might be possible to unlock the disguised number, depending on how the ID had been blocked.

Before Dad and I have even reached the front door, a middle-aged man in jogging sweats and glasses that look like they've survived since the eighties is ushering us inside. I guess PI Krausse doesn't put a lot of stock in dressing for success. Regardless, my dad seems to trust him, so I decide to trust him too. It's not like I have any better options.

The meeting takes under five minutes. We step inside, I hand over the phone, and he tells us he'll be in touch when he has something. It's basically exactly how I'd imagined my trip to the Logansville police would go.

"She needs that back," I say. "So don't delete any of her photos or anything."

"Of course not."

"How soon will you have something?"

He shrugs. "Depends on what I find. I'll be in touch."

I want to press him further, but Dad steers me back to the car.

"Let him do his job, Amanda. We're paying top dollar. We'll hear from him."

I must cringe at the words *top dollar* because Dad gives my shoulder a squeeze. "It's okay," he says. "We'll figure it out."

I spend the rest of the day making a final round of fund-raising calls on my mother's phone while she ties up the landline. Every time she takes a break, I tense up, ready to pounce in case Officer

Lu tries me again, but the kitchen phone doesn't ring. Maybe she has the weekend off.

Just after noon, my new phone arrives via Saturday Express Delivery, and I take it upstairs to charge. My new number will be going to a very select list; if Private plans to continue his reign of terror, he's going to have to find another way to reach me.

At six, it is finally determined that my donor outreach skills have been sufficiently tapped, and I am released to the Sunny Side with Trina and Adele. When we get there, Bronson and Alexander are already inside, holding down our corner booth.

"New number," I announce. Everyone pulls out their phones to key it in. "Delete the old one, phone bit the dust. And don't give it out. To anyone, okay?"

"Huh?" Bronson asks.

"I was getting some weird texts," I explain. I raise my eyebrows at Adele and Trina to keep quiet. "I don't want my new number getting around."

As my friends enter me into their contacts, my stomach does a flip-flop. After making that list with Rosalie last night, everyone seems just a little suspicious. Our waitress drops off a stack of menus, and I page through mine without really looking.

"Where's Graham?" Adele asks. "Not that I care."

"With Ben, I guess," Bronson says. "They should be here soon. Car's in the shop again."

I draw in a breath. How did I miss that? "Since when?"

"Since Monday." Adele looks up from her menu. "I'm starving. Has anyone tried the turkey burger?"

"Since Monday?" I ask at the same time Alexander says, "Go for a real burger. Live a little."

I stare at the four of them, poring over their menus like nothing unusual is happening. Ben's car has been in the shop *since Monday*? As in the day of the accident. Why am I just hearing about this now? Finally, Trina looks up and meets my eye.

"Yeah, I guess he's still having problems with the brakes. Same old shit."

"He never came to the hospital that night, remember, Mandy?" Adele raises her arm to flag down our waitress. "He spent like all Tuesday apologizing. He was stuck in the shop, then he couldn't get a ride out to Mercy 'cause we were all there already. Remember?"

"I wasn't in school on Tuesday. Remember?" There's a bite to my words I immediately wish I could take back. I've been keeping my friends deliberately out of the loop for days. This isn't Adele's fault.

She shrugs it off. "It's been a weird week. Anyway, now you know, Ben's having car trouble, yet again. It's not exactly breaking news." She turns her attention to our waitress, who is standing in front of us with her order pad and a smile. "I'll have the turkey burger, with cheddar and tomato, no onion. And a salad instead of fries."

"You want ranch or the vinaigrette?"

"Both, on the side."

When it's my turn, I can barely focus enough to order a Diet Coke. I have zero appetite. Except for Trina, who was legitimately out of town on a family ski trip, everyone was at the hospital the night of Carter's accident. Except for Ben.

Just as I'm about to excuse myself to run to the bathroom and email Rosalie, the diner door swings open, and Graham and Ben

walk in, grinning and punching each other's arms. Like nothing
fucked up is happening. All the goodwill I've been feeling toward
Ben lately evaporates.

I stare at him, hard. Adele said Carter was out with the guys
the night they met Rosalie. Did they all exchange numbers back
in August? If Ben is Private, that would explain how he got Rosalie's number.

My mind starts reeling. Carter has always been so nice to
Ben. Totally big-hearted in that way that just seems to come to
him naturally. He's always made me feel like a mean girl around
Ben, but what if Carter's been entirely too trusting . . . ? Rosalie's
words from last night come flooding back: *Maybe he's jealous of
Carter? Messing with his relationships would bring him down a notch.
And Carter's probably not playing lacrosse anytime soon.*

They scoot into our booth, Graham next to me, and Ben on
the end. I turn to face him, and I know my words are going to be
sharp as glass.

"Heard your car's in the shop. Brake trouble?"

He cringes. "Yeah, again. Sucks."

"And where do the Gallaghers get their auto work done? The
Kellys are a take-it-to-the-dealer family, but let me guess, you're
a Pep Boys kind of guy?" I sound like my mother, and for once,
I don't even care. If Ben hit Carter, he doesn't deserve anything
close to *nice*.

Ben swallows, glancing around for our waitress, or maybe an
escape. "We go to Mike Parker's dad."

"Supporting local business. Very admirable." My voice is cold,
steady. For the first time in days, I'm one hundred percent in
control. Everyone else shuts up and stares. "So if I swing by the

Parkers' shop, they'd tell me your car was in for brake trouble. And nothing else?"

Ben doesn't say anything. He stares at the table.

"What the hell, Amanda?" Graham is looking at me like I might be the unbalanced one. "What are you getting at?"

"Let him answer," I snap.

Ben finally looks up. "Needed some body work too. Nothing major, but they're still waiting for a part."

"The front bumper, perhaps? A headlight out?"

"Does someone want to tell me what the crap is going on?" Adele looks to Ben, then me, then Graham.

"I think," Graham says slowly, "that Amanda might want to think twice about what she's insinuating, before she says something she doesn't mean."

Adele sucks in her breath.

"Everybody out." Before I can tell Graham I know exactly what I'm saying, Trina is ushering Adele and me along the booth cushions until the three of us are standing. She turns to Adele. "You, stay here. Amanda is coming with me."

She takes my hand and pulls me toward the door. Our waitress gives us a puzzled look as we disappear outside.

"What?" I spit.

"You need to chill. What is this about?"

I eye Trina sharply. I'd rather be talking to Rosalie; she's the only one who would get it. But for now, Trina will have to do.

"You don't think it's a little too *coincidental*? First, Ben doesn't show up at the hospital when one of his best friends gets hit by a runaway driver. Then, we learn he wasn't there because while the rest of us were worried about Carter, he was taking his car into the shop to get the brakes and front bumper fixed?"

"He didn't say it was the bumper."

"I will bet you any money, Trina. Ben Gallagher is a coward. He hit Carter, and now he's trying to cover it up."

Trina slouches back against the front of the diner and tilts her head toward the sky. "Ben's car is always in the shop. It doesn't seem so strange to me."

"You don't think he was acting weird just now? You saw how he could barely answer my questions."

"Probably because he felt like he was on trial! Jesus. You know Ben's sensitive about money. That whole 'my family takes our car to the dealer' stuff? You triggered him, big time."

I need a new tactic. I stare at Trina until she sighs and looks me in the eye.

"Have you ever lent Ben Gallagher your camera?" I ask.

"This again?"

"I'm serious, Trina, think. The week you took those photos of Carter and Rosalie at the gallery. Did Ben use your camera, or did you leave it alone with him?"

"Maybe," she says slowly. "We do have English and calc together. Maybe we went to the diner that Friday; I would have had it at the booth. If I remembered anything, I would tell you."

I press my lips together tight. Either Trina really doesn't remember, or she knows more than she's willing to admit. I watch her face closely, but it remains blank.

"Forget the camera," I say finally. "Think about the accident. Ben was at practice on Monday; he knew Carter was going to CVS. I'm not saying it was on purpose, but Ben would have been on that road. His brakes went out. The snow was coming down. He swerved onto the sidewalk, and he hit Carter. Then he freaked, turned around, drove off, went to the diner to meet up with Graham and Bronson for a bit, perfect alibi. At the hospital, Bronson said that Ben arrived late and left before Adele texted everyone. But we know he didn't go home, right? He lied. He was taking his car to the shop."

As I say the words out loud, they transform from theory to fact. I'm dead sure of it. The only difference between what I tell Trina and what I know in my heart is that it *was* on purpose. Even yesterday, I didn't believe it could be Ben behind the texts, the threats, the hit-and-run. But maybe I've been giving Ben way too much credit. Or, not nearly enough. Rosalie's words ring loud inside my ears: *It doesn't take a lot of guts to send anonymous threats. People will say anything behind the safety of a screen.* And maybe they'll do anything behind the safety of a windshield and a snow-storm too.

For a minute, Trina doesn't say anything. Finally, she breaks my stare. "I suppose it is possible," she admits. "Ben could have copied my memory card. It could have been him behind the wheel. But, Amanda, the roads by the high school aren't exactly untraveled. It could also have been a lot of other people."

"During the middle of a snowstorm? On a school holiday, when the athletes were the only kids there and practice had already let out? How many cars would have been on the road, really, Trina?"

"All I'm saying is, don't jump to conclusions."

"Fine." But it's too late. Trina doesn't know half of the full story, and I'm not jumping to anything. I'm finally seeing what's been staring me in the face for weeks. The truth.

I shove back inside the diner and toss a couple dollars on the table for my untouched pop. Trina follows me over to our booth.

"I'm going home. Everyone have a nice night." I grab my bag and coat.

"Amanda—" Ben starts to speak, but I don't let him finish. I've heard enough.

"Let her go," Trina says. She starts to say something else, but I don't stick around to find out what. I have to get home, email Rosalie, call PI Krausse. It's time to unmask Private.

ROSALIE

SUNDAY, JANUARY 21

I bike hard from God's Grace to Bracken Hollow, the burn in my calves and thighs spurring me on, driving me to pedal faster. I need to get to the library early, before the start of my shift. I need to check my email, something I haven't been able to do all weekend. I can't stop thinking about the screen shots Amanda showed me Friday night. It didn't hit me until I'd gotten off the bus. In at least four of the texts, Private called her Princess.

Which is exactly what Pau's always called her. Princess Amanda.

I don't want the PI to tell me my worst fears are true. But I have to know.

I pedal harder.

At the library, I wave to Marge, then head straight for an open computer station. I draw in a deep breath as my email loads. There's a new message from Amanda, from late last night.

```
Subject: Private
From: Amanda Kelly
To: me


Rosalie!!!


PRIVATE IS BEN GALLAGHER. He was the
hit-and-run driver. I have evidence.


We also got another update. Two group
messages from this afternoon, to you and
my old number. PI Krausse screen-shot
them for me:
```

Your time is running out, ladies.

You need to focus. I don't want to
hurt you, but I will.

You both know what you have to do.
If either one of you lets the hourglass
run dry, there will be blood.

```
Now that I know it's Ben writing that
crap, I want to strangle him. You were
```

right, Friday night. He's jealous. He's
trying to bring Carter down, and us
along with him. You actually met him the
same night you met Carter. Picture all
the guys Carter was with. Ben was the
tall, awkward one.

This thing is almost over. I can taste
it. I'm onto Ben, and now so is PI
Krausse.

Take care, Rosalie. For real. Maybe
don't go out alone, okay?

I'll be in touch.

—Amanda

I close the email and exhale. I don't know what evidence Amanda has about the hit-and-run, but every molecule in my body vibrates with the hope that she's right. That all my suspicions about Paulina have been completely in my head. What if it was never a square, or a triangle either? What if it's just Ben?

I press my eyes closed and try to let myself believe it. If it's true, by Carter's birthday, Ben Gallagher will be in handcuffs. I do remember him from that night. The guy Elissa knew from leadership camp. He seemed . . . nice.

I run my palms back and forth across the tops of my jeans and try to get myself together. If Ben is Private, if PI Krausse is on the case, that solves half of my problems. But when Carter gets out of the hospital, my parents will expect to see him. They'll expect everything to pick up where it left off. And that's not going to happen. Not with Carter, not with any other boy. Never again.

I know in my heart I can't go back, make those choices all over again. Can't do that to Carter, or Amanda, or Paulina. Or most of all, myself. In the end, Pau was right. Graduation is a long time away. And four and a half more months is too much of my life to give to the Fellowship.

I touch the ring on my finger, spin the silver band around and around. In the twelve days I've been wearing it, I almost got used to its presence. How my parents think it's a promise I've made about Carter. How it's another lie. I slip it off and into my pocket.

The computer clock says I have twenty minutes before my shift begins. I squeeze my eyes shut and try to picture myself on the other side of this. Free. Fitted leather jacket, chunky red boots, smile that won't stop. But all I can see is my little sister's face, twisted with anger and pain when she learns I've left her. When our parents tell her why. In my fantasy, we're standing face to face in the middle of the pasture at school. Stretching out behind Lily are our parents, Brother Masters, the God's Grace congregation, and behind them, every member of the FOC, thousands and thousands of bodies strong. Behind me is the barren stretch of woods.

"Homosexuality is a sin," Lily shouts, small fists balled at her sides. The people cheer her on. "When you choose to walk the devil's path, you walk it alone. You're no sister of mine." A burst of applause, voices joined in approval and praise. These are the voices she'll hear when I'm gone. I reach for her hand, but the crowd surrounds her, swallows her. The roar is deafening.

My eyes snap open, then blink against the computer screen light. Twelve minutes until my shift. I open up a Google Doc and start drafting a letter to Lily.

When my shift ends, I remember to call. I ride straight home. I lock my bike in the shed, check in with Dad. Lily and I snuggle together on the den couch, and she reads two whole chapters of *Anna, Banana, and the Little Lost Kitten* out loud, all by herself. I put water on to boil, make a salad, set the table. I do everything exactly right.

Then after dinner, I close myself in my room and start packing. Clothes, shoes, essentials. I leave the items on my dresser untouched, the photos taped to my walls. On the surface, my room looks undisturbed. When I'm finished, I shove my duffel bag in the back of my closet, where it will stay until I can slip out and lock it in the shed late tonight.

I'm strangely calm. This is how it must be in the eye of a hurricane. Before you're hurled back into the storm, the stillness feels like floating.

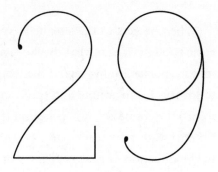

29

AMANDA

MONDAY, JANUARY 22

When school lets out, I pull my hood tight around my face and follow Ben down to the construction site. The benefit is tonight, and I have two hours until I'm on set-up duty with all the good trustee sons and daughters of Logansville. I can barely believe that with all this going on, I'm going to spend tonight clinking glasses with a roomful of arts patrons, but there's no getting out of Linda's benefit.

Ben's kept a low profile since our Saturday night confrontation at the diner. PI Krausse has been stationed down the street from the Gallaghers', keeping watch, but this afternoon he's at the Parkers' shop, looking into Ben's car. I need to head home to shower and get ready, but I can't resist tailing Ben. Just for a little bit.

When he gets to the site, he waves his brother over. I'm not close enough to hear what they're saying, but I can see David dig into his pocket for his keys. If Ben's borrowing David's truck, I'm following. I spin around and sprint up to the student lot. I make it into the coupé and down around the side of the school just in time to watch the truck hang a right at the light and drive off in the direction opposite CVS, toward downtown Logansville. I speed up and follow.

We're told that Carter will be released from Mercy in the morning, as long as he's still stable. Yesterday, I made one last visit to the hospital, where Carter was restless and ready to get home. Our conversation was polite, pinned safely to the present. We talked about how Coach might put him in an assistant coaching role during training and who his parents have invited to Carter's welcome home soiree tomorrow. (Hint: the entire town.) The future can wait until Carter's home and Ben's in police custody.

I stay two cars behind David's truck the whole way into town. Fortunately it's big and blue and easy to follow. I'm a little bit relieved that Carter's not getting out of the hospital today. The benefit will be easier to handle without him on my arm, both of us pretending everything is normal between us.

Tomorrow is another story. Everyone who's anyone will be at the Shaws' to welcome their golden boy home. The party will be big and public—and conveniently right on the eve of his eighteenth birthday. Private's going to expect me to make good on my instructions.

Which is why tailing Ben is so important. If he messes up, just a little bit, it'll be enough for PI Krausse to swoop in and involve the police. They may not be listening to me, but they'll listen to our PI.

Ben drives all the way down to Main Street and pulls into one of the spots in front of the Verizon store with its Logansville-approved storefront in mauve, navy, and gold. I park two stores down and wait.

When he climbs out of the truck, Ben looks over his shoulder and fidgets with his coat sleeves like he knows he's being watched. I slouch down in the front seat, but it's not really necessary. There are five cars between us, and one is some sort of baby Hummer. I crane my neck to get a good view as he disappears into the Verizon store.

He's in there forever. I lean back in the seat and try to get inside Ben's brain. Either his phone is as prone to breakdowns as his car, or Ben Gallagher knows I'm on to him. And after what happened at the diner, I'd say he definitely knows. Can't use the same phone anymore; time to get a new model with a new caller ID to conceal. Too bad for Ben, I turned my phone—and my old number—in to the police. I'm practically twitching in my seat by the time he comes out of the store. *Click click.* I snap two photos of him carrying a plastic Verizon bag. For a moment last week, I actually thought we were the same. Now, I can't believe I ever felt any sympathy for Ben Gallagher.

I wait for his truck to pull out and head back the way it came. I want to keep following him, but I have to get ready for tonight and get over to the museum. Besides, I got what I came for. I shoot off a quick text to PI Krausse with the photos attached, then I put the car in reverse. We're so close to catching Ben in the act, I can almost taste victory.

At home, I make a beeline for the answering machine. There's a second message from Officer Lu, a short-and-not-so-sweet request to contact her immediately. The station is officially filing false reporting charges against me. She says it's a serious offense if I'm found accountable. I can make it all go away if I'll just come into the station with my parents and a letter from my physician. If they don't hear from me by the end of the day, they'll have no choice but to move forward. I am officially obstructing their investigation into Carter's hit-and-run.

What Officer Lu doesn't know is that Rosalie, PI Krausse, and I are the only ones actually moving this investigation forward. I just need a little more time to prove I wasn't falsely reporting anything. I leave the phone off the hook and head upstairs to change.

By the time I get to the museum, I'm in head-to-toe black in a floor-length gown and Jimmy Choos. My hair is twisted up and pinned back with delicate black flowers, and the onyx heart rests against my throat like a promise or curse. I almost take it off, but then I think better of it. My mother will notice if it's gone. This is her big night, not the time to raise questions.

It's a relief not to have Carter here, but at the same time, it's undeniably strange. Since freshman year, Carter has been by my side at every single society event, house party, and gathering in Logansville. Tonight, I'm on my own.

I snap a selfie in the lobby and text it to him with the caption *The Logansville nightlife misses you*. I'm very careful not to say *I miss you*, even though it's a tiny bit true. In my heart, I know it's over. I've known it for days—since his promises at Verde dissolved into lies. Maybe at the time, Carter meant every word. Maybe he believed we'd really start fresh. But for all the goodness in Carter Shaw's heart, the truth is he's also a cheater. And there will always be another Rosalie. My happily ever after is not meant to be with Carter. I know that now, but it's going to take more than a few days to get over three and a half years and an entire future together. And then there's the small matter of my parents. I can handle breaking up with Carter, although the thought makes my stomach twist. But breaking the news to Linda and Jack? My dad might take it okay in the end, but I can already feel the sear of Linda's white-hot fury against my skin. Leaving Carter means leaving my family out to dry. That's how she'll see it. She will never, ever forgive me.

Hands shaking just slightly, I drop my phone into my clutch. If I follow this line of thinking any further, I won't be able to make it through the night. I take a deep breath and head into the classical wing. The benefit won't open its doors to guests until six thirty, but the museum is already buzzing with the caterers, the bar staff, the florist, the string quartet warming up on stage, and of course all the trustees and their families micromanaging the details. I weave through the churn of bodies, searching for my mother.

"Amanda." She spots me first, from her station near a dour-looking Rembrandt. She pauses in her instructions to the catering captain and motions me over. "I need to you check every seating card against the diagram. Last year the Coopers and the Weatherbys were reversed, and it nearly caused a riot."

I nod. "On it."

"And, sweetie? You look beautiful." Tears prick the corners of my eyes, and I blink them back before she can see. I should savor this moment. It might be the last compliment Linda Kelly throws my way in a long time. She gives me a quick kiss on the cheek, and I'm relieved to find a distinct lack of alcohol on her breath.

I take the diagram and head off in search of Table 1. I've always assumed my life would be filled with nights like this. I'd eventually join my mother on her boards, or found philanthropies of my own. As Mrs. Amanda Shaw, it all seemed possible. Inevitable. Now, I wonder how many more benefits the Kellys will chair. With my future title—and fortune—about to go up in smoke, my parents are going to have to find another way to dig themselves out of debt.

It hits me—maybe for the first time—that it's not my problem to solve.

No matter what my mother might believe, joining my future with Carter's is not my job. If you asked her directly, she'd never admit she wants me to marry rich. For days she's been calling Private an opportunist, but she's the opportunist in the family. When Carter and I got together, she saw a solution and latched on tight. But Carter's not the answer, for me or them. They're the adults. They're going to have to figure this out.

I suddenly feel a thousand pounds lighter. I pluck a glass of champagne from the prepoured drinks at the bar and practically waltz to Table 1. My mother is going to scream and rant and say terrible things to me. She's going to cast a lot of blame. She's going to make me feel horrible, and she's probably going to make me doubt myself.

But I need to focus on my own future. And my parents need to figure out theirs. I take a celebratory sip, then another. It's never seemed that simple before. Suddenly, it just does.

I work my way around the tables one by one feeling focused, clearheaded. At Table 12, I find two reversed cards and put Mr.

Windsor back next to his wife. Ben's reign of terror is almost over. Carter will come home, and I'll end things on my own terms. Then, I'll tell my parents. And after all that happens—the screaming, the blaming, the fury—I *will* still have a future. I'll apply for financial aid; I'll take out loans. I'll start over at George Washington or Bryn Mawr or NYU.

I notice my phone buzzing midway through my Table 14 check. Thankfully it's the last table on my list because the doors are open and the museum is filling up. The first message is from Carter, a response to my earlier text.

> Enjoy the benefit, sweets. I know it'll
> be a success.

No emojis, no *I miss you*s, no exclamation points. Three weeks ago, I would have been livid. Crushed. But tonight, it's fine. It's more than fine. Whatever we used to have, it's really over. I take another sip, let the bubbles fizz and pop on my tongue.

The rest of the messages are from Private, except they're not. Instead of Private Number, the header simply reads No Caller ID. I put my glass down and open the conversation.

> It may be 2 days until your boyfriend's
> birthday, but your clock just got reset.

> Carter's welcome home party,
> tomorrow night. You will end things
> in front of all your nearest and
> dearest.

> This is not a request, Princess. If you
> don't break up with Carter, I'll be
> doing the breaking, and I'd hate to
> mess up your pretty face.

I drop my phone on the table like it's burning and lean against the back of a chair. Someone brushes against me from behind, and I spin around. Mrs. Cooper apologizes, and I realize I'm standing at her seat. I retrieve my phone and graciously step aside, trying to get myself under control. The museum is a swirl of black tuxes and red, gold, and silver ball gowns. It's just Ben, I tell myself over and over. Just dorky Ben Gallagher made bold behind a screen. But how the hell did he get my new number? I specifically told everyone at the diner not to give it out.

I step away from the table to fire off a quick text to Adele and Trina. A minute later, Adele writes back.

> Ben wanted to apologize for acting
> weird at the diner, so I gave him your
> number. I thought you meant randos
> when you said not to give it out.
> My bad.

For a second, I'm furious with Adele. But then I realize. It's perfect. Fewer than ten people have my new number, and one of them is Ben. He's basically given himself away. Instead of an apology, he's sent another threat, and whatever he's planning now has a when and a where. This might be exactly what PI Krausse needs to put the nail in Ben Gallagher's coffin. Between the photos in front of the Verizon store and these texts from a different blocked number, that's practically proof that Ben is behind this.

I quickly scan the rest of the Table 14 seating cards and walk over to my mother. "Finished," I tell her. "I just have to run a quick errand."

She glances at the time. "The opening toast is in less than five minutes, and I need you and your father by my side for the photographers. Surely whatever you have to do can wait?"

I press my lips together. I should tell her about tonight's texts, that the PI needs to trace the new blocked number, but this is the worst possible time. The museum is absolutely swirling with people, and she's in her element. I'll stay through the toast, then duck out. I can get to PI Krausse's office and back in forty-five minutes. If he can trace this new caller ID, even prove it came from a Verizon phone, Ben's caught.

I glance back at Table 14 where I realize I've left my drink and my clutch, but I'm already being ushered to the long trustee table up front. My parents and I take our places behind our name cards and fresh glasses of bubbly and smile wide for the photographer. The board president introduces my mother and the other trustees and announces the North African exhibit we'll be able to bring in with part of tonight's proceeds. In the end, Linda Kelly has exceeded her fund-raising goal. In typical Linda style, she used the weekend to reel in the gifts that skyrocketed her total above that of every other board member.

My mother is nothing if not resourceful. Surely, even without me, she will be able to figure something out.

We raise our glasses and toast all the arts patrons in Logansville who made tonight and the bright future of the museum possible.

I scan the crowd, looking for the usual suspects. The Steinways, the Beaufords, the Windsors, and of course the Shaws. Carter's parents are seated at Table 1, directly in front of the trustees. As the board president says a special "thank you" to my mother, Winston's lips part in a boyish grin. It's the same smile that used to light up Carter's face when we first fell in love. Something tightens in my stomach, a small fist of worry.

I take a few polite sips, then put my glass down. The champagne tastes sour in my mouth. My celebratory mood is gone, and besides, I have to drive out to that strip mall. I excuse myself to my mother and retrieve my clutch from Mrs. Cooper's table on my way out.

The first wave of nausea hits in the lobby. My stomach roils, and the air around me shimmers with heat. Or maybe I'm the one who's hot. I stagger against a plush leather bench and force myself to sit—not lie—down. This isn't anxiety; something's physically wrong.

I glance around, but fortunately the lobby is empty aside from an older couple cooing over a tall bronze sculpture near the doors. Everyone else is inside, and the sculpture couple doesn't seem to notice me clutching at my stomach on the bench. My mind searches back, mentally retracing my steps. I didn't have a chance to eat dinner before coming here, but I definitely ate lunch. Well, I had an apple. And some of Trina's chips. That's the problem with early lunch; I'm never hungry. I've had alcohol hit me hard before, but this is different. I don't feel drunk; I feel *sick*.

I need some fresh air. Once I'm outside in the parking lot, I'll feel fine. I'll be able to get it together and drive out to the PI office. I couldn't have had more than one glass. I can't really be this wrecked.

I force myself to stand up straight and walk through the exit doors. The January air hits like a slap. I forgot to stop by coat check on my way out, but I'm not going back inside. I just need to get to my car and turn up the heat and wait out whatever this is so I can get on the road.

It's all I can do to walk in a straight line. I hold on to hood after hood and make my way to the coupé. The air around me is still shimmering, but this time it's definitely not heat. When I get to my car, I slouch against it for a moment without opening the door. I need to open my clutch. I need to get out my keys. I can do that.

I glance up, across the lot. Through the shimmering air, a big blue truck glides out of the lot and onto the road.

I flap my hand uselessly in front of my eyes, trying to clear the air, but the truck is gone, if it was even there at all. I grit my teeth, lean hard against the car, and empty the contents of my clutch onto the hood. My lipstick rolls away, but I grab for my keys and get the door open. Once I'm inside, I know I need to get the car started and turn on the heat, but all I can do is slouch across the seat, face pressed to the fabric. The nausea has turned to stabbing pain that jolts all the way from my stomach through my chest and to my head. I just need to lie down for a few minutes, until this passes. When this passes, I can get my phone to the PI. When this passes, Ben will be sunk. When this passes . . .

ROSALIE
TUESDAY, JANUARY 23

Amanda should probably still be in bed with an endless supply of fluids and *The O.C.* on streaming, but instead she's across the street at Carter's welcome home party while I'm stationed in the Kelly's living room, cordless phone in my lap. My whole body is tense, waiting for it to ring. I try to settle into the silence, but I'm restless, mind retracing the past six hours.

I got Amanda's email at the end of school, then took the first bus home. I checked on my bag, still concealed safely in the shed, and grabbed my bike. My parents think I'm staying with Elissa tonight, one more lie, but soon, I'll tell them everything. Tonight we put a stop to Private, and then I move on with my life. On my terms.

Amanda filled me in on the rest when I got to her house. Last night, when she didn't return to the benefit, her mother went looking and found her daughter passed out cold in the parking lot, slouched across the front seat of her car.

They pumped her stomach and found about .6 fluid ounces of alcohol and trace amounts of two prescription drugs: a heavy sedative and something used to treat infections. The doctors at Mercy think her reaction to the dangerous mix was intensified by the lack of food in her stomach. Amanda's mother seems convinced her daughter's way of coping with the stress of this past week was to "make poor life decisions regarding drugs and alcohol," which had Amanda in hiccupping, hysterical laughter when she told me, since I guess her mother is a raging alcoholic.

But what happened seems clear enough. Amanda was drugged by someone who didn't want her new phone getting to the PI. They managed to delay things overnight, but this morning, her dad drove out to Nathaniel's office to hand it over.

I paced back and forth across her plush bedroom rug while Amanda refreshed her email, fingers tapping the desk. Two hours before she was due across the street, an email from Nathaniel finally came in. We studied the screen shots; three texts that had just arrived to my phone:

> Carter's welcome home party tonight.
> You're not invited, but that won't stop
> you, you little party crasher.

> When Amanda fulfills her part of the
> bargain, you're going to show up
> with some news of your own for the
> party boy.

I want my audio recording. I want the
truth. If you don't do what I say, blood
will spill.

We stared at Amanda's laptop screen, and then we stopped
talking about Private. The PI is doing his best to unblock the
two disguised numbers, and whatever's going down tonight, it's
going down at the Shaws'. So instead of imagining the worst, we
spent a couple hours watching Ryan Atwood and Marissa Cooper fall in love on the Ferris wheel and trying to forget about the
ticking clock above Amanda's bed.

At eight, I helped her pick out a green cocktail dress and heels
and watched her unclasp the necklace she always wears and slip
it into her dresser drawer. Then Amanda went across the street
to keep a close eye on Ben, leaving me in her living room with
Nathaniel Krausse on speed dial.

I sink into the Kelly's plush couch and wait. I don't love the
idea of being split up, but with both our phones gone, someone
has to be reachable on the landline. From their living room, I have
a clear view of Ben's car, which is conveniently out of the shop
and parked down the block. It gleams in the yellow streetlamp
light. Our strategy is simple: Amanda keeps watch inside, and
I'm on alert for anything suspicious outside. Mostly, we're both
hoping the PI comes through with some solid digital evidence
before Private makes a move.

My finger twitches across the phone's keypad. Maybe I should
call Nathaniel now, tell him to get over here. Amanda is certain
it's Ben behind everything, but as much as I want to believe her,
as suspicious as he is, I'm still not entirely convinced he's acting

alone. Which is why before I biked into Logansville, I dug out Amanda's pink sticky note and asked the PI to keep an eye on Paulina tonight.

Just in case.

I shiver despite the blasting heat and roaring gas fire. If I'm right, it's a necessary precaution. But if I'm wrong, I am officially the worst girlfriend ever.

I stare across the street at the Shaw estate. The house and lawn glow bright against the winter dark. People are still arriving, filling the massive horseshoe driveway and lining the street with their cars. This must be the Shaws' idea of an "intimate gathering." My eyes travel to the only car I really need to watch, the gray Ford parked half a block away.

When the Kelly's phone rings, I almost drop it.

"Hello?"

"Rosalie Bell? This is Nathaniel Krausse."

"This is Rosalie." My breath catches. Please let it be that he unblocked one of the numbers. Please let this be over.

"Paulina Flores is on the move. Black Honda Civic headed into Logansville, male driver, early twenties. I'm following."

"That's her brother's car." A giant knot forms in my throat. "Ramon Flores."

"Sit tight, Rosalie. I'll be in touch."

AMANDA

TUESDAY, JANUARY 23

I brush aside the curtain and peek out the bank of windows that line the Shaws' parlor, but the only thing I can see is the reflection of the fire crackling in my living room window. Perfect. If I can't see Rosalie, no one else can see her either. Watching. Waiting for Ben to make a move.

I turn away from the windows and walk across the room to stand behind Carter, who's surrounded by well-wishers. He's stationed on one of the Shaws' stiff parlor sofas in makeshift formal attire: suit pants, shiny gray striped tie, white dress shirt rolled up to the elbows to accommodate his cast. The bandages are gone, and even with the cast, he looks healthy, almost back to normal. He's deep in conversation with his Aunt Patricia, who flew up from Miami for her nephew's homecoming, but he reaches for me absently with his uninjured hand, his fingers closing around mine.

For a minute, I stand behind the sofa, my hand in Carter's. I touch my neck out of habit, but the skin is bare where his onyx heart used to be. When this is all over, when Ben Gallagher is behind bars and Carter and I finally get a chance to talk, will he be heartbroken when I tell him it's over? Or will he be relieved?

I release Carter's hand and reach into my bag for my phone, but then I remember it's with PI Krausse. I'm naked without it. I lean down to give Carter a quick kiss on the cheek, then walk over to my mother, who's standing with Krystal Shaw by the bar. Naturally.

"Any news?" While I'm phoneless, she's supposed to be on high alert for any word from the PI. He has our home number and my mother's cell. But of course there's a glass of bubbly in her hand and her phone isn't even out.

"Oh, Amanda, no. I promise I'll tell you if he calls." She gives me a look that demonstrates exactly how seriously she's taking this. As far as Linda Kelly is concerned, I brought last night upon myself. Not only did they find two prescription drugs in my bloodstream, but there were three loose pills rolling around the bottom of my clutch. The irony of my supposed substance abuse problem is so bitter it's almost funny. Now she's threatening treatment for real; I have an appointment later this week at a private center with a name like Serenity Grove or Coral Vista.

I leave my mother and Krystal to continue dissecting last night's best and worst dressed and turn to my next task: Ben. For most of the party, he's been out in the great hall, kicking it with

Graham. They're standing in the same corner they took over on New Year's, talking about lacrosse or skydiving or comic books like everything's normal. But all night, Ben's been checking his phone.

I leave the parlor and stroll across the hall. "Gentlemen."

Graham folds me into a hug. He's wearing gray slacks and a pale pink shirt. He looks dashing, as always.

"How you feeling?" he asks.

"Never better." I turn to Ben and try to keep my voice level. "Expecting an important call?"

"What?" He looks at me blankly.

"You can see the screen flashing from across the hall. It's like a beacon."

"Oh." Ben shoves his phone into the pocket of his cargo pants, and I scowl. A quip about the dress code dances on the tip of my tongue—the invitation said cocktail party, not trucker casual—but I bite the words back. All this time, I've been hard on Ben for the wrong reasons. He put Carter in the hospital, and yet he has the nerve to be here drinking the Shaws' booze and joking around with Graham. I can feel the anger spark and flare across my face.

"I guess I'm just a little preoccupied," he mumbles.

"That right?" I raise my eyebrows. Ben may have a good five inches on me, but tonight I'm almost at eye level in my heels. I lock his eyes with mine and lean in. "It's a party, Ben. Lighten up."

"Jesus, Amanda." Graham steps between us and puts his hand on my shoulder. "Think you could take a bit of your own advice?"

Ben scowls into the floor panels and I let Graham ease me back a step. Ben looks sufficiently cowed. I'm either riling him up, or calling his bluff.

"You're right," he says suddenly, scowl wiped from his face. "Who needs another drink?"

"I'll come with you," Graham offers. "Amanda?"

"No, thanks. I'm not drinking." Since I woke up in the hospital, I've gone over and over last night's events. Anyone could have dissolved the pills in my drink at the trustee table; the glasses had sat out untouched for at least fifteen minutes before the toast. And anyone could have slipped a few extras into my clutch when I left it on Table 14. In a way, my mother is right. I did bring last night upon myself. I won't make that mistake twice.

Ben and Graham walk across the hall toward the parlor bar. I'm about to duck into the powder room to check my mascara when Carter's dad appears in front of me.

"Amanda, glad I found you."

I smile up at him. "This is such a lovely party, Winston. I know Carter's so happy to be home."

"Thank you." He places a hand lightly on my arm, just above the elbow. "Amanda, I need to ask you for a favor. The pharmacy texted; Carter's prescriptions are ready. Krystal and I are parked in. It would take us all night to get our cars out of the drive. Can you make a quick run to CVS?"

My eyes flicker across the hall to Ben. Trina's with him now, snapping a selfie. Across the room, Adele's settled in on the couch, demanding Carter's full attention. No one's looking at me.

"Of course. Not a problem."

"They'll ask for Carter's date of birth—"

"Winston," I interrupt with a smile. "I've got this."

"Of course you do." He runs a hand through his hair, blond like Carter's, and starting to thin in patches. I duck out and accept my coat from the woman running a coat check in the entryway. Then I slip across the street.

"Just me."

Rosalie's sitting on the living room couch, phone in her lap, exactly as I left her. She has a floppy knit cap pulled down over her ears, mostly covering her hair. It actually looks kind of stylish.

She leaps up when she sees me. "Is something wrong?"

"All quiet at the Shaw estate. I just have to run a quick errand."

She sinks back into the couch and curls her legs into her chest. "Listen, there's something I have to tell you."

I raise my eyebrows.

"Nathaniel called, half an hour ago. Paulina and her brother were on their way into Logansville. They must be here by now."

"At Carter's?"

"No—I don't know. He just said they were headed into town, and he was following."

"Why is he following them? He's supposed to be working on the numbers."

"Right, I know." She takes off her glasses and starts scrubbing at the lenses with her shirt. "I called him, earlier. I think Pau's involved."

"Like working with Ben?" I duck into the hallway and grab my car keys from the hook. "Why didn't you say anything?"

"I'm sorry. I didn't want to think it was true."

She looks tiny and miserable balled up on the couch. Something unlocks inside my chest. It's impossible to be mad at her.

"Fine. I have to run to CVS to pick up Carter's prescriptions. It's two blocks down from the high school. I'll be right back."

Rosalie nods.

"Keep watching Ben's car. And if I'm not back in twenty minutes, call PI Krausse."

"Got it."

For a minute, we both stare out the window. The trickle of new guests has slowed, and except for two of Carter's cousins smoking on the front lawn, illuminated in the porch light, everyone's inside.

I head down to the garage and get in the coupé.

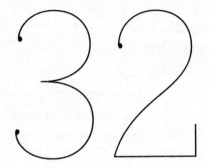

ROSALIE

TUESDAY, JANUARY 23

Amanda's been gone all of three minutes when Ben walks out the Shaws' front door. He pauses to check his phone on the stone patio, and my heart starts to pound. I rush to the window and look down the street, but Amanda's BMW is definitely gone.

Ben switches off his phone and pats his coat pockets, checking for something. Before he puts it away, I try to get a good look. What does a burner even look like? I picture one of those boxy Nokias with a tiny screen and no camera, but I can't make it out in the darkness.

A minute later, he shoves his way through the bushes lining the patio, avoiding the clusterfuck of cars in the driveway and cutting straight across the lawn toward the sidewalk. Toward his car. Amanda must have told someone where she was going, or Ben overheard someone ask her to go. He speed-walks across the grass, head down, and he doesn't look like a killer. He looks like a gangly kid underdressed for a fancy party. In another life, he looks like someone who could be my friend.

I press speed dial five and wait for Nathaniel's voice on the other end. After six rings, his voice mail picks up. No. No no no. I hang up and redial. My feet carry me from the couch to the fireplace, from the fireplace back to the couch. Six more rings, voice mail again.

I throw the Kelly's phone into the couch as hard as I can, and it sinks into the plush cushion with an unsatisfying sigh. I look back outside just in time to see Ben's car disappear at the end of the street. I let Amanda go to CVS alone. And someone is setting her up. Someone who is probably not my girlfriend. Someone who is now following her in a gray Ford.

I sink down on the couch and press my fingertips into my temples. The Logansville police are filing false reporting charges because of Amanda's truly asinine mother, so they're not going to be any help. And the PI who's supposed to swoop in and save the day? Officially following the wrong trail, because of me. I grab the phone and dial Nathaniel again. This time, it doesn't even ring before going straight to voice mail.

"Where are you?" I shout into the receiver. "This is Rosalie. Forget about Paulina and Ramon, okay? You need to get to the CVS two blocks down from Logansville South. Amanda's in danger, that Ben guy followed her, and I'm stuck here with no phone and no car and where the hell are you? Don't call back, just go."

I drop the phone and stand in the middle of the Kelly's warm, dim living room with the gas fire crackling. I can't just stay here and do nothing. Leaving the Kellys' means severing my one line of contact to the PI, but fine. He's off the radar, and I've already made my decision. I grab my coat and messenger bag and run out back for my bike.

I shove off and head down the street, headlamp illuminating the pavement ahead. The high school is the opposite direction from the bus station, I know that much. If I can just get myself off this tree-lined avenue and onto a main road, I'll figure it out. I take the same left that Amanda and Ben took at the end of the street and keep going. More big Victorian houses and lawns that are unnaturally green for the middle of winter. At least most of the snow has melted from last week's storm, and the roads are clear. Up on my right, there's a woman walking her white fluff ball of a dog. I slow down.

"Excuse me, which way to the high school?"

"North or South?" she asks.

"South."

"Take a right at the end of the street, then a left onto Pike. Take your second left onto Foster, and you'll see it from there."

I thank her profusely and take off as fast as I can pedal. Right, then left, then second left. When I get to CVS, I'll figure something out. Go inside and call 911. False reporting charges or not, they'll have to respond to a real emergency. Right?

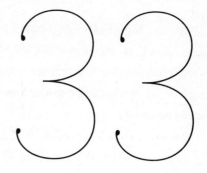

AMANDA

TUESDAY, JANUARY 23

"Picking up for Carter Shaw."

The pharmacist turns to rifle through the bins of white bags, and I reach for my phone, but of course it's not there.

"What time did you request them, miss?" He's empty-handed.

"I don't know. His dad asked me to pick them up. Winston Shaw? He got a text about twenty minutes ago."

"One minute."

I wait while he types something into a computer in the back, shifting my weight from the balls of my feet to my heels and back again. I need to get back to the party.

When he returns, he looks apologetic. "Miss . . . ?"

"Kelly."

"Right, Miss Kelly. Mr. Shaw's physician called in three prescriptions this afternoon, but they haven't been filled yet. They were scheduled for tomorrow morning. Our system doesn't have any record of a message to the Shaws, but we can fill them now while you wait."

I frown. "How long will it be?"

"No more than ten minutes. We're about to close, but we're happy to fill them since you're here."

"Fine. I'll wait in my car."

When I step outside into the tiny front lot, David's truck is in the spot next to mine. He rolls down the window and grins.

"Fancy meeting you here, Amanda Kelly. Shouldn't you be celebrating Carter's homecoming?"

"David Gallagher, as I live and breathe." I glance around the lot, but it's just the two of us.

"Hop in." He leans over to unlatch the passenger's side door.

"Can't. I have to wait for Carter's prescriptions. Then back to the party; you know how it is."

"Suit yourself. I was about to drive around back and light up. You're waiting anyway, right?"

The last time I smoked up with David, I wound up locked in at the track. He probably has no idea what his little brother's been up to, but if Ben came to visit him at the site that day, if David could confirm he was there, that's another nail in Ben's coffin.

"Five minutes, then I have to go back in." He pushes the door all the way open, and I climb inside.

David's truck is the extra large kind with four doors and a backseat, and he keeps it meticulously clean. I remember when he got it two years ago. Despite its age, it still has that new car smell. I lean my head back against the headrest as David backs out of the lot and drives around to the delivery area.

"So, what brings you to CVS?" I ask.

David puts the truck in park right next to the dumpster where I tried to shake down counter boy for teddy bear information. Tonight, the delivery lot is empty except for us.

"Huh?" David asks.

"CVS. The store we're currently patronizing. Never mind, it's not important." I wait for him to turn off the truck and pull out a joint. Instead, he just stares at me.

"I'm sorry, Amanda."

Before I have a chance to ask what he means, two sets of hands are on me. David lunges forward and grabs my wrists, and something dark and scratchy covers my eyes.

"Fuck!" I scream. "What the hell?"

The cloth jerks tight, and I can feel someone knot it around the back of my head.

"You have the ties?" David asks. His fingers are firm around my wrists, crushing them. I try to wrench away, but I can't see anything, and his grip doesn't loosen.

"Yeah, one sec," says the voice from the backseat. "Here, hold them up."

"Ben?" I ask. "Jesus Christ."

Ben just grunts, but I know it's him. "I know your voice, you asshole."

David jerks my wrists up, and something plastic slides around them. It bites into my skin as he pulls it tight.

"Ouch."

"Sorry," he says again, and then I'm being dragged into the backseat and shoved onto the floor. My hands lie useless in my lap. Ben's hands are stiff on my shoulders, ready in case I try to struggle.

"Help! Hel—" I start to yell, but my voice is immediately drowned out by some metal band blasting through the truck stereo. David cranks it up. Then the truck jerks into reverse, and we're backing onto the street.

"Get your hands off me," I growl at Ben over the music.

"Sorry," he mutters, but doesn't budge.

"Is that all you two know how to say? If you're so sorry, let me out of this truck." My heart is pounding. Ben doesn't move.

"You can take off the blindfold," I shout, trying another tactic. "I obviously know who you are."

Ben doesn't say anything. He must have been crouched on the floor when I got in. When I walked right into this. We're stopped at the end of the street. David turns the truck left, away from CVS and South. Of course, the blindfold's so I don't know where we're going. Everything's a little sideways from the floor of the truck, but Logansville is small. Unless we're headed out of town, all I have to do is pay attention.

We stop, and I know we're at the light three blocks down from CVS, at the base of the hill. Then the light must change, because the truck lurches forward. My mind reels. That Saturday at the high school was a setup for tonight, so I'd get in his truck. I imagine Ben and David planning this out. David must have faked a text from CVS while Ben was at the party. I picture Ben, how he kept checking his phone—for updates from David. He knew the Shaws' cars were parked in. He knew mine would be across the street, that Winston would ask me to go.

The truth explodes across the back of my eyelids. I was onto Ben, but not David. It's been both Gallaghers all along.

We turn left again, and my mental map goes blurry. Are we turning onto Oakwood or Clover? We can't be all the way to Bancroft. Right? David makes a right and then two more rights, and by now I'm totally lost. We drive around for minutes or hours. I lose track of time. It can't really be hours, but by the time the truck slows to a stop and David puts it in park, I have no idea where we are or how long we've been driving around. I am totally screwed.

A loud screech. Then something that sounds like scissors or a knife being dragged across cloth.

"What the—" I start to ask, but before I can get the words out, Ben presses something sticky across my lips. Duct tape.

David switches off the ignition, and the car fills with silence. My ears are ringing.

"Sorry, darling," he says, "but we're getting out now. Can't have you yelling up a storm."

"Where the hell are we?" I try to ask, but it comes out as, "Mmrmph . . ."

The back door swings open, and I'm hit with a blast of icy air.

"Time to get out." The guys reach in and pull me to my feet. I want to say I can do it on my own, but I can't say anything. My heart starts hammering again. We didn't get on a highway, I know that. We're definitely still in Logansville. Someone will notice I'm missing, right? Rosalie will have called PI Krausse by now. He'll come to CVS and find my abandoned car. Maybe someone saw me get inside David's truck. They'll put out a search on the vehicle. They'll find me.

Unless no one saw me get in the truck. Unless they have no idea where to look.

I'm sweating through my dress and my legs are shaking as the guys steer me toward wherever we're going. I curse my heels, which aren't making this any easier. We're walking over pavement or cement, something hard. We could be on a sidewalk, but something tells me we're nowhere public. A parking lot?

"Watch your step." David grabs me beneath my arms and guides me over something—a log? But we're not in the woods. "Hold her."

David transfers me to Ben and I give a little twist, testing him. His fingers dig into my shoulders. Then, the sound of a key turning in a heavy lock. A door swings open, and we're moving again. The ground beneath us is uneven now, rocks and dirt? We're inside, I think, but there's no heat, and there's definitely no furniture because everything echoes. It smells a little like cement mix and something earthy.

Suddenly, I know exactly where we are. All that driving around, and we only went two blocks. We're in the construction site at the high school. Of course, David has the keys.

Fingers touch my face, and I jerk, but then the tape rips off in a quick, burning flash. Before they can slap it back on, I scream at the top of my lungs. No one stops me.

"Scream all you want, there's no one here." Ben's voice.

"Bullshit. I know exactly where we are. Construction site. Gymnasium, to be exact."

"Good work." David's voice. "But no one's coming, roof's finished. If it's soundproof enough for hundreds of screaming teenagers, it's soundproof enough for you."

I scream again, just in case, and my voice crashes back at me in a hail of echoes.

Something drags across the floor, and then hands are pushing on my shoulders, pushing me down to sit. A chair, probably the metal folding variety.

"You done now?" David asks.

I don't respond.

"Look," he continues. "I'm real sorry about this, Amanda. But we're not going to hurt you, swear to god."

"Then why are we here?" I ask. "When everyone finds out about this, you're both going to rot in jail."

"Whoa, slow down." David's voice again. "No one's going to jail, because nothing bad is going to happen."

"You assholes are terrible criminals." I can't stop my voice from shaking, and I pray they don't notice. I'm at Logansville South, inside the new and apparently soundproof gym. I'm blindfolded, my wrists are tied up, and no one knows I'm here.

Then two hands remove the blindfold, and I blink hard and fast. It only takes a minute for my eyes to adjust because it's really freaking dark in here. Only the floor is unfinished; the walls and ceiling are complete. A bank of thick, glass windows line the top of a wall where bleachers will eventually go, but it's pitch dark outside.

"Better?" David asks.

I glare at him.

"You asked why we're here," Ben says. "It's simple. We're here to make a phone call."

"Then joke's on you," I say, "'cause I don't have my phone."

Ben reaches into his pocket and pulls out his Android. "That won't be a problem."

His voice is shaking worse than mine. "We're going to call Carter. When he's on, you're going to ask him to put his phone on speaker. Then, you're going to tell him you never loved him, and that your relationship is over. Simple as that."

"No way," I snarl. "You've always been jealous of Carter, admit it. Getting him benched in lacrosse, getting me to dump him? This is pathetic, Gallagher."

David's face is expressionless, but Ben's mouth twists into a scowl. "Make the call, Amanda." He places the phone in my hands. Carter's number is up on the screen. All I have to do is press the call icon.

"No."

Ben reaches into his coat pocket. "I really didn't want to have to do this," he says.

Something metal catches the dim light in the gym, and there's a flash of silver. Ben Gallagher is holding a gun, barrel pointing straight at me.

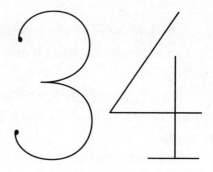

ROSALIE
TUESDAY, JANUARY 23

I'm stopped at the traffic light in front of the school, a long line of cars crossing in front of me. CVS is another two blocks down, but I can see Amanda lit up in the store lights, talking to someone in a blue pickup truck. It's definitely her—green dress flashing through her open coat, and who else wears five-inch heels to CVS? Ben is nowhere in sight. She climbs in, and then the truck pulls out of the lot and disappears up the side street.

My relief at seeing Amanda is immediately replaced by confusion. The light changes, and I close the gap between the high school and CVS, then turn into the lot. I look up the side street, but the truck is gone. Amanda's car, on the other hand, is parked right here. Did she lock her keys inside? Maybe she was getting a ride back to the party. I look through the window, but there's no sign of keys in the ignition or on the seat. I check the tires; no flat.

I'm propping my bike against the store wall when a kid in a CVS T-shirt walks out, shrugging an army jacket over his shoulders.

"Better hurry," he says. "Store's closing."

"Wait." I get in his path, stopping him. "Did you see a girl here a few minutes ago? Straight brown hair, heels, green dress?"

He blinks at me. "Yeah, I saw her."

"Well, she just left in a blue pickup. Did you see who was driving?"

He shakes his head. I'm about to press him further when the truck reappears. I shine my headlamp toward the window, but all I can make out is a guy wearing a baseball cap. He's built, definitely not in high school, and there's no one in the passenger's seat. The truck pauses at the stop sign, then hangs left. As it turns, I catch a glimpse into the back. It's one of those four-door models, and there's someone in the backseat, hunched over. Must be Ben. It looks like he's reaching for something he dropped on the floor. Or holding someone down . . .

As the truck speeds off, I flash my headlamp on the license plate. RTK something.

"I need to use your phone. It's an emergency."

The kid stares at me blankly.

"I need to call nine-one-one. Now." I stick out my hand.

He snaps to life and reaches into his pocket for his cell. I punch in the numbers and wait for the dispatcher to pick up.

"I need to report a kidnapping. A blue pickup truck with

plates starting with RTK made a left onto—hold on." I turn to the kid. "What's this street?"

"Foster."

"Made a left onto Foster at the CVS two blocks down from Logansville South. I saw a girl named Amanda Kelly get into that truck. She's seventeen . . . she's being held by her classmate Ben Gallagher and another guy."

The kid gapes at me. The dispatcher asks about the truck's make and model. Do I know who the driver was?

"It was a Ford I think. I don't know."

The dispatcher wants to know if I saw anything else, am I sure Amanda didn't get into the truck willingly, do I know where they might be headed.

I lie. It's too much to explain, and I need them to start looking. "They dragged her inside. Ben Gallagher and the other guy. Ben's a student at the high school. The other guy was a little older, twenties maybe? Wearing a baseball cap. I have no idea where they were going. Left on Foster, about two minutes ago. Can you please look for the truck?"

When the dispatcher has all she needs, I hang up and return the phone.

"I know that girl," the kid says finally. "She was here about a week ago, asking about these teddy bears? Said she had a secret admirer."

I scowl. "Yeah well, that secret admirer just stuffed her into the back of his pickup truck. Thanks for the phone."

I leave him gaping and grab my bike, wheel it over to Amanda's car, and flip the kickstand down. My pulse is racing; I need to *do* something. But I already called Nathaniel. I called 911. By now, the truck could be anywhere; trying to track it down on my bike would be pointless. If Nathaniel got my message, he'll come to CVS. My best move is to wait here.

I slip my messenger bag off my shoulders and dump it on the trunk of Amanda's car. Then I pull myself up next to it and wait. A few minutes later, a single cop car speeds by.

When I've been waiting for what must be an hour, I admit to myself that Nathaniel's not coming. My teeth are chattering so hard my jaw aches, and there's been no further sign of the police. I need a new plan. The thought of busting into the Shaws' uninvited makes my stomach turn, but someone needs to tell Amanda's parents what's going on. It's not exactly my first choice of missions, but it's something. Maybe *they* can get their useless PI on the phone.

I jump on my bike and start pedaling back up the hill toward the high school. It looks like they're putting on an addition. The school is dark and empty, but the streetlamps cast a dull yellow glow on the half-finished structure. And one blue pickup parked in the tiny side lot. It's barely visible from the road, half obscured by temporary fencing and a hearty pair of pines. If I had been going any faster, I'd have ridden right by it.

I jump off my bike and leave it propped against a planter in the lot. I leave my helmet too, but not before removing the headlamp. It's pitch dark; I'm going to need it. I check out the truck first; it's definitely the right one. I repeat the full plate number beneath my breath, but it doesn't matter now. The truck is right here, and it's empty.

Up close, I can see the half-finished addition is actually two buildings. One is still mostly scaffolding, but the other has walls and a roof. I turn my headlamp on and start walking. They might have taken her inside the school, but it's probably locked up for the night. They're clearly not in the scaffolding structure; I can see right inside. So that leaves the other building.

I walk around the perimeter, trying to stay silent. On one side, it's attached to the school, but the other three sides are exposed. The site is a mess of bricks and buckets and all sorts of materials left out overnight. I guess no one worries about their shit getting stolen in Logansville. There's one door and the only windows are a bank of thick glass cubes up near the top of the building. They're not the kind that open. I think about trying the door, but if I'm right and Amanda's inside, I'll give myself away as soon as I push the handle. What I need is an air vent. Something I can listen to, see if I can hear them. If they're inside, I'll get back on my bike and find someone with a phone. Call 911 again.

Around the back, I find the vents where the heating and cooling system will eventually go. I get down on the ground and press my ear to the wall.

A voice asks, "Better?" Or maybe "bitter?" It's a voice I don't recognize, maybe the driver.

A different male voice speaks next. I can't make out everything, but he says something about making a phone call.

Then Amanda's voice rings out, the loudest of the three. "Then joke's on you, 'cause I don't have my phone."

I suck in my breath. The second voice—must be Ben—is speaking again, saying something about calling Carter, speakerphone, breaking up. Everything's far from adding up, but they're definitely inside with Amanda, and that's all I need to know. Time to find someone who will let me use their phone and let the professionals take over. I start to shove myself up off the ground, but the driver's voice stops me.

"Is that a gun? Fuck, Ben, what the hell are you doing with that?"

He must be closer to the vent; he's easier to hear. Ben says something next, something about taking this shit seriously. Then something about the art museum and Amanda's mom and Carter's dad. I can't make it all out. I hear the words *stealing* and *cash flow* and *scam*. Whatever he's talking about, it's clearly making Amanda upset.

"This is about my *mother*? You're so full of shit, Ben Gallagher. Even if you're right, why do you care?"

I press my ear back to the vent. Ben's voice again, something about "going public." Is he talking about the museum? Or asking Amanda to be his girlfriend?

Then Ben says something I have no trouble making out.

"This gun isn't a toy, Amanda. Make the fucking call."

35

AMANDA

TUESDAY, JANUARY 23

Ben's hand is shaking so hard I'm not convinced he could shoot me if he tried. But I am definitely not prepared to test that theory. I'll call Carter. I'll do whatever Ben says and fix it later. This stopped being worth fighting about the second there was a gun pointed at my head.

"I'll make the call." I twist my wrists against the ties. "If you were any kind of gentleman, you would press the call button for me. In case you haven't noticed, my wrists are bound together." I wonder if he can see my glare through the darkness. All I can see is the pale stream of moonlight from the windows glinting off the gun.

If they were better criminals, they'd just make the call and press the phone to my ear. If they were better criminals, they might have found a place to stash me that wasn't so obvious. If they were better criminals, they'd've cooked up a revenge plot slightly more interesting than making me break up with my boyfriend over speakerphone. As freaked out as I am, I can't help noticing how *bad* they are at all of this.

David lunges for the phone. "I'll dial."

Just then, there's a noise outside, right in front of the door. It's stones or bricks. Something falling. We all jump. Ben spins around, aiming the gun at the door. "The fuck was that?" His hands are shaking even harder than before.

"Wait here." David slips the phone into his pocket and starts toward the door.

"Take this," Ben says.

"Hell, no. Put that thing away, I'm serious. It's probably just an animal. We get raccoons at the site all the time."

Ben lowers the gun but follows David toward the door.

"Stay here with her," David growls. "I'll be right back."

He opens the door slowly, and moonlight mixed with the glow from the streetlamps on Foster floods in. David props the door with a brick and slips outside. I think about running. My wrists are tied, but my ankles are free. I slide my feet silently out of my heels and press them against the unfinished floor. It would take maybe ten seconds to get to the door, tops. But this place is littered with bricks and nails and trash. And I'd have to run past Ben to get out. I wonder if he would really try to shoot me. Before I can make myself stand up, I know I'm not going to test it.

"Where'd you get the gun, Ben?" I ask instead. Now that he— and the gun—are bathed in light, I can see it's longer and skinnier than the little black handguns you see on cop shows. The handle is brown wood, and there's some kind of carving on the barrel. I don't know much about guns, but this looks like a collector's item. Maybe it really is a toy.

He jerks his head toward me. "Borrowed it from a friend. It's a real gun, Amanda. I know how to shoot."

"I bet you do," I sneer. I should probably be more careful, but anger and fear are duking it out inside my brain, and right now, anger is winning. Ben takes a step forward.

"You're really going to shoot me and spend the rest of your life rotting in jail because you're pissed that my mother is *allegedly* enabling Carter's dad to fuel his antique habit?" I ask, a challenge. My mind stutters back to the email I found in her purse and promptly forgot. *N or V. Always V, my dear. In the end, always V.* I'd considered the possibility of an affair, that Winston was my mother's backup plan. But this . . .

"I don't buy it, Ben. I just do not—"

But before I can finish, Ben is crumpled in a heap on the floor and the gun is spinning across the ground in a slow arc toward me.

ROSALIE

TUESDAY, JANUARY 23

I lunge for the gun, which is reeling across the floor toward Amanda, and snatch it up. Then I spin and point it straight at the black silhouette of the driver in the doorway. "Get over next to him, and keep the door open."

He does as I say. My headlamp shines on Ben's slumped figure on the floor. I didn't even hit him that hard. There's a fine line between knocked out and dead, and I was not trying to cross it. Ben's breathing, but he's definitely unconscious. I drop the shovel and kick it toward Amanda.

The gun feels warm in my hand, and really heavy. It's some old wild west model, a revolver I think? Whatever it is, this thing is an antique. Amanda leans down to grab the shovel, and I can see her wrists are tied with some sort of plastic binding. I have a pocketknife on my keys, but I can't hold the gun and slice her ties at the same time.

"Listen, the gun isn't loaded," the driver says. "This all got really out of control."

"You didn't even know Ben had a gun," Amanda spits. "How do you know it's not loaded?"

"I know my brother, okay? He's not like that."

So they're brothers. My brain flashes back to our suspect list. I should have been more open with Amanda about my Paulina doubts. And she should have told me that her number one suspect had a brother.

"Just to clarify," I say, the gun in my hand making me brave, "your brother's not the type to kidnap a girl and tie her up? Or he's not the type to shoot her now that he's got her here? Or was this all your idea . . . sorry, didn't catch your name."

"David," he and Amanda say at the same time. Ben's still breathing deeply at his brother's feet. David holds his hands in the air and crouches down to check on him.

"Fine, David, let's test that not-loaded theory." I turn away from everyone and aim the gun at the ground about five feet to my right. Shouldn't there be a safety? Or maybe not. They probably weren't too concerned with gun safety in the Wild Wild West. I shine my headlamp on the handle, but all I can see are the trigger and a little lever up top. I pull it back with my thumb and it makes a small click. That seemed to do something. Then I point firmly into the ground and pull the trigger as hard as I can.

A loud bang. The gun jerks back in my hands, and the floor erupts into an explosion of dirt and grit. Definitely loaded.

"Fuck." For once, David, Amanda, and I are on exactly the same page.

"Please hand it over," David says from the ground where he's crouched down with his brother. Ben's starting to stir. Guess the sound of a firearm going off in a building with bad acoustics would be enough to wake up your average head injury case. "I know how to unload it, okay?" David says. "I promise that's all I'm going to do."

"Don't listen to him," Amanda hisses.

"Hell, no." I swing the gun back to face the guys. The person with the gun has the power, and a rush of it surges through me. One of these guys was the creep in the woods, and at my house. One of them threatened to out me to my dad. There's no way I'm handing over this gun. "I know what I'm doing now. Lever thing, aim, fire. You two put Amanda and me through hell and back over the last three weeks, and now you're going to talk."

"You've got this all—" David starts to say at the same time Ben says, "It wasn't supposed to be loaded." He's sitting up now, rubbing slow circles against the back of his head. "Rosalie?" he asks, recognition dawning. "How did you get here?"

I glare at him, ignoring his question, and turn to David. "So you're Private? Or you two are some kind of stalker tag team?"

"Who?" David asks.

"The private number," Amanda cuts in. "Anonymous texts? Time to talk, David. Or have you forgotten there's a gun aimed at you?"

"Chill, okay? I promise I will tell you everything you want to know, but I didn't send any anonymous texts. Ben?"

Ben shakes his head. "Not me."

Amanda and I glance at each other. What the actual fuck?

"The gun is Carter's," Ben says slowly. "Well, his dad's, from his antique collection? It's so old, I didn't even think it worked. Swear to god."

"Ben Gallagher." Amanda sounds calm. Dangerous. "Are you telling me you took this gun *from the Shaws* to kidnap me? Carter's going to have your head when he finds out."

"Amanda, he knows." It's David this time. He stands up slowly, one hand still in the air, the other gripped under Ben's arm, helping him to his feet. "This is all because of Carter."

"Yeah, I get that this is about Carter," Amanda snaps. "What do you mean he knows?"

"I mean he hired us," David says.

I turn to Ben for an explanation. "Carter offered to pay me to keep an eye on Amanda," he says. "At first, that was it. Then things kind of . . . escalated. David didn't know anything until today, I swear. I asked him for help a few hours ago."

David looks at Amanda. "The plan was to drive you around for a while, scare you, and then you'd give in and make the call. You were supposed break up with him on speaker in front of everyone at the party, and then we'd all get out of here. No harm, no foul. WVU isn't going to pay for itself. And there wasn't supposed to be a gun." He glares at Ben.

My hands are steady, but my mind is reeling. In the gym's dim light, I can see the same realization start to burn in Amanda's eyes. These guys aren't Private. They're just Carter's puppets, doing what they're told, because it's been Carter behind every threat, every anonymous text. Carter desperate to get what he wants—a brand-new future without Amanda or Shaw Realty or rigid family expectations; a future he thought he'd found with me. Guilt wrings my gut like a limp rag. To say I'd underestimated Carter doesn't even begin to capture it. It's been days since he first said those three little words, but for the first time, I really understand. *I love you, Rosalie.* I'd been so sure Carter saw me as a temporary outlet, because it's how I wanted him to see me. But he saw me as *a way out.*

I close my eyes, and I'm jolted back to that day in the clearing. The deep winter chill. The soft crunch of pine needles and limp, dead leaves beneath my feet. Then, a flash of black and white through the trees. This time, I understand what I'm seeing. Not Trina or someone from the Fellowship or even the Gallaghers— but Carter, all dressed up in a suit and tie, spying on Pau and me before heading off to yet another ubiquitous Logansville social function. I'm sure, now, that it was Carter at my house. The yawn of his shadow made willowy in the dark. Carter other times I didn't even know I was being watched. Carter who sent the pictures to Amanda, knowing how deeply she despised me, banking on the fact that she'd send them on to my dad, do his dirty work for him. Then Carter demanding I confess when Amanda wouldn't comply. Carter desperate to know the truth about Pau and me, but too spineless to ask me to my face.

My mind reels ahead to the two of us at Eat'n Park, how he tried to convince me it was Amanda who had trashed her own locker.

To the day in his car, right before I broke things off. The concerned look on his face when I said someone had been following me.

To his conviction that the car accident was a sign from God, that we should be together. Was that even real? Or was he using my religion to play me?

I try to puzzle it out, get inside his head. He must have thought Pau was some fling, an "experiment" that my deeply religious parents would nip in the bud, pushing Carter and me closer together. That as soon as Paulina was out of the way, we would be Carter and Rosalie, happily ever after. And me none the wiser that it had been Carter who'd come between us. My gut twists harder, but it's anger this time, not guilt, doing all the wringing.

"David, get over here." I dig my keys out of my pocket with one hand, still holding the gun toward him with the other. "There's a pocketknife on my key chain. You're going to cut Amanda's wrist ties."

He walks over to me and accepts the keys. These guys aren't dangerous; I get that now. But just to be safe, I say, "Don't even think about trying anything. Gun, remember?"

He nods. In a minute, the ties are severed and he's handing my keys back. Amanda's just standing there, rubbing her wrists, looking kind of dazed. For a moment our eyes meet, then we turn to David and Ben, who are both staring at the ground, hands shoved in their pockets. They don't bear much family resemblance, but they're both washed in the same shame.

Amanda's eyes flicker to the gun. Slowly, I lower it so it's pointing at the floor. "I think you should get out of here," I say to the guys.

"There is nothing I would love more," Ben says, "but we kind of can't. I have to call Carter. Phone's on silent, but he's been calling nonstop."

"Hey, man. Look, there's a problem."

Ben's on the phone with Carter, but I'm not really listening. I'm not really feeling much of anything, which probably means I'm in shock. Not gun-to-your-head shock, although that happened. But Carter-is-Private shock. Carter-is-*dangerous* shock.

I grab Rosalie's hand, pull her aside. I have to say the words out loud. "Carter is Private."

She nods slowly. "Why did these guys get involved?"

"David just needs the cash. I'm sure Ben thought he was earning a bump up the social ladder by doing Carter's bidding. Or repaying him for all his goodwill." My mind is still reeling, but everything's starting to pull together. "Carter gave Ben that gun," I say. "On purpose."

Rosalie frowns. Her headlamp is shining right in my eyes.

"He's coming here." Ben's off the phone, standing in front of us. "I told him the deal was off, that Amanda knew, and he kind of freaked."

"Let's get out of here." David holds up the keys to his truck. "I'll drive you girls home."

"You're bat-shit if you think I'm getting back in your truck." No chance. I slip my feet back into my heels, but I'm not going anywhere.

"Look, I don't blame you for not trusting me, but believe me you don't want to wait around for Carter. You can drive. Okay?"

"No, thanks," Rosalie says. "Amanda's car's two blocks away. We'll be fine. But we need your phone."

"What?" Ben asks.

"Phone." She holds out her hand. "We don't have one, so give me yours. And clear your password."

David nods toward Ben's Android. He adjusts his settings, then extends it out to Rosalie. "Now get out of here," she says.

"Can I, um . . ." Ben reaches toward the gun, which Rosalie's still holding in her other hand.

"Get out of here," she snaps. He pulls back his hand. Ben and David stare at each other, clearly at a loss.

"Look," Rosalie continues. "No promises that we're not reporting this. But you need to leave. So get in your truck, and go home. Understood?"

A minute later, the guys are gone.

"Thanks. You're kind of my hero." And I mean it. Rosalie Bell is the most bad-ass person I know.

She smiles. "No problem. Now let's go." She slips the phone and gun into her messenger bag and holds her hand out toward me.

"Hold on." Things are moving too fast. "I need some air. I just need a minute to think."

At first, I think she's going to protest, grab my hand and drag me back to CVS. But I must look as messed up as I'm feeling because she nods and lets me step outside, into the moonlight. I draw in a big gulp of cold night air and try to clear the fog out of my brain. The truth is in there, submerged, and I need to claw my way through, drag it into the light.

I squeeze my eyes shut and start with New Year's. *Wouldn't you look better without a cheater on your arm?* Carter sent that text. A piece of truth. I hold it up to my mind's eye, examine it. Carter was warning me *about himself.* Because he thought . . . I try to see that night through his eyes. He thought history would repeat itself, that I'd break up with him again, just like I had after the apple-cheeked freshman. That night, Carter must have thought this would be easy—I'd dump him, he'd be free, and I'd be the one to shoulder all the Kelly-Shaw blame. The thought makes something inside me collapse, a table crashing to the floor. All this time, Carter was setting me up.

Did he ever really love me?

Almost as painful is the realization that he assumed winning would be a snap. When the anonymous texts didn't work, he stepped it up. One by one, snapshots of truth emerge from the fog, show themselves for what they are: The bloodbath at my locker. *Carter.* The January 24th ultimatum. *Carter.* The photos he'd grabbed from Trina's memory card, scattered in the rock garden. *All Carter.*

But *why?* I breathe in and out and wade deeper into the fog. Examining the past three weeks is like staring at one image superimposed on another. On top, there's the boy he let me see: Carter with his arm around me, pulling me close, smiling wide. Carter punching the whiteboard after someone messed up my locker. Carter brimming with promises at Verde, making me believe we could really have a fresh start. Blameless, Loganville's golden boy. If I'd given in, he would have stayed that way. Flawless and charming, betrayed by Amanda.

The first image is an act, a mirage. The fog parts, and underneath I see the true Carter for the first time: liar, coward. A trapped animal, desperate to escape from his life and keep his reputation intact.

I let my thoughts travel then to Ben, and the fog lifts a bit more. You'd have to be really down on yourself to do Carter's dirty work, and I have to admit I'm more than a little to blame for Ben's banged-up self-esteem.

I press my fingertips into my temples, and Ben's role comes into focus. It probably started that day at the track—Carter wasn't getting anywhere, so he brought Ben on board, just to keep tabs on me. I was distracted by David, brain sluggish with pot, but if I had thought hard about it, I would have remembered Ben was there, inside the school. Saturday debate practice. I can see him now, breaking away from mock trials to look out the window. Texting Carter, letting him know. *Amanda's on the field—looks like she's taking a nap?*

Then Ben behind the wheel in the snowstorm—because I was right about that, I'm sure of it—but not because he had it in for Carter. Because Carter paid him, told him to stage the accident so he could play the victim. He thought Rosalie would come crawling back to him out of pity, not that it worked. Ben buying the second burner for Carter while he was in the hospital. Ben spying on me at the gala, drugging my drink. Ben doing it for Carter.

Because in the end, it was *all* Carter.

The fog is almost cleared away. I'm on the edge of understanding everything, but when I think about Private and I think about the boy I used to love, who I thought loved me, the two images hold stubborn at the edges of my sight. Even now, I can't quite make them merge.

A Mercedes passes in front of the high school and pauses at the light. Carter's here. I spin around and run back inside.

"I need to talk to him. Alone," I say. Rosalie's sitting on the metal folding chair in the middle of the floor, waiting for me. "Give me the gun."

"What?" She hugs her messenger bag protectively to her chest.

"He's about to pull into the lot; he'll be inside in a sec. I'm only going to talk to him, promise. But give me the gun, just in case."

For a moment, Rosalie studies my face. Then she reaches into her bag and pulls it out.

"Just give it to me," I insist.

"You don't need to do this tonight," she says. "Why not wait until tomorrow. Broad daylight, public place? Right now, you don't know how he'll be."

"He'll be angry," I say. "And that's what I need. Tomorrow, Carter's going to find a way to explain this all away. Right now is my only shot at the truth." I cringe at the word *shot* on my tongue, but Rosalie doesn't seem to notice. A few yards to our left, a car door slams.

"Fine." She places the gun in my hand, still looking wary. "But

I am not leaving you alone with him. I'll be right outside. Leave the door propped open."

"Obviously," I agree.

"If you need backup, say something about Culver Ridge."

"And then what?" I ask.

"And then I'm calling nine-one-one."

Rosalie switches off her headlamp and tosses it to me, then she slips out the door and into the darkness. I wrap the headlamp's band around my wrist. The skin is still sore where the plastic dug into it, but I am not putting that thing on my head. I walk over to the open doorway and stand next to it, out of sight. My back presses into the wall, and for just a second, I'm strangely calm. I wait for the sound of my heartbeat to fill my ears, but there's nothing. Then two shoes crunch across the gravel outside, and he's here.

"Hello?" Carter steps through the door, into the gym. I still have the lamp switched off, so except for the light spilling in from outside, it's dark in here. I let him walk a few feet inside, then I move into the open doorway, blocking it, allowing the light to black me out in silhouette. He spins around.

"Amanda?" he asks. "Where's David and Ben?"

I ignore him. I switch on the headlamp, hold my wrist up so it's shining right in his face.

Carter flinches. "Is that my gun?"

I'm not going to use it. I would never use it. But it's his turn to feel scared.

"I don't know," I say. "I thought it was your dad's." My mind flashes to Mr. Shaw's antique gun room. Carter had an entire gallery of deadly options at his disposal. I shudder.

"Give me the gun, Amanda. You're going to hurt yourself." He takes a step forward, and I raise it up, point it right at his chest.

"No." A surge of adrenaline rushes through me. I'm in control. "Here's how this is going to go. I'm going to ask the questions, and you're going to answer. Got it?"

Carter looks like he wants to protest, but he crosses his arms across his chest instead. His uninjured arm cradles the one in a cast. "Fine."

"Admit you sent those texts. The ones from the blocked number."

"You're being crazy, Amanda. I'd really feel better if that thing wasn't pointed at me," Carter says.

My hand wavers. If anyone has a right to throw around stigmatizing diagnoses in this scenario, I'm pretty sure it's not Carter. But the gun is heavy and strange in my hand. Maybe I'm not being rational. I am pointing a gun *at Carter*.

"Fine." I lower it to my side, but don't release my grip. "But you still need to answer."

For a moment, he's silent. My hand twitches, and his eyes lock in on the gun. Suddenly it hits me. When he gave it to Ben, he *knew* it was loaded—but he told Ben it wasn't. He actually hoped Ben would shoot me. The realization rockets through every muscle in my body, turning them to rubber bands, and it's all I can do to keep from buckling over.

"I haven't wanted to be Carter Shaw for a while now," he says finally. I force myself to stand tall, meet his eyes. "It's not personal, Amanda. This is so much bigger than you." He laughs, but there's no humor there. I shiver. "So yeah, I sent those texts."

"You could have come to me, Carter. We could have *talked* about this." My empty hand reaches up to my neck, dances across the skin where his heart used to be.

"Talk to you?" he spits. "You must be kidding. You have this whole plan for us. You have since we were kids."

"It wasn't just *my* plan," I spit back. The fact that I don't even want that anymore is beside the point. "It was everyone's plan. Mine, yours, our parents."

Carter shrugs. His face is blank, cold. "So you see? I couldn't just break up with you, or tell Winston I didn't want to work for him anymore. Gracefully bowing out of my future wasn't exactly an option."

I think about my mother's expectations, and for a second, I feel a stab of sympathy for Carter. In a way, I understand better than anyone. But then I remember everything he did to me, the loaded gun he gave Ben, how he hoped Ben would use it, and my hand tightens around the handle. "So you made up a stalker to scare me into dumping you in front of everyone? I'd look like the bad guy, and you'd be the victim. And who would blame you for not going back to me after that." All my synapses are firing now. There's no fog, not anymore. This all makes perfect, sick sense. "And then what? You knew I was never going to keep quiet about what you did to me tonight. So you gave Ben those documents, whatever you have on our parents, and you told him to blackmail me into shutting up. You were just going to throw our families under the bus if I talked. Light a fire, get out, watch everyone around you burn."

He shrugs. "You have to admit, it was a pretty good plan."

"You harassed me!" I practically shout. "You had me kid-napped!"

Carter's eyes narrow. "It's your fault it went this far, Amanda. I tipped you off about Rosalie back on New Year's. But then you had to resist, didn't you? You pushed me. I gave you so many chances. You brought tonight on yourself."

His words land like a slap. I want to scream, *you're wrong*, and *I'm not the one to blame here*, but I should have known better than to leave the Shaws' house tonight. To fall for his kidnapping scheme after I fell for the drugged champagne last night. I'll give him that, but that's the last thing I'll ever give him. As I stare at Carter, the figure of Private and the figure of my boyfriend blur before my eyes. The image leaves me cold.

"Let's just go home, okay?" he says, voice softening. "We'll clean your prints off the gun, pretend this never happened." He's almost cooing. He walks toward me, slowly, his hand reaching out. "No one ever has to know about any of this. You do understand how bad it would look for me, if people found out? How bad this would look for you? Just give me the gun, and we'll leave."

He's three feet away from me now. One more step, and he could make a swipe for the gun. His voice is gentle, but there's something not right about his face—it's hard, like stone. I step back.

"You sure you want to go home?" I ask. My heart starts pounding in my chest. "I thought you'd want to drive out to Culver Ridge. You know, make things right with Rosalie. In Culver Ridge." I repeat our signal, louder this time, but I can't hear anything outside, where Rosalie should be.

"Give me the gun, Amanda." Carter steps forward, reaches for it. I yank it back, away from him, but he grabs my other arm above the elbow and squeezes tight.

"You're hurting me." I stare right into his eyes, but there's no softness there. Only cold. Where ambition and desire—for me, for our future—used to shine, now there's only hate. Something inside him has snapped. My skin breaks into gooseflesh. As he stares back at me, a fresh realization dawns across his face. There's no way out of this for him now. No easy departure from me or his future. There's just Carter, me, and a gun.

He twists my arm behind my back, and I curl over at the waist. Even with one arm in a cast, Carter is bigger and stronger than me. He used to make me feel safe. Now the only thing I feel is sickening, twisting fear. The jolt of pain shoots all the way from my wrist to my shoulder. I cry out; my arm feels like it's going to snap.

"Carter, stop!" I scream, but he doesn't. He throws me to the floor, and my hands reach out automatically to cushion the fall. The gun clatters to the ground, and Carter dives down after it. When I hit the floor, something sharp jabs my thigh. Glass or a piece of broken brick. I bite back the pain and grope around for the gun, but it's lost somewhere in the rubble. My hands are torn up, blood sliding down my leg. I shake my wrist, but Rosalie's headlamp is broken.

Above me, something moves. I look up, tears stinging my eyes. Carter's standing over me, the gun pointed straight at my head.

"Wait." I rub my coat sleeve across my face, but I can't stop the tears. I'm not going to die crying. "I won't tell. I want good things for you. That's all I've ever wanted. I'm not going to ruin that now, promise. We'll go home, just like you said. We'll get cleaned up, and tomorrow's a new day. For both of us."

For a second, I think he's going to take the bait. His face softens, and his arm drops a bit. I force myself to smile up at him. Sweet. Sincere.

"But you will tell," he says. "I know you, Amanda." He lifts his arm and pushes back the hammer. His finger twitches against the trigger, and I scream.

ROSALIE
TUESDAY, JANUARY 23

I tell Amanda I'll call 911 when I hear our signal, but it's a lie. As soon as Carter walks into the building and Amanda steps in front of the doorway, blocking the exit, my gut says this confrontation scene was a terrible idea. I force myself to stay and listen for a couple minutes, to be sure I'm not overreacting. I'm not. I can feel it crackling in the air all around me; something seriously bad is about to happen. Carter admits he's Private, and I'm done. I am not sticking around for the rest of this. I creep silently around the side of the building until I'm back in the parking lot, out of earshot. Then I dig out Ben's phone and dial.

I try to be as clear as possible with the 911 operator. I tell her our location, and that it's Carter—not the boys in the truck—putting Amanda in danger.

"We didn't have a call-back number for you," she says, as if this is going to help anything now.

"I'm on a borrowed phone. A different one. Is someone coming?"

"We have two uniformed officers en route. A marked car will be arriving in a few minutes; I'd like to keep you on the line until they get there, okay, Rosalie?"

"Okay." I stamp my feet against the pavement in a mix of cold and impatience.

"Are you sure you're safe where you are?" she asks.

"I'm fine," I repeat. "Please tell them to hurry."

Carter's and Amanda's voices pitch up from the gym. He's yelling. She's yelling. I'm too far away to make out what they're saying, but my pulse spikes.

"How much longer?" The operator doesn't give me a straightforward answer.

Their voices rise again. Any amount of time is too long—even if I did unload the gun. While Amanda was outside, my headlamp and I found the latch for the chamber, and it popped right out. Five little bullets slid into my hand. The sixth one's buried somewhere in the rubble where I shot it. The thing about handguns is, they're really not so complicated.

But gun or no gun, Carter Shaw is dangerous.

And this is taking too long.

I scan the parking lot. The Gallaghers' truck might have had something useful inside, but it's long gone. The shovel I found earlier is still in the gym. I imagine myself smashing Carter's head in with a brick, and bile floods my mouth. I spit onto the pavement. When I look up, my eyes land on my bike, still propped against a planter. While the operator tries to keep me talking, I squat down next to it and run my fingers along the chain, searching for the quick link.

"Hold on," I tell the operator. I put her on speaker and slip the phone into my coat pocket.

With both hands free, I toss my gloves to the ground and place my fingers on either side of the link. I squeeze. It takes several tries, but finally the links compress and the chain pops open. I run it through the chain guides and around the ring, guiding it off my bike. Laid out long, it's four and three quarters feet, nearly as long as I am tall. When it's free, I dig Ben's phone back out.

"I'm losing the signal," I lie to the operator. Then I end the call.

I look up and down Foster one more time. Two cars pass, but there are no sirens, no sign of help coming. Inside the gym, Amanda screams.

I run.

Moonlight slices one piece of the gym floor into a pale triangle. The rest is darkness. I step silently through the doorway, and at first I only see the white glimmer of Carter's back, hunched over something on the floor. The gun is discarded to his right, glinting and useless in the moonlight. Then I see a flash of green—Amanda is pinned beneath him. His uninjured hand clamps down on her mouth, and his cast cuts a dark line across her neck. He's facing away from me.

I stretch my arms apart, extending three feet of chain in the air between them. The remaining links are wrapped tight around my gloved hands. I squeeze the metal tight and say a quick prayer. *Jesus, if you're listening. Give me strength.*

Then I lunge toward Carter, reach the chain over his head and down across his arms and chest, and yank him toward me. We go flying back and land on the gym floor, hard. He stinks of sweat and rage. I struggle up to a sitting position, bringing him with me, then pull back on the chain, pinning his arms to his sides and his back to my chest. There's a crack as the metal snaps against his cast, and he howls. Through my gloves, the chain bites into my hands. I clench down harder.

"Amanda!" I yell. She's still sprawled on the floor in front of us. In the moonlight, her dark hair spills around her face like a halo. She's not moving.

"Rosalie?" Carter tries to twist around to face me, but I pull the chain tighter. My arms burn and his body heat sears through my coat. It makes my stomach turn.

"The cops are on their way—this is over," I hiss in his ear.

He struggles hard, but the chain holds tight, leaves oily streaks across his white dress shirt. "What the fuck," he spits.

I keep my eyes trained on the still body in front of me. *Come on, Amanda. Move. Breathe.*

Carter squirms again, and this time, he slips down, gaining some leverage. The chain slides up his chest and I redouble my grip. When I first pinned him, I had the element of surprise on my side. Now, I'm reminded of his strength. If he twists again, I'm not sure I'll be able to hold him.

"We should be together," he says through clenched teeth. "Why are you doing this?"

I answer his question with a question. "You knew about Paulina. Why didn't you ask me to my face?"

He whimpers, a trapped animal sound. "You're supposed to be with me," he says, "not her," and my suspicions about the deepness of Carter's delusions are confirmed. Of course, he had no way of knowing what would have really happened if my father had seen those pictures. And that's my fault, because I lied to him, big time. He probably envisioned a stern talking-to that would drive me deeper into his arms. I shudder.

In the distance, a siren wails. We both jerk our heads toward the door. *Please, Jesus. Let that siren be for us.*

Carter gives a massive wrench and my hold on him slips, chain sliding up higher and snagging on his shirt collar. His arms slide free and he grabs the metal to keep it from digging into his neck. I yank back, but the chain trembles in Carter's grasp. Outside, the siren wails louder, closer.

"Don't move."

Amanda's voice is a fragile scratch, a record skipping in the dark. I can hear the damage where his cast smashed down on her windpipe, but she's speaking. She's alive. And when she shoves herself up to a sitting position, she's holding the shovel. Amanda lurches to her knees and crawls, shovel clenched in one hand, closing the distance between us. She leans forward and presses the metal tip into the soft skin at the base of Carter's throat. "Don't fucking move," she hisses.

The sirens pitch up to a high wail, and the sound of car tires screeching into the lot fills the gym. Two doors slam.

"Logansville Police!" a voice shouts. Four feet pound the pavement outside. "Carter Shaw, come out with your hands in the air."

Amanda lowers the shovel, I relax my grip on the chain, and Carter struggles to his feet.

39

AMANDA

WEDNESDAY, JANUARY 24

"Amanda? Are you awake, honey?"

My mother's voice floats through the thick, hot air. My limbs feel heavy, like I took too many sleeping pills. I take a deep breath, and my throat leaps into flames. I gasp, then explode into a series of spluttering coughs. My eyes fly open.

"Here, go slow." For the second time in as many days, I'm in a hospital room. My mother is pressing a plastic cup with water and ice chips to my lips. I feel a lot worse than I did after having my stomach pumped, and that was god-awful. Slowly, everything starts to come into focus. I prop myself up on my elbows and take a grateful sip.

"How long have I been sleeping?" My voice comes out in a raspy croak, my neck bruised and raw where Carter tried to choke me after the gun wouldn't fire. "Where's Carter?"

"He's in custody, honey. You're safe now." She brushes my hair away from my forehead, and I notice her hand is trembling. "It's three o'clock. You've been asleep for a while."

"It's Wednesday afternoon?"

She nods. "You went through a lot; your body needed the rest. Your father had a work call. He'll be back soon."

I sink into the pillows and try to take another deep breath, slower this time. It still burns, but I manage not to cough. Of course Dad had a work call that couldn't wait. At least my mother's here.

"Where's Rosalie?"

"At home," she says. "I assume. They discharged her late last night."

I smile. I thought Rosalie had abandoned me, but she was calling the police, thinking on her feet. She came back for me.

"That girl saved you," my mother says, echoing my thoughts.

"Are we at Mercy or Presbyterian?" I ask.

"Presby. I was not taking you back to Mercy, not now. . . ." She trails off.

"Not now that you believe me? That I was drugged at the benefit? That my life was really in danger?"

She presses a hand to her mouth, stifling a sob. "I had no idea," she whispers. "I should have listened to you."

I push myself into a sitting position and adjust the pillow behind my back. My thigh throbs, and my hands are wrapped in bandages. I'm a mess, and in a different way, so is my mother. She may never be as vulnerable again as she is right now. My throat is burning and all I want to do is go back to sleep, but I have to know.

"I learned some things last night. About you and the museum and Winston Shaw's antique collection. Carter says he has documents. He was going to send them to the media."

My mother's eyes get wide. "He was going to do *what*?"

"So it's true." Her face tells me all I need to know—Ben was right. My mother really was padding Winston's antique gallery from the museum's private collection in return for his help securing major donors. My heart sinks a little. "Does Dad know?"

"Amanda, let me explain. Your father and I, we each have our secrets. Sometimes, that's how adult relationships work. They're messy and complicated, and it's important—"

"No, let me explain," I say, cutting her off. "Because if I have this right, it's really very simple. Winston was using his real estate network to hook the big money for you, and you got all the recognition on the board. In return, the museum would never miss a Restoration-era steeple clock here or a pair of Etruscan serving trays there. When I went to the police, you were scared shitless they'd start digging around. That's why you didn't want them to have my phone. That's why you didn't want them asking questions."

"Amanda, honestly, I thought those texts were a prank. I would never—"

"But you did. You derailed the entire police investigation because you were so afraid your scam would get out. You put your reputation before my safety. You almost got me killed!"

My mind flashes to Winston, his boyish delight over his collection, how he had to keep the pilfered items in storage, the little exchanges with my mother that I'd read entirely wrong.

"One more question." Because I can't let this rest until I know everything. "*N or V.* You had an email from Winston in your purse. What do those letters mean?"

Her bottom lip quivers. "Neoclassical. Victorian. It was our code." Then she bursts into tears, and part of me wants to fold her into my arms and tell her everything's going to be okay. But then I think back over the last three weeks, the times I wanted nothing more than for her to hold me, take care of me. And she never did. I almost died because of her.

Someday, I'll be the bigger person. I'll forgive her. But not today.

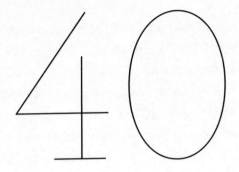

ROSALIE

FRIDAY, JANUARY 26

Three days after Carter is brought into custody, I sit in the Flores's living room with Paulina's parents, an LGBTQ+ youth rights advocate, and my dad. Paulina is out for the evening; her parents thought it would be best if she wasn't here for this meeting, and they're probably right. This isn't about my relationship with Pau, not specifically, although it feels strange and scary not to do this with her. This is about me and my family and taking this major step forward.

The last gasp of late afternoon light filters through the big window behind me. It licks the back of my neck and pools on the carpet at my feet. The cream fibers waver with light or heat or the sense that this is an ending but also a beginning. That my world

is on the verge of shifting irrevocably, permanently, powerfully—
it feels like I'm simultaneously behind the steering wheel and just
along for the ride.

The couch cushion presses reassuringly against my thighs.
Mr. Flores and Ms. Cuesta-Flores are to my left, and Cindy, the
advocate, a warm yet formidable woman in her midthirties, sits
in a chair to my right. Dad keeps standing and sitting back down
in the armchair across from us. The second armchair next to him
is empty. Pau's parents left work early for this, but Mom couldn't
switch her shift to be here, which might be true, and might have
been an excuse not to see me. Not to do this. I don't really want
to know.

My palms itch, and I rub them against my knees. The denim
bites into the spots that are still tender from the bike chain,
and I try to stop fidgeting. Try to be here in the moment, pay
attention to what Cindy is saying. This meeting is important—is
everything—but I can't seem to stay focused on what's happening
in this room with the same barrage of images reeling again and
again through my brain, all the events that led up to today: Carter swerving out of traffic in Bracken Hollow, his bandaged face
through the phone screen, Amanda motionless on the gym floor,
then the gleam of the shovel pressed against Carter's throat.
Paulina's fierce smile, then the hurt in her eyes when I told her I
thought she might have been Private.

And then me, stepping out of the officer's car when she
brought me back to Culver Ridge from the hospital Tuesday
night, onto Paulina's front lawn instead of my own. Enacting my
choice not to go home. Never again.

"Families who provide a supportive environment at home can

work to prevent health and mental health risks for lesbian youth like Rosalie," Cindy is saying. So far, I've let her do all the talking. Sooner or later, I'm going to have to speak up, put my decision into words for my father directly. But I can't find my voice, so instead I press my lips together tight and stare at the shimmering carpet fibers. After a moment, I force myself to look up, study my dad's face. I can tell by the blank mask that's settled across it that he's hearing her, but not really listening.

It's disappointing but hardly a surprise. This is the first time I've seen him since he left for work Tuesday morning, shortly before Lily and I made our last daily walk to the bus stop. On Wednesday, Ms. Cuesta-Flores called my parents to explain that I'm staying here. Mom threatened to call the police, but Dad agreed to this meeting even though he knew what it was, that the advocate would be here. I hold on to that fact like a tiny spark of hope. They've been driving Lily back and forth to school, deliberately keeping her away from me, but Dad's here now. Someday maybe I'll have a relationship with my family again. Someday maybe they'll let me see Lily.

Lily. It's only been three days, and already I miss her with every wild beat of my heart. But I'm safe here. I have to let that be the most important thing.

"Your child's health and well-being is our primary concern," Cindy says, echoing my thoughts. "I'm sure you agree, Mr. Bell?"

My father nods, one quick dip of his chin, but doesn't speak. He's sitting perched on the edge of his chair.

"When a home environment is not accepting and supportive, that's when we step in."

He leaps to his feet. "Rosalie has all the support she needs at

home and in her church community. I don't think you understand—"

"Mr. Bell," she says, cutting Dad off, "Rosalie has expressed
that she does not wish to return to the Fellowship of Christ.
Given your church's reliance on unscientific and frankly seriously
harmful methods like conversion 'therapy,' and what Rosalie has
shared with me from personal experience, we are intervening on
your daughter's behalf."

"She's a child," he sputters. "It's not your place to decide what
my daughter needs." The mask has gone. His face is now alive
with fury, and I sink back into the couch cushions, press my body
away from him.

"The Family Support Network provides pro bono legal services to the youth we advocate for." Cindy stays seated, calm,
doesn't let herself be intimidated by Dad. "When a child is at risk
of physical or emotional harm in their home environment, as
we believe Rosalie to be, that's where we come in. The first step
is a meeting like the one we're having today. If we can't reach
a safe and supportive resolution for Rosalie this afternoon, we
will provide legal counsel on her behalf. Seeing as your daughter
will turn eighteen in just over a month, I can assure you that the
courts will be very much on Rosalie's side in whatever choices she
makes for her future. Frankly, Mr. Bell, you do not have a case."

Dad sinks back into his chair, mouth slightly gaping. He's
been in the Flores's living room for almost half an hour, and we
haven't exchanged a word beyond hello. I've waited long enough.

"Dad," I say, the sound squeaking from my throat. I rub
my palms against my jeans again, and every head in the room
turns to look. "I want to stay here. For now. Until graduation.

Over the summer, I'll move to the city for college."

When I arrived on their doorstep in the middle of the night, unannounced, the Floreses took me in, no questions. I'd never doubted the sincerity of Pau's offers to stay with them, but I didn't realize how much she'd told her parents. How vigorously they'd step in to help, the second I asked.

Until this moment, staying with them has felt temporary. A duffel bag with a few changes of clothes on the floor of Ramon's old room. Eating meals in their kitchen. Smiling and laughing with them, everything out in the open and perfectly okay. It's felt too good to be true.

"Come home, Rosalie," Dad says softly. "Let us help you."

Let us help you. He means *let us try to change you.* I can't let that happen again.

"I'm a lesbian, Dad." The words stick to my tongue, don't want to roll free, but they do. Coming out isn't something you get to do just once. It doesn't matter that I already told him five years ago. It's just as hard now, but it's not the same. Then, I was terrified. Now, every cell in my body is coming to life. "It's not a choice, not something I could change if I wanted to. And I don't want to. This is who I am."

"Rosalie—"

"Let her speak, Richard." It's Ms. Cuesta-Flores's voice, and I turn my head to look at her. She's holding her husband's hand, and he places his other hand on top. "It wasn't easy for us when Ramon came out. We're Catholic. I understand how it feels when your faith says one thing and your heart says another. We weren't perfect, but we learned from Ramon, and we were able to support Paulina from day one. Rosalie needs you, and that means supporting her decision to live with us right now. I promise we'll take very good care of your daughter."

She nods at me, encouraging me to continue.

"I'm not coming home, Dad," I say. "I need to be away from the Fellowship, and that means taking some time apart from you and Mom. I love you a lot. I just need you to trust me right now."

The words hang heavy in the air. I'm asking my dad to trust me, the way I should have trusted Pau. Instead, I sent the PI on a wild-goose chase to a basement club with loud music and no reception—Latin Night, all ages. Paulina had even invited me to come along, but somehow, I'd forgotten. She hasn't totally forgiven me, and I don't blame her. I haven't forgiven myself either.

Dad stands again, but he's not angry this time. I know this conversation is over. Cindy's warning about family court chastened him, even though I'm not sure what she could do if he tried to drag me out of here. But he won't. I can see by the slope of his shoulders that he's defeated. I've won, but without Lily, it's only half a victory.

I remind myself that I'm working on a plan. Wednesday morning, I sent two emails. The first went to Lily's school account, my attempt to explain what was going on in a way she could understand.

Dear Lils,

Remember that time you asked me if I liked Carter? I didn't give you a real answer, and I'm sorry. I owe you that. The real answer is no. I don't like

Carter, not like that, because I don't like boys. The Fellowship says romantic love is only between a man and a woman, but sometimes even churches get it wrong. I like girls. The Fellowship says that's a sin, but I don't agree. I hope someday you can make up your own mind about that. I know this is a lot for you to process right now, but just promise me you'll think about it, and keep thinking about it. Mom and Dad aren't going to let me see you for a while, but I'll find a way, soon. Promise. I want you to know that I love you so much, and I miss you something fierce.

Love,
Rosalie

For a whole day, she didn't write back, and my heart pulsed like liquid lead in my chest.

Then on Thursday, I got a reply: *I miss you too. Duh. Love, Lily*

The second email went to Miss Larkin, the former FOC teacher at Lily's school. We're meeting for coffee tomorrow.

Now, as Mr. Flores shows Dad out, as he closes the door, as Cindy slips her hand into mine, the reality begins to settle in. I don't know what's going to happen with Lily or my family next week or next year or in ten years.

But I'm safe. I got out.

AMANDA

FRIDAY, AUGUST 24

It's our last Friday night of the summer, and we're here, but really, we're all already somewhere else. We're in our usual booth at the Sunny Side, the big round one in the corner. Tonight the four of us could have fit around a regular table, but it's tradition. To my right, Graham's arm is draped across Adele's shoulders, his fingers running idly through her freshly highlighted hair. Figures they'd finally get together at Bronson's graduation party, now that we're all about to leave for college. Next week, Adele's off to join the University of Wisconsin-Madison's newest crop of Badgers. She's been sporting her new favorite red-and-white hoodie with little rhinestones bedazzled around the *W* non-stop since her campus visit in April. Graham's staying on the

East Coast to study political science at George Washington, so something tells me their love won't last past Thanksgiving, but maybe I'm just cynical. Given my history, I'd say I have every right to be.

I glance to my left, where Trina is polishing off a basket of curly fries and scrolling through Instagram. In a week, she'll be moving to Manhattan to start her BFA in photography at the School of Visual Arts. She got into all the top programs where she applied—SVA, RISD, UCLA—but I'm glad she chose New York over LA or Rhode Island. What's even in Rhode Island?

"Holy crap, that's gorgeous." She holds her phone out to show me a series of pictures Bronson just posted to his feed. The University of Washington has some weird quarter system that doesn't start until late September, so he's hiking Angels Landing in Zion National Park with his mom and half sisters this week.

"Wow." I scroll through. "Who knew Utah could be this stunning?"

"I need to get out there to shoot," she says. "Trip over break?"

"For sure," I agree, but it probably won't happen. Next week, I'm leaving for Paris, and I'm not certain I'm coming home for winter break. I'm not sure I'm coming home ever again.

I look up from Trina's phone, and at first I'd swear every eye in the diner is trained on the four of us, barely filling out our big, round booth. But I know better now. Sure, a few of them are looking at me, the girl who almost died. But mostly they're looking at the empty spaces around us, taking in the ghosts of the people who aren't here. Bronson and Alexander were going strong until last month, but Alexander said the strain of leaving for college was starting to get to them, and they split up mid-July. I think Alexander and I will still stay in touch.

And of course, they're hardly the most conspicuous absentees from our booth. Ben graduated with us in June, but he's been keeping a low profile while logging his mandated hours at an organization for impoverished kids in the panhandle this summer. He messages me a lot, and sometimes I even write back. I know he feels terrible about all the shit he helped Carter do to me, and I'm practicing this little thing called forgiveness.

David lost his job at the construction site, and I haven't seen him around in months. I've been trying to find out when his sentence starts, but Ben says they don't know yet. It's just for six weeks; he took a plea. My mother says they're both lucky. Kidnapping. Accessories to attempted murder. Ben could have easily been tried as an adult. They could both have been locked up for a long time. Thinking back on that night still sends chills down my spine, but I can't spend the rest of my life being mad at them. The only person I really blame is going to be locked up in a youth reform center for a really long time. He should probably be in prison, but apparently there's no limit to what Shaw money can buy.

Last week, the Shaws finally closed on their house. So when I'm home over break—*if* I'm home over break—no more Winston and Krystal across the street. They're moving to Charleston, which is apparently a more centrally located headquarters for Shaw Realty, but please. Everyone knows it's because staying in Logansville was hardly an option. Carter's case was a leading news story for weeks. They have to start over. I'd almost feel bad if their son hadn't tried to kill me.

Things at home have been tense, but better than they've been in a long time. My parents finally admitted to themselves that we're deep in debt, and my mother fessed up to Dad and stepped down from the board of trustees. She got off pretty easy. Winston and Krystal will never tell for obvious reasons, and everyone else who knows about their scam is a criminal. She started a new position as a development officer for the symphony, and now that she has an actual paying job, things are looking up. Either way, it's their problem to figure out, and I think my mother has finally accepted that I'm my own person, not her ride up the social ladder. I know she wants me to forgive her, but I'm not quite there yet. One pardon at a time.

I take a big sip of Diet Coke and try to ignore the room full of eyes. In three days, I board a plane to Paris. In three days, I'm leaving all of this behind. I got into a program called Global Liberal Studies at NYU, and they're letting me spend my entire first year at the campus in Paris. I owe my guidance counselor about a million thank-you notes. My French is going to go from proficient to totally fluent. I could be a UN interpreter when I graduate. I could be literally anything other than the wife of Carter Shaw. I might be paying off my student loans for the rest of my life, but it's worth it to get as far away from here as possible. Carter may be locked away, but the ghost of who he was—and the horrible truth about what he tried to do to me—is everywhere.

"I'll be right back." I grab my bag and squeeze past Trina, out of the booth, then out the front door and into the parking lot. The bright August sun burns down on my shoulders, and I lean against the cool diner wall while I dig my phone out of my bag.

Hey. Carter moment.

Three dots spring up right away.

Hey. Glad you texted me.

ROSALIE
FRIDAY, AUGUST 24

It's our last Friday night before orientation kicks into full gear on Monday, but Pau and I are treating it like any other night of the summer, sitting in our regular booth at the "O," sharing a basket of fries. It's been almost three months since we moved into an apartment walking distance from Pitt with two adorable junior chem majors, Max and Bea, who we met through a Rainbow Alliance movie night on campus last spring, a few days after getting our acceptance letters.

The semester starts next week, but I'm not waiting for anything to begin. My life began again the day I left the Fellowship behind.

When Amanda's text chimes on my phone, I hold the screen up to Pau. For the past seven months, I've been doing everything I can to win back her trust. She says I'm going overboard with the openness thing, but it's not just about making it up to her. For years, secrets overshadowed my life. I'm done with secrets now.

"I'm just going to check in with Amanda real quick."

"Sure thing." She slurps the last drops of her Dr. Pepper and heads to the fountain for a refill.

I had to step outside the diner. It's like
I can feel him inside, watching.

It's okay if you need to leave.

I know. But I can't let him ruin it for
me. He's everywhere.

Yeah. I'm at the O with Paulina. I know
what you mean.

For a minute, she doesn't write back. Then, three dots hover
on the screen.

You're stronger than I am, Rosalie. I
don't know if I could go to college so
close to home.

Pittsburgh was never about Carter. It
was always about Pau and me.

 I should get back. Tell Paulina hi, okay?

"Amanda says 'hi,'" I tell Pau when she slides back into our
booth.

"Cool. She in France yet?"

"Monday." Sometimes I forget that Amanda's actually leaving, probably because nothing between us is likely to change.

I've only seen her a couple times since she got out of the hospital last winter; mostly, we text whenever one of us has a "Carter moment"—that deep chill only the two of us would understand. Carter could have been the worst thing that ever happened to us. He got really close to destroying both our lives. But if Carter hadn't almost ruined everything, Amanda wouldn't be going to Paris. And I wouldn't be the happiest I've ever been—out, living in Pittsburgh, not looking back. I cross my feet at the ankles beneath our booth, chunky red boot over chunky red boot. I got them at a vintage shop in Oakland our first week here. I'm never taking them off.

"Any news from Lily?" Pau asks.

"Yeah." I grin. "I'm chaperoning the second-grade field trip to the aquarium next week." Miss Larkin has been helping me see Lily as much as possible. The summer has been rough, but now with the school year about to start up again, it'll get easier. This is one secret I feel okay about keeping.

My Extradition formally took place in May. I received a letter from Brother Masters himself, which I framed. Paulina said we should hang it above the toilet in our bathroom, which was tempting, but I hung it above my dresser instead. Every time I look in the mirror, I look at the letter too. It's supposed to be a sanction, but to me, it's a letter of freedom. *Rosalie Bell is no longer a member of the Fellowship of Christ.*

I know it hurts Lily that I've been Extradited, and that she doesn't fully understand, but she hasn't kicked me out of her heart. Someday, when she's old enough, I hope she'll make the choice to leave the Fellowship too. But I haven't lost her, and for now, that's enough.

Some evenings this summer, when I'm out walking in the city, my feet take me to the majestic Catholic cathedral on North Dithridge and Fifth. After the noon mass, it's mostly empty inside, just a few worshippers praying. I like it in there, sitting quietly in the back, pew sturdy beneath me. The cathedral hall is white and gold, ceiling soaring and filled with light. It hums with history and a kind of peace.

I'm not planning to convert. I don't think organized religion is right for me, not right now. But inside the cathedral, I feel alone with God. For the first time in a long time, I feel His eyes on me, filled with love, bathing me with light.

"You go somewhere?" Pau asks.

I glance at the booth in the far back of the "O," the one Carter and I sat in the first time I came here. It's filled now with a family passing around baskets of chicken strips and bottles of ketchup and mustard. For just a second, I let myself remember the girl I was with Carter, the mask I wore like a shield until it almost broke me. Then I let the memory fade and reach across the table for Paulina's waiting hand.

A Note from Kit Frick

Rosalie and Amanda live very different lives only a few miles from each other, but the two girls are united by the shared experience of intense pressure from their families and communities to play prescribed—and deeply harmful—roles. For Amanda, escaping that pressure means accepting that her parents' financial situation is not her problem to solve and choosing her own path despite the guilt that comes with that decision.

For Rosalie, however, choosing a healthy and happy future comes at an even higher cost: She must leave her family and undergo excommunication from the conservative Christian church community in which she was raised. The Fellowship of Christ is a fictional denomination,[1] but its beliefs are representations of those held by real evangelical congregations with

---

1 God's Grace Fellowship of Christ bears no intended relationship to the Fellowship of Christ HeartSync Ministries of North Carolina Evangelical Presbyterian Church or any other church organization that may bear a similar name.

fundamentalist interpretations of Christian scripture.[2] Similarly, while the term *Ecclesiastical Extradition* was created for the FOC, the practice of church excommunication and the corresponding mandate to sever ties with family members is very real and drawn from practices such as the Jehovah's Witnesses' policy of disfellowshipping members for perceived "sexual immorality"[3] and the Scientologists' policy of declaring members Suppressive Persons for a number of behaviors considered counter to the church, which results in removal from the organization as well as cutting off all contact with those still inside.[4]

If Rosalie's experience with so-called conversion "therapy" struck a chord, please keep reading. Known variously as conversion therapy, reparative therapy, ex-gay ministry, sexual reorientation, and Sexual Orientation Change Efforts (SOCE), the practice of attempting to change a person's sexual orientation or gender identity is both ineffective and harmful.[5] The experiences depicted in Rosalie's story are drawn from the real stories of conversion therapy survivors, but are by no means representative of every survivor's individual experience nor inclusive of all the damaging techniques employed by various "practitioners." I am grateful to the survivors who shared their stories through the National Center for Lesbian Rights

---

2 https://ag.org/Beliefs/Statement-of-Fundamental-Truths and https://ag.org/Beliefs/Topics-Index/Homosexuality-Marriage-and-Sexual-Identity

3 https://www.huffingtonpost.com/rodney-wilson/i-am-now-a-ghost-jehovahs_b_9764478.html and https://www.jw.org/en/publications/magazines/w20150415/disfellowshipping-a-loving-provision/

4 http://exscientologykids.com/glossary/ and https://www.scientology.org/faq/scientology-attitudes-and-practices/what-is-a-suppressive-person.html

5 http://www.nclrights.org/bornperfect-the-facts-about-conversion-therapy/ and http://www.hrc.org/resources/the-lies-and-dangers-of-reparative-therapy

#BornPerfect Survivor Network[6] and through various news and media outlets.[7]

The hard truth is that as difficult as Rosalie's experience was and as difficult as it may have been to read, she was lucky to have Paulina, the Flores family, Miss Larkin, and an LGBTQ+ youth rights advocacy organization to support her once she made the hard decision to leave her family and church. Many people—especially youths—subjected to conversion "therapy" face equal or even more difficult psychological, emotional, and logistical challenges when coping with the aftermath of conversion therapy's harmful effects, when separated from their families, and when navigating the world outside their religious communities. Conversion therapy can inflict serious, long-term harm. Studies show that risks range from depression and guilt to self-hatred and hostility to suicidality.[8] Compared to those who are accepted at home, young people rejected by their parents for their sexual identity are "more than 8 times as likely to have attempted suicide; nearly 6 times as likely to report high levels of depression; more than 3 times as likely to use illegal drugs; and more than 3 times as likely to be at high risk for HIV and STDs."[9]

As *All Eyes on Us* goes to press, the harmful and unscientific

6 http://www.nclrights.org/bornperfect-survivor-stories-and-survivor-network/
7 http://abc.go.com/shows/2020/episode-guide/2017-03/10-031011-A-Boy-Named
-Lucas, https://www.salon.com/2017/03/21/conversion-therapy-is-torture-lgbt-survivors
-are-fighting-to-ban-pray-the-gay-away-camps/, https://www.theatlantic.com/politics
/archive/2015/04/how-christians-turned-against-gay-conversion-therapy/390570/, and
https://www.huffingtonpost.com/entry/realities-of-conversion-therapy
_us_582b6cf2e4b01d8a014aea66
8 https://www.apa.org/pi/lgbt/resources/therapeutic-response.pdf
9 https://nccc.georgetown.edu/documents/LGBT_Brief.pdf

practice of conversion therapy has been made unlawful in only fifteen states, plus the District of Columbia. The practice is additionally banned in fifty US cities and counties, and legislation has been introduced, but not yet passed, in several more states.[10] While this is an important and encouraging start, there's still a long way to go. In 2018, researches at the Williams Institute found that approximately 698,000 adults in the United States had been subjected to conversion "therapy"; 350,000 were adolescents at the time. Even in states with statutory bans, the legislation applies only to licensed mental health care providers and sometimes to others who practice conversion therapy in exchange for payment. The laws do *not* generally apply to religious or spiritual advisors who practice conversion therapy within their clerical capacity.[11]

Youth in West Virginia, Rosalie's home state, and thirty-five other states remain wholly unprotected. There is no scientific evidence that sexual orientation can be changed; conversion therapy practices are both ineffective and seriously harmful, even fatal. As a nation, we need to do better to protect LGBTQ+ youth.

How can I help and get help?

If you are an LGBTQ+ youth in crisis, there is help available. If you or someone you know is in immediate danger, please call 911.

---

10 http://www.lgbtmap.org/equality-maps/conversion_therapy and http://www.nclrights.org/bornperfect-laws-legislation-by-state/ — As lawmakers work to ban conversion therapy in additional US states and cities, please continue to check these resources for the most up-to-date information.

11 https://williamsinstitute.law.ucla.edu/wp-content/uploads/Conversion-Therapy-LGBT-Youth-Jan-2018.pdf

TrevorLifeline: 1-866-488-7386. Trained counselors are available 24/7 to young people in crisis, feeling suicidal, or in need of a safe and judgment-free place to talk. (Free.)

TrevorText: Text the word *Trevor* to 1-202-304-1200. Available Monday through Friday between 3 pm and 10 pm ET; noon to 7 pm PT. (Standard messaging rates apply.)

TrevorChat: Enter the online portal on the Trevor Project's website: https://www.thetrevorproject.org/get-help-now/ Available 7 days a week between 3 pm and 10 pm ET; noon to 7 pm PT. (Free.)

TrevorSpace: https://www.trevorspace.org/ An online community safe space for LGBTQ youth ages 13 to 24. (Free.)

LGBT National Help Center Youth Talkline: 1-800-246-PRIDE (1-800-246-7743). Available Monday through Friday 4 pm to 12 am ET / Saturday 12 pm to 5 pm ET; Monday through Friday from 1 pm to 9 pm PT / Saturday from 9 am to 2 pm PT. For teens and young adults up to age 25. (Free.)

LGBT National Online Peer Support Chat: https://www.glbthotline .org/peer-chat.html Available Monday through Friday 4 pm to 12 am ET / Saturday 12 pm to 5 pm ET; Monday through Friday from 1 pm to 9 pm PT. (Free.)

Trans Lifeline: US: 877-565-8860 / Canada: 877-330-6366. Available 10 am to 4 am ET; 9 am to 3 am CT; 7 am to 1 am PT. Volunteers may be available during off hours. Peer support hotline run entirely by and for transgender people. (Free.)

The Southern Poverty Law Center: If a church or school official rec-
ommends conversion therapy to you or someone you know, please
contact: https://www.splcenter.org/issues/lgbt-rights/submit

Childhelp National Abuse Hotline 24/7: 1-800-4-A-CHILD (1-800-422-
4453). (Free.)

National Suicide Hotline: 1-800-273-TALK (1-800-273-8255). (Free.)

If you are a survivor, consider sharing your story with
#BornPerfect: http://www.nclrights.org/bornperfect-what-you
-can-do/#SURVIVORS

If you are a legislator or LGBTQ+ leader in your state, please
contact the NCLR #BornPerfect campaign at BornPerfect@
NCLRights.org. You can also reach out to the Southern Poverty
Law Center at https://www.splcenter.org/contact-us about
becoming involved with their efforts to expose and end conversion therapy.

If you are involved with an organization for mental health,
faith, civil rights, youth advocacy, or reproductive justice, talk to
your organization leader about joining the more than one hundred
leaders and organizations who have signed on to the effort to end
conversion therapy by contacting BornPerfect@NCLRights.org.

If you want to get involved as an LGBTQ+ community member, ally, or advocate, several national organizations are working
to end conversion therapy:

The National Center for Lesbian Rights: visit http://www.nclrights
.org/our-work/bornperfect/ to learn more about #BornPerfect: NCLR's

Campaign to End Conversion Therapy or http://www.nclrights.org /bornperfect-campaign-supporters/ to become a campaign supporter.

The Southern Poverty Law Center: visit https://www.splcenter.org /issues/lgbt-rights/conversion-therapy to learn about the SPLC's work to protect the safety of LGBTQ+ youth.

The Human Rights Campaign: visit http://e-activist.com/ea-action /action?ea.client.id=1954&ea.campaign.id=43545&ea.tracking .id=or_gnr_hrc_support_volunteer to become involved with the HRC's efforts to educate, mobilize, expand the LGBTQ community's voice and visibility, and end hate and discrimination nationally.

Acknowledgments

Writing a second novel and ushering it into the world is no easy feat (said every author everywhere). To get to do so is both a considerable accomplishment and a tremendous gift. A world of thanks to my editor at McElderry Books, Ruta Rimas, for guiding *All Eyes on Us* through a revision process that encouraged the girls and their stories to take the lead, and for your fantastic support every step of the way. It is a privilege to get to work with you.

Much gratitude to the entire McElderry Books team: in particular, Justin Chanda, Audrey Gibbons, Nicole Fiorica, Bridget Madsen, Ellen Winkler, Chris Gage, Greg Stadnyk, and the brilliant sales and marketing force. This book could not have found a better home.

Endless thanks to my agent, Erin Harris, for your immediate enthusiasm for this story and for your constant guidance and wisdom on bookish matters large and small. We make quite a team. Huge thanks as well to the whole crew at Folio Literary Management / Folio Jr.

Enormous gratitude to my early readers: E. Latimer, Karen M. McManus, and Rachel Lynn Solomon, whose feedback at various stages was absolutely invaluable.

To Osvaldo: your boundless support and enthusiasm mean the world. You are my perfect partner person.

To my family, particularly Mom and Dad, Aunt Sally, Sonia, Lissette, and Angel: your ongoing encouragement and love mean so much. And to my friends: thank you for being excited for me and for just being you.

Heartfelt thanks as well to the writing communities of which I'm lucky to be a part, namely the Electric Eighteens and Pitch Wars. Please keep filling my feed with bookish joy. I also owe a thousand thank-yous to the MacDowell Colony, where I had the great fortune of spending a month working on *All Eyes on Us* in a beautiful studio in New Hampshire. It is impossible to quantify how deeply and richly the book benefited from that time and space to work.

I cannot adequately express my gratitude and awe to the survivors who have shared their stories. My heart is with you and the countless survivors whose stories have not yet been told. My immense admiration goes to the lawmakers and organizers working tirelessly to put an end to conversion therapy practices nationwide, and internationally. A world of thanks, as well, to the many religious organizations worldwide who support and embrace the LGBTQ+ youths and adults in their communities.

Finally, to my readers. Thank you for coming along for the ride.